Colin II

Edward Frederic Benson was born in 1867, at Wellington College, where his father, later Archbishop of Canterbury, was Headmaster. Brother of the equally prolific Arthur Christopher and Robert Hugh Benson, Fred, as he was always known to his family and friends, was author of more than one hundred books – autobiography, biography, social satires (notably the famous Mapp and Lucia novels), thrillers, tales of the macabre and the supernatural and short stories. E.F. Benson died in 1940 and his rediscovery commenced in the 1960s.

Millivres Books has also reissued *David of King's*, *The Inheritor*, *Ravens' Brood* and *Colin*.

Peter Burton is the Commissioning Editor of Millivres Books, author of *Rod Stewart: An authorised biography*, *Parallel Lives*, *Talking to . . .* and *Amongst the Aliens: Some aspects of a gay life* and co-author of *The Boy From Beirut*, *Vale of Tears: A problem shared* and *Drag: A history of female impersonation in the performing arts.*

Colin II

E.F. Benson

New Introduction by Peter Burton

Millivres Books
Brighton

Published in 1994 by Millivres Books (Publishers)
33 Bristol Gardens, Brighton BN2 5JR, East Sussex, England

Colin II first published by Hutchinson, 1925

A CIP catalogue record for this book is available from the British Library

ISBN 1 873741 20 0

Typeset by Hailsham Typesetting Services, 4-5 Wentworth House, George Street, Hailsham, East Sussex BN27 1AD

Printed and bound by Biddles Ltd., Walnut Tree House, Woodbridge Park, Guildford, Surrey GU1 1DA

Distributed in the United Kingdom and Western Europe by Turnaround Distribution Co-Op Ltd., 27 Horsell Road, London N5 1XL

Distributed in the United States of America by InBook, 140 Commerce Street, East Haven, Connecticut 06512, USA

Distributed in Australia by Stilone Pty Ltd, PO Box 155, Broadway, NSW 2007, Australia.

Introduction

'I have just finished *Colin.*' Lord Halifax wrote to E.F. Benson on October 6th 1923. 'I have been deeply interested in it – first rate plot and most exciting. Colin is a real devil – rather *he is* the devil – and yet one is interested in him and something more than interested, quite abominable as he is. One ought to *hate* him, but somehow I didn't and don't. Now I am longing for the sequel. Please be sure to make the next volume as good as the first . . . I do hope the next volume will be soon out. I can hardly wait.'

Described by David Williams in his useful *Genesis and Exodus: A portrait of the Benson family* as 'arch-champion of the Anglo–Catholics', the second Viscount Halifax (1839-1934) was an old family friend and something of an authority on the supernatural. 'He was intensely interested, as his collections of genuine ghost stories show, in apparitions and supernatural phenomena, but he also loved the ghost stories of fiction, whose only object is to terrify,' Benson wrote in his posthumously published autobiography, *Final Edition* (1940). 'I wrote several, as desired for his special discomfort, and read them aloud to him. He was getting rather deaf, and sat close, with his hand up to his ear; and, if the story was fulfilling its aim, he got more and more uncomfortable and entranced. "It's too frightful," he said. "Go on, go on. I can't bear it!" The Noble Lord had to wait almost two years between publication of *Colin* (1923) and *Colin II* (1925), which concludes this epic of evil ascendant.

Once again Benson adroitly moves his narrative between the deceptive rural calm of the Stanier ancestral mansion overlooking Rye in Sussex, the hedonism and sheer decadence on the Italian island of Capri in the Bay of Naples and the city of Naples itself – home to the thoroughly beguiling, thoroughly corrupt British Consul, Mr Cecil. With his taste for 'wine and obscenity' and his 'extensive knowledge of subterranean life . . .', Cecil is undoubtedly a sybaritic homosexual (he could have ever-so discretely entertained Oscar Wilde and Lord Alfred Douglas when they stayed in the city in 1897). There can be little doubt that Cecil's locked cabinet would have included reproductions of the more *outré* Pompeiian frescos and a cache of photographs by Baron von Gloeden, Fred Holland Day, Wilhelm von Plüschow, Rudolf Koppitz, Vincenzo Galdi and Gaetano D'Agata. The Mediterranean was a seductive lure to homosexuals up to – and beyond – the First World War.

Paganism suffuses *Colin* and *Colin II*. In fact, for the son of an Archbishop of Canterbury, E.F. Benson possessed a curious fascination with paganism and pantheism, dominant themes in at least two further novels, *The Inheritor* (1930) and *Ravens' Brood* (1934).

An interesting exchange between Colin's Aunt Hester and wife-and-cousin Violet occurs very near the beginning of *Colin II*, showing at once where Benson's sympathies lay and indicating why the compellingly evil Colin is yet so utterly appealing.

'"Aunt Hester, you're a pagan," observed Violet.

'"I always was, my dear,' said she, "and it's pagans who make the world go round. It ain't for long that anyone's fit to look at, so while youth lasts, for God's sake let them make the most of it. There'll be time for them to lead a godly life when no one asks them to do anything else. That's what I say."

'With which atrocious sentiments, Aunt Hester walked briskly off to get her good perspiration to prepare her for her cold tub and her dinner.'

Although he blithely tosses in the adjective 'atrocious', it is clear that – as always – Benson's biased towards the young and the beautiful and all for deflating the pretentious, stuffy and mentally middle-aged.

Mention is made of a portrait of Colin painted by the most famous artist of the day . . .' Possibly Augustus John, though I rather imagine Colin looking like the W. Graham Robertson of Sargent's famous 1893 portrait, now in The Tate Gallery, London. Tall and slim and wrapped in a long and tightly fitting overcoat (underneath which he was virtually naked, due to the heat, he tells us in his enchanting memoir, *Time Was,* 1931), Robertson stands with one hand on hip and the other resting on the gold top of a walking cane. Like Benson's Colin, here is an epicene young man, fully aware of his beauty and of the power that beauty invests in his.

Colin and *Colin II* are particularly vivid books and a whole series of images come to mind as character and incident spring to life. The Colin Stanier who founds the family fortunes after making a pact with the devil in the days of Elizabeth 1 could be a portrait by Nicholas Hilliard; the decadent Colin Stanier whose story forms the main narrative of these two novels could be a portrait by Sargent or John or William Rothernstein – as could his beautiful son Dennis. And any of the Italian youths who fleet through the books – Nino in particular – could have stepped from the Taormina photographs of Wilhelm von Gloeden or any of the other essentially Northern European photographers who flocked to Southern Italy to capture for eternity the likeness of naked or barely veiled young men.

Circulating amongst gay men of the period (and consistently reprinted even today), these photographs were at once pornography *and* art – the former when served up for erotic titillation at private gatherings of like-minded men, the latter when published in such high-minded magazines as *The Studio.* In either one or the other circumstances, Benson would have seen the photographs – and he would have had first-hand knowledge of boys like Nino from his own experiences of Capri and the holiday villa he shared there with John Ellingham Brooks and W. Somerset Maugham. Nino, loyal and loving, is brilliantly realised. He is dedicated to Colin – 'He did not want any visitors: he much preferred being bullied by Colin to not seeing him, and it had entered his curly head that his master was just as happy alone with him as with his guest' – and is too naive to see that this devotion will be his doom.

As Colin sinks further and deeper into diabolism, the narrative gathers speed, moving inexorably towards a climax that is shattering but just. And as the tale moves towards its inevitable conclusion, Christian imagery, always evident in the background, moves to the fore.

Colin and *Colin II* present a detailed and chilling portrait of seductive evil. Neither book is a shocker in the style of Stephen King or James Herbert. Unlike those modern masters of the genre, E.F. Benson is sparing with his effects. Perhaps it is this subtlety which makes the story of the Staniers all the more persuasive.

Peter Burton
Brighton, 1994

There are two societies devoted to the life and work of E.F. Benson and anyone wishing for further information should write (enclosing a sae) to: The Secretary, The Tilling Society, Martello Bookshop, 26 High Street, Rye, East Sussex TN31 7JJ ***and/or*** The Secretary, The E.F. Benson Society, 88 Tollington Park, London N4 3RA.

COLIN II

INTRODUCTION

WITH the declining wheel of the sun to the west, the shadow of the great yew-hedge began to flow like some tide, dark and clear, over the paved terrace which since morning had basked in the blaze of the July day. It had been planted by Colin Stanier first Earl of Yardley, when he laid the foundations of his house in the time of Elizabeth, and the three-sided serge rampart, now thick and solid as a fortress-wall, ran out from the corners of the façade, and formed a frame for the lawn below the terrace. Beyond, the ground declined in smooth slopes of short-cut turf to the lake. This lake also was the creation of the first Lord Yardley, for he had built the broad dam now clothed with rhododendrons across the dip of the valley, so that the stream which flowed down it was pent to form this triangular expanse of water. At the top end it was shallow, but by the sluice in the centre of the dam fifteen feet of dark water reflected the banks of blossom.

Beyond again and below the hill-side tumbled rapidly down to the heat-hazed levels of the Romney marsh, and over all the great house kept watch, stately and steadfast as the hill from which it sprang, a presiding presence and symbol of the three centuries of unbroken prosperity which had blessed the fortunes of the Staniers. Whatever uprooting tornado of revolution had swept across England, devastating or impoverishing the great families of the past, they seemed anchored and protected beyond all power of ruinous vicissitudes. They were no fat or brainless race, who but battened and dozed in material magnificence, but served their country well in public ministries. As for their private lives, the Staniers have always considered that such were their own concern.

The family rose to the splendour which it still enjoys in the reign of Elizabeth. Its founder was one Colin Stanier, the son of a small local farmer, who, on the occasion of the Queen's visit to Rye as she toured her Cinque Ports, went into the town to see the pageant pass. As Her Grace rode down the steep cobbled way from the church, her horse stumbled, and the boy, some eighteen years old at the time, had the privilege by his quickness to save the Queen from a serious fall. She looked on his amazing comeliness with an admiring eye, and bade him wait on her next day at the Manor of Brede. . . . That night, according to the family tradition, as he worked and slept in a shepherd's hut on the marsh, busy with the midwifery of his father's ewes at lambing-time, he was visited by a personage even greater than the Queen, one no less than Satan himself, who, for the signing away of his soul, offered, not only to him but to those of his descendants who chose to associate themselves with the bargain, health and wealth and honour up to the fulness of their hearts' desire. A deed was thereupon executed between the two which Colin signed with the blood of his pricked arm and which is supposed still to exist, let into the frame of the famous portrait of him at the family seat at Stanier. This curious story has been known from that day to this as the Stanier Legend.

The advent of Colin's good fortune made no long tarrying, for early next morning, after his interview with His Satanic Majesty, he waited on Her Susceptible Majesty at the place appointed. Ruddy and fair he was to look upon, and even as the Lord took David, as he followed the ewes great with young, and made him King in Israel, so from the sheepfolds did Elizabeth take Colin Stanier and made him her page, and presently her most confidential secretary, and conferred on him as the age of twenty-five the monastic lands of Tillingham with the Earldom of Yardley and the Knighthood of the Garter. So, whether the student can accept or not as true the Stanier Legend, he is forced to credit Colin's rise of fortune which is hardly less miraculous, for certainly he was a shepherd-boy one day, and a page of the Queen the next, and thereafter, while still a young man, attained a position such as few subjects have ever enjoyed. He wrote a voluminous memoir of his life which is preserved in the library at Stanier, and, yet unpublished, contains some very curious matter. In it he recorded without reticence or shame the manner of his days, his ruthless cruelty and relentlessness to those who crossed him, his building of the great house at Stanier, his ceaseless quest for pictures and tapestries, for statues and furniture, and described with the faithfulness of detail the bargain that he struck with Satan, and his conviction that he owed to it all the good fortune and prosperity that so unfailingly attended his earthly pilgrimage. That belief was confirmed by the characters of his descendants who by his bargain came under the diabolical protection, for in all history you will not find a family so consistently prosperous nor one so infamous. For more than a century after his death, the eldest son of the house made, on his twenty-first birthday, his formal choice as to whether he accepted for himself the legendary bargain, or dissociated himself from it, and during that period one only, Philip, the third Earl, would have no part in it, and he, within a month of his accession to his lordship, was smitten with a mysterious and terrible disease of which he soon died.

The rest all claimed their inheritance and mightily prospered, but in the eighteenth century their belief in so extravagant a legend faded in the light of more modern materialism. The solemn ritual of choice was performed no more, but, though the formality was given up, the subsequent successors to the bargain mostly acted up to the spirit of it, and their lives, if not their lips, acknowledged it. For, in general, their wickednesses have been so notable as their prosperity; pity, and its greater kinsman, love, can find no seed-cranny in their hearts where they can take root, but both alike wither in that iron soil. The Staniers have always been loveless folk, and it is strange that, though love is alien to their natures, they have often so madly inspired it, and with a glance have kindled in others the fire which is powerless to warm them. They sate their passions, and, when that is done, toss the outworn minister away, or, if that minister is wife and mother to their children, she freezes in the Arctic cold of lovelessness. Many a bride has come to Stanier all ardent and a-flame, on whom that congealing blight has fallen, which has turned her into a figure of ice doing the honours of the house with stately courtesy, wearing the great jewels which are the insignia of her servitude, and bearing beautiful sons for the perpetuation of the race. The love that adorned her advent was frozen, maybe, into hate and horror of him with whom she was indissolubly one, and whose soul was in pawn to Satan.

The Staniers have never run to large families: two or at the most three children have been born to the Lord Yardley of the day. In the last generation there were three: Philip the eldest, a daughter Hester, and Ronald, father of Violet Stanier, now

Countess of Yardley. At the time of her birth Philip, who had quarrelled with his intolerable sire, and was still unmarried, was living at a villa he had bought on the island of Capri with an Italian girl whom he had made his mistress. She was with child by him, and less than a month before her delivery news came to Philip, that this younger brother of his had begotten a daughter. He thereupon married Rosina Biagi, who soon presented him with twin boys. Philip telegraphed the news of his marriage and their birth to his father, and the despatch arrived as he and Ronald, heavy drinkers both of them, sat tipsily over their wine. Lord Yardley had had a stroke some two years before, and now he fell forward with a crash among the glasses and died without speech. Within a few weeks Philip's wife died also, and he came home with his two sons to enter on his inheritance.

Of these the elder by half an hour was Raymond, a dark and ugly fellow, black of temper, and between him and his brother Colin, as they grew up, flowered an implacable enmity. On Colin the gods had lavished the utmost of their gifts; he was the beloved of his father and of all who came near him, and Raymond, the uncouth and unpleasing, envied and detested him. This hatred was hotly returned by the other. Raymond was an abomination in Colin's eyes, not only for what he was but because, thanks to that half-hour's seniority, he was heir to all that he himself so passionately coveted, title and revenues and, not least, the lordship of the wonder-house at Stanier. Through all their generations the Staniers have adored the place: it is said that none of them is completely happy if he is away from it for long. That passion was shared by Violet, who was an exact contemporary of her twin-cousins, and was brought up with them there, and it was for the sake of being its mistress that, at the age of twenty, she promised to marry Raymond. But her heart was already not her own to give, and, though as yet she scarcely knew it, Colin held it.

Then he beckoned to her, and, discarding the graceless Raymond, she married him, and forthwith, as if a lamp had suddenly been lit which showed her his black heart, she knew that, in loving him, she loved one in whom the Stanier Legend found such fulfilment as none of its inheritors had manifested yet. In person he might have been the very incarnation of their Elizabethan ancestor, who had founded the house, for there in life was the matchless beauty of the great portrait, the gold hair, the beautiful mouth, the dancing azure of the eyes in which gleamed the greeting of his enchanting grace; in him blossomed the fairest that Nature and inheritance could bestow. Luck favoured him, even as it had favoured his ancestor, in all he did, for shortly after his marriage Raymond was miserably doomed as he skated on the lake at Christmas-time, and within a few months his father died also, and Colin his son reigned in his stead. He and Violet, fair as a spring day, numbered but forty years between them; they were an April couple with all the splendour of the summer waiting for them.

But the dawn of love for Violet had been the dawn, too, of a nightmare of unfathomable darkness. For Colin, excelling all of his race who had been merely indifferent to love, knew very well what love meant, and bitterly hated it. He was not content to shrug his shoulders at it, and pass on to gratify his pleasures, for the sweetest of them to him was love's discomfiture, and his joy to strike at it and wound it. . . . Often Violet wished he could have killed her love for him, for then would have died withal that eternal struggle within her between love and her horror of him, whose soul, whether in fulfilment of the legend, or from his inherent wickedness, was as surely Satan's as if with his own blood he had signed the fabled bond. Yet as often as she wished that she cried out on herself at so blasphemous a desire, for she knew that by love alone, though in some manner inscrutable, could redemption come to him.

That creed was inscribed on her heart's core: it was the fabric on which was stitched the embroidery of her days.

PART I

CHAPTER I

THROUGHOUT this hot afternoon of July the terrace had lain empty and soaked in sunshine, and it was not till the shadow of the yew-hedge had crept half-way along it from the west, that Violet Yardley stepped out of the long window of the gallery which lay along the front of the house. Colin was in town; he had said he might possibly return to-day, but, if so, he would telephone. Violet had just asked if any message had come from her husband, and it was with a feeling of relief and remission that she had heard that there was none.

She paused in the doorway with puckered eyelids, as she emerged from the cool dimness of the house into that reverberating brightness. She was bareheaded, and the gold of her hair was so pierced by the sun that it looked as if it shone from some illumination within itself. She had the blue eyes of her race, its fineness of feature and arrogance of bearing, and so like she was to Colin that they could still almost have repeated that jest of his school-days when, on the occasion of a fancy-dress ball, the two had changed costumes with each other half-way through the evening, and had been undetected till Colin's sudden spasm of half-cracked laughter, when a school-friend of his had made a suitable speech to so enchanting a girl, had given them away. . . . She had changed very little since then, her figure had still the adorable slimness of girlhood.

There was a small encampment of chairs, with a table laid for tea at the shady end of the terrace and she seemed to be the first to come out from the coolness of the house. Aunt Hester would be here soon or perhaps Violet's father still hobbling from a rather sharp attack of gout, and presently Dennis, her fourteen month-old baby, would be wheeled up and down the terrace by his nurse for his evening airing, and make some more of those intrepid experiments in voluntary locomotion, which were meeting with an increasing but still hazardous success. He appeared to consider his legs as an impediment more than an aid to movement: they got in his way and caused stumbling, but he was rapidly teaching them not to interfere. Colin would be pleased to see the progress his young son had made in his fortnight's absence.

Violet's eyes wandered from the terrace to the blaze of the flower borders round the lawn below, and beyond to the bright surface of the lake. So still was it and unruffled by any breeze that it might have been covered with a sheet of ice that gleamed blue with the reflection from the sky. At the thought of ice on the lake, there started unbidden into her mind the memory of that terrible morning, only eighteen months ago, when Raymond, Colin's elder twin brother, had taken his skates down there and had never been seen alive again. She and his father had followed him not long afterwards, and had found his boots on the bank, and a great hole in the ice at the deep end by the sluice, where the rhododendron bushes hung over the lake. It had been terrible, and was there something more terrible yet? Had no one ever seen Raymond alive after the moment when he left the house? Colin had once said something of casual application, about a drowning man coming up to the surface not three times, as popularly supposed, but once only, and somehow that had suggested to her that he had seen Raymond struggling in the water. There was no cause why so ghastly an idea should ever have occurred to her; it was more like the unsubstantial remembrance of a nightmare than a waking thought, but it had the haunting vividness of dreams.

There came the brisk tapping of heels along the terrace and Aunt Hester approached. She was small in stature, and carried her sixty years with a dainty lightness. She had on a gay print dress, short in the skirt in true modern fashion, which shewed to great advantage her neat slim calves and tiny ankles. On her head was a broad-brimmed straw hat, a garden of monstrous blue convolvuluses, and her face was hidden beneath swathes of pale pink veil. Her tripping gait suggested a bird scouring the lawn for its breakfast, and her speech was the argot of smart young ladies in the mid-Victorian epoch.

"Well, thank God, this wretched sun's got behind the trees at last," she said, "and I can take off my veil. Sunshine's a plague to the complexion, my dear. How you stand it, I don't know. Give me my cup of tea, there's a good girl; I'm as dry as the desert."

She unpinned her layers of veil, as Violet poured out her tea, disclosing the prettiest little face, pink and white, of porcelain delicacy.

"Girls to-day ain't got one decent skin among a score of them," she observed. "They go playing golf and smoking cigarettes till their faces are like kippers, and then they make them twice as bad by smudging themselves with rouge and powder and muck, till they're in such a mess as never was. How a young man nowadays can bring himself to kiss one of them without wanting to wash his face afterwards, I don't know. I like my tea strong, my dear. Hope it's been standing."

Violet held out the cup.

"Will that do, Aunt Hester?" she asked. "Or will you wait a little?"

"No, I'll take that," said she, "and the next cup will be a bit stronger. Then I shall go for my walk, and get a good perspiration, and have my cold tub, and be ready for my dinner. That's the way to keep well."

Violet laughed.

"You're a marvel, Aunt Hester," she said. "Colin always says he'll never be as young as you, even if he lives to be a hundred."

"Colin's a wretch," said Aunt Hester, selecting a piece of hot buttered bun. "He's making fun of me, pulling my leg as they call it nowadays. Anything been heard of him? Is he coming down to-night?"

"He hasn't telephoned to say so."

"Well, I wish he would. Stanier ain't really Stanier when Colin's not here. I shall have to run up to town and see what he's after; mischief I'll be bound. But Colin's sunshine's the only sunshine I've any use for. Lord, how his father used to dote on him. And pleased he was, my dear, when you gave poor Raymond the chuck, and took Colin instead."

"I was thinking about Raymond just now," said Violet.

"Well, I should have thought you could have found a pleasanter subject than that," said Lady Hester. "He was a sulky bad-tempered boy was Raymond, and I daresay God knew best, when He let him drown. Not but what I'm sorry for him, but as for pretending to like people just because they're dead, I call that bunkum, and if I ever die, my dear, which God forbid, I hope you and Colin won't talk any trash about me, and say I was the model of all the virtues. Such a pack of nonsense! But don't let's talk about that."

She looked round, and her eyes sharp as a terrier's noticed what Violet had not seen yet. At the far end of the terrace had appeared a wheeled chair pushed by a woman in nurse's costume.

"Why there's my mother," said Lady Hester. "Fancy her coming out!"

This was indeed a most unusual appearance. Old Lady Yardley, mother of Colin's father, of Lady Hester and of Ronald Stanier was now seldom seen until the hour of dinner, when she with her bath-chair was brought down in the lift from her rooms, was wheeled into the long gallery, and, with the help of her crutch-handled stick, transferred herself to the brocaded chair by the fireplace near the dining-room. In the grate, whatever the weather, a couple of logs smouldered into white ash, and by it she sat till the rest were assembled. So she had done for sixty-three years, when first as a bride of eighteen she came to the house, waiting till all were ready when, according to immemorial usage, the major-domo threw open the doors of Lord Yardley's room at the far end of the gallery, and he entered. That had been the custom in the days of her father-in-law, and when her husband reigned, and when her son reigned, up till now when Colin, her grandson, still kept up the ancestral tradition. She seldom spoke but sat through dinner, eating in silence what was put before her, and, in the manner of the very old, regarding now one, now another of her companions with eyes blank and unwinking, but half-veiled with the drooping lids of age. After dinner she played a couple of rubbers of whist, and when they were done she was conveyed back into the silence and sequestration of her room again. There she remained, thickly rimed by the Stanier frost, until the hour came round for her again to put on her jewels and her evening gown, and wait by the fireplace for Lord Yardley, be he father-in-law or husband or son or grandson. Colin alone had always the power to galvanize her into life; his presence blew away the white ash that seemed to cover her mind, as it covered those smouldering logs in the fireplace, and disclosed some mysterious pale fire that still burned within. She would nod and smile at him when he kissed her, would listen with pleasure to what he said to her, would ask him sometimes some question about his doings. She might enquire what he had actually done to-day: equally well she might enquire whether he had been out with Raymond, who had been dead this year and a half, or whether his grandfather, who had fallen lifeless across the dining-room table, on the very day that Colin was born, would make one of their whist-table that night. Colin always had some answer that pleased and satisfied her, and sometime next day or maybe a week afterwards she would shew she remembered it by some further question or comment. But she seemed to have no cognizance of any of the others, unless she wanted to know something about Colin. She ate her dinner in silence and in silence played her whist, and waited for the next evening.

She was wheeled now half-way down the terrace, and there her nurse would have turned again, but she gesticulated and pointed to where Violet and Lady Hester were sitting.

"I can't make out what she wants, my lady," said the nurse to Violet. "She told me she wished to come out. But it's so warm, it can't hurt her."

Violet went to the side of the bath-chair.

"Well, Granny," she said. "Have you come out to have tea with Aunt Hester and me?"

Old Lady Yardley looked at her in silence: then transferred that unwinking gaze to Lady Hester. Lady Hester particularly disliked this grim silent observation: it gave her 'the creeps.'

"I'll be going for my walk," she said. "Whatever Mamma wants, my dear, she doesn't want us."

"Where's Colin?" asked old Lady Yardley.

"He hasn't come, Granny," said Violet. "I don't think he's coming to-day."

"Yes, he's coming to-day," said Lady Yardley. "Is he here now? Is he with Raymond? I want Colin."

"Granny dear, he's in London," said Violet. "We'll let you know the moment he comes."

"Just a fad she's got, my lady," said the nurse. . . . It was impossible to speak of old Lady Yardley as if she was there. There was no one truly there, unless Colin was there, too. The nurse turned to her charge.

"You'd better let me take you back to your rooms, my lady," she said, "and have a nice rest till dinner-time. You've seen for yourself that his lordship isn't here."

Old Lady Yardley paid not the smallest attention to this. "I shall wait for Colin on the terrace," she said to Violet. "I shall wait there till Colin comes. He is coming."

"Wheel her up and down then," said Violet to the nurse.

To Aunt Hester's great relief, old Lady Yardley consented to have her chair turned round, and be wheeled away again.

"She gives me the creeps, my dear," said Aunt Hester, "though I know she's my own mother. But there it is! Ever since I can remember she was cold and dead: the iceberg your Uncle Philip and I used to call her. A beautiful woman she was, too: it's strange that your Uncle Philip and your father were such plain men."

"You took all her good looks, Aunt Hester," said Violet. Aunt Hester loved firm little compliments, laid on with the full spade.

"Well, I had my share of them," she said, "but beauty ran to prettiness in me, and that's a sad seeding. The Stanier style skipped my generation and I daresay that's why it came out strong in the next. Your Uncle Philip and your father, as I say, two plain men if ever there was one, and yet one was the father of Colin, and the other of you. You two have got it all: that's what happened. There was never such a pair of Staniers as you, and as like as two peas. Make haste, my dear, and have a dozen sons and daughters, and there'll be a dinner-table worth photographing when you've got your family growing up. Let them all be as wicked as hell, and as long as they have the good looks of their mother and father I'll forgive 'em. There are enough plain folk in the world already who can be models of piety, but when I see a handsome boy, I want to see him kissing a pretty girl, as I'm too old for him now."

"Aunt Hester, you're a pagan," observed Violet.

"I a ways was, my dear," said she, "and it's pagans who make the world go round. It ain't for long that anyone's fit to look at, so, while youth lasts, for God's sake let them make the most of it. There'll be time for them to lead a godly life when no one asks them to do anything else. That's what I say."

With which atrocious sentiments, Aunt Hester walked briskly off to get her good perspiration to prepare her for her cold tub and her dinner.

The Staniers had always been patriarchal folk, and indeed in that immense house there was room for the exercise of this family virtue, without any inconvenient jostling of the generations: it was an asylum and almshouse for the antiquated members of the family. Four generations indeed were now installed there: old Lady Yardley represented the earliest, and next in succession came her two children, Lady Hester and Ronald Stanier with his wife, all of whom inhabited what Colin called the Dowager wing. If he wished to say something special about Violet's father, he called it the Home for Inebriates, or if her mother had to be characterized, the Home for Decayed Gentlewomen. Old Lady Yardley was a permanent inmate: since her husband's death twenty-one years ago, she had never left Stanier, and Ronald, Violet's father, was scarcely less constant, for he only absented himself for a curative month at Aix or Marienbad every August, which should enable him to continue eating and drinking too much for the remainder of the year, or passed a occasional fortnight in his much less comfortable flat in town. When there he spent most of his time at his Club presenting the back of his head to St. James's Street, and dozing over a succession of morning and evening papers: the morning and evening papers were for him the current day. When Colin and his wife were in London, he would still stay on here, dining nightly in silence with his mother, and sitting with her afterwards, nodding and snorting under her steady and malevolent gaze till she was wheeled off by her nurse, and he would fuddle the rest of the evening away over a couple of cigars and the whisky bottle.

Ronald's wife, Margaret, also was usually in residence here, an eclipsed and negligible presence, whom it was difficult to be aware of, and impossible to miss. There had never been any real parental or filial relationship between her and Violet. She behaved with controlled propriety on all occasions, sad or festive, and emotion withered in her immaculate vicinity. The Stanier frost which falls on those who marry into that family had long ago congealed her: there was no telling what (if anything) lay beneath that cold chalky surface. She drank hot water with her meals (though it never thawed her), always replied if spoken to, took a walk every morning in the Park, if the day was fine, and if not, sat in her sitting-room in the Dowager's wing and played Patience. Her career in life was to write out the menu-cards for the dinner-table in French, with accents where required. Violet made occasional efforts to get in touch with her, but there was nothing to touch; her hand merely became numb with the cold mist in which it groped. Margaret Stanier went with her husband to Aix for his yearly cure: she kept house for him in London, but for the greater part of the year they were here, not welcome exactly, but not unwelcome, merely part of the house like stair carpets in unfrequented passages which were sometimes taken up, and then laid down again. It had always been so at Stanier: brothers and sons of earlier generations were part of the house, if they chose to make themselves so, until the day came when they were borne on their short journey to the family vault in the church that stood not two hundred yards away.

Lady Hester was the fourth but less chronic inhabitant

of the Dowager's wing, for she had still a lively appreciation of the gaieties and stir of life, and chiefly confined her visits to the times when "that wretch" Colin made things "go a bit." "For where's the use, my dear," she used to say, "in my sitting to be stared at by Mamma, or in watching poor Ronald fuddle himself? I like a bit more spunk than that." But she, like Violet, like Colin, like her brother, had that feeling about Stanier, just the place itself, which for generations all the family have shared. To them all it meant something intimate and indefinable, something for which Violet, for instance, had been willing to marry the dark uncouth Raymond, if, by that, she might become mistress of the house. True, that had not been required of her: she had married Hyperion instead of the Satyr, and had harvested love and that deep-set terror that prowled about in the darkness below these magnificent surfaces. Had she been challenged as to whether she believed in the legend in any literal sense, she would perhaps have denied it, but she would have given her soul to deny that, as regards Colin, there was no spiritual significance in it. Whether it was actually true or not, did not matter: that belonged to the dust of mediævalism. But there was a darkness deeper than that. . . . None of the others, not Aunt Hester with her gay paganism, not old Lady Yardley with her half-closed eyes and steady gaze, knew Colin as she knew him. They saw the charm of him, the beauty, the sunshine of his gaiety, and just occasionally winced under the quick lash of his tongue. But none of them shuddered at what lay below his sunshine.

There came out of the gallery door that presence which alone had power to scare off these black ill-omened birds of thought from Violet's mind. Here was the fourth of the generations that inhabited the house, Dennis in his perambulator being wheeled out for his evening airing and for whatever fresh discoveries about the use of legs might reward his daring. Just as he came out, the bath-chair with its withdrawn and antique occupant was passing the door, and dramatically enough, so it seemed to Violet, the two were face to face across the gulf of eighty years which divided them, both attended and conveyed, the one owing to the infirmity of faded energies, the other from he immaturity of them. Occasionally old Lady Yardley seemed o take some notice of Dennis; the faint dawning of the smile with which she looked on his father, would begin to hover on her mouth, and the heavy eyelids lifted a little. To-day, as Violet saw, that blink of recognition was there, but immediately Lady Yardley's face clouded again. "No, that's not Colin," she said to her nurse, "but he's coming." Then as the bath-chair in its peregrinations came close to the tea-table again her eyes were alert to see if he was there, but for Violet they had no spark of recognition. It was always for Colin that she searched: no one else could reward that silent scrutiny.

Violet got up when the bath-chair had turned and gone back, for here was the perambulator with Dennis in it. Her baby was the emblem and incarnation of those early days of her marriage, before she believed in that spiritual fulfilment of the legend which since had clouded the fair morning of her love with its gross darkness, and there lived for her again the hours when Colin was her adored lover in Southern nights at Capri, where, at his father's villa, they had spent their honeymoon. Dennis was to her the untainted blossom of those days.

There he was, drumming with his hands on the apron of his perambulator, demanding with shrill cheerful crowings to be let out to make fresh discoveries about the laws of motion. He saw her coming towards him and the crowings swelled into enraptured squeals.

"Take him out, Nurse," said Violet. "Now, Dennis, come and walk to me."

That was precisely what Dennis wanted to do if he could, but the squeals subsided over the extreme seriousness of the undertaking. He stood, swaying slightly, as his nurse's arms released him, and regarding with fixed attention the two dimpled sandalled feet which certainly had some share in the proposed excursion, though it was still a matter of doubt as to what that share was. After having examined them both, he decided to put his best foot foremost. This was a complete success, and he shouted "Daddy!" which wasn't quite so clever. That effort somehow disturbed his equilibrium, and he fell down.

"Clumsy," said his mother. "Try again, Dennis."

Dennis had not the slightest intention of trying again just now. There was a crack between two paving-stones which was more interesting than the problems of locomotion. But destiny, in the habiliment of his nurse, set him on his feet, and Violet moved a little nearer in order to make the tremendous gulf of yards that separated them yawn less impossibly. Then staggering like a ship at sea, he launched himself again, and after a wild semi-circular career he fell against her skirts.

But exploration is exhausting work, taxing to the nerves and imagination as much as to the muscles, and presently he was wheeled away again for bath and bed. But still up and down the terrace, now pausing, now moving on again, went Lady Yardley's bath-chair, as she waited for Colin to come and bring her back out of the mists where she moved into the clear twilight, which, though veiled and dim, rendered visible the phantoms that peopled it. But when the dressing bell sounded she spoke:

"Take me in," she said. "Colin will be here for dinner, and I must not be late."

To-night Ronald Stanier was the first down. He had been something of a buck in his earlier years, and the habit of impressing the world with his gallant appearance, had remained with him through dishevelling age and a remarkable fondness for food and drink had rendered his task more difficult. His forehead and crown were completely bald, but he grew his hair, of a bright suspicious auburn and unflecked by any line of grey, very long on one side of his head, and espaliered it carefully over the shiny pink skin of his pate. He wore clothes that were meant to make him look slim, but only succeeded in looking tight themselves; a monocle, a large solitaire and a carnation were the other salient points of his decorative scheme. His face, loose and fleshy, had a trampled look about it, as of a muddy lane over which a flock of sheep had passed: he limped a little as he came down the gallery. His wife, thin and dry, followed him shortly after, and presently old Lady Yardley was wheeled in. She took no notice whatever of the others, and, with the help of her stick, transferred herself to the brocaded chair by the fireplace, where that invariable couple of logs sent up a vacillating thread of blue smoke. Why on so hot a night a fire should have been there was beyond conjecture; but so it always was: perhaps a hundred years ago someone, when they assembled here for dinner, had unexpectedly found the room chilly.

They all sat silent. Why should any of them speak, and put somebody else to the trouble of a reply? Nothing had happened since, twenty-four hours ago, they had last met here: no fresh interest had stirred the toneless tranquillity. Ronald's slight attack of gout was certainly better, and he meant to drink his port again to-night: his wife's Patience had 'come out' twice; as for Lady Yardley, was she living in to-day at all, or in times long buried beneath the years? Then Lady Hester joined them, brisk from her walk and her 'tub.' She asked Ronald how he was, she told them where she had been, and then she, too, succumbed, and sat silent. Violet followed, made a general apology for being late, and the doors into the dining-room were thrown open.

"Will you take Grandmamma in?" she said to her father, and the other three followed.

Though the evening sky was still radiant, and there was light enough to have dined with unshuttered windows, curtains were drawn and the room lit with many candles, for Staniers dined by candlelight, quantities of candlelight, whatever the sun happened to be doing. Round the panelled walls were a dozen family portraits, each with its concealed electric illumination that made them look as if they had stepped forward from the walls, and were part of that little knot of their heirs and inheritors who sat round the table. For all their unbroken continuity, the Staniers had always grown on a slender stem, and to-night, with Dennis rosily sleeping upstairs on the floor above, only Colin was wanting to complete the full number of the clan. From generation to generation all collateral lines descended from daughters or younger sons had died out, but the silver cord of the direct descent had never been broken. Now from the walls, the past ages joined the present: here seated in the soft glow of candles was the fruit and distillation of the years, Ronald with his heavy wine-bibber's face, Hester, in whom, as she had said, beauty had run to seed in prettiness, and Violet. The other two, Ronald's wife and old Lady Yardley, had been, so to speak, but the fuel that made the Stanier fire burn. The younger, Violet's mother, was no more than a burned-out cinder in the grate, she had done her part, and the dustman would sometime call and remove her; the elder, watchful and alive below the ash, still glowed with some inscrutable vigour. Through her had passed the spark that now blazed in Colin and Violet alike, and something of it still lived in her embers. For more than sixty years, Stanier and all that it stood for had soaked into her: she had become a sort of incarnation of the Stanier consciousness, and, sunk far below the surface, except when Colin was present, into whose gay hands she could resign her watchful responsibility, she witnessed and recorded.

The stately silent meal went on, unutterably dull, and

impeccably exquisite. A vagabond or a hungry tramp would almost have preferred to go unfed than to have his cravings so joylessly satisfied, but then the Staniers were not tramps or vagabonds, and this was the way they had dinner. Alone with Aunt Hester or even with the additional incumbrance of her father and mother, Violet could have hoisted the standard of ordinary human sociability, and made a normal little festival of the meal, but neither she nor Aunt Hester could struggle long, without the dispelling influence of Colin's beam, against that paralyzing effect of old Lady Yardley's presence, her silence and her steady watchfulness. It was like talking in the presence of an open coffin, where lay something corpse-like yet alive. . . .

Violet, as usual, had begun dinner with her invariable effort to pull them all out of that deadly pit into which they nightly descended.

"Dennis walked at least ten yards this evening, Mamma, without falling down once," she said to Mrs. Stanier. "Colin will be surprised to see how he has got on."

For a second Lady Yardley's eyelids flickered at the name of Colin.

"He will get on quickly now," said Mrs. Stanier. "When babies once begin to walk, they soon pick it up."

This was a very just observation but lacked any initiative touch.

"I think he's rather forward," said Violet. "He's only fourteen months old."

"Yes, just fourteen months," said Mrs. Stanier. "Fancy!"

Violet wheeled to Lady Hester.

"And where did you go, Aunt Hester?" she said. "Did you find any coolness? It's the hottest day we've had this year."

"Yes, my dear, it's like an oven," said Lady Hester. "I hate the summer. It broils my bones, and then there's a thunderstorm, which scares me stiff."

"Yes, a glass of sherry," said Ronald. He took up the menu card and held it up to his monocled eye.

A short silence fell. Violet tried again.

"And when are you going off to Aix, father?" she said. "I hear it's tremendously full this year."

"Next week," said Ronald.

Violet let her eyes sweep round the pictured walls. Just opposite her was the picture of Colin, painted by the most famous artist of the day. He more than any of the other portraits seemed to have drawn close to the dining-table. He had stepped boldly forth, in another moment he would be standing at old Lady Yardley's elbow. . . .

Lady Hester made an effort. The midges had bitten her during her walk, and she felt what she would have called 'scratchy.'

"Well, I could never see the sense of filling yourself up with stinking waters," she said, "and being pounded as if you were a heap of clothes at the wash."

Ronald put down his menu card. Always he pretended not to be deaf.

"Beg your pardon, Hester?" he said.

There are many things which it is easy to say once but impossible to repeat. This seemed one of them, and the next silence was rather longer.

"You will like your game of whist to-night, Granny?" asked Violet at length.

Lady Yardley did not answer. She held up her finger as if listening, not to what Violet said but to something inaudible to the others. Then she turned to the butler.

"Give me my stick," she said. "I hear wheels. That is Colin."

"No, Granny, he's not coming to-night," said Violet.

Lady Yardley grasped her stick and had half-risen from her place, when there came a step along the gallery floor, and the door opened.

"It is Colin," said she.

Colin entered: it was as if the sunlight came in with him. The room seemed to leap into brightness.

"Ah, what a dreadful time to arrive!" he said. "Don't get up anybody, or I shall go away again. Violet, darling! How blessed to see you! Granny, my dear Granny! Aunt Hester . . . everybody. Just push me a chair in, and let me sit down with you. Where shall it be put? I don't know. I want to sit next everybody."

He sat down between old Lady Yardley and Hester, and ran his hand through his hair.

"I'm dusty, I'm dirty, I'm dishevelled," he said, "but I needn't go and wash, need I, Granny? I want dinner. Don't send me away to wash, and brush my hair, as you used to do when I was little."

"I knew you were coming, Colin," she said. "I told them all you were coming."

"You're a witch, Granny," he said. "I'm not sure you oughtn't to be burned. You shall have your game of whist afterwards, and then we'll make a fire of the cards and burn you. But you expected me, didn't you? I telephoned, or somebody telephoned surely?"

Colin knew that he had not telephoned, or told anybody to telephone: the fact that his statement was not true, made a mild reason for uttering it. It had only occurred to him a couple of hours ago to come down, and he had driven straight off with Nino, his young Italian servant. The image of Stanier, spacious and cool among its woods, had drifted across the reek of the grilling streets, and gave him the impulse: he never resisted an impulse. . . .

"Darling Aunt Hester," he said, "I couldn't get on without you a minute more. Everyone in London was old and cross, and I wanted to feel young again. Good gracious me, have you got to dessert already? You mustn't wait for me. My fault for being so late. Uncle Ronald will keep me company over his wine. No, I don't want any soup. Give me some cold ham or something. Granny, I'm going to be like you for the future, and never leave Stanier any more. We'll grow old together."

She was leaning forward, listening to him, and laid her hand on his.

"No, Colin, you must never grow old," she said. "You mustn't grow old or die. It isn't good to die. And you haven't brought Raymond with you, have you? I don't want Raymond."

Colin patted her hand.

"No, he's not come with me," he said. "He couldn't manage to come."

He spoke quickly and low to Violet.

"Get up, dear, and take her away," he said. "I want to have my dinner in peace."

"What is that you're saying, Colin?" asked Lady Yardley.

"Nothing, Granny. Now you go and sit in the gallery, and presently we'll have our game of whist."

"But I want to have my dinner with you," said she.

Something ugly and impatient gleamed in those blue eyes of his for a moment, but it sheathed itself again.

"Nonsense, Granny," he said. "You've had your dinner."

Violet had come round the table.

"Won't you let her stop with you," she said quietly. "She's been looking out for you all the evening."

"No, darling, I won't," he said. "Not much competition for her, eh, Vi? Take her away . . . Go on, Granny, Violet's waiting for you. Uncle Ronald and I will come after you when we've had a glass of wine together."

The door closed behind the women, and Colin sat down again.

"Granny seems to be immortal," he observed. "That's a great score. She'll see you and me into our graves, Uncle Ronald. The gout's better, I'm glad to see, and permits you to have port again. Have some more?"

"Well, perhaps another glass, while you're eating your dinner," said Ronald. He was never very comfortable alone with Colin, but he wanted port. Though not a person of very quick perception, he felt as if he was in the presence of some lithe fierce creature, which might suddenly snap at him. When other people were there, they served as bars.

"That's right," said Colin. "You see if you can get through a bottle of port by the time I've finished dinner. I'll bet that you can. Aren't we a sadly degenerated race, Uncle Ronald? I hardly ever touch wine. Tell me about the old days when you and my grandfather used to sit soaking at this table hour after hour. Bring another bottle of port," he said to the butler.

"No, indeed, Colin, there's plenty here," said Ronald. "Just one glass more for me, and then I've done."

Colin felt himself scintillating with evil purpose. The atmosphere, the environment of Stanier was always charged with currents that vivified and stimulated him. If no more subtle entertainment offered itself at the moment, he could at least induce Uncle Ronald to drink more than was good for him. Perhaps he would get tipsy, perhaps his gout would begin jabbing him again: it would all afford amusement.

"Oh, I know what your one glass more means," he said. "Besides you're going to Aix soon, and that will set it right. I think I must learn to drink, for there's clearly pleasure in it, and it is criminal to deny oneself a pleasure. Ah, there's the fresh bottle. Sunshine, you know, Uncle Ronald. It was the sunshine that brooded over some vineyard before I was born that produced that wine. Without the sunshine there would never have been any wine that year. There's romance for you! That's not a bottle of wine really: it's a bottle of sunshine and the warm air of the South. Just what's so good for gout."

Ronald took a few seconds to follow the course of this admirable reasoning; then he gave an appreciative chuckle.

"Upon my word, that's a new way of looking at it," he said. "Makes it seem as if it will be positively good for me."

"Of course it will," said Colin. "That's the whole system of modern physics. If you think anything is good for you, it does you good."

Ronald clapped his loose lips to the glass, and smacked them.

"Nectar!" he said. "You miss a lot, Colin, by not joining me. But not a word to your Aunt Margaret, mind—I should get a scolding if she knew I had had more than one glass."

"No, I won't tell her," said Colin. "We'll see if she discovers it without being told."

Ronald, twiddling the stem of his wine-glass, faintly wondered what Colin meant. Certainly it was a wonderful bottle of port that had been brought him, and it did not matter much what Colin meant. He emptied his glass and with an absent air refilled it again.

"Much going on in town?" he asked. "Dances? Dinners? Ah, when I was a young fellow I don't suppose I dined at home once in a month, nor got back there till three or four in the morning."

Colin found his fingers twitching with sudden dislike of this buckish old wine-biber. Why, after all, did he let him and his thin-lipped scarecrow wife feed and board themselves here? Her return for her keep was to write out the menu-cards, his to consume, as fast as was reasonable to expect of any one man, all the best bins. True, it was a custom in great houses at one time to keep a professional fool on the premises for entertainment, but when he became a bore, you sent him down to the scullery, or wherever he lived. He must really consider the question of conveying to Uncle Ronald and his wife that their visit had been rather a long one, for they had lived here since before Violet's birth. He might begin now.

"Oh, it's been quite lively," he said. "And I daresay you'll have a gay autumn. I suppose you and Aunt Margaret will settle down in London when you get back from Aix."

Ronald finished his glass in rather a hurry.

"Bless me, no," he said, "there's no thought of that. My London gaieties are over, but for a week or two occasionally, and naturally I couldn't think of leaving your grandmother."

Again Colin's fingers twitched with dislike. Why should he at this moment be sitting here with this boring old man with his tremulous hand and his plastered hair, who couldn't think of ever leaving Stanier? He might be assisted to think of it. . . .

"Couldn't you, indeed?" he said. "Why, of course, that settles it, doesn't it? Let me fill your glass for you."

Ronald made a clumsy feint of putting his hand over the bowl.

"No, upon my word, not a drop more," he said.

Colin inserted the lip of the decanter between his glass and the covering hand, and filled it up again.

"Of course that settles it," he repeated.

This reiterated observation seemed to give Ronald food for thought. He began to see that Colin might be speaking ironically; he did sometimes. But his glass was full again, and it was wiser to not pursue an uncomfortable topic at a convivial hour. Better to be genial and companionable.

"And if you haven't filled up my glass again!" he said. "Well, Stanier was always a hospitable house, and very worthily, my dear fellow, you carry on the tradition."

Colin got up. Uncle Ronald's little doxology might be brought to bear on the hospitality he had enjoyed for so many years.

"Kind of you to say so, but I have my limits," he observed. "Perhaps you had better finish your wine, Uncle Ronald, or we shall have my grandmother back looking for you. You mustn't leave her, as you said just now."

Ronald got to his feet. He was still a little lame, and Colin moved towards him.

"You'd better take my arm," he said. "Or Aunt Margaret will see you've had another glass of port without anybody telling her."

Ronald gave his gross chuckle.

"That would be a singular thing," he said, "if a Stanier couldn't carry the drop of wine I've drunk without inconvenience. It's only the fag-end of my attack of gout that makes me lame."

Colin, however, pressed a friendly arm on him, and together they went into the gallery.

"Granny dear, we've left you a long time," said he, "but Uncle Ronald was so amusing that I couldn't tear myself away. Now, Uncle Ronald, you sit quietly there on the sofa."

Colin steered his uncle to the sofa, thus conveying the impression that there was need for guidance.

"Now, Granny," he said, "we'll get to our whist. Whom shall we ask to play with us? Here's Violet and Aunt Margaret; oh, that leaves Aunt Hester out."

Aunt Hester instantly disclaimed any desire to play. She had got hold of a number of '*Vogue*,' with a very dainty picture of a young lady on the cover, with a hat that she thought would suit her. . . .

At half-past ten old Lady Yardley's bath-chair was wheeled in for her, and as soon as the second rubber came to an end she was taken off. Ronald had already left his sofa and drifted away, without doubt to the smoking-room. Aunt Hester, who had cut into the second rubber, gathered up her winnings.

"And I'll be off, too," she said, "or I shall lose my beauty-sleep. Bless me, have I won all those silver shillings! Somebody will want to marry me for my money."

"Aunt Hester knows that every handsome young man in London would like to marry her if she hadn't a penny," observed Colin.

"You're a sad rascal," said Aunt Hester, fearfully pleased. "Good night, everybody."

Aunt Margaret followed, and Violet would have done so, but at the door Colin stopped her.

"Not five minutes' chat, Vi?" he said. "I haven't had a word with you all the evening. . . . Ah, that's dear of you. Come out on the terrace. Let's take a stroll. I want to talk to you."

"Anything special?" asked Violet.

"Oh, just bits of things. Mayn't a man want to talk to his wife sometimes?"

He paused for a moment as they stepped out. The moonlight shone full-orbed on the front of the house in vivid but colourless illumination, making a warm neutral tone of its mellow redness. Below the lake gleamed silver grey, across it was ruled the velvet blackness of the yew-hedge, and beyond, the marsh stretched level to the sea. Colin's eyes sparkled as he looked on the heritage that he loved, but came back quickly to Violet.

"My word, you're a beautiful woman!" he said. "I was in luck, wasn't I, with my wooing? Did you hear Granny ask me if Raymond had come? I wish he had. I often wish Raymond was here to look on our happiness."

He took her arm, and began walking towards the yew-hedge. Stanier always stimulated him to be himself, and it was through some little revelation of himself that he could most surely make her wince.

"I often thought of telling you something about Raymond," he said, "which perhaps you never guessed. Do you know I actually saw him drown? Only just for a second but such an interesting one. I can see it now, like some scene on the movies. I had gone down to the lake after him, heard the crash of the ice, and there he was in the water. There was nothing to be done. If I had jumped in after him I should only have drowned as well, and you wouldn't have liked that. Nor would I."

Violet felt herself shudder, not at what Colin had done or what he had not done but at what he *was*. . . . That trembling passed down the bare arm in which Colin had linked his.

"That's not really news to me," she said. "I guessed it."

Colin pressed her arm.

"I wondered if you had," he said. "Characteristic of me, wasn't it, to be in at the death. My dear, how horrified you are at me. You're trembling. I rather like your being horrified at me, and yet I rather resent it. What odd people we are, to be sure. . . . Are you glad to see me, Vi? Pleased I came down? Rather a difficult question, isn't it? I make you shudder sometimes; I make you freeze. And yet you love me. That's what tortures you. . . . Look, there's the door in the yew hedge! It was exactly there you stood, when you found out you loved me. And the next morning you threw Raymond over. I adored that morning. However, we'll leave these romantic reminiscences, and come on to this evening. Cigarette? My God, Violet, what an evening!"

He offered her his case, and then took one himself, nursing the match in his hollowed hands. His face vividly lit, glowed with some elfish glee.

"What a menagerie!" he said. "I don't suppose if you searched through all England, and goodness knows there are monstrosities enough everywhere, that you'd find such a collection. The whole lot of them ought to go into Barnum's show. Look at Granny! She would be the 'World-famous Animated Corpse.' She's not alive, she's been dead for centuries, and I've got some uncanny power of animating her. Is she immortal, do you think?—an immortal corpse? Will she see us all out? I shouldn't wonder."

Colin sat down on a bench by the yew hedge drawing Violet gently with him.

"But after all she only comes on for her evening 'turn,'" he said, "and it rather amuses me to hear her talk about

Raymond. She's almost a museum piece, isn't she? They'll send down from the British Museum some day, and say her case is ready for her, and they'll put her in some room full of Anglo-Saxon remains. Really I'm rather proud of her: she's a bore, of course, but there are worse things than bores. Aunt Hester, for instance. What an awful old woman! What a grizzly kitten! She's prinking before the glass now, I'll bet, because I said all the handsome young men in London were in love with her. There's an object lesson for you, as to how not to grow old. A cocotte of sixty—I think I shall tell Nino to make love to her. She would marry him, I'm sure, if he asked her."

Colin paused, and Violet could guess what was coming next.

"Yet there's a sort of entertainment about Aunt Hester," he said. "It amuses me to see how silly and preposterous she can be. But what about your deadly old father, darling? What can be said for Uncle Ronald?"

He waited to see if Violet could find anything to say for Uncle Ronald.

"Don't bother your head over trying to find a decent point about him," he said. "It's so comfortable being able to talk him over quite frankly with you, because you've never had the slightest real feeling for him, and so I can say what's in my mind without fear of hurting you. And probably I know him better than you, for it's my privilege to sit over the table with him when you've taken the female part of the menagerie out of dinner, and to see him at his most characteristic moments. He's really himself you know then, when I entice him out of his eclipse of sobriety, and he gets a little squiffy. He comes out then: the shadow of temperance passes off his bloated old face."

She interrupted him, still shuddering at him.

"Ah, you're dreadful!" she said. "Why do you let him get like that? You encourage him to: it amuses you in some horrible manner to see him degrade himself."

"Lord! He doesn't need much encouragement," said Colin. "I fancy he encourages himself quite sufficiently when I'm not there to help him. To-morrow I shall just look at the cellar-book, and see how much he has encouraged himself since I've been away. Don't misunderstand me now, wilfully or unintentionally, and think that I grudge him drinking a bottle or two of port every night, even though he's rapidly finishing all the 1860 vintage which is quite irreplaceable.

What I object to is that I should have to sit there and see him growing more purple and nauseous while he's doing it. But clearly, as long as he's with us, I can't be so inhospitable as to stint my own uncle and your father of the only thing he cares about. Certainly I wish he would take to whisky, so that other guests of mine might get a few glasses of wine before he has finished it all, but Uncle Ronald doesn't begin on whisky till he goes to the smoking-room. . . . The filthy old pig. Cigarette, darling? It will soothe you."

Violet got up.

"Colin, I can't stay and listen to you talking about my father like that," she said. "It amuses you to make him drink, and it's horrible of you."

Colin lit his cigarette with great deliberation.

"Well, if you can't stay and listen to me," he said, "you can go away. But you're not going: you want to hear what I've got to say next. Ah! You sit down again, I notice."

He threw the match away, and again put his arm through Violet's.

"I don't grudge him his wine," he said, "because I want everybody to do as he pleases. He may drink himself into his grave as soon as he likes or sooner for all I care, and in fact I give him the shovel, so to speak, to dig himself in. But what I do grudge is the damnable infliction of his company on me. And Uncle Ronald seems to think that Stanier belongs to him. I hinted, ever so gently to-night, that I supposed he would settle down in London when he comes back from Aix, and he said that was out of the question, because he couldn't possibly think of leaving Granny. Now I hated that. To begin with Granny has no more use for him than she has for a toothache, and also it's quite untrue. Supposing Granny—it doesn't seem likely—were to die, he wouldn't dream of leaving Stanier, unless I kicked him out. And what I hated most was his notion that he has a right to live at Stanier, and guzzle and snore his days away. He's got a house in London; let him go and live there, and since he can't leave Granny, I suppose he'll take her with him. Aunt Margaret will go too then, though it doesn't matter what Aunt Margaret does, as it's impossible to tell whether she's there or not. Sometimes I'm afraid of sitting down on her by mistake: it's dreadfully difficult to be aware of her. Of course when one is aware of her, she's a crashing bore. She fills up space somehow, without putting anything there. Such a lady, too! All her nature is swallowed up in being a lady. After all, Vi, they've paid Stanier a nice long visit. Something over twenty years, off and on, and chiefly on. But isn't it time almost that the menagerie went to a new place? Barnum used to travel, you know: they all do."

Violet had never contemplated any possibility of such a thing, nor imagined that Colin would. Always at Stanier there had been this background of relatives; what would it be like to be here alone with Colin? As if he had heard her unspoken thought, he answered it.

"And you and I are never together alone, Vi," he said. "Never since our honeymoon at Capri have we been alone."

"Do you want to be?" she asked.

He laughed.

"No, darling: I should hate it. I only wanted to see how you would look if I suggested it. You looked just as I imagined you would. But I daresay that won't often happen: don't be alarmed. . . . Now I've inserted into Uncle Ronald's mind the notion that perhaps, when he comes back to England from Aix, he might live at his own charges for a bit, and I want you to-morrow, to touch on it again. In a little while he will get it into his head. . . . Not at once, of course: one couldn't expect that. Tell him he may take away all the 1860 port that he hasn't already drunk. That may be an inducement, or there mayn't be much in it: I will go through the cellar-book. Granny, I'm afraid, won't go with him, though he can't leave her. We shall have a lot of people here all the autumn, I expect, and Uncle Ronald isn't—well, he isn't really up to parties any more. He behaves as if he was alone: he makes windy noises in his throat. And we'll begin to ask Aunt Hester for certain dates, don't you know: the twelfth to the seventeenth, underlined."

"Stanier has always been a home to the older generation," said Violet. "I don't know how Father will take it."

"He'll take it neat, probably," said Colin. "But I really don't see why, because Stanier has always been a geological museum for family fossils, it should continue to be. That's all about that, darling. Please do as I tell you. Ah, and how's Dennis?"

"Very flourishing, and learning to walk so quickly."

"That's good. And any signs of character yet emerging?" asked Colin.

"Only the desire to investigate and explore. . . . Colin, about the other matter——"

He interrupted her.

"I know what you are going to say, darling," he said. "You will tell me to do my own dirty work, though, of course, you'll put it much more politely. Was that it?"

"Yes. It's your house, and if you choose to turn my father and mother out you must do it yourself."

Colin patted her hand.

"Well, well: don't let us quarrel on the very evening I come home," he said. "I just note that you don't intend to do as I ask you, but I daresay you'll be very glad to before long. Now about Dennis. He likes investigating and exploring, does he? That's like me. We must feed him with plenty of material, direct his attention, as he grows, to all sorts of things. Early impressions are so important: they form a child's character and mind, so psycho-analysts say. And you never can tell what may be impressing itself. I must see a lot of Dennis."

He laughed quietly to himself, a soft purring laugh, and a sudden wave of terror came over her at this beautiful and awful boy—he looked no more than a boy—whom she loathed and loved. To her there was something sinister and menacing in his saying that he must see a lot of Dennis, that a child's character was determined by its early impression. What impressions would he feed Dennis with? . . .

"Oh, Colin," she cried, clutching at his hand, "for God's sake, let Dennis escape the curse of the legend. Don't make him evil . . ."

Colin threw back his head and laughed aloud.

"Was there ever such a ridiculous woman?" he cried. "What on earth do you mean? You speak as if I was intending to mix brandy with his milk to give him a taste for drink, or bid him look at Aunt Hester to get a taste for cocottes, or at dear Aunt Margaret to stunt his intelligence. Really, darling, the moon must be exercising a lunatic influence on you. You're not very complimentary, you know; in fact I should say you were damned rude, only I never say that sort of thing. You tell me I'm a wicked fellow with a taste for corrupting the mind of a baby at the bottle. Let's go indoors, or there'll be a mad-woman to add to the menagerie."

CHAPTER II

Colin woke next morning to a serene sense of well-being; while still too drowsy to question himself on the cause of this sunny sleepy happiness, he knew it was there. Then he remembered that he was at Stanier, which alone might account for this content at waking, and one after another fresh interests and anticipated amusements came bubbling into his mind. That talk with Violet in the moonlight last night embodied several of them, but there was another which interested him more.

He drew himself up in bed, and took from the table by it a great pile of typewritten sheets, the perusal of which had caused him so late and absorbed a session last night. There was the transcript, now made for the first time, of the memoirs written by his Elizabethan ancestor, to whom and to whose bargain the fortunes of the house were wondrously due. When last he went to London he had taken the original volume with him for reproduction in more legible form, for the text was written in a strange, crabbed hand, the ink of which was dim with age, and was so difficult to follow, that the mere decipherment of it occupied the mind to the exclusion of the appreciation of the text. But the fragments which he had puzzled out were so sprightly and entertaining that he had determined to procure a less distracted study of the whole.

Colin had read last night with fascinated glee the account of the early life of his ancestral namesake, who analysed his own nature, not in tedious terms of abstract tendencies, but by the far more convincing method of putting down just what he did, and letting his actions analyse for him. He admirably sketched his boyhood in the days when the marsh was still largely undrained, and the white-plumed avocets bred there, when the tall ships came up full-sailed on the tide to Rye, and the smugglers brought in barrels of Hollands, and if caught were summarily hanged. His father, Ronald Stanier, whom he succinctly described as "a drunken sot" (how charmingly did heredity reproduce the type) was a farmer with fat acres and full flocks, who dissolved his substance in drink. He was barbarously harsh to the boy and to his wife, whom he tamed from her shrewish ways into obedience and silence, and used to beat them both till there came a day when Colin had no mind to take any more strappings, and soundly thrashed his own father. "And this I did," he wrote, "with great pleasure, not only because I served him as he had served me, and with a stronger arm, but because I had always hated him." He described his own queer power over animals: a savage dog would never bite him, an unruly horse behaved itself when he came near it, "and that was strange, because I had no love for animals, and indeed no love at all. I made good pretence, for so folk were kind to me, and I liked a wench well enough for my own pleasure to which she ministered, but all I loved was my own strength, and my own beauty, which they loved too. . . ."

Colin had got to this point last night, and now, sitting up in bed, ran over the pages again. How amazingly history repeated itself; there more than three centuries ago was Ronald Stanier the drunken sot, and the tamed silent wife, who was the mother of Staniers: and there above all, three centuries ago, was his very self, incarnate surely in the bodily tabernacle of his ancestor, he and his handsome face which the wenches loved, and his heart which hated love and loved hate.

And then came the story of the Legend, told with sober conviction by the beneficiary himself. The boy had gone that day (it was a week before Easter) to see the Queen pass through Rye, and luck attended him, for he had been at hand when Her Grace's horse stumbled, and she would have had a fall had he not run forward and caught her in his arms.

"And I knelt, after she had released me from her flat bosom," he recounted, "and gave her just such a look as I would give to a wench at a fair, and I saw this pleased her." She told him to wait on her at the Manor of Brede next day, and he went back to the lambing, for the ewes were fruitful, and his father was drunk, and all that afternoon and deep into the night he was busy with his midwifery, and finally he threw himself down on a heap of straw in the shepherd's hut, for a few hours' sleep before morning. He woke, while it was yet dark, but, dark though it was, he could see that a fine tall fellow dressed in red stood by him, who revealed himself as none other than Satan. He promised him all that his heart could desire, of health and wealth, of beauty and honour and affluence, if in return for these gifts he would sign away his soul. "I cared little for my soul," so ran the account, "and I cared much for honour and wealth, and further he did promise me that our bargain should hold good for the heirs and descendants of this my body, if they should choose to take advantage of it. So quickly we were at terms, and he gave me pen and parchment and I pricked my arm for ink and signed in my blood the deed he had prepared, which deed he bade me keep as testimony to our pleasant bargain. Then shone there a strong flash of light in my eyes, and I cried out and fell back on the straw, where I had been sleeping, and he was gone from me, and the night was yet black round me. But this was no dream, for the parchment was in my hand, and then came a blink of lightning, and I saw that my signature of blood was still wet."

Colin gave a gasp of pure pleasure and surprise. What an inimitable touch of veracity was that! No one could have invented that; the experience, fantastic and dipped in mediæval superstition was absolutely and literally real to the writer. He described what he saw. In this first-hand contemporary record, the legend of Faust lived again in unadorned and literal simplicity. Since then it had come into sad disrepute, becoming merged in cooked-up tales and elaborate myths: Marlowe had made a tragedy of it, and Goethe fishing it up had built a dreary and tedious philosophy on it, and Gounod had made an opera of it. But here was the same story plain and vivid without comment or moralizing. Faust himself was describing just what *happened*. . . .

Colin turned the page. Authentic and eye-witnessed surely as was that touch about the blood being still wet, there were difficulties, insuperable ones, about accepting the story of the Legend in connection with the parchment now let into the frame of old Colin's portrait. Here was a perfectly ignorant shepherd-boy, who almost certainly could neither read nor write, subscribing his name to a document which was, if the parchment was authentic, written in Latin. The most credulous could hardly swallow that. . . .

He read on: "I had no skill then either to read or write, but there still wet and red was what I had written. After that I slept soundly, and in the morning I got home and hid away the parchment, and went to wait on the Queen's Grace as she had bade me, at the Manor of Brede. Of that I will tell presently, but here first will I tell of the parchment, and what befell. For presently I was attached to Her Grace's Court, as her page, and there I learned both to read and write, and Latin I learned too, for she loved to speak in Latin, and show her wisdom and learning which indeed was no great affair. Then could I see that though, on that night in the sheepfold, I had no knowledge of writing, yet I had signed my name, very scholarly and clerk like, and in the hand that was mine when I had learned to write. Then, too, I could read what therein was promised me, riches and honour, all of which came to pass. As for the parchment itself, I kept that secretly, and told no man of it, for they burn at the stake those who have had dealings with my Lord and benefactor, and I had no wish to suffer such a fate. For my soul I have no care; I do not reckon my soul at the worth of a doit, but it would be a grievous thing to be burned, though I, while my life was yet strong in me and the lusts of the flesh sweet. So I told no man of the matter, except only in after years my two sons, each of them, when he came of age. I had brought them up with both precept and example for their profit, and they knew what manner of man their father was, and how mightily he prospered, and how it went ill with those who crossed him, and so, when their time came to know of the parchment, and to make their choice, it was no wonder that they chose with wisdom and prudence, even as I had done. . . . Now let me write what so wonderfully befell when next morning I walked to Brede and waited on the Queen. . . ."

Just so far had Colin got in his reading, when Nino, his valet, came in to call him. Usually Colin slept like a child till he was roused; often Nino had to twitch his bedclothes or rattle with cans before he could raise him out of these tranquil deeps.

"Awake, signor?" said Nino in surprise.

"Yes, very much so," said Colin. "Morning, Nino, I've been reading about what I was like rather more than three hundred years ago."

Nino put his letters and the morning paper by the bedside. There was no one in the world to whom Colin felt more akin than to him. Nino was Southern and gay, and had the morals of a sleek black panther. In the Italian fashion, he had made Colin his chief interest in life: he was devoted to him and was quite without fear of him. In Nino's eyes whatever Colin did was right.

Nino beamed over this unintelligible remark. All that mattered was that Colin was pleased.

"And used I to call you in the morning then?" he asked.

"No one called me in the morning as far as I've got," said

Colin. "I was a shepherd-boy with bare feet. What sort of a day is it, Nino?"

"I brought it straight from Capri," said Nino. "Hot, hot, ever so hot."

"I'll bathe then," said Colin, getting out of bed. "Bring some clothes along, Nino. Just flannels. Come and bathe, too. I hate bathing alone. And bring my tea with you. I'll drink it after my bath."

The morning as Nino had said was already very hot, but the dew of the night before had been heavy, and in the shadow the grass was still shining with it, and the smell of the wet earth was fragrant with liquid freshness. Colin kicked off his shoes for the pleasure of walking barefooted; and for very lightness of heart ran whistling down the grass slope to the lake. There was a bathing shed on the bank towards the deep end with steps and spring-board, and next moment he had stripped off his pyjamas, and stood poised to cleave the deep water, where the rhododendrons and the white balustrade of the sluice were unwaveringly reflected. Taut as an arrow of sunlit limbs he flicked outwards from the board and disappeared in a fountain of foam.

He rose to the surface and struck out into the lake, swimming with overhead stroke, his shoulders gleaming as they lifted themselves alternately, his golden head now a-wash and now glistening in the sunlight as it emerged. Then when he was halfway across the lake, and opposite the sluice, he turned and swam straight towards it. . . . There the water was deepest, and there it slept in the shadow of the bushes, and now he dipped his head and dived, scooping with his arms, and pulling himself downwards. Down, down he pressed, till the twilight of the depths closed round him, and the bright surface above was veiled and dim. The water was markedly colder here, and he thought how cold it must have been to Raymond when the ice was thick above. . . . Then turning he kicked out, and shot upwards again into the sunshine and the sweet air.

Nino had followed hard on him, bringing his clothes and his tea, and as Colin came to the surface again, there he was on the header-board ready to dive. Colin swam towards him.

"See if you can get to the bottom, Nino," he said, "where it's deep opposite the sluice."

Nino rose from his plunge, and laughed, shaking the water from his face.

"Scusi, signor," he said, "but I do not like the depth below. That is the place for the dead."

Colin laughed back at him.

"So it is," he said. "'Down among the dead men': there's a song about it. I don't insist on your going there yet."

"Grazie: molte grazie!" said Nino.

Soon Colin paddled to land, and lay basking on the grass. Never had he felt the current of life run more strongly through him, tingling for some outlet of self-expression. And yet just to be alive was enough, here in the home of his inheritance, which he, about whom he had been reading last night and this morning, had built to the glory of himself and those who came after. And it was more than kinship he seemed to claim with that engaging ruffian, it was identity; the memoirs shewed him his own mirrored self, astonishingly revealed. There was much more of them to come, at present he had but read a chapter or two, the sincerity of which he could vouch for by the picture it gave not of the writer only but of himself. He burned with his passions, bubbled with his hatreds, revelled in the largesse of 'his Lord and benefactor.' He had his son, too, whom one day he would initiate into the evil sacrament, and like Colin of old he would let Dennis see how mightily his father prospered in his allegiance, and how it went ill with those who crossed him, so that when the time came for Dennis's choice he would choose with wisdom and prudence, as old Colin's sons had done. As yet he was but a baby, scarcely able to walk, but soon he would learn what splendid paths were hewn for him, how royal a road. . . .

The future lay before Colin wrapped in this sunlit mist, much as the plain of the marsh lay swathed in pearly vapours. Soon the heat would fold up that soft mantle of the cool night, and the plain glitter in the sun-steeped noon; and just so with him would the future emerge and shew its discovered delights. He had no wish to brush the mists away, or dive and grope into that obscurity. All would grow clear as his own life rose towards its noon . . . as for the evening and the decay of day which would follow, it was idle to give a thought to them. Days were long in summer, and the day was given for enjoyment: he was a fool who wasted its goodly hours in thinking of what came next after it was done: sufficient unto the day was the good thereof.

He lay back on the cool green grass, while his body and

limbs, still wet with his bathe, drank in the kindly heat, purring with sheer physical satisfaction. The activity of his vigour for the moment was satiated with his plunge and his swim, the bodily demands desired nothing more than this freshness and effulgence which soaked through his skin into his very marrow, and fed it with youth and pliant strength. Sinew and nerve and bone lay still and sunned and stretched, content with this blissful passivity. It could not last long: soon their vigour would stir and twitch in them again; and, even as they drowsed and purred, so for the moment his soul and the desires that lay behind the body were satisfied with the mere fact that he was at Stanier, in the midst of all that was his. Uncle Ronald with his gaping cod-fish mouth, Aunt Hester with her ridiculous sprightliness, his grandmother, that image of death in life, Violet even with her horror and love of him were mere puppets of a show over which he pulled down the curtain.

But this quiescence of the spirit was less lasting than that of his physical vigour, and even while he lay slack and stretched with his arm over his eyes to shield them from the glare, and his body still sunned itself without asking anything more than to lie open and naked, alertness and the twitch of activity began to beat in the pulses of his brain again. There was a broth of immediate interest bubbling there. . . . Violet had been tiresome last night: she had said she would not give a hint to her father and mother that they were not wanted; he must move in that matter himself then, and make her sorry she had struck that filial attitude . . . and then there were the memoirs to read, which revealed him to himself . . . and there was Dennis.

This stirring of his soul began to react on his body; it was delicious to lie here with the cool grass below and the sun above, but one could not do that for ever. He rolled over on to his side, and saw Nino sitting by him.

"Nino, it's almost like basking at Capri," he said. "I shall come down again after breakfast.—What time is it?"

Nino pulled a watch out of the pocket of his coat that lay on the grass.

"Ten o'clock," he said.

Colin sat up.

"Then why the devil didn't you tell me it was getting late?" he snapped.

"I thought you looked happy," said Nino. "What does the time matter, signor, if you're happy?"

Colin laughed.

"That's a very sound observation," he said. "But you ought to have told me I was already late for breakfast. Never mind, give me my clothes. I've got a lot to do. Yes, shirt and trousers and shoes. That's all I want."

Nino, but for a towel round his loins, was still as Nature had made him. But she had done it very nicely, and as he handed his master his clothes, Colin looked at his shapely shoulders and broad chest.

"You'd make an awfully good bronze statue, Nino," he said. "You'd look nice in a museum, covered with verdigris, and with an arm and leg missing. How would you like to be an antique?"

"I like better being young," said Nino.

Colin pulled his shirt over his head.

"So do I," he said. "But Time's a thief, Nino, and you can't insure against his burglaries."

This was too much for Nino's English, and he raised a puzzled eye.

"You understand what I mean, though you don't understand what I say," observed Colin. "Do you believe in God, Nino?"

The boy crossed himself.

"Si, signor."

"Then why are you such a dreadful bad lot?" asked Colin. "Don't you know that He will punish you when you're dead?"

Nino shrugged his brown shoulders.

"May be," he said, "but I'm not dead yet."

Colin laughed.

"Nor am I," he said. "But why talk theology before breakfast?"

"Scusi!" said Nino. "But who began?"

Colin leaned against him as he stepped into his flannel trousers.

"I did," he said. "Do you know, you're extremely like me, Nino? I think you must be a Stanier. I wonder if the old fellow I've been reading about had an Italian mistress from whom you're descended. We both believe in God, and are determined to go to the devil. . . . There you are talking theology again, and I told you to shut up!"

"I am dumb as a sheep," said Nino.

"Ba-a-a," said Colin.

Colin found his menagerie at breakfast, as he came in coatless, with his hair drying back into curls again, and his shirt open at the neck, with sleeves rolled up to his elbow. There was Aunt Hester, looking, so he thought to himself. like some aged hag under the delusion that it was still springtime with her, the absurd old woman with her short skirt and girlish blouse, and beribboned hat. And there was Uncle Ronald, bleary-eyed and unsavoury beyond all words, in a velveteen coat, with his gouty knobbed hand all a-tremble as he lifted his tea-cup. And there was Aunt Margaret, looking, as she always did, as if the bells were ringing for church on Sunday morning, and she was just ready to start. . . . "I wonder what she finds to accuse herself of in the Confession," thought Colin: "a want of diligence over her Patience, I suppose. . . ." And there, with face suddenly and involuntarily lit up at his entrance, and as suddenly clouded again, was Violet.

"Good morning, everybody," he said. "I'm late, and I'm not dressed, and I'm not sorry because I've been enjoying myself. Darling Aunt Hester, why didn't you come down to bathe? You would make the most seductive water-nymph. And why has nobody got a complexion like yours? Give me a kiss, if you don't mind my being unshaved."

"Face like a peach," said Hester. "Talk of complexions——"

"Aunt Hester, we mustn't flirt with so many relatives present," said Colin. "You'll shock Violet. Uncle Ronald, you look awfully fit this morning. That's the effect of good Doctor Colin coming home and seeing that you took that medicine for your gout. Now I'm going to make a nice dog's dinner for myself, fish and bacon and a poached egg all on one plate. What's everybody going to do this morning?"

"Sit in my skeleton, like that wag Sidney Smith," said Aunt Hester.

"When and where?" asked Colin. "I want to come and look. You must have got a delicious skeleton, Aunt Hester. I needn't ask what Violet's going to do. She's going to attend a three-hours' service of baby-worship. Violet and I talked about Dennis last night, didn't we, darling? She wants to make him a string of amulets to keep off evil spirits. Sensible idea: it's a wicked world. And Aunt Margaret's going to write out menu cards, and Uncle Ronald's to take a glass of my famous sun-medicine at eleven. You're all provided for."

"Well, and what are you going to do?" asked Hester.

"Me? Studious morning, Aunt Hester, over my books."

"Books, indeed!" said Aunt Hester. "Where's the use of reading books when you're young? When you've got to sit by the chimney-corner and keep your feet warm, then's the call for books, for they pass the time and make you drop off and have a snooze. I've not taken to books yet, thank God."

Colin laughed.

"My dear, you talk about taking to books as if it was like taking to drink," he said. "Doesn't she, Uncle Ronald?"

"Eh, what, I beg your pardon, Colin," said he. Uncle Ronald was not very bright at breakfast, he liked to be left alone to drink several cups of strong tea. After that be could toy with a little toast and marmalade.

"I was only saying that Aunt Hester regards reading as a vice in the young, like drink, and hopes I shan't take to it yet."

Colin let his laughing eye dwell on Ronald long enough to be assured that he took in some of this, and then on Violet to see that she had arrived. . . . Then he turned to Aunt Hester again.

"One of the books I am going to read this morning is entirely about drink, Aunt Hester," he said, "and nobody can guess what it is. There's nothing but drink in it from beginning to end. Guess, Aunt Hester!"

"Oh, one of those rubbishy novels," said Hester. "Seven and sixpence worth of gibberish. Don't ask me!"

"Not a novel at all," said Colin. "Every word in it is true. In fact it's the cellar-book, and I shall see how much gin you've drunk, Aunt Hester, since I've been away. And then if I find you've drunk it all, so that there's none left for Uncle Ronald and me, I shall go down to the lake and drown myself, and haunt you ever afterwards. Oh Lord, I wish somebody would stop me talking such awful drivel. Tell us about your new Patience, Aunt Margaret."

Mrs. Stanier folded up her napkin very neatly. She would do the same with the napkin given her at lunch. She would fold up her napkin when the Last Trump sounded. . . .

"I'm afraid I haven't got a new Patience, Colin," she said.

"Ah, the old is better. You must teach me one of your Patiences some day. Violet and I must learn Patience, to occupy the autumn evenings when we're alone here."

Colin was half-inclined to reconsider his plan for sending the menagerie on tour. Just as the lover is happiest when the object of his affection is with him, so dislike and contempt sun themselves in the presence of their derision, for it supplies them with fuel. It was amusing to plant little stinging darts, to speak of drink to Uncle Ronald, to flick Violet with an allusion to their solitary evenings in the autumn, to make everybody uncomfortable with the threat that he would drown himself in the lake, for that reminded them of Raymond These darts were feathered with his gay inimitable geniality, which charmed and enchanted, with that sunniness that warmed their cold old bones, for so the point stung more smartly. Certainly that allusion to the time when he and Voilet would be alone here gave them all something to think about. . . .

Colin, before settling down to the Memoirs again, sent for his butler and the cellar-book, and rather enjoyed the fact that Uncle Ronald had been consuming the 1860 port at a steady average of a bottle and a half a day. He was a sodden old brute, of course, but, as drink was all that he cared about, it shewed sense to annex as much as possible of the very best, for he always, it appeared, asked for that memorable vintage. But, though it was an agreeable diversion to look at his tremulous unsightliness of a morning, it did not counterweigh the heavy burden of his presence, and he had better go. . . . Violet would have to convey that to him, if only for the reason that she had said she would not. Colin thought he had a persuasive device about that. . . .

All this was very trumpery, and, with a sense of turning to something better worth his attention, he took up the Memoirs again, and soon found himself delightfully absorbed in them. Never was there so sincere and unvarnished an autobiography; the author rejoiced in his presentation of himself. Most men when they paint themselves cannot avoid dipping their brush in the medium, if not of conscious falsity, at least in that of self-deception. They view themselves with a kindly eye, they gloss over or tone down, even to the point of omission, their uglier characteristics; they emphasise what is creditable, they find a sympathetic reason for their occasional frailities. All this may be honest enough in intention, for the reason that they have hoodwinked themselves and really see themselves in such and such a light, but here Colin found an honesty transcendent and diverting. For this ancestor of his had no desire, conscious or subconscious, to fashion an edifying image of himself; he had no mind to be decorated with virtuous phylacteries, and with plain deft strokes he presented this evil and sincere picture of himself. That picture was mirror as well as portrait, and it took Colin's breath away to see himself so unerringly delineated.

. . . So the shephered-boy waited on the Queen next morning, at the Manor of Brede. He had not dressed himself up in his best, but came in his shepherd's garb, shirt and breeches and shoes, and he carried with him his crook and a young lamb. The varlets would have driven him from the door, but that he said it was by the Queen's orders that he presented himself, and they, knowing the whims of that fiery dame, sent word to the Controller of her household that a lousy lad demanded audience of Her Grace. "Lad indeed I was," indited the writer, "but no lousy one, for I had washed the muck of my lambing off me, and had bathed myself in the Rother, and I was cleaner and sweeter than any of they. So out came the Queen's Controller, a pursey fellow, and he too would have shoo'ed me away, but I told him fairly there would be trouble for him, if Her Grace knew that I had been turned from her door. He went to tell Her Grace, and presently came back faster than he had gone, and brought me speedily into the Queen's presence, me and my lamb and my crook. There she sat at the end of a great table, where she had been holding a Council, and she said never a word, but watched me. So I bent my eyes on the ground, but I lifted up my heart to my Lord and Benefactor, and prayed that he should guide my doings, and well he counselled me. I put myself in his hands, and thought no more what I should do or say but trusted him, and I walked past the long table towards where she sat, and the rushes on the floor pricked the soles of my feet, for I had left my shoes outside. Once only did I look up, and saw her still watching me, out of those sharp eyes, with their high eyebrows. How little was her face, I thought, and how red her hair, and how fine her ruff and how yellow her skin, and this was the Queen of England. Then I looked down again, and walked until I saw close in front of my bare toes the tip of her shoes set with pearls. And then I knelt down, and bowed myself and said:

"'A lamb, madam, which is the first fruits of the spring. My crook which I lay at your Grace's feet, and myself who am not worthy to lie there.'

"Then I raised my eyes and looked at her, gay and bold, as I look at the wenches, for wench she was, though the Queen of England. And then once more, as if blinded by her splendour, I abased myself, and she spoke.

"'Look at me, Colin Stanier,' she said.

"'Madam,' said I.

"'Well, what next?' quoth she impatiently.

"'My body and soul, madam,' said I. And I made my eyes dance at her, and my mouth to be eager. . . . She bent towards me, and drew her hand down my cheek.

"'And is your desire to be my shepherd-boy, Colin?' she asked. 'You desire to be my page?'

"'I am sick with desire,' said I.

"'I appoint you,' says she. 'I greet and salute you, Colin Stanier.'

"Now I had just that pause for consideration as she stroked my cheek and tweaked my chin, but even then, when I was but a downy boy, I never thought long whether I should do this or that, or should forbear, and I knew that a man fares better by taking risks than by shunning them, if he has his way to make. I knew, too, how a wench looks at a lad when she would like to be kissed by him, how her neck goes forward to him, and she turns her chin, and Queen or whore they are all like to that. So my mind was made up, and straight I kissed her cheek, for she had saluted me as her page, and was I not to salute my Queen? Which when I had done, I abased myself again and kissed her smelly shoe.

"'You bold dog!' says she. 'Stand up, I might well have you whipped for that.'

"'And I should still be the infinite gainer, your Majesty,' said I, and she laughed.

"That good thought then was the first of the benefits which my Lord gave me, and there was no whipping for me, but for the slap she gave me on the ear, and Her Grace clapped her hands, and in came the Controller of her household.

"'Colin Stanier is my page,' said she, 'and attached to my person. See to it. And at the feast of Easter, I will dine off his lamb. Begone, Colin Stanier, and learn your duties, and see that you serve not the wenches as you have served me!'"

So there was Colin Stanier who last night had been among the ewes translated as at the wave of a magician's wand into the Queen's page. He returned home only to take from its hiding-place the bond he had signed, and within a week he had his fine new clothes and was in waiting on his mistress.

Never for a moment, such was the conviction that inspired the record of his swift advancement in the favour of the Queen, and in the idolatry, no less, of the Court, did he doubt to whom he owed his amazing good fortune. Swiftly he acquired the art of reading and writing, and by the next Easter time he was the Queen's page no longer, but her private and confidential adviser and secretary. The same felicity which had marked his first audacious dealing with her in the character of wench, never failed him, but he had a true appreciation of her fiery magnificence and courage as well as of those aged tendernesses of a childless woman who makes an idol of a boy or a lapdog to quench the thirst of her virginity. No lapdog indeed, was Colin, he could stand up to her in her foaming rages with her ministers, when they gave her spiritless advice in her dealings with trouble at home and political crises abroad, and with an oath she would say, "I cannot abide their twittering diplomacy: I shall go my own way, for when all is said and done I am Queen of England. Eh, Colin, am I not in the rights of it?" and she tweaked her secretary's rosy ear, as he sat at her elbow. Very often she was not in the rights of it, and then Colin would indicate further arguments, prefacing them by saying, "As Your Grace has sagaciously told us, there is this too to be considered," with such deftness that, though she had but so lately affirmed the flat contrary, he would make her believe that she had pointed these things out herself. Whoever rose or fell in that fickle favour, Colin remained there firmly rooted, and his advocacy with the Queen was the surest way to secure the granting of a boon, or the lightening of her displeasure.

"My Lord of Leicester came to me one day," he recorded, "for he was sadly out of favour with Her Grace, and besought me to intercede for him. Nothing that he could do or say would meet with her approbation, he feared she would deprive him of his offices and worse than that, if her anger against him blazed up. He knew well that a word from me would cause it to do so, for I had but to tell her that he had laughed at her Latinity, and said that any youth in King's College at Cambridge would be whipped for such grammatical errors as she made. It was pleasant to me to remind him of that, for not long before he had called me an upstart and a bumpkin from the marshes, and now he was a suppliant to the bumpkin. And well he had to pay for the bumpkin's good word with the Queen, and it was not for that alone that he must sue to me.

First, by reason of his insolence, he must make me his friend, and bleed for his unwisdom in slighting me. Otherwise, I threatened him that it would be my sad duty to inform her Grace how poorly he thought of her Latinity. He was wise enough to see with my eyes, and rich enough to load my pocket, and so I bled him famously, and when I supped alone with Her Grace that night, and had delighted her with the bawdy talk that she loves, I told her that my Lord of Leicester was the unhappiest of her subjects, for she had withdrawn her light from him, and, fool though he was, he had the wisdom to know that he must presently perish of cold, if the beam of her favour was not restored to him. She was loathe to hear me at first, but I pleaded with her and let her cuddle me, and said it befitted not her splendour to grudge a ray to my lord's sorry dunghill. No flattery was too gross for her; she would believe she lit the stars at night, and presently I had my way with her. And I was wise in keeping faith with Lord Leicester, though it would have pleased me better to have taken his money, and then have told the Queen that he thought very poorly of her Latin, and I doubt not that my Lord and Benefactor would have liked me so to do, but I had yet my way to make and my future to see to, and none would sue to me if I did not keep my bargains."

"Sheer blackmail," said Colin to himself as he turned the page. "And he delights in it. That was half the fun. I wonder what my Lord of Leicester paid him! . . ."

While he was yet but five and twenty, the Queen created him Earl of Yardley, decorated him with the Most Noble Order of the Garter, and bestowed on him the monastery and lands of Tillingham, where soon he built the house of Stanier. She often told him that it was time for her Colin to take a wife to himself, but in this, with a sure wisdom, he positively refused to obey her, saying that Venus herself had no charms for him while Gloriana's light was shed on him; and thus, though he disobeyed the letter of Her Grace's command, she did not disapprove of the spirit which prompted his obstinacy. But he sought and copiously found consolations for his celibacy, and he devoted a long section of his memoirs to the account of them and of the diversions of his bachelorhood. He gave a list of the women whose favours he sought and obtained, "but indeed," he commented, "it was they rather who sought me, though I was nothing loathe, for youth is the time for pleasure," and enumerated their charms or their defects. As in his dealings with my Lord of Leicester his favours must be paid for, "though I accomplished some pretty seductions for my own pleasure of which I was speedily weary." Never a hint of love, of devotion, or of affection seemed to have dawned on him; he sought his own pleasure and profit, and what above all made to him the spice of these adventures was their wickedness. . . . He described at length how the spectacle of the love and devotion between a certain Sir James Bland and his young wife irritated him, and how, with a view to wrecking it, he first made friends with the husband, thereby to gain an intimate footing in their house, and cover his ulterior purpose, while he made himself cold to his friend's wife. "She was accustomed to draw the eyes of men after her, though she had no eyes for any but her lord, and it piqued her to see I was indifferent to her. Presently, for all wenches are alike in heart, she must needs lay herself out to attract me and I softened towards her, so that there were not three gayer folk in all London than this devoted pair and their attached friend. This way and that I drew her into my net, so that she cooled to her husband, and became weary and restless and discontent. And then my Lord and Benefactor whispered to me that the time was ripe, and before long nought would restrain her but she cast herself at my feet, and so I gave her her way once or twice, but very soon she was tedious to me. But I was very merry all that month."

Colin threw back his head and laughed. "I was very merry all that month" . . . how well he knew the inward glee that this old kinsman of his must have experienced at the accomplishment of this pleasing design. He had been in harmony with himself all that month: that was what made him merry. And, of course, when the thing was done, it was done, and who, that was truly alive, cared to dwell on an achievement? He had bitten into the fruit, and swallowed its mellow flesh, and now there was but the rind and the stone, which he spat out. There were plenty more such fruits when he felt thirsty: no need then to mouth the stone and squeeze out the last drop of juice from the rind. Naked cruelty and the pleasure of seeing others suffer gave the savour to this and other adventures, and he described how he had gone to see a recusant tortured on the rack, till the joints were wrenched from their sockets. . . . Colin could understand that too.

He got up out of his chair, stretched himself and strolled to the window which looked out over the terrace and the lake. There was Aunt Hester sitting in the shade of the yew-hedge looking like some foolish autumnal butterfly, and close at hand on the terrace was Dennis in his perambulator. Some day Colin would read these Memoirs with him and explain what he did not understand. There would be some years to wait yet, eleven or twelve perhaps, till Dennis had been a term or two at school. That kneaded the dough of a boy's mind; it was ready then to be moulded: it was soft and pliable and leavened. . . . Then Violet came out of the house, she stood close to the window out of which Colin looked. She did not see him for her eyes were on her son.

"Take him out of his pram, Nurse," she called, "and see if he can get as far as me. Dennis! Come to me, Dennis."

Dennis was lifted out paddling in the air and set down on the terrace. Again Violet called, and he looked this way and that, unable to localize the sound, though recognizing his name. Suddenly he saw his mother, and giving a crow of delight staggered towards her.

Colin forgot about the Memoirs for a moment. There was Violet stooping down with arms outstretched to the boy, her face all radiant with motherhood and love, and, at the sight of her, Colin felt that exasperated impatience which love always provoked in him. It was not for anything that Dennis could give her, that this beam transfigured her, it was just because he was Dennis. From her he looked at the child maintaining that difficult balance, which every moment threatened to topple, and there, too, in that dimpled laughing face, bright with the glory of this heroic adventure, there shone the same. That was even more exasperating to his mind. While a child's intelligence was as elementary and undeveloped as this, there was this instinct triumphantly asserting itself. Love seemed to be as natural as breathing, and far more natural than walking.

Dennis had now got on the high seas; the safe harbour of the nurse with the perambulator was to him hugely remote, and equally remote was the harbour for which he was steering, and though he was progressing bravely across the billows of this perfectly level sea, the awful loneliness of his position suddenly overcame him. He staggered, he put his advancing foot in a most untenable position, collapsed on the ground, and sent up a signal of distress in a piercing yell. Before Colin knew what he was doing, he had opened the window.

"Not hurt is he, Violet?" he called.

She looked round, her face still all aglow. But her brightness faded as she saw him.

"Oh no, I'm sure he isn't," she said. "Put him on his feet again, Nurse. Come, Dennis, you're half way already."

Colin waited a moment longer, till the adventure outside was happily accomplished, rather astonished at himself for having taken any notice of it. He had felt, he supposed, just a sporting interest to see whether Dennis would stay the course: he was sorry when he came to grief. Then he went back to his far more congenial occupation.

He embarked now on the account of the building of Stanier, and the collection of its treasures: this, for the next two years, was clearly the great diversion and achievement of his ancestor's energies. The Queen's death, which occurred when he was thirty, was but casually mentioned, with a shrewd recognition of her greatness, and an impatient gibe for her vanity, and a congratulation for himself for having used her weakness as a quarry for the building of his own wealth and splendour. Her last gift to him was the great sapphire, that flawless and unique stone, which the Queen had worn every day when her fleet was out to meet the Armada. Priceless in itself, it was supposed to be a talisman which brought its owner prosperity in all he undertook. After her death there had been an attempt on the part of the Crown (renewed again when the Hanoverian dynasty came to the throne) to repossess itself of the jewel on the grounds that it belonged to the regalia, and so could not be bestowed, but both times these efforts had failed, and the winking cornflower splendour still reposed in the jewel-safe at Stanier, a queen's gift worth a king's ransom. "Lucky it was," said the Memoirs' author, "that so few days before Her Grace's death I had so mightily pleased her, for that was her last and noblest gift to me, and that was the finest fruit that I had plucked from my bargain. To my Lord and Benefactor I owe it, who shewed me how to please Her Grace so mightily that she gave me the most precious of all her jewels." Equally cursory was the mention of his marriage with the daughter and heiress of Sir John Reeve, though he gave a detailed list of property which this ill-fated young woman brought to the house. Two sons were born to him, and soon after, having secured these great estates, he secured his wife's divorce, and presently married the only daughter and child of Lord Middlesex. She gave him no further heirs, but brought considerable addition to his estates. "An unseemly woman," so ran her husband's comment, "and of a most unseemly temper, of which I would have none. She was red as a fox, but rich."

But these events (apart perhaps from the birth of his two sons) were no more than acts of routine in his career, his passion was the creation of his palace and pleasaunce of Stanier. Only twelve years had elapsed between the day when he had gone, a bare-footed shepherd boy with his crook and his lamb, to wait upon the Queen at Brede, and now at her death he retired from Court life and came back, Earl and Knight of the Garter, to his estates at Tillingham. His father's farm was close by, where the "drunken old sot" still lived, and Colin, coveting it for the completion of his gardens, found a way to dispute the ownership, claiming that it was part of the monastic land devised him by the Queen, and turned the old man out. He gave him, however, a decent enough dwelling-place for a man of his station, and adequate maintenance, and further allowed him to draw on his brewery for unlimited ale, making only the provision that the old man should never attempt to see him or obtain access to him: otherwise his maintenance should be withheld. This indulgence in the matter of the brewery may have been kind in intention, for assuredly the old man was fond of beer, but the effect was that he did not long enjoy the bounty. He was oftener drunk than sober, and, before the year was up, he had a stroke of which he died. Meantime the great house was rising rapidly, and in two years was complete up to the lettered baulstrade, where you might read in Latin that, unless the Lord built the house, their labour was but lost that built it, and into it Lord Yardley poured the treasure that he was constantly acquiring: Oriental carpets, and French Tapestries, Chinese porcelain, Greek marbles, and Italian pictures: all arts and ages were sought by him, for there was kinship in all fine work, and a Greek relief of Heracles and Hylas might be flanked by a crucifixion by Tintoret on one side, and a portrait by Rembrandt on the other. He made, too, a wonderful collection of occult and magical books, that told the student how he might acquire supernatural powers, and among them was a missal, as Colin read "of wondrous blasphemies". . . . Out of doors the work was pushed forward with the same expedition: the great terraced garden to the south of the house was levelled and stepped and encircled by the yew-hedge; below, the dam was pushed out across the dip of the valley in which had stood the house of his youth, and the lake formed. He planted, too, on the bare upland east of the house the oaks that flourished there now.

At this point in the type-written manuscript, there came an annotation directing him to a certain page in the original Memoirs, and Colin turned it up, and found that it referred to a loose sheet in the book dated 1642, which was the year before the author died. On this page was a rough sketch of the house and gardens as designed then, and as they existed now, but with the addition of certain buildings which apparently had never been erected. But while the plan of the house as it stood was only roughly indicated, this addition was drawn with considerable care and detail. It looked therefore, as if, after the completion of the house, this building was contemplated and planned, but never carried out. It consisted of a long passage, leading out of the room where he now sat, which had always been Lord Yardley's private room, and communicating with a small house that stood, at the distance of sixty yards, on a knoll just outside the gardens. It was one-storied, and consisted of three rooms en suite labelled 'parlour,' 'bedchamber,' and 'dining-room,' with a kitchen and quarters for a servant. But on the south side of it there was a spacious oblong room, equal in length to the three rooms adjoining, with a descriptive word attached to it. This was only faintly pencilled in, and was difficult to decipher. The initial letter 'S' was clear enough: the second might have been 'o' or 'c': then came a long letter that might have been either 't' or 'l,' followed (with room for another letter between) by 'arium,' which was distinct and legible. Colin puzzled over this, and then a very reasonable solution struck him; the word no doubt was 'Solarium,' implying an open gallery, facing south on the long side, as this did, and either open to the air or fronted with big windows, a winter-sitting-room, a sunning place. . . . Simultaneously, with a laugh, the significance of this discreet little establishment struck him. No doubt it was intended to be the quarters of the companion for the time being (for he soon wearied of each) with whom Lord Yardley solaced his leisure. There would be an impropriety perhaps in her being actually housed in the same dwelling as his wife and his sons; convenience and propinquity were alike served by her having her pleasant little establishment (with its solarium) at a short distance from the house and communicating with his own room. The interpretation was reasonable, simple and entertaining, but, to be sure it did not seem very characteristic of his ancestor's methods to be so tender of the feelings of his wife, and guard the morals of his sons from loose presences, and though Colin was pleased with his explanation and his decipherment of 'Solarium,' he was not quite satisfied with it, and put a slip of paper in the place, meaning to refer to it again. He turned back to the typewritten copy, of which now not many pages remained for his perusal.

There was a short description of how, on the coming of age of his two sons, they each chose to be associated with the bargain he had made in the shepherd's hut, and indeed, from the few details given about their characters and their escapades, the choice could not have been a matter of much difficulty to these young gentlemen. The younger, in especial, attached to the Court of His Majesty King James, seemed to have been as perfect and appalling a young rogue as even his father could have wished. Then there followed the entry that to-day was the author's sixty-ninth birthday, and, thanks to the ever-constant goodness of his Lord and Benefactor, his health and strength were still unabated, and the pleasures of his youth still his. He blessed the day, now fifty-one years ago, when he had chosen so wisely and well, as the parchment, now preserved in his strong-room, testified, "How would I rejoice," he wrote, "to build some shrine in honour of my Lord, where I would worship him who has wrought so great benefits upon me, some sanctuary, where I might worthily adore him"—and then suddenly in the middle of a sentence the Memoirs came to an end.

Colin put down the last sheet of the manuscript, and leaned back in his chair. He felt as if, Narcissus-like, he had all the morning been regarding himself as shewn in this Elizabethan mirror of his ancestor's confessions. It was his own spirit so undeviatingly reflected there, and the contemplation of it was an act of self-recognition. All that he had read was a three hundred year old portrait of himself, even as he might have sat for the great picture in the hall, into the frame of which was now inserted the signed parchment of the bargain. Whatever was the literal and the material truth about that (his ancestor, clearly, who might be expected to know, confirmed it) there could be none about its spiritual authenticity.

No one who had seen the Memoirs could possibly have any doubt about that, and Colin knew that he, like most others of his race, eagerly associated himself with the bargain. He knew, too, that his choice was solid and real and no fantastic imagining; there was God on one side, there was Satan on the other. He had rejected God, and, not only for the benefits attached, but because he preferred evil to good, he had chosen Satan. Hate and evil were dear to him, he had no use for love.

There came the sound of the bell for luncheon, and he got up. . . . It was a strange thing that anyone so diligent in evil as the old man had been, should at the end of his life have turned coward and twitterer in the way he had done. His last year on earth had been a terrible one, for, so family tradition averred (and indeed the thing was attested), terror of what was coming fastened on his flesh like a monstrous growth, and he wrote no more in his diary of the sins that were so dear to him. He practised pious and charitable deeds, restoring the monastery church, on the altar of which he had often played dice. He endowed almshouses in Rye. He bought great tomes of the works of Christian fathers, and of the meditations of the Saints, and hour after hour he used to sit in the library to study these under the tuition of a priest who resided in the house, and ministered at the church, and no doubt it was then that he destroyed or dispersed that great collection of magical and occult works which he had brought together, for no vestige of them was now extant here. He cut himself off from the pleasures of youth, he fasted and prayed, in the hope of turning away, the fate at which all his life he had mocked, and it was said that when on his knees he attempted to address the God whom he had rejected, no prayer or holy words would come from his lips, but that he mumbled unspeakable and obscene blasphemies. He seemed in fact, so it appeared to Colin, to have gone crazy, and though he continued throughout that year in the full serenity of his physical health, he let himself be the prey of his disordered and terrified soul, turning and truckling, not in love but in abject fear of the destiny he had chosen, to Him whose spirit he had defied. It was firmly rooted in his head, that (he would die on his seventieth birthday, and that indeed no doubt because he so firmly believed it) came to pass, and in an appalling manner. For he gave a feast that night to his tenants in honour of his birthday, and had risen to speak to them at the end of supper, when he put out his arms, as if pushing away some invisible presence, and shrieking "No, no!" fell forward, dead across the table. At that moment there came a blinding flash of lightning, which certainly struck the hall, but those who were nearest to him said that his seizure had preceded the flash, and that it and the roar of thunder that followed were rather the endorsement of that judgment than the judgment itself. That year, anyhow, thought Colin was a common and craven conclusion to his brilliant life; he did not fancy that he himself would suffer so deplorable a collapse, legend or no legend. But in the interval, he had more than all his ancestor's lust for pleasure, and his hatred of love. . . .

He put the manuscript in a drawer of his table, and with it the original copy of the diary, for he was not satisfied about the plan of that establishment with the 'Solarium.' It seemed unlikely. . . . But if the word which designated that building was not 'Solarium,' what on earth could it be?

CHAPTER III

COLIN went back to his room after the invariable rubber of whist that evening, with the intention of studying this plan more minutely, but, though the others had gone upstairs he was not surprised to hear his door open, and Violet asking if she could speak to him. Indeed, he almost expected that interruption, and he smiled to himself when she entered. . . .

There had been a horrid little scene at the close of dinner, a dovecote-fluttering in the menagerie, arising from Colin's having instructed Nino to dispense the wine, and to be lavish in his ministrations to Uncle Ronald's glass. The wine in question was Dagonet 1880, to which he was incapable of putting up the smallest resistance, and Nino did his duty so thoroughly that Uncle Ronald had got on very quickly, and had told a story which might possibly have passed with a snigger in a smoking-room of broad-minded men. Even Aunt Hester, who was as broad-minded as most people, had said "Better hold your tongue, Ronald; you're disgracing yourself," while that perfect piece of Patience, Aunt Margaret, bridled and folded her napkin and diligently perused the menu card which she had so neatly written out, though at that period of dinner its information was obsolete . . . And then, when the women had adjourned, Uncle Ronald, having been told that there was not much 1860 port left, had partaken so freely of what there was, that he had become wonderfully voluble about the old days when he and his father used to sit here together. Colin had taken Nino's place as dispenser of wine, and so sedulous was he that Uncle Ronald presently lost the power of coherent speech altogether, and, when he tried to rise, leaned lamentably against the table, and was assisted upstairs by the butler and Nino, which again was quite in accordance with the tradition of the house. Colin had joined the ladies alone, and said that his uncle had gone to bed with a nasty cough, such a troublesome cough, which made him feel a little giddy, and clogged the free functioning of the vocal chords.

All this, of course, was directed against Violet, who must be taught that if Colin expressed a wish that she should undertake some little mission, like telling her father and mother that they must no longer consider Stanier their house, she must be a good wife and obey. . . .

Colin was just unlocking the drawer where he kept the Memoirs when she entered, and he hailed her with a smile and a word of welcome.

"That you, Vi?" he said. "Have you come for a little talk? That is nice. Sit down."

She looked at him in silence as he brought the book out, continuing to stand.

"I thought I told you to sit down," he said.

"No, I'll stand," she said.

He glanced at her still smiling.

"You had better do what I tell you," he said. "That's right. How simple, isn't it? Now what have you come about? It's something tedious, I suppose. About your father, eh? Wasn't he horrid at dinner? He made me blush for his dyed hair. Such a story! Awful for you and Aunt Margaret. Granny, too, at her age! And the servants."

She looked at him again in silence, then dropped her eyes.

"I suppose it is your plan to make him tipsy every night," she said, "until I tell him that he and my mother are not to come back here after their visit to Aix."

Colin nodded at her with that sunny smile of his.

"Absolutely correct," he said. "How well we understand each other, dear! And you've come here to tell me you're going to be good, and do as you're told. Is that it?"

"Yes. I can't sit by and see my father as I saw him to-night. What do you want me to say to him?"

"Oh, just that. Say that you understand that he'll be settling down in London for the autumn, or for ever and ever. . . . Just a little tact and pleasantness."

"Colin, it's awfully hard on him," she said. "He and mother have practically lived here since their marriage."

"Yes, darling: a nice long visit, as I said yesterday. He must put his name in the visitors' book, Saturday, 1890, or whenever it was, till Monday, 1913. And though I don't often criticize you, I must remind you that you shouldn't always think of yourself."

"What do you mean by that?" asked she.

"I'll explain. You've got no real filial feeling for either your father or mother, and that pricks your conscience. So, to mollify that smart, you take their side and want them to have a comfortable home here. That doesn't cost you anything, and it gives you an atoning feeling inside. It is your cheap manner of making amends to them."

There was just that grain of truth in this which made it impossible for Violet to deny it completely. She had not consciously thought of that, but, when he pointed it out, she knew it was so. There were plenty of other reasons, kindliness, affection, compassion, which prompted her, but he with his amazing subtlety had put his finger on the smallest and meanest of them all.

"You are an adept at seeing the worst side of everybody," she said.

"Would it be rude if I suggested that the reason for that is that the worst side of people is so much more to the front than their best?" asked Colin. "We all put our worst foot foremost. . . . And then think of Dennis, Vi. Would you like him to have among the early recollections of his boyhood the memory of his grandfather telling bawdy stories and reeling up to bed after dinner in a squall of hiccups? And then, last and least, there's myself. Your father bores and disgusts me. I hinted to him that he was not perhaps such a fixture here as he seemed to imagine, and now, please, you're going to repeat that timid conviction, so that he may see that on this, as on every point, we're at one. Mind, the suggestion has got to come from yourself not from me: otherwise he will think that I have asked you to make it. Now we've spent too much time and speech already over a trivial matter. You think I'm a brute, but then you often do that. I'm used to that: getting almost callous about it."

He held up the sheaf of typed pages which had occupied him all the morning.

"I've had a delicious day," he said, "for I've been reading the Memoirs of old Colin. I had them type-written, and they're entrancing. He realized himself so wonderfully. There was neither false shame nor conceit about him. He was neither proud nor the reverse of being such a devil. I thought of letting some learned Antiquarian Society publish them. Odd, isn't it, how all the puritanical, pure-minded people, chiefly women, who shiver and are shocked at what they call a bad man, and won't visit him or have him to dinner, and heave any sort of brick at him, greedily devour any indecent memoir, and simply roll in it, like dogs when they've found some putrescent muck. . . . You'd have thought that, if they shudder at wickedness, they wouldn't care to read about it. But they say it's the historical interest that makes them devour it, which isn't true. It's the insatiable fascination that wickedness has for prudes. However, the Memoirs are enchanting: they ring so absolutely true: you feel you are looking at the very man himself. I even found myself believing in the literal truth of the legend. Sit down and dip into them, darling; you won't find a dull page anywhere. Meantime I'm puzzling out a curious plan of some projected addition to the house, which he never executed."

"I won't read them to-night," she said. "It is rather late."

"Very good. I won't insist on that as you've been a good girl otherwise. But you must read them some day. I want to know if a certain thing strikes you as it struck me."

"What is that?" she asked.

"Why, that old Colin was a sort of prophet. I felt all the time as if he was writing not about himself but about me. How types repeat themselves: there is another character he mentions which so closely resembles someone we both know. Old Colin's father in fact, Ronald Stanier, whom he describes as a drunken old sot. Good night, darling. Not a kiss? I suppose I don't deserve one. You're punishing me for being such a brute."

She paused at the door. There he stood, looking gaily and yet wistfully at her, with his mouth a little open, and the soft fire of his youth burning in his eyes, and she yearned for him. Surely it was not only his beauty that she adored, that physical perfection of him. There was somebody, surely, imprisoned there, who called to her through the bars of his nature and its love of evil and its hate of love. As often as she had tried to reach that prisoner it was as if the guardians of his soul, monstrous and terrifying, pushed her panic-stricken away. She hated and feared them, and their ruthless wickedness, but in spite of them she knew that she would never cease from trying to get past them, and rescuing him who lay there in iron bondage.

She turned back into the room, her eyes troubled and eager, full of love, full of fear. Some gust of inspiration came to her.

"Colin, you hate love," she said, "and I can't help giving it you. I pity you so, you know; all my heart pours itself out round you in pity. You've tried to kill my love, but you can't. It's so much stronger than either you or me——"

He whipped round on her.

"Good Lord, you must have misheard me," he said. "I asked you for a kiss, not a sermon. But I don't want either. Go to bed."

The door closed behind her, and he stood there a moment, simmering with anger and contempt at her undesired homily, with its puerile message. He could have laughed at the idea of love being strong: love was the most helpless and defenceless of all the pieces on the savage chessboard. It was vulnerable at every point, you could wound it wherever you thrust at it. Any clumsy stroke penetrated and made it bleed. Or you could rope it down to the rack, and quite without effort pull the lever that wrenched and distorted it, and made it white with silent agony. . . . But how strange that just now Violet should give vent to gabble like this, when a moment before she had shrunk from him and his brutality in his dealings with her and her father! In her small way she was like the martyrs praising and blessing God, as their limbs writhed with anguish, that they were accounted worthy to suffer for His sake. She was like that comely smoothed-limbed S. Sebastian in the gallery, for which Nino might have been the model, who seraphically smiled while he was being made a pin-cushion for arrows. Certainly Colin had tried, as she said, to kill her love, and often he had wounded it, though none of those thrusts, it would seem, had proved mortal . . . He shrugged his shoulders; there were plenty more weapons in his armoury. Above all, there was one which as yet was not ready for use, for its blade was still soft and unannealed. But he wondered if her love would survive the thrust when Dennis was a sword of wickedness in his hand.

He brought out again the sketch-plan that had puzzled him, and examined it through a magnifying glass. Certainly the word which he had conjectured to be 'Solarium' did not stand this closer scrutiny, and now when he looked again at the plan itself, this oblong room, thus conjecturally labelled, could not be a solarium, for on the south, where you would expect it to be open, or to present a row of big windows to admit the sun, there were but two very narrow apertures marked there. At the east end, however, there was indicated a very big window, which took up nearly the whole length of the wall.

Colin turned his attention to the written word again. 'Solarium' it certainly was not, for the second letter was a 'c' surely, not an 'o,' and there was a faint cross-stroke over the 'l' which made a 't' of it, and another letter, quite illegible, preceded the final 'arium.' "S,c,t," thought Colin . . . and suddenly a new solution dawned on him. It must be 'S'ctuarium,' abbreviated from 'sanctuarium,' a chapel, a shrine. As he scrutinized it, he was more than ever certain that he had hit on the true decipherment, but this only complicated the puzzle instead of solving it. For how was it possible to account for the author of these Memoirs planning to build a sanctuary? Sanctuary, however, it certainly was, and this identification explained the narrow lancets on the south wall, and the big east window.

He considered the history of his ancestor's last year on earth, how, as the time approached for his death, he turned to God, not from love of Him but from fear of hell's damnation. He broke off the chronicle of his iniquities, he built almshouses and indulged in fastings and charities with a view to avert the destiny that he had chosen and rejoiced in. That all fell in with the notion of his building a chapel, which communicated with his own room in the house, so that he could go there by day or night, for cowardly prayer and search for forgiveness of his trespasses. Then, too, on this assumption, the little dwelling-place that adjoined it could be explained: no doubt he intended that a priest should reside there, as domestic physician of his soul.

For the moment this hypothesis seemed to account for the whole project, and Colin unwillingly accepted it. It was disappointing: it was just another instance of that collapse and cowardice which came over his ancestor, and made his last year on earth such a pitiful surrender. And yet . . . why did he not then put his plan into execution, if this was the design of it? For a whole year after the date recorded on this drawing, he practised his belated pieties and yet never a sod was cut nor a brick laid in the erection of this chapel. Surely he would have hastened on the building of it with the same speed and enthusiasm with which he had built the house for his own glory. Clearly, if this solution was correct, and he had intended to build a chapel here with lodging for a priest, he abandoned it. But why, if his soul was set on pieties and repentance?

Colin got up from the chair in which he had been sitting for the last half-hour since Violet had left him, frowning and puzzling over this riddle. He felt that there was a key, which would fit the facts, and that he was hovering round its discovery. It was close at hand, but some sluggish mist of his own mind obscured it. He paced up and down his room for a minute or two, then went to the window, open behind its tapping blind, which he drew half up. Only the faintest night-wind stirred, the sky was bare, and the full moon rode high in the south among the stars. Just in front the terrace lay grey, and the garden dark, but beyond the square black line of the yew-hedge the lake shone so bright in the moonlight that it seemed a sheet of pale flame, brimming and molten. To right and left rose the swelling uplands of the park, and all this spacious stateliness within and without was the creation of that ancestor of his who had planned a sanctuary. Colin felt no doubt that his spirit survived in some remorseful hell, and what more poignant hell could there be for it, now shorn of its pomp and prosperity, and naked in the immaterial world, than the splendour of its earthly habitation where it no longer had a place? Somehow his spirit seemed close and ready to communicate: could it not give to one who so rapturously claimed kinship and sympathy with it, some hint, some expression of itself that should awake in him the comprehension of its strange desire to build a sanctuary? . . .

Colin stood quite still, looking out on to the silent tranquillity, not cudgelling his brain with conjecture any more, but letting it lie open and quiet to the midnight, to see if, from outside or from its own subconscious activity, there did not emerge what he was seeking for. It was curious that a satisfactory solution of this point seemed of such immense importance, but, rightly or wrongly, he believed that it held some great significance. . . . And certainly there was a power abroad to-night, something that tingled and throbbed in his veins. It was hard to keep still under it, not to let his brain busy itself with ingenious surmise, but he had done that already to the utmost of his power, and now, with this stir of force round him, he must let himself stay passive and receptive. . . .

Suddenly the faint stirring of the night-breeze grew stronger, it ruffled his hair, it blew the cracking, flapping blind out horizontal into the room, and the pages of the manuscript on his table whispered and shivered, as if they were talking to themselves and giggling together. And then the mist that had obscured his mind was whisked away, and he knew he had the explanation for which he had been seeking. In a couple of steps he was back at his table, and, open in the manuscript he had been reading all day, there lay before his eyes the final words of it which he had read uncomprehendingly before, but now saw to contain the key he looked for.

"How I would rejoice," he said aloud, "to build some shrine in honour of my Lord, where I would worship him who has wrought so great benefits upon me; some sanctuary where I might worthily adore him——"

There was no need to search further: all was clear. It was indeed a sanctuary he had planned, in honour not of God but of him who had given him all that his soul desired. Clear, too, at last, was the reason why he had never built it, for just then, when it was freshly planned, fear began to darken round him, and the shadows to stalk, and he turned from his Lord and Benefactor, and wrote no more in his praise, but prayed and fasted in impious piety.

One o'clock had already sounded, and Colin replaced the Memoirs in a drawer and turned the key on them. The gust from outside that seemed literally to have blown the mist from him, so that he saw sharp and distinct across the sundering centuries the purpose of this design and the sure reason for its abandonment, died into stillness again, but the night seemed charged and alive with consciousness. All day he had put himself to soak, so to speak, in the spirit that infused these Memoirs with so sympathetic a vitality: now, even when the book was finished, it was friendly round him, stimulating and quickening him, so that reinforced with its vigour the idea of the physical refreshment of sleep seemed ludicrous. To sleep was to abandon your consciousness for the sake of its recuperation: it was the expression of his consciousness that he needed.

He put his hand on the low window-sill, and vaulted out on to the terrace, where he had watched Dennis's early essays in locomotion. In the stillness, past and present seemed melted into one: the centuries no longer represented the movement of time, they had not been borne away on its stream, but were static as if portrayed in a picture. It might have been on this very night that the original bargain was made, it might have been here and now that his ancestor was devising the sanctuary on the little plateau that lay among the oaks which he had planted. In the moonlight Colin could almost visualize the windowed corridor that had been planned to run from the corner of the room which he had just quitted, till it joined among the trees the west wall of the sanctuary. What a symbol would that shrine have been of old Colin's life, what a jubilee of the dedication of himself! There without doubt he intended to celebrate those Satanic rites, that worship of evil for evil's sake in which they, to whom the sacred service of love was a thing abhorred and derided, renewed their allegiance to the enemy of God, and in the blasphemy of the Black Mass drew near to their Lord and Benefactor, who strengthened and refreshed their souls. The shallow, the indifferent, who just made as pleasant a pilgrimage as possible out of life, or who, from vague instincts, tried to be good, or merely fell into evil because they were weak or self-indulgent, could have no part in that; it would be savourless as bran to any who had no living belief both in God and in Satan; for blasphemy signified nothing to souls who did not hate the sublime majesty of love. They who took part in its dark mysteries were they who believed in God, and who, by their deliberate choice, rejected and hated and defied Him. Old Colin would have been a fit worshipper there, had not that senile panic, hoisting the white flag of his surrender, overtaken him before his bond was due. It was a craven, pitiful end: it was not love of his life-long Enemy that drove him to that camp, but fear of him who had so magnificently befriended him.

Colin had wandered in the moonlight past the end of the terrace, and now stood on the plateau, where, according to the plan, the sanctuary was to have been built. Round him rose the tranced forest-trees, the grass, drenched with dew, glimmered like a spread sheet of moonstone. Then, suddenly springing up again, the wind warm and caressing made the branches of the oaks whisper and sway, and through him ran a great exaltation. He raised his hands, spreading his arms out wide.

"O Lord and Benefactor," he said. "How will I rejoice to build a shrine in honour of thee. . . ."

Colin woke from his dreamless sleep next morning, to find Nino's hand on his bare shoulder, gently stirring him. His clothes were in a heap on the floor by his bedside, for when he came in he had but stripped himself and wrapped a sheet round him in which, cocoon-like, he had lain unstirring. He was conscious of a strong glow of happiness as he was thus recalled, and his lazy strength came soaking into him.

"Oh, Nino, what a nuisance you are," he said. "You spend your beastly life in waking me."

"Will you sleep again, then?" asked Nino.

"No, the mischief is done now. What's the morning like? What's the news?"

"A telephone message from Mrs. Hunt," said Nino. "She would know if she may come down to-day for Sunday."

Colin grinned. The moment Nino had said "telephone message" he had guessed from whom it came.

"Well then, she mayn't," he said. "Damned cheek! It would never do, would it, Nino?"

"She will be very happy, she said, if she may come," observed Nino.

Colin raised himself a little, and drew his hand down his arm. The fact that he had decided that Pamela Hunt should not come, made him see causes for re-consideration.

"Just rub my arm," he said, "I've been sleeping on it, and it isn't awake. Of course, if it would make her happy, that's a different thing. We ought always to make people happy, Nino, except when we're making them miserable. Tell her she can come then. What's the morning like?"

"*Splendore,*" said Nino.

"I shall bathe. I wish you'd carry me straight down to the lake and drop me into it."

"Sicuro," said Nino.

Colin looked at him, yawning.

"Get on then," he said, wondering what he would do.

Nino bent down, and putting one arm below his neck, and the other under his knees, lifted him up.

"Right about turn," said Colin. "March."

Nino carried him as far as the door, and was evidently perfectly ready to bear him, with the sheet folded round him, down to the lake. He held him as easily as a child, and his face was all wreathed with merriment.

"I am your nurse," he said. "You are my bambino, signor."

Colin laughed.

"Oh, but this won't do," he said. "Put me down, Nino. People would think it so odd. There are enough oddities in the house without our adding to them. And go and telephone. Don't keep a lady waiting."

"But I was busy attending to my signor," said Nino.

"I know. You're a good boy. You shall come off to Capri with me before long. Follow me down when you've telephoned. I know there's something I want to ask you about, and I shall remember it when the water has awakened me."

As Colin ran downstairs, he was in two minds again as to whether he should allow Pamela Hunt to be happy or not. Their friendship, quite a recent one, had been founded on laughter and good looks and high spirits, but, since then, he had become aware that she was searching for more from him than that, was digging below those flimsy foundations of liking and laughter for something more profound. He did not really care about her in the least, but she was eminently ornamental, and he liked the bland unscrupulousness with which she pursued her way. Her suggestion, indeed, that she should come down to Stanier for the Sunday, where she knew he was in retreat in the bosom of his family, had a daring innocence about it which was rather attractive. Their friendship had already been a matter of extensive public comment in London, and it showed a charming disregard of the usual conventions that she should propose to share his domestic tranquillity. It was no secret from him that she was in love with him, and he was guilty of no fatuous gratification about that. In fact it seemed to him a pity, for he had nothing whatever for her, and beyond doubt she was getting serious and eager. However, she had proposed herself, and he had permitted it, and, after all, there might be some amusement out of it, some chilling disappointment for her, some ludicrous dénouement derived from his own indifference or, possibly, exasperation if she became tedious. He had not given her the smallest encouragement but that of laughter and chatter, and, if she chose to attempt to hunt him down, any consequences were of her own seeking. Then, too, how would Violet take it, in case some kind friend had whispered warnings to her? It might be an amusing Sunday.

He stepped out on to the terrace, already grilling in the sunshine, but it looked less real now than a few hours ago under the moon. The stage then had been alive with dark forces brewing drama, whereas now, in this sane freshness of day, it was mere paint and pasteboard, like that same stage seen next morning, when the actors had left it, and no drama vivified the splendid setting. But as he walked along the terrace to the yew-hedge it gained reality again. Just there would be the windowed corridor, and there close at hand was the plateau among the oaks. Yes, it was growing real again.

And at that he remembered what he had wanted to ask Nino. A couple of years ago when he was staying for the night with the very lively little English Consul at Naples, who had shewn him such curious Neapolitan diversions, he remembered his having said something about a cabaret, in a room behind which were held certain Satanic rites. . . . Possibly Nino might know, Nino had much gay native knowledge of an unexpected kind, and had many local stories to tell of the doings of the monstrous Emperor Tiberius, who took such wonderful holidays from the cares of State in Capri. These Satanic rites were as old as religion itself: in fact they were the earliest form in which religion, the belief in the supernatural, appeared, for originally the supernatural was an evil power to be propitiated. It was later that mankind had conceived of it as beneficent and loving. . . .

Colin was out of the water when Nino came down.

"Well, have you made her happy?" he asked. "What an age you've been, Nino!"

Nino's mouth twitched, and broke into a smile.

"Sis-signor," he said. "She is very happy."

"And what are you grinning at?" asked Colin.

"She thought it was you at the telephone," he said. "She thought I had gone to fetch you."

"And what did she say?" asked Colin.

Nino schooled his mouth into gravity.

"She said—scusi—but she said 'Colin, darling, how perfectly sweet of you!' So I said 'Signora,' and I think she understood for she—she rang away."

"Rang off," said Colin, "you're thinking of 'ran away.'"

"She is running away here," said Nino.

Colin lay back on the grass.

"Why do men get in such a fuss about women?" he asked.

"Chi sa? There are plenty for all," said Nino.

"Yes. Tell me more tales such as you told me at Capri about Tiberio."

Nino laughed.

"Why does the signor love to hear of Tiberio? He was a fat old man."

"Yes, but full of ideas. He liked wickedness: the sort of man who would worship the devil."

"Sicuro!"

"Italy's a very wicked country," said Colin. "I believe they worship the devil still in Naples."

Nino crossed himself.

"So it is said."

"Why do you do that?" asked Colin. "I don't believe you really think it protects you. It's only a habit. Tell me about the worship of the devil in Naples."

"I know little," said Nino, "and though others find it diverting, I would not find diversion in it. Why do they want to behave like street boys, and make faces at holy things? And it is not prudent. May not lightning strike them, or madness come on them? There are many things which the priests say offend Il Padre, which are diverting. But this is not one of them."

Colin gathered up his knees in his arms, his skin still shining with his bathe. What nonsense, as he often thought, were the English ideas of 'class.' Here was he, talking to his own valet on terms of perfect equality, and Nino accepting that as perfectly natural, though had Colin next moment said "Get me my shoes," Nino would have jumped to his feet, his most obedient and respectful servant. These Southerners had fine breeding in their bones, whereas so many Englishmen of his own class had only got it on the skin. His brother Raymond, for instance, what a howling cad compared to Nino! Or Uncle Ronald last night telling a smoking-room story, so that one really sickened at his grossness. Nino talking about the much more awful deeds of Tiberius was not gross at all. He was only gay.

"Nino, why do we talk theology before breakfast?" he said. "We did yesterday, and here we are at it again to-day. I was very theological last night: I suppose that's it, and this is an overflow. . . . But don't you see that it's diverting to defy Il Padre, and be rude?"

"No, that is not diverting," said Nino.

"Well, everyone must go to the devil in his own way. So

if I wanted you to do something wicked, which didn't divert you, I suppose you would refuse?"

"I shall always wish to please you," said Nino.

"Well, you can please me now. I want to hear about the Black Mass. I think it might make me happy. Have they a book? Have they a missal?"

"Yes," said Nino.

"Nino, you're rather annoying. You're becoming serious."

Nino shook his head.

"I have no use for it," he said, "and indeed I know little of it. They have a book, there is a priest, but he must be one who has been turned out of his office. But where is the good of it all? It is enough for me to do what is diverting, and wipe my mouth after, till I want to be diverted again."

Colin reached out for a towel. The mere fact that Nino found something revolting in the idea of the Black Mass was naturally a reason for causing him to interest himself in it, but if he did not feel the fascination of defiance, he could be no true worshipper. . . . And somehow Nino was so perfectly delightful as he was: it might spoil the gaiety of his Paganism to tamper with his instincts. He only cared for diversion, there was no devotion about him. . . .

"Nino, we're wonderfully alike in some ways, as I've told you," he said, "but we're wonderfully different in this. I don't believe you like hurting people, for instance. That's where the difference lies."

"Not if I am fond of them; only when I hate them," said Nino.

"Oh, you're no good," said Colin. "Give me my shirt."

Nino scrambled to his feet, and held it up for him.

"Have I displeased you?" he said.

"No. You're a nice boy, but I believe you want to go to heaven when you die."

"Sicuro," said Nino.

Colin mentioned casually at breakfast that Pamela Hunt was arriving that afternoon.

"She telephoned this morning," he said. "So of course I said we should be delighted. I forget if you know her, Vi."

He, Violet and Aunt Hester were the only three down yet. The latter looked up from her well-furnished plate, for Aunt Hester always had a fine appetite for breakfast, and couldn't bear the silly rubbish of those who said they were better without. Whether Violet knew her or not, it was evident that Aunt Hester knew something about her. . . .

"Pamela Hunt coming here!" she said. "Well, I never!"

Colin turned to her with his most radiant smile.

"What is it that you 'don't ever,' Aunt Hester?" he said.

Lady Hester returned to her plate. She had no desire to make mischief, but really, the way Pamela Hunt had run after Colin, and his perfect readiness to be caught! . . . They were always together: the whole world noticed it.

"Well, I hope we shall have a fine Sunday," she said.

Colin, shooting a glance at Violet, saw that her attention had been aroused. Probably it could not fail to be aroused when Pamela arrived, but what on earth had that to do with this old Victorian creature, whose morals, as everybody knew had been of the most indulgent order in her own affairs? Her old age and her wit had begun to whitewash her now, but it was a little too much that she should wish to change her name to Mrs. Grundy. It wasn't nearly such a pretty name as Hester Brayton, nor did she look the part. However, he would deal with that soon.

"I hope so, too," he said. "We'll go to church together, Aunt Hester, and sing 'A few more years shall roll.' That's so encouraging, isn't it? Good morning, Uncle Ronald. Your cough's better, I trust."

Uncle Ronald presented a rueful appearance. People ought not, thought Colin, to be allowed to spoil the appearance of a room like this. Presently Aunt Margaret joined them: all the menagerie was here now except Grandmamma. . . . He turned to Aunt Hester again, with all his sunniest good humour.

"Aunt Hester, you're got up to kill," he said. "I never saw anything so saucy as your hat. Should I look as nice if I wore a hat at breakfast? I think I shall have breakfast in a bowler. Have you been out already?"

Aunt Hester felt encouraged. . . . It had been a mistake to make that ejaculation on the subject of Pamela Hunt, but it had 'popped out.' But Colin bore her no grudge, bless him: such a good-natured boy, he was, and she felt it would be quite easy to speak to him after breakfast, and beg him to reconsider the propriety of letting that baggage come down here. Of course Staniers weren't saints, and she herself wasn't a prude, thank God, but to bring that wench down here with Violet in the house was a 'bit thick' as they said nowadays. . . .

She had finished her breakfast, and got up. Colin immediately followed her, and they strolled along to the shady end of the terrace.

"And now, my dear, I'm going to talk to you like a mother," she said.

Colin took her arm.

"Ah, do," he said. "That'll be lovely."

"Well, my dear, you're doing what you shouldn't," she said. "All the world and his wife have been talking of the way that Pamela of yours is running after you. Don't think I blame her for that, for that's her business and yours and nobody else's. But everyone's been saying that you and she—well, with that snuffy old husband of hers, no wonder she's wanting to make the most of her youth."

They sat down in an encampment of chairs under the trees. Colin had wanted an excuse for getting rid of Aunt Hester, and she was evidently going to give him one. . . . It was so pleasant of people to dig their own graves. His eyes were soft and gay as he spoke.

"Dear Aunt Hester!" he said. "Go on."

"My dear, you're charming to me. I was afraid you looked vexed for a moment when that silly speech of mine popped out. So there it is—and it ain't quite decent of you, my dear, to bring her down with Violet in the house. I don't know what your relations with the woman are, though of course you'd tell me there are none, but whether there are or not doesn't affect it. You oughtn't to have her down here, for, even if Violet knows nothing about it now, there'll be a host of kind friends to tell her, when they know that Pamela's been to stay at Stanier, and it makes a fool of her. Don't you ever make a fool of anybody, my dear, for they'll heave it back at you sooner or later. That's my experience."

Colin felt a sudden inexplicable impulse of affection for this damaged old butterfly, which ought to have been hibernating. She was such a pagan, and she had enjoyed herself so in her time, and she had shrewd wicked little eyes like an elephant. But that softening towards her only made him impatient of himself, and he rallied against this insidious intrusion. Just a little more from her first.

"I suppose you're right," he said.

"Yes, my dear, I am, but it's nice of you to listen like this to an old woman like me. You ring her up, or get that young

Italian ruffian of yours to ring her up, and say you've got the influenza. I've not forgotten what it's like to be young and kick over the traces a bit, but down here you know. . . ."

Colin sighed. He had got rid of the intrusive affection. She was just like an improper little doll.

"There's one thing I want to know, Aunt Hester," he said.

She looked at him a moment. Really he was the handsomest and most attractive boy she had ever seen. Anyone so endowed ought to have carte blanche to do as he pleased.

"Tell me, my dear," she said.

"I will, as we're talking so pleasantly and confidentially. I've been wondering what the deuce you've got to do with it. I believe I'm master here: I fancy I can invite anyone I choose. Perhaps I'm wrong: perhaps I'm only a dummy stuck at the head of the table, and the place is run by a syndicate of aged relatives. Certainly it seems to be, for there's Uncle Ronald drinking the cellar up, and telling me he couldn't dream of leaving Granny, and there's Aunt Margaret, as adhesive here as a postage stamp, and now there's you dictating to me about my morals and my guests. As for what you tell me the world and his wife say, how can you expect me to be interested in the gabble of a pack of your foul-minded old friends? You always liked gossiping in the gutter."

Colin jumped up from his chair, and shook off Aunt Hester's hand which lay on his arm. Cruelty is a whet to itself: it grows sharper with use.

"Do you know, I'm not going to stand it any longer," he said. "I've already told Violet to get it into Uncle Ronald's head that he mustn't expect to be here all the rest of his life, and now I tell you the same. You've got houses of your own and you can all go and live in them. As for telephoning, if there is any telephoning to be done, it'll be you to telephone to your housekeeper to say you've got influenza and are coming home. I don't want you to do that; I hate rushing things. But if you stop here a day or two longer—I shall be quiet pleased if you do—you must first apologize for your damnable interference in things that don't concern you. Really, Aunt Hester, for you to set yourself up as a guide to the young, is just a shade too grotesque."

Aunt Hester sat still, her hands tight on the arms of her chair, and her mouth holding itself in. Into her eyes there came the small difficult tears of the old. She wiped them away with a little pink-bordered handkerchief, and got up.

"I'll be telling my maid to pack," she said.

"Just as you please," said Colin.

"That's what I please," said she.

Colin felt a spasm of impotent fury with her. He could not have been more invincibly brutal, but he had not won. She went down with her flag flying, she was sinking unsubdued.

"Good-bye, my dear," she said, "I was always devoted to you, and I thought you liked me. But you hate me, else you couldn't have spoken to me like that. I'm sorry I was wrong about you. And I thank you for my visit."

"So good of you to have come, Aunt Hester," he said.

Violet had come out of the dining-room and was now close to them.

"I've got to go up to town, my dear," said Aunt Hester, turning her back on Colin. "I must see to my togs."

Violet cast one glance at Colin, who stood there all debonair and smiling.

"But you'll be back this evening?" she said.

"No, my dear, not so soon as that," said Aunt Hester, and tripped off to the house.

Violet turned to Colin.

"Has anything happened?" she said. "Why is Aunt Hester going?"

Colin followed the retreat of the sprightly little figure for a moment in silence. Then with a sigh he looked at Violet, shaking his head.

"It's all wretched," he said. "Yes, Aunt Hester's quarrelled with me. She took it on herself to tell me I had no business to ask Pamela here. She said everyone believed I was having an affair with her, and that it was an insult to you to ask her here. Now that doesn't happen to be true. Do you believe that, darling?"

Violet looked at him with that direct limpid gaze, so like his own.

"If you tell me so, of course I do," she said.

"I do tell you so," he said. "Even if it wasn't true, what on earth has it to do with Aunt Hester? But her talking to me like that—she called it talking like a mother—gave me the opportunity I wanted, so I told her I was tired of being ruled by aged and parasitic relatives. I said I wasn't in a hurry for her to go, but that, if she wanted to stop a bit longer, she must apologize. So she went to pack. That's all."

"Oh, Colin, poor old thing!" said Violet.

"Me, or Aunt Hester?" he asked.

"Aunt Hester. She didn't mean to insult you."

"I suppose then she did it by accident," said he. "If so, she ought to have said she was sorry. How about the others, by the way? Have you spoken a seasonable word to Uncle Ronald?"

"Yes. He understands. He and my mother are thinking of going to-day. They would be off on Monday anyhow."

"Golly: the animals are going out three by three," observed Colin. "You and Pamela and I will be *à trois*. A quiet peaceful Sunday. I hope it will be fine, as Aunt Hester said."

Violet turned towards the house.

"I must go and see Aunt Hester," she said.

"What for? To commiserate with her for having a brutal nephew?" asked Colin.

"No, Colin. To say I am sorry she is going, but that, if she can't see her way to apologize to you, there's nothing else to be done. I believe what you tell me, and, that being so, she has wronged you."

Colin paused.

"And supposing now I told you I was in love with Pamela?" he said.

Violet's eyes wandered away from him a moment, and mused alone.

"I believe that at the bottom of my heart I should rejoice that you were in love with anybody," she said.

Colin's beautiful mouth curled with derision.

"God! That's the last word in wifely devotion," he said.

"But it's true," said she.

Ronald and his wife had decided not to alter their plans, but to stay till Monday, and thus Pamela's arrival left the party numerically as they were. But her presence brought into it some sort of emotional intensity; flippant as was her speech, Violet divined a certain force behind the flippancy, below her wit there was will. Certainly she was extremely good-looking, black of eye and hair, olive in skin, a wonderful contrast to the fairness of Staniers. And flippancy and force alike, wit and will, were all shooting at one target. . . .

"London is getting addled," she was saying. "It always does half-way through July. The hens, that is the hostesses, sit and sit and sit, but nothing comes out, except a few engagements of their sons and their daughters, or rather of their fathers and their mothers. That would be nearer the truth. There was a summary of the ages of newly-married people in *The Times* the other day. There were six over seventy, three over eighty, and one of ninety-two."

"Deaths, surely, deaths," said Ronald. Pamela had been making him feel young: he was glad he had settled to stop till Monday.

"No, dear Mr. Stanier, marriages," she said. "The people who died were much younger, I noticed it particularly. How do you explain that, Colin?"

"That marriage keeps you young is the only explanation," said he.

"No, my dear, you don't grasp it. They were already wonderfully old when they married. Being old keeps you young is the only explanation I can think of. We must get old: otherwise we shall die instead of marrying."

"And what was the age of the babies who were born on this remarkable day?" asked Colin.

"How can you ask? Babies are the oldest things in the world. You can't compute their age, it is infinite: they are age itself. But by degrees, through experience, they get young. We come into the world all red and wrinkled, and we go out all white and wrinkled. We've been bled, that's all."

All the time, Violet felt, she was talking at Colin. These sprightly trifles, unreal as stage-dialogue, were but the steam that rose over what lay below. Whether she addressed Ronald or his wife or Violet herself, the steam blew always towards Colin. She talked impartially to one or another, just as she looked impartially at one or another, so that out of that very impartiality she might look at Colin, too. But on him her hovering glance settled for a moment. A woman always did that if she was in love with a man. She talked here and there, she glanced here and there, in order to make it natural that she should glance everywhere. But when she came to the face that she sought, she hovered no longer, but, just for a moment, she settled.

As certainly Violet knew that Colin was not in the least in love with her; he had never spoken a truer word than when he had told her that. He was amused with her, he looked long and very openly at her: he did not disguise his admiration. But he had no secret message for her, as she for him. . . . Lady Yardley's voice broke in: she had been perfectly silent throughout dinner.

"Why is Hester not here, Colin?" she said. "Has this lady who has been amusing us all come to live here instead of Hester?"

Colin nodded to Violet, who rose.

"No, Granny darling," he said. "This lady has only come to live with us till Monday, unless you can persuade her to stop. Now it'll be time for your whist in ten minutes. Go on with Violet."

Colin took a delicate pleasure that night in not allowing Uncle Ronald to drink more than one glass of port. He had told Violet that he would make him tipsy every night till she did as she was told and informed her father that he was not to regard Stanier as his home any longer; now, since she had been obedient, he would see that Uncle Ronald was lamentably sober. He could play whist to-night in fact, and Violet and her mother must make up the table for old Lady Yardley. This left him and Pamela free, and presently he strolled out with her on the terrace.

"It was delightful of you to propose yourself," he said, "though, upon my word, I felt it was very selfish of me to let you come. How can I prevent your having a fearfully dull Sunday with nobody here? You've missed Aunt Hester: she adds a little spice sometimes to the plain family pudding."

Pamela glanced up at the noble façade of the house. "And to the suburban villa," she said. "No wonder you adore it. Be it ever so humble, Colin, there's no place like home."

Colin had been reflecting what he should do with Pamela. He had seen all that Violet saw, but his opportunity did not allure him. She was magnificently handsome, but she conveyed nothing to his senses. She was all very well as a unit, in the general crowd; she talked nonsense, she made him laugh, but he had no earthly use for her beyond that. He knew very well what she was after: what she was after walked by her side now, and his own entire indifference to her made that appear an unwarranted liberty. In his summary of her, she wanted—that was so characteristic of some women's love—she wanted to possess him, by making herself indispensable to him. That was the way a woman worked. She put it that she gave herself to a man, whereas in reality she aimed at just the opposite, for she meant the man to give himself to her. She wanted always to undermine a man's independence, and subject him to herself. She used her beauty, her wit, her short skirts, her powder-puff all for the same end, to enslave him to his desire for her. That sapped his strength, it sheared him of his manhood, even as Delilah cut Samson's mane, so that he was helpless in her hands. A woman's avowed abandonment of herself, her yielding, her weakness were all fetters of steel with which she cramped and enchained the man: her weakness, indeed, was precisely her strength. And she called this rapacity tenderness! It was the tenderness of a leech which softly fastens itself and softly clings till it is satiated with the blood of its victim. Then full-fed it drops off.

Thus at any rate he judged her quality, a quality greedy and common, that called itself self-surrendering. She was out for what she could get, and Colin had a certain sympathy with that, for it was sensible and intelligible. It had not, at any rate, anything in common with Violet's love for him, which sought to give and not to get. That was wholly alien to him: its manifestations bored him, its spirit, just because it was so unintelligible to him, he hated and defied. . . . Pamela was not like that, nor again was she light, she did not think of this physical desire, which she called love, as a diversion. Had she offered him a part in a comedy, he might have accepted it: comedy was a pleasant pastime. But it was not that which she wanted: she was engaged, so he construed her, on nefarious designs against his liberty: and these must be met with counter plots, which would lead her on to some final debâcle.

They paused a moment as she looked up at the house. The moon to-night had only just risen, tawny and large on the horizon.

"Yes, I adore it," he said. "It casts a spell on us all, you know. I would sooner be here than anywhere on this earth, but, as you know now, there are certain drawbacks to it."

"Drawbacks? Shew me some," she said.

"Ah, you're too polite. Polite Pamela. . . . But imagine what dinner would have been like if it hadn't been for you! Granny, Uncle Ronald, Aunt Margaret——"

"My dear, you've left out Violet," she said. "I think she's too fascinating."

Colin saw that his counter-plot was positively opened by her. He put his arm through hers.

"I feel sure you have seen," he said, "and I'm sure you're sympathetic. Give me a drop of pity, Pamela. That'll be rather healing, and then we'll be gay again."

"But pity? Why pity?" said she.

Colin stopped.

"Violet detests me," he said. "Yes, I know you saw that, and naturally you couldn't say it. But it's said now. It's sad, isn't it? Just a little sad? It's not her fault: any more than it's my fault that I love her. And I suppose I shall get used to it. They say one gets used to anything. Wounds heal if you give them time. But, oh, how easily they're torn open again! Look, here where we stand in the shadow of the yew-hedge is the very spot where Violet first kissed me: it was here she said she would marry me. Come away. I bleed."

He saw her eyes sparkle and soften. They sparkled first: that was the genuine symptom. Then they softened: that was womanly sympathy. Her arm just pressed his encircled hand, and that perhaps was both. All this he read so easily, with that adeptness derived from the birthright of his inheritance. No saint of God could find good in people with such dexterity as he could find evil.

"My dear, I'm so sorry," she said. "I hadn't seen, more shame on my blindness. And really it never occurred to me that sorrow could come near you, for you always seem so robed in joy."

"I'm glad. I mustn't lose hold on joy," said he quickly. "But what atrocious manners I've got! There's nothing so thoroughly rude and middle-class as to tell your friends of your troubles."

"There's no greater compliment that you can pay, than to do just that," she said. "But I should never have guessed, Colin, you're a wonderful dissembler."

He laughed.

"I'm a wonderful grouser," he said. "Grouse too, Pamela. Be sociable: tell me the secret sorrows of your domestic life."

"You know quite well I haven't any. My husband and I are the greatest friends. Whenever we meet, which is about once a year, we have the most delightful talk, and always hope we shall meet again soon. In the intervals we hear of each other occasionally. I hear about his little affairs, and I suppose he would about mine if I had any. But I can't behave as so many women seem to."

Colin gave a little shudder.

"I should hate you if you did," he said. "Don't make me do that."

That certainly was not part of Pamela's plan.

"I promise that you shan't for that reason," she said. "But we won't talk about me. . . . Oh, Colin, I hate your being unhappy. What can be done, my dear? You've got so much, too: you've got so many people who are devoted to you."

He looked at her with eyes brilliant and wistful.

"Have I?" he said. "I don't feel as if I had. People are friendly, I know, but I am only one in a crowd to them. They come down here in shoals in the autumn—next time you come, you shall really have some more amusing people to meet."

She interrupted him.

"No, don't do that," she said. "The shoals of amusing people aren't anything to me."

"Ah, that's nice of you," said Colin.

They stood there a moment in silence: then he turned quickly to the house.

"We must go in," he said. "Granny will have finished her whist, and then my uncle likes a chat in the smoking-room. You never knew I was such a domestic character, did you, Pamela?"

"I always knew you were a dear," she said. "And you do like me a little, don't you?"

Colin, when he found himself alone—Uncle Ronald was gloomily consuming whisky to make up for the dearth of port—was as pleased with his terrace-talk as his companion had been. There was the little side-show (gratis) of representing himself as yearning for Violet, but that was only an ante-chamber, so to speak, which he and Pamela were passing through, and there she saw him, the gay trappings of his brilliance stripped off him, hungry for love. And already Pamela—how well he read her—was at his side. Closer and closer must she get till she could not exist without him. All the time she would be posing as the consoling friend, the healer of wounds, and all the time to the truer vision she would be the hunting leopard hungry for the hot blood of its prey. And just as she thought she had got it, it would be the prey somehow that turned on her with derision and mockery. With the exact manner of that furious turning of the tables. Colin did not trouble himself: it could not be settled now, for it must depend on developments. Before long he would be going out to Capri: he might ask her there perhaps, for at Capri everything always turned out well. How often had he made plans, lying there on the beach between the bathes, and how surely had their accomplishment justified the design! The fruit was not ripe yet, though the moonshine on the terrace had brought it on towards maturity. To-morrow ought to be a nice growing day, too. . . .

What a high morality he would then exhibit, and how delightful would be the mockery of it! His plan, thus vaguely outlined to himself, was a derisive parody of morality, in which a decent married man would be seen resisting the improper seductress: what could be nicer? It would be a veritable tract about a Messalina and a Galahad. And then you looked closer, and saw that hate and the desire to hurt twitched in every gesture of Galahad. There was the cream and felicity of it, for it would all be a defiance of love, a campaign of hostility and rebellion.

Colin stood up, stretching himself slowly and luxuriously. He had taken out again from its locked drawer, the plan of that annex which his ancestor had never erected, to study it further, but there was really no need of that. He had sent for his architect to come here on Monday morning, who must get to work on this outlined sketch-plan, and devise something in the style of the house, using old brick and weathered stone and timber. That would all be talked out on Monday, and the building of it begun at once. For to-morrow's employment there was church in the morning, where he always read the lessons if he was at home, and after that there were fruits to be ripened, and very soon after that, certainly during this week, he would go off with Nino to Capri, for a month of basking and bathing and, he made no doubt, a moral interlude, for he meant to ask Pamela to visit him there. And researches must be made in underground Naples: that red ridiculous Consul, Mr. Cecil, would have to lend his friendly offices. He would get him to come over for a night to the island.

Colin looked round his room. Just there the door would be pierced that led into the corridor communicating with the sanctuary.

CHAPTER IV

Colin woke from his siesta very gradually. He had not the slightest idea when the first faint glimmerings of consciousness began to return, where he was. He scarcely knew who he was, and with a deliberate quiescence of mind he tried to prolong this vague sense that what lay here was alive and happy, without orientating it or attaching it to any fixed point. Nirvana, he thought, must be like this, mere awareness of existence and content.

But this Nirvana began spontaneously to break up: from outside his window a whisper of wind and a stir of sun-winnowed air spiced with indefinable Southern odour flowed across to the bed where he lay in shirt and trousers, and at the end of his bed, very curiously, he saw two bare feet. It was still unconjecturable, to his drowsiness, to whom they belonged and what they were doing there, but now a fly settled on one of them, and he made the great discovery that it was his own foot which twitched to dislodge it. This snapped the chain of his identity round his neck and he knew he was Colin. Then the hot Southern scent and the whisper of wind in the pine outside localized him, for nowhere else, but in that beloved villa on Capri, did a pine whisper like that. Yes, he was in Capri: of course he was, for he had arrived late last night, and had spent the morning in the sea.

When once the sluices of sleep were raised, memories began to pour through, and he let them flow as they would without direction. He had come here first only two years ago with his father, and instantly his Italian blood had initiated him into the magic of the South; the lizards basking on the walls, the grey olives, the stone pines, the steep cobbled ways were as home-like, even when he saw them for the first time, as the thrushes that scudded across the lawn at Stanier, and the yew-hedge and the lake. Of course his father's presence, and his father's devotion to him, had been tedious at times, but he had borne that very indulgently. Then he had come here with Violet on his honeymoon, and here she had begun to learn something of his real nature, and that cold terror she had of him, which so inexplicably existed side by side with her love, had first laid a finger on her. Strange, to think how that hand of ice had never frozen her love, nor squeezed it out of her heart. . . . And then he had come here a third time, after Raymond had been drowned, but had stayed here only one night, for waiting him—welcoming him?—was the telegram to say his father was dead. He had not wanted his father to die exactly: he was quite content to wait a few years yet, but how his heart had leaped to know that already, while he was not yet of age, his great inheritance had come to him. Surely Capri was a lucky spot for him: yet was there, where he was concerned, such a thing as luck? Luck, as it was generally understood, was a fitful visitor, with rare capricious advents, and long absences. But with him it abided always.

Colin yawned, till the whole half-circle of his milk-white teeth was disclosed, with his tongue lying like a curved rose-leaf between them, and when his mouth closed again, it closed into a smile. He slewed himself off his bed, and barefooted stepped across the cool tiled floor to the next room where tea was waiting for him. This siesta through the hot hours of the afternoon, when it was impossible to go out, made two days out of each twenty-four hours; you awoke as to another morning, with body refreshed and brain alert. Already the sea breeze was stirring, and the westering sun was off the front of the house, and presently, cup in hand, he strolled across to the window, and pushed back the closed green-slatted shutters, which had kept the room cool during the heat. In came the flooding freshness, spiced with sea, and chasing before it the stagnant air of the house which had been darkened against the tropic blaze of the noon. It heralded the approach of the caressing Italian evening and the star-sown night.

Nino entered to clear away the tea-things. The house was entirely run by him and his family in true Italian fashion, for his sister was housemaid and his stepmother, the second that his father had provided him with, was cook, and she was abhorred by the boy with a genial intensity, for there would be no patrimony left when his father had finished with this brisk succession of wives, each of whom feathered her own nest before she died.

"Well, Nino, and how's Mamma?" said Colin.

Nino, who had been audibly exchanging compliments with his stepmother in the kitchen, drew his eyebrows inward and down, and muttered something which with certain prudent expurgations indicated a pious wish about desiccated and barren stoats.

Colin laughed.

"Well, you wouldn't like her to be a fruitful stoat," he observed.

"Scusi, but I would," said Nino, "for surely she would die in childbirth, and there would be one coffin for the two."

"I thought I heard you kissing in the kitchen," observed Colin.

"I would sooner kiss the gridiron," said Nino.

"Well, go and kiss the gridiron then if you prefer it. And take the tea-things away, Nino. And when you've finished kissing the gridiron come back. I want you."

The Southern smile broke through. Colin could always make Nino laugh, even when the stepmother was in the picture.

"Sis-signor," said Nino. "I will kiss the stoat and the gridiron."

"We shoot stoats in England," said Colin, "and hang their corpses upon trees."

"Eh, she'd look nice on the pine there," said Nino. "But, Dio, the stink, when the scirocco blew!"

Nino departed with the tea-things to kiss his stepmother or the gridiron or anything he chose. That was the true spirit in which to live here; you never bothered your head as to what you were proposing to do; you just did exactly as you liked whenever an amusing opportunity suggested itself. And yet it was a wonderful place in which to make plans, thought Colin. You lay on the beach after your bathe, and without effort your brain seethed with ideas. The sun seemed to liquefy the contents of its cells, and the secret juices, scarcely known to yourself, oozed out in the clear broth of thought. And fruitful too, was the night, when the wind whispered in the pine, and the great furry-bodied bats with wings of stretched black parchment wove silent circles in the air. . . .

There was a power abroad then, Colin knew well, and if you were in tune with it, you caught, like some wireless receive, strange messages from the midnight. Not less surely did he know that there was power abroad for those who sought it, whenever above the altar the lamp burned before the tabernacle that held the sacramental food, which is the Bread of Angels. But unless your heart lay open in faith and loving adoration, the power which in itself was infinite was no more than a fragment of water, or a sip of wine: faith set that vast engine of love and redemption at work, and across the sky, from horizon to zenith, the worshipper beheld how Christ's blood 'streamed in the firmament,' and adored the divine miracle. So too with the power that whispered in the pine and poured itself out on the midnight: unless you believed in it and by faith laid hold on it, there was for you nothing there but the night wind and the wheeling bats.

There was the truth of the legend, a truth eternal and irrevocable, a matter of choice, not for him alone but for the whole world. He could not so passionately have loved evil, if he had not known there was a definite choice to be made. He might have drifted into any sort of sin and self-indulgence from the mere fact that they were pleasant, but the only thing that could have given him his furious zest for evil in itself, was the terrible conviction of the existence of God. If evil had been the dominant power in the world, he would, without the sense of choice, have lain and soaked indolently in it, but he chose it because he loved it, and because in its service he defied love.

Colin made no pretence of doubting the existence of good and evil and the original living causes of them. They were principles perhaps, but since they certainly lived, and daily and hourly manifested themselves, he could not conceive of them otherwise than as Persons. With the same faith that he believed in the power that inspired evil, he believed in the power that inspired good, which had once been incarnate in man, and in some mysterious way suffered for the redemption of those who desired it. For those who believed (and Colin was among them), He was Love, infinite in power, but choice was given to every man, and His Sacrament of Love, to those who abhorred Love, became the Sacrament of Hate and the adoration of evil. Those who had chosen thus could receive it in mockery of love, and to them their decision was an act of faith, through which they dedicated their powers and their will to the service of evil, and drew therefrom the strength that inspired them.

These thoughts were no more than the stream which ascended from the bubbling liquor of his mind, and he did no more than just watch, for this idle moment as he waited for Nino's return, the familiar wreath. And here was Nino's step on the stairs, and it was time to put these general principles into practical shape. He had come to Capri, no doubt, primarily, for a month of that basking amphibious life, which always put him into harmony with himself, but there were other projects as well which now, in strict accordance with these principles, presented themselves for execution, projects no less dedicatory than diverting.

"Nino, we're going to have two visitors here," he said, "and we must arrange about them. Mr. Cecil is coming from Naples to-morrow for two nights and next week there comes the pretty lady, who'll bring a maid. Let's go round and inspect."

The villa was deficient in accommodation for more than a very small number of persons, for Colin, during this last year, intending it to be no more than his own Hermitage, had thrown rooms together, and had converted a spare bedroom into a bathroom. Downstairs, therefore, nowadays there was only the kitchen, and the long vaulted dining-room, originally two rooms. Upstairs there was a large studio running the length of the house, the bathroom, Nino's bedroom, with Colin's next door, and, *en suite*, the sitting-room with the balcony where Colin had been having tea, and a slip of a room beyond, opening out of the sitting-room. This latter would do for Pamela's maid, but where was Pamela to go? Nino's stepmother and sister always went home in the evening after dinner, returning again early next morning.

"I'm afraid you'll have to turn out, Nino," said Colin, "while pretty lady is here, and go home in the evening with your dear gridiron. Then you can make love to her on the way."

"Grazie," said Nino.

"Or scrag her in the dark," said Colin. "No, you mustn't do that, or how should we get breakfast next day? But what room can pretty lady have except yours? I'd sooner have you in the house, though."

The fell prospect of walking home every evening and coming back every morning with his stepmother sharpened Nino's wits.

"The signor does not really want that sitting-room next his bedroom as well as the studio," said he. "Could not that be the signora's bedroom while she is here? Then she will have her maid next door."

"Good boy," said Colin. "We'll do that. There'll be the maid at the end of the passage, then pretty lady's bedroom, then me, then you. And you won't be able to flirt with the maid without passing through the signora's room. Very good for your morals, Nino."

Nino laughed.

"If it is the maid the signora brought to Stanier, she is like a broomstick," he said.

"Then don't fly away on the broomstick," said Colin. "Well, that's settled. But when you're married, Nino, I shan't turn out of my sitting-room for your wife. . . ."

Colin was always charming to those who were in a position to serve him, and Mr. Cecil found a most cordial welcome when he arrived next day. He was a convivial little cad (so Colin would have described him), gratified that Lord Yardley should have asked him to spend a week-end at his villa, and delighted to get out of that frying-pan of a town for a couple of days. In person he was a round red bachelor, with a taste for wine and obscenity. Colin supplied the one, and Mr. Cecil had as his contribution a considerable fund of local lore not quite suitable for children. Usually dinner was served under the pergola in the garden, but to-night the weather was uneasy with hot puffs of scirocco, and instead they ate indoors. In this heat it was impossible to shut the windows, but the Venetian shutters were closed and little blasts of hot moist air, entering through the slats, hovered and fluttered bat-like about the room.

"Yes, yes," said Mr. Cecil, mopping his flushed forehead after the relation of one of these curious episodes, "a bad piece of work. But picturesque, undeniably picturesque. My belief is that the girl was possessed. That sounds a queer thing to say in the twentieth century, when physiologists have proved that every disorder of mind or body alike is due to some microbe, but what microbe covers the facts, eh? Shew me the microbe, that's all, and let it produce that effect again on a guinea-pig."

Colin pushed the decanter towards his guest.

"Awfully curious," he said. "And it would be even more curious to see a guinea-pig behave like that girl. Lord! Wouldn't it look funny? Besides, aren't there diseases and disorders of the spirit, as well as those of the mind and body?"

"Of course there are. What makes one fellow a saint and another a devil? Is that a microbe?"

Colin laughed.

"The microbe that makes a man a saint is a devilish rare beast," he said. "I never saw a case of sanctified possession, did you? But possession, yes. The devil was in the girl: give the devil his due. Anyhow, they believe in him in Italy, don't they? Evil eye, all that sort of thing."

Colin spoke in the lightest possible manner, flicking the ash off the end of his cigar.

"Yes, and it goes much deeper than that," said Mr. Cecil.

"How interesting! You mean they take the devil really seriously, as a force to be reckoned with, to be fought, or sided with?"

"Quite, quite," said Mr. Cecil. "Fought, of course, in general: the Church has a very strong hold."

"And, by exception, sided-with," said Colin. "The direct worship of Satan really goes on still, doesn't it, in—in holes and corners?"

Mr. Cecil evidently did not like the subject more than Nino. By now the puffing wind had increased into a roar, which rattled the shutters, and screamed round the corners of the house.

"One does hear of such things," he said.

The hot wind strangely exhilarated Colin: he felt it tingling in him; he vibrated to its friendly violence. On Nino, who entered the room now to see if the signori were not disposed to quit the table, so that he might clear away, it seemed to have an opposite effect. Like all natives he detested scirocco, and looked jaded and washed-out.

"Black Mass, for instance," said Colin to Mr. Cecil.

Nino, at Colin's elbow, clicked his tongue against his teeth. Colin turned round.

"Oh, don't hang about, Nino," he said. "Go to bed: you look cross and tired. You can leave the things here till the morning. Good night."

Nino had no answer for him, but sullenly withdrew.

"Your servant doesn't seem to like the subject," remarked Mr. Cecil. "He looked as stuffy as a thundercloud when you mentioned the Black Mass."

"I know. Nino twitters with superstition. He's a son of the Church: he fears the devil without believing in him. The Black Mass now. Do tell me what you know about it. I don't believe there's anything you don't know about these wonderful Southerners."

Mr. Cecil certainly prided himself with reason on his extensive knowledge of subterranean Italian life, and it was hard to resist justifying his conviction.

"Well, as a matter of fact I have some little knowledge of it," he said. "Indeed I possess a copy of the missal. An extremely rare book."

"Ah, that's interesting," said Colin. "What language? Latin? Italian?"

"No, strangely enough it is in English. In fact the book is probably unique. It was printed in London in the early seventeenth century. How it got into a bookstall in the Via Maurizio I haven't any idea, but there I found it."

Colin leaned forward over the table, his face all alight with eagerness. Such exactly might have been the missal in use in that sanctuarium at Stanier, had not his ancestor turned his back on his Lord and Benefactor, and striven by craven acts of loveless piety to shuffle out of his contract before it became due. . . . Now, three centuries later, it looked as if it was given to him to atone for that lamentable surrender, and here was an opportunity for the furnishing of the chapel that was already being built. Sitting there, with his face vivid and eager, in the matchless charm of his youth and beauty, he looked, in contrast with the flushed little Silenus opposite him, like some young god in whom was incarnate the spirit of physical perfection. Surely no such gracious creature had ever been fashioned in the image of God.

"Mr. Cecil, you're the most wonderful person," he said. "You know everything. Take some whisky: what's that damned boy of mine done with it? Ah, there it is."

Colin got up to fetch the bottle. As he rose the catch of the shutters gave way under the press of the wind; they swung wide, and with a triumphant whoop the scirocco burst into the room, like some vivid invisible presence. Colin laughed aloud with exultation, and ran to the window, where he wrestled with the shutters. Then, just as suddenly, there came a complete lull, and he fastened them back into place and closed the windows.

"The wind had been wanting to come in all evening to join us," he said. "Now it has had its way, and it will be content. There's your whisky: now tell me all about the missal. You will have to let me see it, too."

Mr. Cecil helped himself.

"Well, certainly it's a curious book," he said, "and I take an antiquarian's interest in it. But naturally that's all. To you and me, of course, it appears a mere farrago of ridiculous blasphemy, because, though we're delighted to amuse ourselves, eh? and perhaps are not always as moral and monkish as we might be, we don't want to be wicked for the sake of wickedness."

"Just so," said Colin.

"In order to appreciate what the missal and the mass mean to the worshippers," continued Mr. Cecil, "we must try to imagine ourselves—if it were possible—delighting in evil for its own sake. We must realize that to such ruffians as these, evil is the Mecca of their every thought and deed. They worship it, and, in consequence, detest and mock at all that you and I hold sacred, though we may not live up to our beliefs. Still we hold them."

Colin was bubbling with amusement and impatience. He wanted Mr. Cecil to get on, but, on the other hand, it was wonderfully diverting to hear him talk like this. He took a hand in it.

"I think I can see what you mean," he said. "These ruffians, as you so rightly call them, are fanatics in the cause of evil. But do such people really exist?"

"Yes, and all the time they believe in God," said Mr. Cecil. "Their creed is of defiance, as well as worship."

Colin liked knowing that his theories of yesterday were so wonderfully confirmed, but it was all stale stuff to him: Mr. Cecil was instructing a master in the rudiments of his art.

"And now for the contents of the missal," he said.

"As I say, it will seem to you only a farrago of blasphemy," repeated Mr. Cecil, "but interesting as a human, or rather a devilish, document. It follows the English use, it is a parody in fact of the English use. The exhortation, I remember, begins, 'Ye that do truly and earnestly delight you in your sins, and intend to lead a vile life' and so forth. Then follows the Confession, addressed, of course, to Satan 'We acknowledge and bewail' so it runs 'our manifold good deeds and loving actions, which we from time to time have most grievously committed against thy Divine Majesty, provoking, most justly, thy wrath and indignation against us. We do earnestly repent' . . . it follows the words of the Confession in our prayer-books."

"But what of the priest?" asked Colin. "Is he really a priest?"

"Certainly; he must, as is stated in the preface, be a duly-ordained priest, on whom the Church has bestowed the power of Absolution and of Consecration. If the celebrant was not a real priest, the blasphemy of the Black Mass would be meaningless."

"I see," said Colin. "Horrible . . ."

"Then follows the Absolution, and a Satanistic rendering of the Sanctus. And then we come to what the Romans call the Canon of the Mass, and the Consecration. And that really is so shocking that I can't tell you about it. But the point is this, that when the priest has consecrated the elements, he desecrates them in a manner laid down in the Rubric. That is the crowning and awful infamy. I don't say I'm a very religious man myself, but when I came to that, I really felt the sweat come out on me."

All the time that Colin's eager face had been raised to his, the brightness and beauty of it was something amazing. Never had he felt himself so truly in harmony with the spirit that inspired his life. Here, under the symbolism of this rite, was his own spirit revealed to him, his hatred of love, his love of hate. Here was the strengthening and refreshing of his soul: the renewal, mystically, of the bargain made in Elizabethan days. . . .

He recalled himself from that flash of perception: there was Mr. Cecil, looking really shocked, and he lowered his dancing eyes.

"How absolutely awful," he said, "you make me shudder, Mr. Cecil. And how well and vividly you are telling it. But, horrible as it all is, I think you must let me see that missal. I've got gruesome tastes, you know. I like to be horrified. When will you let me see it?"

"You shall see it whenever you like. You will be passing through Naples on your way home, and I should be delighted to shew it you. We could have another bachelor evening together, as we had before. Dear me, I quite forgot that you were married now, Lord Yardley: I should never have said that. But if you will persist in looking like a boy of eighteen——"

Colin was on fire with impatience to see this missal, but he did not in the least want to spend another evening, such as he had done before, with this sprightly elderly sensualist in the cafés of Naples. Passionately evil though he was, there was not a grain of coarseness in him: he had no objection to others wallowing in mere animalism, poking and giggling and prying, but he had no mind for it himself: that was not his brand. What was imperative was that he should get hold of this wonderful book without delay: literally he thirsted for it, and his thirst must be assuaged. He would want to make a copy of it, unless, as he determined to try to do, he could secure the original. He could not wait. . . .

"Ah, yes, bachelor-evenings are not for me any more," he said gaily. "I'm a father, a heavy father, Mr. Cecil, and I read the lessons in church on Sunday mornings. Imagine if some respectable neighbour from Stanier saw me razzle-dazzling in shady places in Neapolitan slums! I should be thought such a hypocrite. But this missal: couldn't I send Nino across to Naples to-morrow, with a note from you to your housekeeper, telling her to look on a certain shelf, and let him have a certain book?"

Mr. Cecil gave a complacent little giggle.

"I'm afraid that would hardly do," he said. "That book is locked away in a cupboard, and there are some other things there I should hardly like my housekeeper to see. One or two of those terra-cottas from Pompeii; not quite in my housekeeper's style. You remember her? Comes from Aberdeen; Aberdeen granite I call her."

Colin had to continue propitiating this dreadful little man till he had got what he wanted.

"Excellent!" he said. "What a knack you have of hitting a person off, Mr. Cecil. I remember her perfectly. Aberdeen granite! Awfully good! . . . But I've got to go to Naples soon. Would it bore you too much if I came across with you on Monday?"

"By all means do that, and I'll shew you the missal. But it's queer to me that you are so anxious to see it. What was my phrase for it just now? A mere farrago of blasphemy. That's all it is."

"Somehow, you've interested me in it," said Colin. "Well, what do you say about bed? I've got no amusing little night-haunts to shew you in Capri. We're innocent Arcadians here, Mr. Cecil, who eat lotuses and go to bed at ten."

Colin shewed his guest to his room, and went to his own. The scirocco, which an hour ago had been raging, had quite died down, and he threw open his closed shutters, and looked out on to the 'darkness, thick and hot.' That furious wind which had clamoured round the house, until it had burst open the Venetian shutters, and then, as if its purpose had been fulfilled, had ceased altogether, seemed to have charged the night with power; it tingled round him in bubbling eddies. . . . He could hear the sea, maddened by that fierce tempest, buffeting along the rocky coast to the south, and surely not far away the wind still yelled. But just here there was calm as at the centre of some cyclone. . . .

Colin accompanied Mr. Cecil to Naples on Monday morning, and they went straight to his house. Presently the cupboard containing the objects which were not fit for the stony eyes of Aberdeen granite was open, and Mr. Cecil drew out a very thin quarto volume, finely bound in tooled morocco, but much worn.

"There's your book for you," he said. "It's quite a long time since I set eyes on it: a fine binding, and I see, what I had forgotten, that there's a coronet and a coat of arms on the back."

Colin, before opening it, looked at the cover. There was an earl's coronet, and below—— He jumped out of his chair, his eyes wide with wonder.

"But, Mr. Cecil!" he cried. "This is the most amazing thing, the thing's a miracle. Those are my arms. And there's the date, 1640, the book must have belonged to the founder of the family; the Elizabethan Colin, who made the bargain with Satan. . . . No one could have put the coronet and his arms on a book in 1640, except him. He died in 1643."

Then, in a flash, the whole history of the book dawned on him; the theory was as incontestable as a mathematical proof.

"I've got it!" he cried. "As you know, he built Stanier, he collected pictures and bronzes, and, as I read the other day only, in the Memoirs he himself wrote, he collected a quantity of magical and occult books, and mentions among them a missal of 'wondrous blasphemies.' They don't exist at Stanier nowadays: probably he disposed of them."

"Dear me, dear me!" said Mr. Cecil, reaching out his hand for the book. "Your arms, are they? And the date, and the coronet. . . . Yes, I see. Go on, please, my dear fellow."

"Well, he lived an awful life," said Colin. "I will show you the Memoirs when you come to England and stay with us, as you must promise to do. He enjoyed the benefits of his bargain to the full. And he certainly contemplated—this is rather private family history—he contemplated building a sanctuary for Satanic worship. Then, the year before he died, he got into a state of terror about the future. He wrote no more about his awful deeds in his Memoirs, and he did not build the chapel, of which he left the plan, with a priest's lodging adjoining. . . . Now doesn't that fit in completely with the disappearance of the collection of magical lore, and the book of wondrous blasphemies? He fired them out of his library, and read lives of the saints, and that sort of truck: those books are there, yards of them. And now the missal of wondrous blasphemies has turned up again. There it is in your hand."

Mr. Cecil looked at the device on the cover.

"Well, upon my word, that does seem a very sound hypothesis," he said. "Really, if I had known——"

Colin laughed.

"You needn't finish that sentence," he said. "What is in your head is that you would never have shewn it me, if you had known that it came from Stanier."

He sat down again, and, laying his hand on Mr. Cecil's arm, summoned all the charm and persuasion of which he was master.

"I must have that book you know," he said. "I should

have tried to get you to let me buy it from you, anyhow, but now, I really have the right to acquire it, haven't I?"

Now this reconstruction, so ably sketched by Colin, had considerably increased the pride of possession in Mr. Cecil. It gave an immense interest to the missal to know that it had once belonged to so historical a Faust as the first Earl of Yardley.

"I don't see that there's any question of right about it," he said.

Colin bridled his impatience. Once the book was in his possession, he wanted no more of Mr. Cecil, who, for all he cared, could burrow in underground Naples to his heart's content, until somebody knifed him.

"Perhaps 'right' is too strong a word," he said. "Let's say suitability. Surely it's very suitable that the book should go back to Stanier. As for price, if you'll tell me what you paid for it, I'll give you five times what it cost you."

Mr. Cecil laughed.

"I fancy I bought it for five liras, say four shillings," he said. "I don't know that twenty-five liras would tempt me very irresistibly."

"Five liras!" said Colin. "My goodness, I wish I had been shopping with you that day! Of course, that makes my offer ludicrous. But how about getting it valued by Quaritch or somebody who knows? I should then be delighted to pay you twice its estimated value."

Mr. Cecil shook his head.

"I don't really want to part with it," he said. "Charmed to let you read it——"

"But I want to own it," said Colin quietly. "In fact I must. After all, it is only a question of terms. Please name your terms."

Mr. Cecil, for answer, merely put the book in the cupboard from which he had taken it, and turned the key on it. Colin's insistence had increased his determination to keep the book; as a strong sub-current in his mind there was the notion that here was this enormously wealthy young man, who, for some reason of his own, intensely wanted the book. There was no harm in running up the price. . . .

"Ah, my dear boy, you don't understand the collector's spirit," he said. "He is as obstinate as a mule when he has got hold of something he values. The book is not for sale."

Colin felt one spasm of furious rage. It was for the honour of his Lord and Benefactor that he was engaged, and at that moment he would have stuck at nothing to get his desire. From the depth of his heart he let some voiceless intense petition issue.

As that silent prayer welled out of his inmost soul, his anger fell off him like dead autumn leaves, and through him there spread the clear consciousness of the presence of the power which two nights ago had infused the riot of the wind, and brooded in the calm that followed. What had made him angry was the sense of his own impotence to get what he wanted; what gave him now this sense of perfect confidence, was the knowledge that an all-encompassing power possessed him. He spoke as it was given him to speak, without thought or reflection, but with the irresponsibility of inspiration. His smile came back to his lips, and to his eyes that boyish charm and brightness.

"Ah, we mustn't quarrel, Mr. Cecil," he said. "Surely you are wise enough to see that. People who quarrel with me have no luck ever afterwards, and, believe me, I should hate to be the cause, the unwitting cause, I may say, for it is none of my doing, of what might befall you. Don't force me to break you to atoms—yes, you may stare, but I mean just that, and at the bottom of your heart you know I mean it, and you're afraid already. Well you may be, for you are beginning to guess what stands by me."

Indeed, Mr. Cecil was staring at him, and indeed he knew that he was afraid. As he looked, some nameless inexplicable terror began to stir in him.

Colin paused: the power that gripped him grew in intensity as he yielded himself to it, and it now completely possessed him, so that he had no volition of his own, and no consciousness of himself apart from it. Once more he spoke, and though with his outward ears he could hear the words he uttered, he did not grasp their import. He was a mouthpiece only of the power that used his lips. He had no idea what he was saying: all he knew was that his voice uttered the syllables, which, as they were spoken, he heard, but which, once said, passed from his mind altogether. But as he spoke he saw Mr. Cecil's face change, the ruddiness of it blanched to a deadly glistening whiteness, and suddenly, with a cry, he started to his feet, and fumbled for his keys, and opened the cupboard door.

"Stop, stop! that's enough," he said. "For God's sake, for God's sake! . . . Here; here's the accursed thing. Take it and begone."

The power that possessed Colin ebbed and sank, and he felt his own individuality restored to him. He did not know what he had been saying; but, whatever it was, it had been sufficient, for this gross little man was as white as paper, and, shaking, he thrust the missal into his hand.

"That's delightful of you, Mr. Cecil," he said. "I thought, I was sure, in fact, that when I put the case to you, quite simply like that, you would agree with me. Now I will take this to Quaritch's, or wherever you choose, and send you their estimate of what it would fetch at a good auction, and with that I will send you a cheque for double the amount. Its value to me, as perhaps I told you, is quite inestimable."

Mr. Cecil mopped his face.

"I will not receive a penny for it," he said hoarsely. "It is for me to thank you for taking it off my hands."

"Oh, I can't accept such generosity," said Colin.

"I must ask you to. And in your turn you can do me a favour."

"Willingly: it is yours," said Colin.

"Then never let me set eyes on you again," said Mr. Cecil.

Colin rose and picked up his hat.

"Delighted," he said. "Why on earth should I want to see you again? You didn't think I liked you, did you?"

He found a letter from Pamela waiting for him on his return to the villa with his treasure that evening, in which she announced her arrival in a couple of days. This letter, to his mind, was thoroughly typical of her type, reeking with subconscious falsity, cloaking the obvious with the transparent, and pretending that it did not shew through. Was it worth while, for instance, to ask whether Violet was with him, when she knew so well that her visit was based on the fact of Violet's absence? And was it worth while to say that she wondered whether she had not better stay at an hotel? She knew perfectly well that she had not the smallest intention of staying at an hotel, she would not have come to Capri for that. Colin could imagine the blankness of her face if, when he met her, he told her that he had taken a nice room for her at the Bella Vista, or that Violet was with him at the villa. . . . Or should he telegraph and put her off altogether?

He carried this question still undecided down with him to the beach next morning, and, as he swam, turned it coolly over in his mind, and, as he basked on the hot shingle, let his decision liquefy and declare itself. For himself, he did not in the least want her here, neither as comrade nor as lover had he any use for her. Her beauty made no spell for his senses, and the very fact that it was his for the asking discounted it to a zero. If she had been difficult of access, he might have found pleasure in the chase; as it was, it was only himself who was being chased. . . . On the other hand, as he had already sketched it out, the prospect of some ludicrous and humiliating dénouement for her attracted him: it would be amusing also to play the part of the outraged moralist, the unsuspecting and devoted husband. How his face would pass from amazement to indignation, when she made her meaning clear! Or perhaps some intolerable humiliation. . . .

He turned over on to his back, and threw an arm across his eyes, to shield them from this resplendent glare of the noonday, and let his body and limbs drink in the light and the heat. These were the allurements of the South: the hot basking and the plunge into that liquid crystal, the mouldering fragments of Roman masonry, with lizards basking on them, and tufts of fragile campanula springing from the crevices, dusty roads with walled-in paths leading through the ripening vineyards, stories of Tiberio, wine decanted from perettas into bottles stoppered with green folded leaves, ripe figs, and the warm dusk of evening, saunterings on the piazza among dark-eyed boys and smiling girls, gay and friendly . . . all these made up the Italian spell of exquisite conditions and effortless existence. To his loveless nature mere physical passion was an affair of kisses and laughter and light caresses, to be enjoyed and forgotten and renewed. If you adored a woman's personality, you would need her, body, soul and spirit, but without love to inspire passion she provided no more than a pastime. And love was his enemy; whether it was such love as Violet's or such as Pamela's, its only office was to give quarry for his sport. He liked laying traps and ambushes for it, he liked hurting and humiliating it. . . . Sometimes, of course, the claims of the body were insistent, you desired satisfaction, if only to rid you of its unease. Just so, if you had a corn, you would go to a corn-cutter, who would make you comfortable. . . .

"Yes, Pamela shall come," he said to himself, "and God knows in what plight Pamela shall go." That would all be settled for him, he thought, some inspiration would come, not out of his own contrivance and ingenuity, but, like those words which he had spoken to Mr. Cecil yesterday, out of a subtler wisdom than his. Never had he been able to recollect them: they were spoken in some ecstasy, and how well they had done their work! He had seen how the man's face changed to damp ash as he listened; would Pamela's suffer some such change?

He raised himself on his elbow: the air over the hot white beach was tremulous with the heat; a few yards away the sea, still as a lake, sent no tiniest ripple to its liquid rims. Within it, like the fire in some precious stone, a network of light played over the pebbles that lay below, and, more than ever this morning, Colin was conscious of the fire within himself, which, like that radiance within the sea, made a dancing light deep in his soul. He had read and re-read that missal of wondrous blasphemies, and like Faust it fed his soul. In the devotion of worship was the true expression of the spirit, and with what knowledge of its needs had the compiler framed the ritual of mockery and defiance! The vestments of the priest and his acolyte, the gestures and genuflexions with which he accompanied his acts, the atrocious symbolism ordained for the decking of the altar, all stirred the imagination to the lust of evil. Those impious orisons! How they prepared the soul for the culminating act described in the rubric the very reading of which had made Mr. Cecil sweat with horror! To Colin it had given a gasp and spasm of delight: it expressed in visible symbol the core and spirit of his being. . . . Here was the fire and the dancing radiance that worked within him: presently, when the building which his ancestor had planned at Stanier was erected, it would blaze up, a beacon of self-dedication.

Well, it was time for a final swim, for he was roasted through and through, and already Nino with the boat that should take him back to the Marina was approaching, and, running over the hot pebbles, he fell forward into the sea, and lay floating with arms and legs spread wide, and face submerged. His own shadow hovered below him on the bottom with flickering outline, and the water clear as air seemed to hold the sunshine in solution. For the moment the cool tingling touch made him forget the missal and the traps to be laid for love; the sheer exquisitness of bodily sensation contented all his needs. If only that sensation could be preserved in all its first sharpness, he could imagine himself happy, without his burning love of hate and his hate of love, in this Nirvana of liquidness and sun.

CHAPTER V

COLIN was lying full length in the shadow of the ruined walls and tumbled masonries that crowned the cliff at the east end of the island. A few yards away was the wind-bitten edge from which the huge rock plunged sheer into the sea. Pamela sat by him leaning on her elbow: at the moment her hand was foraging in his breast-pocket for his cigarette-case. She would find it for herself, she said; he need not disturb himself. His shirt was unbuttoned at the neck, and the raising of his left arm, to make a pillow for his head, delved a cupped hollow of suntanned skin above his collar bone.

He had just told her that this ruin of walls was one of the palaces of Tiberius.

"He had seven palaces on the island," said Colin lazily. "Wasn't that imperial? One for each day of the week, perhaps—oh, they didn't have weeks, but it doesn't matter—and this was the Sunday one!"

Her fingers found the cigarette-case: it lay against his chest, and as she withdrew it her finger-tips perceived the steady beat of his heart. Presently, when she put it back, they would dwell there again for a moment.

"Why his Sunday palace?" she asked.

"Oh, just the best and biggest, the one he enjoyed most. The better the day the better the palace. He was awfully Tiberian here: Nino told me all about it: such goings-on! It was a sort of Sunday school. He used to send for some samples of nice young things to stay with him from Saturday till Monday, and if he got tired of the girl he chose, he had her brought out and chucked over the edge. Just as you throw away a paper bag when you've eaten your sponge-cake."

"Colin, what a horrible story," she said. "I think I had better move further from the edge, in case you feel you're tired of me."

"Now that's unkind of you," said he. "I've been doing my best as host, not only to amuse you but to enjoy myself, which is the first duty of a host——"

"I wonder if you have enjoyed my being here," she said in interruption.

"Don't stop me in the middle of a sentence," said he. "As I was saying, I've been trying to do my duty as a host, and the impression I've left on my guest appears to be that I am tired of her!"

She put the cigarette-case back. Even if his pocket had been full of red-hot pebbles she could not have prevented her fingers from lingering there to feel that slow steady pulsation below. But it did not quicken under her touch, and how she longed for that!

"No, I don't believe you're really tired of me," she said. "I was fishing for a compliment. But I don't seem to have used the right bait."

"But, my dear, why should you fish for compliments from me?" he asked. "Great friends, like us, don't pay compliments to each other."

"Sometimes I wonder if we are great friends," said she. . . . Colin waited for this train of thought to develop itself: if he took no notice of what she had said, it was certain that she would carry it a step farther, or at any rate repeat it. . . .

She had been here a couple of days, during which she had never let go of herself at all. She had been quite cool and comrade-like. Violet might have listened to all that they had to say to each other. But to-day there had been signs that her self-control was becoming difficult to her. She had sulked—no less—at luncheon, and that was a sure sign: it always meant that a woman wanted to be asked, ever so delicately and affectionately, what was the matter. He knew quite well what was the matter, and so had not asked, but remained good-natured and maddeningly unconscious of her mood till she gave that up, and apologized for being so silent. Then to make amends (as if he cared!) she had been effusive with protestations of how much she was enjoying herself, of how good it was of him to ask her here. . . . And now again this wondering if they were great friends indicated a certain perturbation . . .

"Tell me, are we great friends?" she asked.

He knew she would ask that again: women are such damned fools, and he leaned lazily towards her.

"And tell me!" he said. "Don't you know it?"

His face must have reassured her, for she let her eyes dwell on it, and broke into a smile.

"I suppose I do," she said. "You wouldn't have asked me

to stay with you otherwise. What a bore we women must be! We always want to be reassured about the things a man takes for granted!"

Colin turned over on to his side.

"I never take anything for granted," he said. "It's really much wiser not to expect anything, and not to count on anything till it's given you."

He knew she would attach a certain meaning to that. She did.

"Colin, what nonsense!" she said. "Why, you're the one person in the world who always gets what he wants."

He sat up, plucked two long stems of grass, and threaded them together, with that rapt intentness which must mean to her that he was thinking of something else than this task of his fingers.

"Not a bit," he said. "I have so often expected to get what doesn't come to me, and then what comes instead is a disappointment. Moral: never ask, never expect! Take what is given you and be thankful, and if nothing is given you, do without it. But, my dear, I didn't bring you up here to bore you with mild philosophical homilies."

He threw away his threaded grass stems, and appeared to throw away with them his unspoken preoccupation.

"To get back to our topic," he said, "I was telling you that Tiberius pitched the favourite of the night over the edge of the cliff. I always make pictures in my mind of Nino's stories of Tiberius: he tells them so vividly. It was just here it happened at dawn, when the rising sun came over the top of the hills there above Sorrento so that it shone on this palace on the peak, but below it was still clear dusk. And Tiberius came out of the palace, rather bored and rather sleepy, followed by two black slaves who dragged his—his discard along. Then he made a sign to them, and they picked her up by the wrists and ankles and swung her once or twice and then let go. Out she went, a glimmer of white limbs, like a starfish, clutching at the empty air, and turning slowly over as she fell. She passed out of the sunlight into the shadow below, and then there was a little splash, just a little white feather on the sea, and that was all. Or, perhaps, if they did not swing her far enough, she would fall on the beach, and there would be no splash. Tiberius peered over the edge, and then went in to have his early morning tea, or whatever they took then, and probably dozed for a little. Perhaps the chill of the dawn had made him sneeze. . . . I shall write a picturesque guide-book to Capri some day, and send you a copy from the author."

Pamela hastened to fit herself to his mood. He did not want to talk about the only thing that interested her, which was their personal relations to each other, and she was wise enough not to bore him by an insistent return to them. Men were like that; even if they were tremendously in love with a woman, they did not want to discuss it all day. They kept their other interests alive and intact: they played golf just the same, or talked politics, or ate their dinner. Whereas a woman when she was in love thought about nothing whatever else. But she did not make a man any fonder of her by limiting her conversation to that. And if he was not in love with her, she ruined her chance if she irritated him by bleating. She had to be sympathetic and interested in what occupied him, if she was to get her way with him. But how increasingly hard it was to be intelligent and companionable when only one thing mattered, and it was the part of wisdom not to mention that.

"Do write a guide-book to Capri," she said. "You're quite horrible about Tiberius and his Sunday palace, but you make it tremendously picturesque. You're frightfully pitiless, you know. You haven't a grain of sympathy for that poor white starfish. What had she done to be chucked over the edge?"

"Why, she had bored him!" said Colin lucidly. "After all, what more horrible outrage can we commit on each other?"

Pamela's mind switched back to personal matters. She mustn't bore Colin. . . .

"Well, it was his own fault for having chosen her," she said. "He ought to have seen she would have bored him!"

"Quite so. Of course he became more savage just because it was his fault."

What a nuisance she was, he thought. Whatever he said to Pamela, she wanted to be bright and discuss it, and argue and interest him. . . . It was his fault also that he had allowed her to come here, and that had the same effect on him as on Tiberius.

"Yes, that's quite true. We always are angry with others when we've been mistaken in them or have injured them," she said.

Colin suddenly registered the fact that he hated her. The knowledge seemed to spring from no particular source; it was blown to him perhaps on this evening breeze. In consequence he exerted himself to charm and attract her, for that was the path that led to the completest outrage and humiliation for her. He hated her passion for him, and therefore inflamed it, so that she would pay the more for it.

"I don't believe you ever wanted to injure anybody," he said. "You've got the most adorable nature, do you know?"

"My dear, how about compliments?" she asked. "Great friends don't pay each other compliments, you told me."

"Well, I wanted to let you know that I had noticed it. Leave it at that. . . . Ah, look; the loveliest light of all is beginning. Just before sunset sea and sky and land all get inside an opal. The hard wearisome brilliance of the afternoon fades, and you have ten minutes of pure fairyland. Everything is unreal and exquisite: you can hardly believe in the beauty of it. I could almost jump over the cliff myself for the sheer joy of falling, free and unfettered, through the air. One is too much anchored when one is on land. Swimming you get some feeling of being unattached to anything, but think if one was falling, falling through the air. And what does it matter if there's death at the end? One would have had a perfect moment. Fancy being happy, though only for a few seconds!"

He sat with knees drawn up to his chin, looking outwards over the bright gulf of air, below which the sea lay blue and unflecked, and he heard her take a quick breath as she looked at him. Then, turning, he saw the fire in her eyes so nearly breaking into flame.

"Fairyland!" he said. "And you look a real native of it, Pamela. . . . My dear, 'real native'! It sounds as if I were calling you a Whitstable oyster. And then, as one fairyland fades—look, it's going quickly—another, the fairyland of night, begins. I could sit here, at least so I believe this moment, all night with you, watching the stars wheel, and fancying I could hear the rustle of the world as it span through space, until it came out of the tunnel of the night into morning again. But you would have to be close by me. I couldn't do it alone; I should get self-conscious, and that's the ruin of magic. My dear, how bored you would get before sunrise."

He saw the fire begin to leap in her eyes, and he did not want it to burst out yet. There must be some greater abasement for her than his mere solitary derision, if he let her now say what was trembling on her lips, or if under the impulse she could barely resist she clasped and clung to him. That fire must be damped down for the present: the core of it would only grow the hotter for that. . . . He laughed and went on without pause.

"What dreadful positions I put you in," he said. "You are almost bound to say that you would be delighted to stay here all night with me, and your tongue would be blistered for that thumping lie. How bored you would be before morning! I shall get Nino to come instead: poor Nino, he would have to do as he was told, and I shouldn't care how bored he was. Or your maid, perhaps she would come, or Nino's stepmother. But a companion would be necessary: just somebody, just anybody."

She got up, stung to the quick, but Colin was quite undismayed. The fire burned all right, that blast of cold air only made the core of it turn white-hot, as the surface of it for the moment ceased to glow. Perhaps she was going to sulk again. . . . But apparently she had not found that of any use: instead, after that one moment of averted face, she laughed.

"You're a savage," she said. "I wouldn't trust myself up here for a night with you. You would get tired of me, and push me over the edge."

He sprang up: this was how to treat her, with romance and sweetness one moment, and the next with this callous indifference, and then with gay affection again and encouragement and nonsense till she was dizzy with desire and bewilderment and pique.

He could play on her like a lute, which presently he would dash down and trample on. The manner of that was beginning to form itself in his mind. It would serve her right for coming to Capri in this compromising way.

"Ah, you're really unkind," he said. "That's the second time you've told me you were afraid I should commit a murderous assault on you. I'm a savage: there it is. How you bully me! But I forgive you. You're one of those blessed people who will always be forgiven whatever they do. Sunbeams of life: you melt whatever you shine on! Blessed ray from that celestial luminary! . . ."

Colin's sudden pomposity was irresistibly funny. He spoke with a throaty pious intonation.

"Oh, what nonsense you talk," she said. "Are you ever the same for two minutes together? Just now you were in fairyland, and then you snubbed me, and now you're a dreadful sort of parson. When are you Colin?"

Colin continued to be the dreadful parson.

"Dear friends," he said, "let us ask ourselves in all humility of heart how often we are our own true selves. I would fain we were our true selves oftener. What is it that the Swan of Avon says, 'To thine own self be true, and then you will be true to everybody else.' Truth and lies! How wholly unlike they are, the one to the other. Let us sing the hymn 'The sun is sinking fast' . . . Golly, so it is, Pamela and the antiquarian lecture I meant to give you hasn't been begun yet. Let's go home. And my hair is full of grass-seeds with lying down."

"Stand still, and I'll pick them out," she said. She perceived in his sun-warmed hair the faint fragrance of the sea, and longed to bury her face in it.

"No, it doesn't matter. Perhaps they'll sprout. I should like to have a hay-field on my head. I would sit in the hay. . . . Then, to skip a few centuries, when the Christians came to the island, they built a little shrine up here, and erected that bloated statue of the Virgin. I suppose they thought her image would disinfect the place from its Tiberian memories. But it doesn't; it's Pagan in spite of all their statues. You're a Pagan, too, Pamela. That's why you fit in so well up here."

"Yes, I've never believed in anything," said she. "How can one believe in anything one doesn't know of? I believe in what I see, and hear, and touch and feel. I know of nothing else but these things. I'm a flame that throws a little light round itself, so that it perceives. And then it's blown out. All the more reason for making the most of it, while it's alight."

They had begun the downward descent of the steep path, too narrow for two to walk abreast. Colin, just behind her, found his muscles twitching with intolerance of her shallowness.

"Then you don't fear death?" he asked.

"Of course not. As long as things are pleasant, and I don't have toothache or cancer, I don't want to die. But if I was fearfully unhappy I shouldn't think twice about dying. Or if——"

She paused a moment: the path had broadened out, and there was room for them both.

"Or if——" said he, stepping to her side.

"Or if I was terribly happy," she said softly. "It would be dull to go back to ordinary pleasantness after that. To flare up, and go out. Not a bad fate, Colin. Who wants to gutter away into old age?"

He laughed.

"Then all your friends must keep you gently simmering," he said. "You mustn't be allowed to be terribly happy or terribly unhappy. Or you'd blow yourself out like a candle. But I don't agree at all: I shall like being old; I shan't then have desires and expectations which I fear to put to the test. I shall be a gentle old man with a beard, and a bath-chair, and some grandchildren, and some gout, and no memory, and no desires. But, enough of that. Let's observe the features of the landscape. There's the town beginning to twinkle with lights, and there's the Marina with the evening boat just coming in. And there's that wonderful Monte Solaro, where we'll go to-morrow if you like a long walk. At the top you can see fifty thousand miles in every direction, and there are tawny lilies in the grass, also quantities of insects with quantities of legs. And here's the villa. Blessed place but rather sad. Yet I have been awfully happy here sometimes. You know I spent my honeymoon here with Violet."

That was designed to prick her, and excellently well it did so, for Pamela had not forgotten that little tragedy of Violet's dislike of him, which he had talked of on the terrace at Stanier. And now he clearly conveyed to her that Violet's coldness had infused the villa with the bitterness of sweet memories. As they entered together in the cool dusk, there was lying on the table just inside the door a letter for him, and she heard him mutter to himself rather than say to her, "Ah, that's from Violet," and, opening it, he instantly became absorbed in it. To Pamela that was the definite challenge: it was as if Violet's glove had been thrown on the floor between them, and all aflame she went on up the stairs, and into her room, which stood at the head of them.

So it was Violet for whom he still ached and thirsted, and the knowledge was a spur to her passion. The cause of his cool friendliness to herself, vague and indefinite before, was firmly outlined now; she knew what stood in her way, and what must be demolished. After all, he had asked her here alone; that argued strongly in favour of her success, and it was up to her to make good the footing he had given her. It was still the thought of Violet which occupied him. . . . Now that she knew that, she could act on her knowledge: she must use her utmost seduction, not alone for her own enhancement but to point the contrast between Violet's lovelessness and herself. And without doubt she held an advantage: he and she were alone together in this spell-struck island with all the setting for passion; they were both young, and she was a beautiful woman. . . . His preoccupation with Violet had blinded him: he had not seen with what intensity she wanted him. He had said that he never counted on anything until it was given him: what could that mean except that he was not certain about her? There should be no further doubt about that. . . .

Colin read his letter through twice. As a matter of fact it was not from Violet at all, but how well he played on that poor lute with his muttered information! He knew just what effect his absorption in a letter from Violet would have on his companion. But there was nothing false about his absorption in his letter, for it was from his architect, and told him of the progress of what was in building at Stanier. The walls were rising apace: he had plenty of old weathered bricks for the facing of it, and assuredly the addition would be quite in keeping with the south front of the house.

So that was good, and in the meantime there was plenty to occupy him. He went up to his room, where Nino was waiting for him to come and dress, and his tactics for the evening were all settled now, though he had scarcely given a conscious thought to them. The plan, whatever its success might be, had ripened of its own accord like a fruit hanging on a sunny wall, and he longed to set his teeth in it. Surely his project would be successful: what came to him like this always succeeded.

As he dressed he looked round the room. The door from the passage was opposite the window; in the wall to the right was the door into Pamela's room, converted from its usual habit of sitting-room; in the wall to the left the door that led to Nino's room. There was but little furniture; there would be plenty of space for Nino's bed along the wall of Pamela's room. His own was on the other side, in the corner by the window, head to the wall. Beside it were two switches that turned on the light above his bed and that in the middle of the room, suspended by a cord from the arch of the vaulted ceiling. That would do nicely. . . .

"Well, Nino," he said, "I haven't seen you all day. I don't have so much time to bully you now I've got a visitor to attend to. Don't you hope she'll stop till we go back to England?"

Nino grinned. He did not want any visitors: he much preferred being bullied by Colin to not seeing him, and it had entered his curly head that his master was just as happy alone with him as with his guest.

"I can do without visitors," he said.

"Well, I expect you will very soon have to," said Colin. He pulled his shirt over his head, and went softly to the door into Pamela's room. It was shut.

"Nino, you don't say your prayers before you get into bed, do you?" he asked, "or snore when you're asleep, or have any monkey tricks of that kind?"

"No, neither prayers nor snoring," said Nino. "You have never heard me pray or snore."

"I don't think I have, and don't let me."

He came close to the boy.

"I want you to sleep in my room to-night, Nino," he said. "Isn't that odd? But I do, and I'll promise not to pray or snore either. Bring in your bed when your sister has done the room, and put it alongside that wall there. Be in bed when I come up. Can you keep awake?"

"If you wish me to," said Nino.

"I do. And when I've got into bed and put out the light, I want you to lie quite still whatever happens. I don't suppose it will be for long. And if by chance afterwards I turn on the light again, I want you to sit up in bed and look cheerfully round, and laugh or do anything you like. Do you understand?"

"I understand what the signor says, but I do not understand what he means," said Nino.

"Well, perhaps you will . . . and then after that you can go to sleep. Poor Nino, how I bully and sweat you. Aren't I a queer creature? You're sure you quite understand what I say? Say it over to me! And then run downstairs, and see if dinner's ready."

Colin finished dressing and, when Nino returned, tapped on the door that communicated with Pamela's room.

"Dinner's ready," he called out, "and if you are, come in here a minute. You've never seen my room, have you?"

Pamela entered. For the last two evenings she had only put on a tea-gown for their garden-dinner, but to-night she was resplendent in a blue silver-shot magnificence, cut very low and clinging close to her beautiful girlish figure. Over her arm she carried a cloak of pale pink feathers.

Colin stood open-mouthed.

"You perfectly glorious vision!" he said. "You're superb: you're dazzling!"

"Do you like it?" she said. "I was tired of being so dowdy."

"Like it? I adore it," said he. "It's really almost worthy of you."

She looked round the room.

"Oh, Colin, what a nice room!" she said. "Just a rug and a bed and a washing-stand and a couple of chairs. Tremendously like you, somehow."

He laughed

"I'm a penny, plain," said he, "and you're quite twopence, coloured. I bet you that gown didn't cost less than twopence. Come to dinner. I shall walk backwards in front of you and stare at you."

"You won't. You'll give me your arm."

The table was set at the end of the pergola, lit by electric lights half screened in the vine-leaves, among which the bunches were beginning to ripen. Curtains of brown sailcloth were hung between the pillars, and Nino had drawn all these but one, so that their table was screened from the house, and the road below. This one square opening looked westwards where the last crimson of sunset was fading, and across it rose the black stem of the stone pine, and, though the night was windless here, some murmur as of the distant sea stirred drowsily in its branches. Nino, serving them, slipped noiselessly to and fro, and presently he brought them their coffee.

"Shall I draw the other curtain, signor?" he asked.

Colin glanced at Pamela, and there was no need to ask her what she preferred.

"Yes, Nino," he said. "And clear away now. Just leave the cloth."

All through dinner they had been gay on trivial topics, and again and again she had known that battery of swift glances like signals that he had cast on her, as if unable to take his eyes off her for long. Now she pushed back the cloak that she had thrown over her shoulders.

"Ah, that's right," he said, more to himself than her.

Though he laughed at himself for doing so, he often listened to the sound of the breeze, as if to a wordless and friendly counsellor.

"What a delightful evening you're giving me, Pamela," he said. "You wean me from myself with your splendour and your gaiety. I declare that since you came into my room before dinner I haven't once thought of that letter I found waiting for me."

"From Violet?" she said.

His eyebrows contracted as if with a twinge of pain.

"Yes. Oh, no bad news. Excellent news: she's getting on wonderfully well without me. Hopes I am enjoying myself very much——"

"I join her in that wish," said Pamela.

"I know you do, bless you, and it would be black and ungrateful of me if I didn't recognize that. My dear, you've been such a godsend, coming here to sit on the perch with the moping owl."

"You mustn't mope," she said. "You're an owl for moping, Colin."

"I don't mope except with you," said he. "It's shocking bad manners, I know, and yet it's one of those involuntary compliments. Ooh, the relief of getting somebody who understands."

His eyes left her face, dwelt hovering over her breast, and came back again.

"Help me, Pamela," he said.

She leaned forward over the table. She loved this weakness and this appeal.

"Violet has used you abominably," she said.

"No, no: you mustn't say that," he interrupted.

"But I must say that. I want to help you, my dear, and ah, how lovely it is that you ask me to try—and you must lay hold on that. She gets on wonderfully well without you, you told me. Let that rouse your pride. Don't let your happiness suffer shipwreck over that. Heavens, if I found that anyone I was fond of got on wonderfully well without me, that would make me determined to get on just as well without him. I saw how charming and gentle you were with her at Stanier, and she gives you a stone——"

"She gives me nothing," said he, in a voice suddenly harsh and bitter.

She put her hand on his as it lay on the table, and he felt her pulses leap at the contact.

"I like to hear you say that," she said. "Say it again and again till the truth of it stings you. Realize it, make it part of yourself instead of looking at it from outside and mourning over it. Oh, my dear, have some pride! You aren't going to let all your power of love and of happiness pour itself away into the sand of a desert! You've got enough power of happiness to light up the midnight. Don't waste it."

("She's going it rather well," thought Colin, "and I'm not doing it badly.")

"I know you're right," he said.

He raised his eyes to hers.

"Of course I'm right," said she. "Oh, youth passes so quickly and with it all power of real happiness, though you may tell me that you will like to be old. . . . Ah, what nonsense! . . . Colin, you're so different to what I thought you at first. When first we met and made friends, you were all laughter and enjoyment. Who could have guessed that you knew sorrow or unrequited love?"

She paused a moment: in that gaze of his there was a light she had never seen there yet. So suffocatingly sweet to her was it, that she panted for breath.

"Don't fence yourself in," she said, "and mourn over ruins. Build with them: use . . . use the stones you spoke of, to make a pleasure-house. Laugh to see them serve your end."

He looked at her in amazement. There was enchantment and force in her, and her beauty was enough to make a man's senses reel. Was this the strength of which Violet had spoken which was more potent than all else in the world?

Pamela leaned back her head, pushing the heavy black hair from her forehead.

"Open the curtains, Colin," she said. "Let's have some air; I'm stifling."

Was she going to faint, he thought, or adopt some mean feminine device of her weakness to escape from the situation that was closing round her, and which she had done her best to provoke? That would be tragic. . . . He pulled back the curtain with a rattle of rings, and the still tide of the night swept in.

"Ah, that's delicious!" she said.

"Not faint?" he asked. "Not overtired?"

"Not a bit. It was just a breath of air I wanted: our lovely little tent was concentrated, overcharged. . . ."

"Are you sure?" he said. "Hadn't you better go quietly to bed? It would be wretched if in return for the help and strength you bring me—ah, such help, such strength. . . ."

If all the kingdoms of the world had been his, he would have staked them against a penny-piece on her answer. It was her hour, she was winning, so she thought, all down the line. This was not the moment for the victor to ask for a truce.

She rose from her chair and stood by him. The flame burst out from her, enveloping her in fire.

"It's all yours," she whispered. "All . . . all."

She swayed towards him, and he caught her close; her face was against his, and she sought his lips. No word, no whisper even came from her: dumbly she clung to him, and, exultant, he betrayed her with a kiss. The best and the worst of her, love, trust, and all that was merely sensual as well, were his.

For one second he wavered, and reconsidered. Partly it was the mere beauty and physical intensity of her that gave him pause, partly also something akin to what he had felt when he saw Dennis staggering on the terrace at Stanier. Then back, stronger than ever from the gathered force of that check, came his hatred of love.

"We must go in," he said. . . . "Pamela, you adorable thing. Your pity first, and then your love."

They paused at the head of the stairs. Not a word had passed since they left the table.

"But your maid next door . . .?" he queried, and her smile told him she understood.

Colin went softly into his room. There was Nino's bed along the wall, and Nino there already, awake and silent, and eager for any adventure of Colin's contriving. He tore off his clothes, and, as he undressed, once or twice his eyes caught Nino's, and he had to check himself from laughing aloud. He slid into bed, and clicked off the light.

There was no long waiting: there came a faint rattle from the door into Pamela's room, but in the darkness nothing was visible there, and Colin heard the door close again, and the key turned. He could just hear her feet on the bare tiles of the floor, and then from close at hand a little bubbling laugh and his name softly called. The sheer happiness of love sounded in that whisper: it might have been Violet's voice speaking to him on one of the nights of their honeymoon here, and he hated the inimitable thrill of it. . . .

He reached his hand to the switches and turned them both on.

She was standing in the middle of the room just under the light from the ceiling. In that strong illumination the thin silk nightdress, which was all that covered her, was transparent as a veil of sun-pierced mist; her figure crowned by that bright flame of her face was clearly visible, and her apparelled magnificence was pale beside this luminous revealed perfection. Colin almost regretted that he had prepared this hellish surprise for her to-night. To-morrow would have done as well . . . and yet, what thrill of physical love could rival this gorgeous humiliation? How superbly moral it was! The woman had tempted him, coming to him at solitary midnight in the blaze of her beauty, and for once the man, master of his soul, derided her seduction. But the infamy of the brothels of Sodom was nearer salvation than his chastity.

She heard a stir behind her and half-turned. There was Nino sitting upright in bed. Simultaneously Colin spoke.

"Hullo, here's a pretty lady!" he said. "Has she come to visit you or me, Nino? I'll pretend to be asleep, if you like."

She turned her back towards Colin as he spoke, and there came over her face just such a blanching, just such a stark terror as had struck the colour from Mr. Cecil's. Colin's laughing mouth, his dancing blue eyes, were close to her; in his hurry to be ready for her he had not put on his nightclothes, and over his slim suntanned body, as he sat up in bed, the skin-sheathed muscles rippled as he breathed, and at the sight, as if the horror of the Gorgon's head had been shewn her, she turned to stone. Her arms made one stiff movement, as if drawing a cloak round her to hide her, and she went back to the door through which she had come. A violent trembling seized her; she could scarcely grasp the key in her fingers.

"The lock's a little stiff," said Colin. "Ah, that's right. What a short visit! Good night, dear Pamela."

Colin jumped out of bed the moment she had gone, and briskly turned the key.

"We'll have no more visitors to-night, Nino," he said. "The bold slut! There's a lesson for her. What's the matter, Nino?"

Nino's face was buried in his pillow. He had given that once glance at her as she stood under the light, and then, for very pity, had hidden his eyes from her intolerable shame. Now at Colin's voice he looked up.

"Ah, the poor lady!" he said. "You were terrible to her, signor."

Some ecstasy of wickedness possessed Colin. Naked as a young Greek god, and as fair, he capered round the room in an abandonment of glee.

"Oh, the poor pretty lady!" he cried. "What a pleasant hour she had planned, and what a disappointment! But how naughty of her! She shocked me. What will she plan next, do you think? I would bet on a slight headache in the morning, and breakfast in her room. Or will she make an effort, and catch the early boat? *Chi sa?* Good night, Nino."

He jumped into bed; Nino could hear it shaking under the gusts of his smothered laughter.

Colin, according to his wont, slept dreamlessly, and woke to find Nino's hand on his shoulder, rousing him.

"Wake, signor," he said.

Colin yawned and stretched himself.

"I'll raise your wages, Nino, if you'll go away," he said.

"The signora——" began Nino.

Colin broke off his yawn and began to laugh.

"Good Lord, yes," he said. "Well, what about the signora? I hope she had as good a night as I."

"She did not sleep in her bed," said Nino, "and she is not in the house."

"Well, what then? She's gone by the early boat; I thought she very likely would. So cool in the early morning. Probably she has left a note for her maid to say so. Look and find it. I'll have breakfast out of doors."

He got out of bed, and while he dressed basked in the wonderful memories of the night before. Just here had she stood for that short moment . . . and then with that odd gesture of folding something round her had turned. . . . What a horrid humiliated night she must have passed, too badly stung to sleep, and only eager for the morning, and the boat that left at six o'clock, which would carry her away from the island. He wondered whether, if he had received a slap like that, he would have turned tail. Certainly it would have been an embarrassing breakfast next morning; they would have had to talk with great perseverance and animation. He rather thought that he would have stopped and brazened it out to show he didn't care. . . .

Nino entered again.

"I've found a note, signor," he said, "but it is addressed to you not to her maid. It was on the breakfast table in the pergola."

Colin held out his hand for it and opened it. It was quite short.

"I was terribly happy here," it ran, "and I have been terribly unhappy. So it is good-bye, Colin."

He knitted his brows. Surely he had heard something very like this only a few hours before. . . . Then he remembered.

"No one knows of this but you, Nino?" he asked.

"No, signor, I found it and brought it to you."

Colin stood crumpling the note in his hand. A contingency had presented itself with the reading of that note, which he wished to be prepared for. If the implication there hinted at was true, he did not want to stew in that ebullition of scandal and gossip which would boil up if last night's adventure were known. Three people knew of it, possibly only two now, himself and Nino. . . . For a few seconds he thought intently, then his face cleared.

"Now, listen to me, Nino," he said. "You have found no note for me, you have brought me no note. The last you saw of the signora was when you brought us coffee last night after dinner in the garden. That's all you know. . . . Ah, wait a moment: your bed. Move it back to your room, where of course, you slept last night as usual. I'll help you. Now——"

Colin laid his hands on the boy's shoulders and looked him in the face.

"When did you see the signora last?" he said.

Nino's eyes were wide with some unspoken terror.

"Last night," he said, "when I brought your coffee after dinner."

"And you found nothing on the table when you went to lay my breakfast this morning?"

"No, signor."

"Good boy. Now be quick with my coffee. I long to be in the sea this morning."

Colin swam and basked and swam again, spending the whole morning on the beach. He was convinced that when Pamela wrote that note to him she had intended, at any rate, to take her own life, for the wording of it reproduced too closely for any explanation of fortuitious resemblance what she had said to him the evening before as they came home. Very likely she had not done so, for there was a big gulf between such an intention and its execution. It was one thing to feel that you were terribly unhappy, and quite another to put an end to your unhappiness. Most people preferred any amount of unhappiness to forcing an entry through the door that led no man knew whither. Even if it led into nothingness, anything that could happen to you was better than nothingness.

Colin came up out of the water, and, after brushing the wetness off him, sat down on the hot shingle. Supposing Pamela had done what her melodramatic little note implied, what would he think of her, or what (which concerned him more) would he think of himself?

Of course he had never dreamed of such a possibility, but if she had done it what a swift and surprising drama? Yet how abominably stupid, and how, if you looked at it clearly, how self-conscious! There was revenge in it, too: she meant, at fatal cost to herself, to overwhelm him with remorse at this great final gesture. Was it a sign of love, to do that which might be calculated however mistakenly to bring misery on the adored? Yet, after all, it was not love of him that might have driven her to the desperate act, it was no more than self-love and self-pity for that unexpected exposure. He remembered just how she had looked when he turned up the light, and she heard Nino stir. If he had supplied a determining motive at all, it was fear.

Misery . . . remorse. . . . What had he done to be miserable or remorseful for? The woman was a slut and she had come to stay with a respectable married man, who had assured her that his heart's devotion was consecrated to his wife, and, knowing that, she had deliberately tried to seduce him, coming into his room at midnight and offering herself. There was a fine story to tell the world, if so he chose, and Nino, with a wink from him, would testify to the veracity of the crucial episode. And the stern morality of his own attitude, his scorn of her intrusion! That was the cream of it! The missal of wonderful blasphemies itself contained no mockery so distilled.

And then supposing she had done nothing desperate at all, but simply gone for a nice walk to think things over and console her wounded vanity? It was easy to realise what he would feel then. Mockery, sheer mockery and contempt at the fiasco. She had written that note to indicate what she meant to do, and when it came to the doing of it she had squealed and shied off at the idea of going out alone into the dark of nothingness or whatever she imagined was the next scene. Probably she thought that nothingness came next: that was the usual conclusion of such shallow folk. He knew better than that. . . .

The dense stupidity, the blindness of those who did not believe in the hereafter of heaven and hell! He knew his hereafter well enough, the eternal hate, or, if love was too strong, the eternal spectacle of love, and to have no share in it, to sit in a cave of ice, and in an everlasting numbness of cold to behold the sun. . . . But the very thought of that, the certainty that in the end God would somehow beat him, gave the spice to defiance. Safe in the protection of evil, as long as life lasted he would enjoy and deride without remorse or fear. He chose evil because he loved it, and because he hated love, even when it was such love as Pamela had tried to enchain him with, for it partook in its narrow greedy sphere of the true essence, in that she wanted somebody not herself, and if she longed to get, she also longed to give.

Through the windless calm there came the sound of some rhythmical movement, and sitting up he saw a boat approaching with swiftly-dipping oars. The sun was bright on the water, and it was only a vague black speck, but soon he saw who was rowing in such a hurry. . . . He had said he would come back for lunch, so why had Nino come down to the bathing-place? News of some kind, perhaps.

Nino beached the boat, and jumped out.

"The signora," he said.

"So she's come back," said Colin. "I knew she would."

Nino looked at him with wide eyes of horror.

"They brought her back," he said. "Two fishermen found her in the water below the high cliff where Tibero's palace is, the palace you call the Sunday palace. . . ."

PART II

CHAPTER I

COLIN got out of his motor when it stopped at the lodge-gates at Stanier, and struck into the woods through which a short cut led to the house. He had been in London for the last month, and had driven down after lunch on this April afternoon through glints of sunshine and scuds of windy rain. But now with the fall of day the sky had cleared, and, after the pavements and fogs of the town, he longed to immerse himself in the sense of Stanier and spring woods and bird-song.

All round him were the melodies and the enchantments of the spring. The turf underneath the foot was elastic with the thick growth of the young grass, and vivid with little round cushions of greenest moss, and the small of the damp earth was fresh and fragrant. Neither oak nor ash were yet more than budding, but the great hawthorns that studded the slopes up from the lodge to the high ground were covered with the varnished clusters of young leaf, the hazels and alders by the stream that ran into the lake were gay with pendulous catkins and mole-skin buttons, and the copses of birch and hornbeam were full-fledged. Clumps of primroses and sheets of anemonies were in flower in plantations where the young trees had been felled last year, and outside on the turf the wild daffodils bloomed among the curled heads of the young bracken. Once and again a copper-coloured cock pheasant scurried away from beside the path with head low and stealthy stride; in the covers thrushes were vocal with evensong, and in some remote tree-top the chiff-chaff was metallically chirping. From the firs pigeons started out with clapping wings, and a heron, disturbed at his fishing, flapped ponderously away.

The path rose steeply, and presently he came to the top of the ridge, and passed through the deer-fence into the Old Park. Here the trees, planted by Elizabeth's Colin, on what was once bare down, were of statelier growth, and more widely spaced, so that between their trunks broad stretches of the reclaimed marsh-land below could be seen, and beyond, the faint melted rim of the sea. A warm spring air out of the south-west flowed up from the plain, seasoned with saltness, and he drew in long breaths of its refreshment. Ten minutes more brisk walking along the height brought him to the end of the ridge, and below, he saw the roof of Stanier and its red walls smouldering in the clear dusk. The thrill of home vibrated in him; he could never look on Stanier, after an absence, without a smile of pleasure and welcome on his lips.

There came into his mind, vaguely and distantly, the memory of someone looking at Stanier with him, and ironically saying to him, "Be it ever so humble, there's no place like home." That had happened on the terrace one night in an after-dinner stroll, and almost immediately he recalled the incident wondering at the tenacity of the memory. It was Pamela Hunt who had said that, when she came down here, at her own suggestion, for a domestic Sunday in the country. How infinitely remote and meaningless was the recollection of Pamela! He did not suppose he had thought of her half a dozen times in the last half-dozen years. After all there was no reason why he should have thought of her, for it must be close on twelve years since he had seen her. Yes, when August came it would be twelve years since she had paid him that visit in Capri. . . . That had been an affair of ludicrous tragedy: long ago it had lost all personal connection with him, and had become no more than a sensational episode, which, though no doubt it had happened to him, might equally well have been something he had been told or something he had read in a book of short stories, a book of sketches and episodes . . .

He sat down on a fallen tree-trunk—several of old Colin's oaks had blown down in the fierce gales of March—and as his eyes wandered over the wide plain and distant sea below, his mind dwelt idly on that remote month in Capri. What had affected him far more intimately than Pamela's death was the sequel that Nino had refused to stay in his service. Nino had been utterly devoted to him, but something strange had come over the fellow from the hour that he learned of Pamela's melodramatic suicide. He had simply frozen up: his gaiety and devotion had been replaced by some sort of abject terror of Colin; he had become like one of those women on whom the frost and blight of Stanier had fallen. He started and stammered if he was spoken to: he looked at him with eyes behind which lurked some deadly fear. . . . He had no answer to give when he was asked what ailed him: he said "Nieute, signor," and quaked. Finally, within a week, he had said he could stop with him no longer. Colin had used his utmost persuasions, but without avail, and from persuasion he passed to warning and to threats, reminding him that it did not go well with those who crossed him, as Nino had seen not so long ago. But there was no keeping him, and Colin naturally resented Nino's desertion, for his companionship, his gay paganism thoroughly suited him. Yet he seemed to himself to have done no more than let this resentment flow where it willed without conscious direction. Certainly he did not concentrate and aim it at Nino: he but shrugged his shoulders, and said to himself "Well, it's Nino's fault if anything happens." And sure enough Nino sickened of that ill-defined fever which was rife in the island and in Naples that summer, and not long afterwards Colin had to give his cook and his housemaid a half-day's holiday to attend his funeral. . . .

It had served Nino right, thought Colin; for if he had remained up at the villa he would have not gone back to live in that insanitary hovel by the Marina, where the fever was so prevalent, and he wondered whether, in a sense, it had served him right too, for there was no denying that he had been really fond of him, and that was an offence to his Lord and Benefactor. To-day the memory of Nino was far more vivid than that of Pamela, who was a tiresome woman, greedy and graceless, and often even now, when he lazily awoke in the morning, he found himself sleepily imagining that it was Nino who was moving about the room. . . . It had been very stupid of him to behave like that: Colin had always been kind to him: he need never have feared for himself. It was Nino's fear that had driven him into danger: if he had only stopped where he was, and remained gay and companionable, he would have run no risks. But his fright, his mad attempt to escape, had been his undoing, he had run underneath the very wheels like a startled fowl on the high-road.

That month, in fact, had been full of incidents, tragic for others, but strangely prosperous for himself: episodes had taken place then far-reaching in consequence, that fitted into each other with more than casual coincidence. At Stanier, before he left, for instance, there had been the discovery and certain solution of that pencil plan in his ancestor's diary, followed, when he got to Capri, by the finding of what beyond doubt was old Colin's book of wondrous blasphemies, of which he had so easily possessed himself. And the chain of odd occurrences had not been broken there, for within a week of his having obtained that he saw for the first time Hugh Douglas, now librarian at Stanier.

The memory of that was very vivid, and had none of the episodic insignificance of his recollections about Pamela or indeed about Nino. . . . He had gone down to the Marina one evening to meet Violet, from whom he had received a telegram immediately after the catastrophe saying that she was starting at once for Capri. That had been both wise and kind of her; she had not previously known that Pamela was there, and had seen one day in the daily Press the notice of Pamela's death when staying with Lord Yardley at his villa at Capri. With quite admirable wisdom, she had thereupon sent notices to half a dozen papers that she was returning from Capri in a fortnight's time, and had instantly started. Colin had no taste for the foolish scandal of wagging tongues, and Violet's prompt action, making it appear for the benefit of the world at large that she had been with him all the time, was a most effectual silencer. Even those who knew that she had not been there when the catastrophe occurred would look on it with quite different eyes when they knew that she had gone there at once, and Colin had unreservedly applauded her intuition. No doubt, by now, any scandal that might then have arisen would have been as episodic and obsolete as the cause of it, but Colin in this lazy retrospect of that marvellous month permitted himself to stand aside a moment and say "Well done, Violet."

He took up the thread of the far more significant happenings and let his mind dwell on each, recalling details, fingering them like a rosary. . . . He had gone down, as he had recalled, to meet her, and waited on the quay for the disembarkation in small boats of the passengers from the steamer. There she was, and as she stepped out of the boat, at the quay side, he saw a young man put out to her an assisting hand. She did not avail herself of it, and Colin's eye met that of the man who would have helped her. Instantly he knew that the glance had some significance for him. The face he saw was alert and clean-shaven, and it had stamped on it that unmistakable quality of a priest's face, a quality impossible to define and impossible to miss. He was not in clerical dress, but that detracted nothing from the certainty. If the man had worn spangles and pink tights, he would have been a priest. . . .

Day by day, as Colin had seen him, always alone, at the café, or lounging in the piazza, or at the bathing-place, the conviction of his calling and of his significance (whatever that should prove to be) in his own life, grew stronger. He entered into casual conversation with him, introducing himself, and saw at once there was reserve and suspicion to be overcome. But the young man gave him his name, Hugh Douglas; he was out for a holiday, he said, and expected to be here some weeks. As they idly talked, sitting at a café in the street, it so happened that a priest came by. At the sight of him Douglas rose to his feet and deliberately spat on the ground, and in his eyes was a smoking blaze of hatred.

"So you are a priest," thought Colin, "with no love for priesthood."

Then Colin asked him up to dine one evening after Violet's departure, and set a wonderful example of frankness and unreserve. He told him about the legend, and saw his interest kindle; he felt he was somehow on the right track, though still he did not guess where it led.

"But the old fellow was craven at the last," he said, "and tried to escape from his Lord and Benefactor. He abandoned the building of the shrine he had planned where, beyond doubt, he meant to celebrate some Satanic rite——"

He paused a moment with intention. The other turned quickly to him.

"That is most interesting, Lord Yardley," he said. "You have no notion, I suppose, of what he contemplated?"

Colin laughed.

"Indeed I have," he said. "In fact there has lately come into my hands a book, which beyond doubt was actually his, for it bears his coronet and arms of the correct date, and I feel sure he intended to use it in his chapel. A missal in fact, through following the English use. He refers to it in his memoirs."

Douglas's face was alight with eagerness.

"Indeed!" he said. "Have you it here? I should enormously like to see it."

Colin leaned forward to him across the table.

"Yes, I have it here," he said, "and perhaps I'll show it you, for I feel that I'm meant to show it you. But first, doesn't it strike you that I'm telling you a good deal, and that you're telling me nothing?"

Instantly the man shrank back into himself.

"There is nothing that could interest you," he said. "I have no profession——"

Colin felt on absolutely sure ground.

"Yes, you're a priest," he said quietly.

"I am nothing of the kind," said Douglas.

"Oh, once a priest, always a priest," said Colin. "No man nor any body of men can take from you the power that has been given you of doing the great miracle at the altar. . . . You were a priest, Mr. Douglas: and you know that perfectly well. I'm not the least inquisitive, and I don't want to hear why you no longer wear priest's dress, unless you care to tell me. You hate the priesthood now, I saw that for myself the other day, and perhaps you hate that which makes a priest a priest. . . ."

Colin summoned all that gave him his charm, and all that gave him his force.

"Aren't you wrong not to trust me?" he said. "Hasn't our meeting, and what I hope will be our friendship been wonderfully contrived for us? . . . How can I make you trust me? I am building, I may tell you, what my ancestor left undone."

At that he saw the man's soul leap in fire to his face, and not only without shame, but with pride, as to one who would appreciate, he told his story. Ever since he was a boy, he had been conscious of his secret love of evil just for its own sake. His own profanities horrified him, and yet below his horror there was love. Under the whip of his horror he had striven to mortifying that lust for evil within his soul, and yet all the time that he tried to suppress it he looked on himself not as a sinner but as a martyr. He had taken orders in the Catholic Church, had joined an English community with vows of obedience and chastity, and the joy of sins, secret and abominable, became all the sweeter because, in the name of all that was holy, he had renounced them. He felt himself like a spy in the camp of the enemy, talking their language, practising their manœuvres, and making war on the powers to which his heart's allegiance was given. Only a few weeks ago, exposure had come, and he left England for fear of a criminal prosecution. . . .

All this came out in gasps and jerks of speech. Sometimes there was a pause, and the pause would be succeeded by the pent, exultant torrent of what had never been told yet. At the end, Colin got up.

"I see we shall be friends," he said. "I will show you the book I spoke to you of. . . ."

All these things were welded together like links in a chain, the discovery of the plan of the Sanctuarium, and then of the missal, and then of the priest. Each linked on to the next. Indeed it would be an imbecile who saw in these events a mere grouping of fortuitous circumstances. And there was more, too, a chiselling and chasing of these links, decorative detail you might say. . . .

Nino, in spite of persuasions and threats, had gone, so soon to sicken of the fever, and Colin had let it be known that he wanted a servant to take his place. There were many applicants, for it had been seen how Nino, just a barefooted boatman's son, had become almost a signor himself with fine clothes to wear and money to spend, and the friend and companion as much as the servant of the marvellous youth rich and noble and beautiful as a god, for the sake of whom, Capri made no doubt, the English lady had popped herself over the high cliff. Among them was a young Neapolitan, employed during the summer season as waiter at one of the hotels, shrewd and monkey-like in face, some incarnation of pure animalism. Hugh Douglas was with Colin when he came up to be interviewed, and the boy made his obeisance as to a priest.

"Why do you do that?" asked Colin. "Why do you behave as if this gentleman was a priest?"

The fellow looked at him once more and smiled. When he smiled his ears moved, and Colin noticed how pointed they were.

"But I am not wrong, am I?" he said. "When I was a boy, I was an acolyte."

Douglas rose.

"I'll leave you," he said, and he nodded at Colin as he went out.

The boy had spoken in perfect English, and when the door had closed Colin came up to him, put his hands on his shoulders and smiled into his eyes. What he was going to say was derived from no process of reasoning in his own mind, scarcely even from observation. . . .

"Let me see, your name's Vincenzo, isn't it?" he said. "Well, Vincenzo, I like your face: it's the face of a devil. Did no one ever tell you that? You must have been a queer sort of acolyte.

Did they choose you for your sanctified face? And when you crossed yourself did you cross yourself like this?"

Colin made the sign backwards.

"Like that was it?" he said. "I have never been to a mass where they did like that. . . . I should like to see you serve mass, for I shall have a chapel at my house in England, and maybe I shall wish you to serve again. And you were right about that gentleman. He is a priest; so go to him now and tell him I have sent you to say you will serve him. . . ."

How vivid it all was to him still, and most vivid of all that which took place that very evening. . . . He had been hitherto like someone receiving instruction merely, now he was received into the church of his religion. The room where Pamela had slept, and to which her body had been brought, was decked as a chapel, and in symbols and desecrated rites he set the seal on his faith. He had bought not long before in Naples a cope of fifteenth century needlework, in which the celebrant was vested, and Douglas read from the missal of wondrous blasphemies. He threw his cope wide when Vincenzo censed him. . . . As the supreme moment approached some ecstasy stirred in the very centre and shrine of Colin's being, and from there spread to his mind and his physical frame. Would God permit the approaching defiance and blasphemy? He did not doubt that He could by some swift judgment assert the infinity and the omnipotence of Love, and it was just that belief which spiced the defiance. Or was Love itself powerless against this supreme act of Hate and Mockery?

Colin rose from his seat on the fallen oak, and began the descent of the long smooth slope towards the house. Never before that evening at Capri or ever since had he attained to so clear a realization of the spirit of evil: his initiation had also contained the ultimate revelation. Often in the years that followed he had, here at Stanier, attended the Black Mass, but, his allegiance once definitely and symbolically made, the repetition of it had progressively failed in fervour. It was not so with those whose souls worshipped Love: the more they mystically joined themselves, in acts of faith and worship, to their Lord, the more closely, if you judged from the chronicles of the Saints, were they knit to Him. Had Love, then, some quality which Hate lacked? Hate had often seemed to him as infinite as Love, but now he wondered if you could attain to the absolute in Hate, to the realization of pitch darkness than which nothing could be darker, whereas you could never attain to absolute Light; for some fresh sun from all the millions which Love lit and moved would add its spark to the illumination. Or was there, on the other hand, no such thing as absolute darkness of the spirit, just as scientists assured you that there was no such thing as absolute physical darkness? Did some ray always penetrate it? Was there no place utterly devoid of God? In either case you arrived at the utmost possible in Hate, and could go no further.

Colin let the question go unanswered; the abstract never much concerned him compared with the concrete and the practical. . . . How purely episodic his life had been, and how full of prosperous conclusions. Episodes of his boyhood, episodes in Capri, episodes here and in London, strung like beads on the thread of his own personality, but each distinct from the other, accounted for the whole of it. He desired nothing for long; he got it, whatever it was, so quickly, sucked it dry and threw the rind away. All that wealth and position could bring him, all that health could bestow were his; no desire of his went unfulfilled: all he had to do was to find something he wanted, and if it was the gift of his Lord and Benefactor—and wide was his bounty—it was his as soon as he cared to put out a firm hand to take it. And yet in spite of this perfect freedom, which he had used to the uttermost to do exactly what his desire or fancy prompted, to eat any fruit on the tree of evil without fear of scruples interfering, like a seed or a stone, with its lusciousness, he knew that this liberty was somehow built on the foundation of a slavery which enchained him. He was in pawn and in bondage to evil, and these episodes were links of his fetters. . . . As fast as one was hammered and welded, there would be another one, an appetite gratified, or perhaps an account revengefully squared, as in the case of Raymond his brother, and of Pamela. Often, as in the case of Raymond, the catastrophe fell without his active intervention at all: it just followed on his wish: or again the victim might bring it on himself, as that wretched Nino had done. . . . Episodes, just episodes. To find things to wish for, to find experiences and expressions that excited and absorbed him! He had already begun to recognize that this was not so easy as it had been. Life was full of amusements, his vigour, now that he was in his thirty-fifth year, still retained all the elasticity of youth, but it was hard to find for it experiences that were not staled by custom. He had to find those, it appeared, for himself. His Lord and Benefactor did no more (as if that was not enough!) than give him what he wanted. Well, there were a dozen people coming to-morrow, and for the Easter vacation the house would be crammed from cellar to garret with a huge party and diversions would spring up like mushrooms. . . . And then he remembered that Dennis was at home for his holidays, now in his fourteenth year and at school at Eton.

Colin had come to the east end of the building which he had erected in execution of the plan he had found in his ancestor's memoirs. He had stopped long in Capri the year that was built, and when he came back the fabric was complete. Before he left he had shewn the plan to Violet, telling her that this was an addition to the house, planned in Elizabethan times, and never executed. There was a little apartment, he said, for a priest, and a sanctuary adjoining. It was this which was now to be built. . . .

"A sanctuary?" she had said.

"Yes, darling, a little chapel. Old Colin was a very fervent sort of man. It was for his private devotions, no doubt, that he planned it."

He thought that she had understood, and this impression had been born out by the fact that never had she alluded to the 'little chapel' again. She knew that it was approached by a corridor from his room; she knew that this librarian, Mr. Douglas, whom he had brought back with him from Capri, lived in the apartment there, but she had never asked Colin anything about it, nor had he volunteered any information. But that she guessed the general purpose of it, he had no doubt: 'old Colin's private devotions' was sufficiently explicit, and she had understood.

"Violet takes no interest in what means so much to me," he thought now. "Shall I try to make her a litle more sympathetic?" She had had a very easy time lately, with him away so much, and perhaps it would be a good thing to wake her up to her wifehood.

As he passed he saw that the chapel was lit within. The last window was of plain ruby-coloured glass, frosted on the outside so that none could see in, and he lingered there a moment, and thought he caught the sound of a voice within. Douglas, his chaplain and librarian, was there, and perhaps Vincenzo, who had driven down from London with his master, was there also in his more ecclesiastical capacity. The shrewd, monkey-faced boy of twelve years ago, had grown into a dark-faced silent man, wonderfully efficient as a servant. But as a server. . . . Colin had never seen anything so like possession: the ape-like gestures twitching and vehement, the rapt surrender, the tearing animal passion of devotion. And when the rite was over, he lay sometimes on the alter step, panting with gleaming eyes of a surfeited ecstasy. Then the mask of humanity covered him again, and he became the impassive watchful valet, anticipating Colin's wants almost before he was conscious of them himself. But these seizures (for they were really nothing less than that) were terrible. Colin wondered sometimes if he himself would ever know such physical frenzy, such mingling apparently of torture and exaltation.

He passed on round the corner of the yew-hedge: he was late for whatever was going on, and indeed he had no particular mind to be present. But he felt as if some force like that of a great engine that beat in pulsations momently increasing in power was at work there. Then the bell in the turret sounded three strokes, and, in the pause that followed before those strokes were repeated he felt himself thrilled and charged with the mysterious dynamic energy that spread through the still air in invisible waves of inspiration and into his mind there came the vision of himself kneeling there at some such moment as this with Dennis by him. That, of course, would not be yet: the boy was at present far too young to understand even the nature of the moral choice on which the rites were based. Not yet did he know the force of love and hate; he only liked and disliked. He had to feel the power of love, before he could loathe it or comprehend the infinite seduction of evil. The essential qualities of love had to be apprehended before they could be rejected and mocked at. He must know them first, he must know too what hate meant, before he could realize the presence of its inspirer. That, and the things which some day Dennis would see with his father in the chapel there, would be inexplicable and indeed meaningless to him until in his blood there was developed the perception that gave them life. Certain of these rites would seem to him merely grotesque or disgusting till he was hot with the passions of which they were a symbol.

He would be puzzled: he might even be amused at these grimaces and contortions of Vincenzo. He would want explanations, and even then would not understand. . . .

All this was not so much a train of thought in Colin's mind, as a flash of perception that vibrated through it at the sound of the bell in the turret of the chapel, and, dismissing principles, he let himself into the door on the garden front that opened into the long gallery. Principles would take care of themselves provided your practice was in accordance with them, and, with the thrill of home-coming to this beloved Stanier, he stepped out of the glimmering dusk into the lit house.

He got one comprehensive glance at the two who were there before his entrance was perceived. Violet was sitting in a low chair by the fireplace at the far end of the gallery, her face all alight with love, and on the floor, full length in front of the fire, was Dennis lying. His head was bent back and he looked up into his mother's face, as he told her something in his boyish voice, high treble one moment, and suddenly cracking into a man's tones. Whatever it was that he said, it made her suddenly burst into laughter, and she threw herself back in her chair.

"Oh, Dennis, how wicked of you," she said. "Go on, darling. What did the master do?"

Colin stood very still. Was it really Violet who could laugh like that, with that pure abandonment to amusement? Was it she who shone with that serene and radiant love? . . .

She sat up again after that burst of laughter, and saw him. In an instant her face changed to the face he knew. It changed from the face of a mother, girlish still, though that big boy sprawled there, to the frozen beauty which she presented to the world. No faintest glint of laughter lingered on her mouth or in her eyes. And yet, amazingly, they were still alight with love. Something that had beamed there for Dennis still beamed there for him, though it was shrouded, like a gleam of fire through smoke, by the blight and the frost.

"Ah, Colin," she said. "There you are! Get up, Dennis: here's your father."

For a moment, sharp as a stabbed nerve, and coming from some ice-bound cave of consciousness a pang of regret shot through Colin that it was not in his nature, nor in theirs, that he could join the group of mother and son, and partake of their mood, their laughter and their ease, and all that it implied. They looked so jolly, and his hunger for pleasure always envied those who were enjoying themselves, for all enjoyment ought to belong to him. But the instantaneousness with which Violet's care-free laughter had withered from her face, shewed that she instinctively recognized the inconceivableness of that. It was not to be wondered at, after all: she always froze in his presence.

And then he looked at the boy who had jumped to his feet, and pride at having begotten anyone so beautiful supplanted for the moment every other consideration. He was very tall for his age, already his head was nearly on a level with his mother's, and, bred as he was on both sides from Stanier blood, he seemed the very flower of his race. Loose-limbed and lithe he stood there, with shoulders low and broad, and neck rising square from them, and there was the small head, yellow-haired and blue-eyed, the straight short nose, and the mouth as perfect as Violet's own. Colin had not seen him since the Christmas holidays, in the interval he had greatly grown, and his boyhood had emerged from the sheath of its childish sexlessness: now the father saw in his son his own magnificent youth carried to a stage finer yet; physical perfection could go no further. . . . And, on the heels of that exultant pride in his son's beauty, there came the vision again of going with Dennis up the corridor from his room and into the chapel. What a peerless offering to bring his Lord and Benefactor!

The boy had always been much fonder of his mother than of him, and here at once was a thing to be taken in hand. Dennis must learn to be at ease with him, to open his heart to him, and eagerly to receive what was good for him to learn. That was the first requisite: hitherto Dennis had been rather shy with him, and apt to be on his good behaviour. He must be charmed out of that and learn to be comfortable with him and lie on on the floor and tell him stories about school.

He put his arm round Dennis's neck and kissed him.

"Why, you dear boy," he said. "This is nice. Dennis, you've grown in a perfectly indecent manner. Stand up there with your back to your mother——"

Suddenly he remembered that he had not yet said a word to Violet. Violet had Dennis's heart at present, therefore Dennis must see how dear she was to his father, for that would predispose him favourably.

"Violet, darling," he said, kissing her. "How are you? I needn't ask, though. You're always well, thank God. And such shrieks of laughter, as I heard, when I came in! What was it all about? Dennis I believe you've been telling your mother something quite unfit for a parent's ears. So you must tell me too, and let me judge. My word, it is nice to be home again!"

"Have you had tea, Colin?" she asked.

"Now have I, or have I not? I don't believe I have, but I don't want any. I shall sit on the floor, if Dennis can make room for me. Lie down again, Dennis, exactly as you were before, and we'll all be fearfully comfortable. Now what's the story?"

"Oh, it's only a rotten yarn, Father," he said. "The master I'm up to doesn't like mice. So—so someone bought a clockwork mouse and wound it up, and set it running in small circles—you know how they go—just under his chair. You never saw anything so funny. He thought it was real till he heard it buzz."

Dennis had sat down again on the floor: Colin, with a shout of laughter, put his fingers in the back of his collar, and pulled him down across his knees.

"I think I've got hold of that 'someone' by the short hairs," he said. "What brutes you boys are! What shall we do with this brute? How long are the holidays, Dennis?"

"Three weeks and a bit."

"And where do you want to spend them?"

"Oh, here, of course."

"You're just like me. I never want to go away from here, unless it's to Capri. Now let's talk in a whisper, so that your mother can't hear. She doesn't like Capri, Dennis. She's not been there for twelve years. That summer, don't you remember, when you were one year old?"

"Of course I don't remember," said Dennis.

"That's because you didn't attend. You must be more attentive next time you're one year old. But there it is: she'll never come with me—we're still talking in a whisper— so next summer, if you'll promise not to put mice in my bed, perhaps I'll take you."

"Oh, I say, how ripping!" said Dennis. "You bathe all day, Mr. Douglas told me."

"Except when you're basking in the sun. How is Mr. Douglas, by the way? I haven't seen him. May I ask him to dine to-night, Vi? I know you don't like him, darling, but he has a pretty lonely time when we're away. I think we ought to have him in as often as we can when we're here. He shall sit next Granny; he shan't sit by you. And how is Granny?"

Dennis was finding a father that he had never known before, and he felt himself expanding to him. Colin had released his hand from the boy's collar, but Dennis's head still lay contentedly on his knees.

"Granny's dotty, I think," he observed. "I mean your granny, Father."

"Dennis, dear!" said Violet.

She turned to Colin.

"Granny's been expecting you all day," she said. "She always knows when you're coming. She was out on the terrace this afternoon in her bath-chair, and when she saw Dennis, she thought it was you——"

"Yes, Mother, that's what I mean by dotty. It is dotty," said Dennis.

Colin tucked his hand under the boy's head.

"You shouldn't call your aged relatives dotty, Dennis," he said. "Your mother's quite right. When I'm as old as your great-grandmamma, which will be in a week or two for time goes so fast, I shall be exceedingly vexed with you if you say I'm dotty. So there, old boy. She probably thought you were dotty when you told her you weren't me——"

"And then she thought I was Uncle Raymond," continued Dennis. "That just shews——"

"It just shews that you're an ugly little devil," observed Colin. "When you come down to dinner to-night——"

"But I don't," said Dennis. "I have supper upstairs——"

"Well, I ask you to come and have dinner with me to-night. Don't drink too much port like your grandfathers and great-grandfathers. . . . What was I going to say? Oh, I know. Nip round, like a good boy, to Mr. Douglas's rooms, and ask him to come to dinner to-night. Say it's to have the honour of meeting you."

"He's probably in the library, isn't he?" asked Dennis.

"No, he's probably not. And then come back here, and I'll have a game of billiards with you."

Colin waited till Dennis had gone, then turned to Violet.

"How the boy is growing up!" he said. "Was I as big as that at fourteen, darling? He's a splendid fellow, we ought to congratulate ourselves. He'll develop swiftly now. How interesting to watch that, eh, dear Violet, and to train and influence him? . . . You've kept him all to yourself hitherto. It's time that a father's care——"

She had long feared this moment, and, now that it had come, it roused in her not her womanly motherhood alone but something of the tigress-motherhood that will fight for its young, with any who threatens them, even if he is her own mate. . . . But it was the woman who spoke first.

"Oh, Colin, leave me Dennis," she said.

He laughed.

"How funnily you said that," he remarked. "You speak as if I were meaning to take him away from you. You speak as if it was a piece of private property of yours. Mayn't a father take an interest in his own son? And, as I say, he's growing up. He knows nothing of his inheritance at present, or of his family history. He must learn. Yes, yes, he must learn."

Colin shifted his position, and leaned his back against the chair in which Violet was sitting.

"I feel awfully remiss," he said. "I feel as if I had neglected Dennis shamefully. But surely he's grown suddenly, not in inches only, but in sex and temperament. I seemed to feel that. He's entrancing: my heart goes out to him. But he must be moulded and educated, mustn't he? What a wonderful fruit of our love, Vi! What joy for us to see it ripen! And physically, what a young Apollo. You and I were rather a pretty pair at his age, but Dennis beats us hollow."

He leaned his head back to see Violet's face. Well he knew what he would find there, for he had felt his words go home. But he was not prepared for the fierceness of it.

"You shan't have him," she said. "And you know what I mean when I say that. He's a manly, sweet-hearted boy. Oh, as naughty as you please, but he's a good boy. That's the part you shall never have."

She got up, stepping sideways away from him.

"Colin, we've been strangers for many years now," she said. "You've frozen me with horror at what you are. But you've never frozen my power of love. It's there, and it's always melting the ice. And by that I know that you won't get Dennis, for it's stronger than you."

Colin raised his eyebrows.

"Well then there's no more to be said about it," he remarked. "I hate arguing, anyhow. If one wants to prove a thing, the simplest plan is to go and do it, and then it proves itself without any palaver. Ah, there was something else I wanted to talk to you about, but here's Dennis back again. . . . Well, Dennis, will Mr. Douglas have the honour of meeting you?"

Dennis was looking excited.

"Oh, yes, that's all right," he said. "And Vincenzo was there. He was lying on Mr. Douglas's sofa, looking—looking like nothing at all. Looking awfully queer. But Mr. Douglas said he would be all right soon."

"I expect he knows," said Colin. "Vincenzo's devoted to Mr. Douglas. . . . Dennis, I've been catching it hot since you left me. Your mother's been scolding me. Whose side do you take? Hers or mine?"

Dennis looked from one to the other. But he moved towards Violet.

"I don't know," he said. "But aren't we going to have a game of billiards?"

The Dowager's wing at Stanier, of which Colin had made so summary a clearance twelve years before, had never become repopulated again. Aunt Hester was still alive, very much alive, indeed, but never, since the morning when she had 'interfered' about Pamela, had she set foot in Stanier. "Colin behaved like a devil to me, my dear," she had said to Violet of that occasion. "He meant to turn me out and made that his excuse. Well, you don't catch me going where I'm not wanted. I hope I've got too much spirit for that." Violet, however, often took Dennis to see her when they were in town, and he had lunched with her and been handsomely tipped by her to-day on his way from Eton. Aunt Hester adored Dennis; she saw in him the Colin she had loved, and Dennis, for his part, thought her one of the most enterprizing old ladies he had ever come across. Why she did not come to see them at Stanier, he did not know, and she was remarkably brisk at changing the subject when it came up, but he meant to ask his father about it.

Of the others, Ronald Stanier and his wife, though deprived of their permanent domicile, had been occasional guests here, till when, a year or two ago, on one of their visits, he had had a stroke one night, as he sat over his wine after dinner, quite in the traditional Stanier style, and had gone down with the decanter flying. His widow, strongly reacting, had gone to live at Winchester where she drove out daily in a brougham, gave small sad little dinner-parties, from which everyone went away at half-past ten, and was similarly entertained by her elderly guests. Once or twice a year she came to Stanier for a few nights, and played patience, and put some flowers on her husband's grave, but she had no real existence. Stanier, as it had so often done to those who married into the house, had frozen her or perhaps rather burned up all such inflammable material as she had once possessed, and she lay now, so to speak, in the fender, clinking a little from time to time as she cooled, and disintegrating into ash. . . .

But the fourth occupant of the Dowager's wing was still there, and still every night old Lady Yardley was wheeled down to the long gallery five minutes before dinner-time, and sat by the fireplace near the dining-room till the others had assembled, and then with the aid of her two sticks went in to dinner, and afterwards played her phantom game of whist. She was now over ninety years of age, she ate and she slept, she had her sight and her hearing, but she lived in some withdrawn twilight, peopled it would seem by shadowy figures of her century of memories. Certain rays could still illuminate that crepuscular kingdom: Colin's presence was a sure lamp there, and Dennis was beginning to be another, perhaps from his likeness to Colin twenty years ago, perhaps because she realized that in him lay the perpetuation of the house, for the dim archives of her mind contained only the records that concerned Stanier. . . . Strangely enough. Hugh Douglas was the third who could lighten that black darkness; probably she did not know his name, and he belonged to the later years of which she had normally no memory, but it was clear that she regarded him as somehow significant, and often, if he dined with them, she would sit looking at him with that unwinking gaze that saw no-one knew what, and begin speaking of days of fifty and sixty and seventy years ago. Others, her nurses, for instance, and Violet, made no reaction on her mind: she was no more directly conscious of them than she was of the chair where she sat, or the carpet she walked on, and they cast no shining glimmer on the memories that reached back and back, to years when not only were none of those present born, but not even her own children of the generation before, Colin's father, and Violet's, and Aunt Hester, and when she herself was newly come as a bride to Stanier. Physically, by some miracle of vitality, she was upright still: and her skin, instead of hanging in parchment-like laps and folds over her face, was one with it: she looked as if she was made of bloodless, imperishable alabaster. When she sat motionless and without speech she seemed scarcely alive, and then her wrinkled eyelids would lift and she spoke in that quiet uninflected voice of those who had been dead sixty years and more, as if they were still here. To her, they probably were.

Colin felt a sort of fascinated pride in her—"She's clearly immortal," he said, "in fact she's a sort of totem—isn't that what they call it?—a tribal god. She belongs to myth and legend, especially legend. I wonder if she signed a bond too. . . ."

To-night she was in her place when Violet came in. As usual she took no notice of her, and Violet sat down with the evening paper and did not see Douglas's entrance, till suddenly old Lady Yardley began to talk.

"My grandson Colin came home from school to-day," she said. "He has grown——"

Violet looked up.

"Ah, good evening, Mr. Douglas," she said. "Colin and Dennis have been playing billiards, but they'll be here in a moment. You saw Dennis, I think?"

Douglas shook hands with her. More markedly than ever was his face that of a priest. He knew very well that Violet disliked him: dislike perhaps was too superficial a word. He had seen just that same horror in her eyes when she looked at her husband. He wondered sometimes what she knew. . . .

"Yes, Dennis came up to my flat," he said. "How he has grown. Developed, too, I thought, as well."

Dennis and Colin came in together.

"Dennis's fault that we're late," he said. "He took so long to beat his poor old father. Well, Granny, how are you? I believe you grow younger every day. Dennis and I are going to take you in to dinner, one on each side."

She got out of her chair, and stood erect.

"Ah, I knew Colin was coming," she said. "I told them Colin was coming. Now all will be well at Stanier."

She pointed at Douglas.

"I want him," she said. "He must sit by me, because he and Colin know, and I know. Those who know must sit close and talk in whispers."

Colin laughed.

"So we will, Granny," he said. "Dennis dear, you take in your mother; Granny's got no use for you."

Dennis put Violet's arm within his own.

"Lord, what pomp!" he said. "Shall I always come down to dinner now, Mother? Oh, and I beat Father at billiards!"

"Well, don't trample on me, now I'm down," said Colin. "You've no feeling of chivalry for the aged, Dennis."

Old Lady Yardley looked from one to the other. They dined at a small round table; Colin and Douglas were on each side of her, Dennis and Violet between them. Her eyes travelled past Violet as if there was no one there, but at Dennis she looked long. To-night the stimulus of these three was strong; and she began to say things she had never said before.

"The boy there," she said. "That's my Colin before he grew to be a man. He's come back to us as a boy. He doesn't know the legend yet."

"Oh, but I do, Granny," said Dennis. "It was when the devil——"

"No, dear, you don't know it yet," said she. "You've only heard it, that's a very different thing. My son Philip never knew: he only heard——"

Colin intervened.

"Now, Granny, eat your soup," he said, "or we shall never get through dinner. Tell us about it afterwards."

He looked up at Dennis, just one passing glance, and saw that the boy's attention was violently arrested.

"And does Mr. Douglas know?" asked Dennis, "Is that what you wanted to whisper about? Father, what is it that you know and I've only heard?"

It was odd how the atmosphere was suddenly charged with impalpable tension. Lady Yardley alone, whatever she said, could not have produced it; it required Dennis and his innocent boyish inquisitiveness at the other end.

Violet interrupted. Dennis mustn't ask, Dennis mustn't know.

"Dennis dear, you saw Aunt Hester to-day, didn't you?" she said. "Didn't she send any message to me?"

Dennis's whole mind was fixed on this other puzzling matter. But at his mother's voice he seemed to detach himself.

"Yes: her love," he said. "And I'm going to write to her

to-morrow—so's Father: two letters, and a motor's going up to London to take them to her. And it'll bring her down here, we think."

Colin turned to Violet.

"Darling, you'll be nice to her, won't you?" he said. "It's so long ago, all that misunderstanding. . . . And she loves Stanier. I was going to tell you, of course."

Violet felt there was no need for explanation; she knew Colin. He had represented to Dennis evidently that Aunt Hester never came to Stanier, because of some bygone quarrel between herself and her. Dennis had asked why she never came—it must be like that—and that had been the answer. Then Colin had concocted just such a plot as a boy loves, to ask her in spite of it and bring Mother and her together. . . . Colin was the peacemaker, she was the person to be propitiated. . . .

The wonderful falsity of it all! There was nothing too small nor too great for Colin in the accomplishment of his ends. Here there was no question of what his ends were: they were the wooing of Dennis by him, the detachment of Dennis from herself.

She could not sit down under this.

"But it was you who turned her out, Colin," she said. "You quarrelled with her; you sent her away. What have you been telling Dennis?"

Colin was seated next her. He laid his hand on hers.

"Darling, before the servants . . ." he said gently. "Besides, it's all over, years ago."

Old Lady Yardley was looking fixedly at Dennis again.

"He's growing up," she said. "Soon he must make his choice. Staniers will never fail as long as they choose wisely and well. I am an autumn leaf now on the old tree, but the sap hasn't left me yet, and though the leaves fall, fresh leaves come. This is a beautiful young leaf: it is spring-time with the tree again, and the birds are singing in its branches. It will always be spring at Stanier, if they take care of the young leaves."

Colin turned from Violet to her.

"Granny dear, the spirit of prophecy is upon you, but you really mustn't prophesy at dinner. Everyone finds it so disconcerting, darling. Now there are some friends of mine coming to-morrow, and you must promise me not to prophesy at dinner. Otherwise you shall have dinner upstairs and no whist at all."

For once she paid no attention to him.

"I watched them building twelve years ago," she said. "They made a chapel for the prosperity of Stanier. Aha! That makes the legend thrive——"

Colin saw Dennis's wide-eyed gaze, fascinated and puzzled. He had settled that he did not want the boy to know anything about that at present. . . . And yet surely you sowed in winter the seed that did not germinate till the spring. How marvellously dramatic, too, that Dennis, still hardly free from the soft enveloping sheath of childhood, should learn the beginning of wisdom from this aged Sibyl. It was like taking a child to learn about Druids from Stonehenge. . . . But Dennis was too young yet: it would never do to initiate him into the final revelation, till he had learned the rudiments and the alphabet of the creed. Simultaneously Violet spoke to him.

"Oh, Colin, stop her," she whispered. "She mustn't go on. She mustn't tell him about the chapel."

. . . So Violet knew: he always guessed she had known. He turned to old Lady Yardley again.

"Granny, you're being very naughty," he said. "I promise you you shan't come down to dinner again unless you're quiet. I won't have it: do you understand? Now go away with Violet. If you say a word more, you shan't have any whist at all. Take her away, Violet."

Violet got up.

"Come along, Granny," she said. "And you too, Dennis."

"Nothing of the sort," said Colin sharply. "Dennis is going to stay with us."

He waited till Violet and the old lady had gone.

"Dennis, old boy," he said. "You were quite right when you said your great-grandmother was dotty. She was talking gibberish. There wasn't a word of sense in what she was saying."

Dennis looked unconvinced.

"But she must have meant something, Father," he said. "Did she mean the chapel by Mr. Douglas's rooms?"

Colin was always swift in invention.

"Very likely. But you know all about that. I built it, as I've told you before, to complete the original plan of the house. Very likely old Colin intended to be buried there. Memorial chapel, you know. Just think of the old lady as dotty. She's got the legend on her mind. She always had. Why, I really believe that if Satan came to her now, and said 'Sign, please,' as they do in shops, she'd find one drop of blood in her body still and use it up. Give Mr. Douglas some port, and take half a glass yourself. Not more, Dennis: we can't have you like your grandfather Ronald before you grow up."

Dennis gave that delicious half-treble croak of laughter.

"Good Lord, I shouldn't like to be like Grandfather Ronald," he said. "He was a rum 'un. . . . Father, did he know about the legend, in the way Granny meant?"

"No, Dennis, I should say he didn't. But we've finished with the legend for to-night. Someday I'll tell you more about it."

"Hurrah! When?"

"When I think that you will be able to understand it, Mr. Douglas and I will set you an examination paper."

"Oh, not in the holidays," said the boy.

"You won't know it's being set you," said his father.

"That's an improvement on the Eton plan," remarked Dennis.

Dennis was sent up to bed when old Lady Yardley had had her two rubbers of whist, and presently Mr. Douglas went too.

"And now we're alone, Vi," said Colin, "and I haven't seen you for a month. Mayn't we have a little talk? In fact, I've got several things to say. About Aunt Hester now."

"Yes, I think you owe me an explanation of that," said she.

"Darling, don't talk about 'owing explanations,' in that way. You speak as if I had run up a bill with you, and wouldn't pay it. Probably that's just what you do think."

Colin moved across to the fire where the traditional log smouldered.

"I hate explaining," he said, "and really you can understand for yourself. But if you insist on it, it's this. Dennis asked me point-blank why Aunt Hester never came to Stanier. Well, I couldn't tell him about her impertinence with regard to poor Pamela, her imagining that I had an intrigue with her. . . . Good Lord, didn't the sequel exculpate me? An edifying incident, wasn't it?"

"You know what I think about that," said she.

"Yes: I remember your saying you wished I was in love with Pamela. And I kept telling Pamela that I was in love with you. But she rushed on disaster. Odd—I was thinking only this afternoon how long it was since I had given a thought to Pamela, and now she comes up in connection with Aunt Hester. Well, I couldn't tell Dennis about that. You would have been very much shocked with me if I had. I couldn't tell him that the woman was in love with me, and his mother wished I was in love with her. Such a dreadful thing to tell a young boy at the most impressionable age! You agree?"

"You distort it all," she said. "But I agree."

"Oh, distortion!" he said. "Everyone else's point of view is distorted when viewed from one's own. We all have our own individual perspective, which shews everybody else's out of drawing. But, as you agree, I had to give some other reason. I gave one that naturally occurred to me, namely, that you resented and found unforgivable something poor Aunt Hester had done. I was pleased when I thought of that."

"You always think of everything," she said.

"Yes, darling, I am pretty thorough. And you see why I was pleased, don't you?"

"Perfectly well. You wanted to give Dennis a new impression of me, as being hard and unforgiving, and of yourself as kind."

Colin softly clapped his hands.

"Ah! I knew you really understood," he said. "I knew you didn't need any explanations. But why not have said so at first? You shewed you knew at dinner."

She moved the screen that stood by her. That might have been to shut out of her eyes the flame that had broken out from the smouldering log, or it might have been to shut out his face . . .

"I didn't mean that when I asked for explanations," she said. "The explanation I wanted, if there was one, was any justification for what you did."

Colin stretched out his hand to the blaze; the shapely smooth fingers looked redly luminous as the fire shone through them.

"The justification is that it was part of my policy," he said. "Dennis is devoted to you at present. I must detach him. He must be devoted to me: he must love what I love and hate what I hate. No man can serve two masters."

She slid from her chair on to her knees, holding up her hands to him. The face of the future, now that it was coming close, was terrible.

"Ah, Colin, no, no!" she cried. "Your soul's your own, and you've chosen for yourself. But Dennis's soul is his: his and God's. You daren't tamper with it."

Colin laughed.

"Oh, but you're inconsistent," he said. "You've told me that love is stronger than me, and that I'm powerless. Now you seem to be afraid that there is something pretty powerful to back me. Have faith, darling."

She had no personal fear of him now that Dennis was in question: the instinct of protection swallowed it up.

"I know you've got something powerful to back you," she said. "You've got the power of Hell to back you. No one who believes in God dares despise that; he hates and fears it."

Colin drove the poker into the blazing log, and a squib of sparks shot up. His face in that brightness seemed to shine from some inward illumination.

"Very wise," he said. "Now another thing. It's clear to me that you know about the sanctuary. Clever of you, darling, because I've only once mentioned it to you, when I settled to build it, telling you old Colin had planned it for his private devotions. Did you guess then I wonder? Did you imagine for what purpose he had planned it, and for what purpose I carried out his plans?"

"It wasn't a guess," she said. "I knew. In whose honour must he have planned it, and in whose honour must you have executed it?"

"That's logical, certainly," he said. "But how about Grandmamma? I never said a word to her, and I don't suppose you have. But yet she knows. Has she got some sort of second sight, do you imagine? Is she a sort of incarnated genius of Stanier, so that by instinct she knows all that concerns the welfare of the house? Sometimes I scarcely believe that she's human at all. Will she go on living for hundreds of years, a sort of priestess? My word, we're an amazing institution, you know."

Colin turned round away from the fire, and yet it seemed to her that his face glowed.

"I wish my family were more with me in my convictions," he said. "Dennis doesn't know, and you don't sympathize. Supposing Dennis was to die before he had come to the full knowledge? Once he had chosen, he would be protected——"

Violet felt her mouth go dry.

"Colin, you're not meaning to take Dennis there, are you?" she whispered.

"Aha, now we come to the root of it," he said. "Of course I mean to take Dennis there as soon as he's learnt, well, the rudiments of the faith. I see he's not fit for it yet, but he soon will be. He's got high spirits, and the lust of life is beginning to bubble in him. That just has to be directed. Then the moment he is ripe, and a boy like that ripens quickly——"

Violet's face whitened and hardened.

"You daren't," she said. "That would be the sin for which there's no pardon. Don't you understand?"

Marvellously Colin's eyes glittered. It was as if they were faceted and caught a hundred points of light.

"And don't you understand," he said, "that that's the very reason for my doing it? I pine for unpardonable sin!"

From outside there came the sudden stir of wind. It rattled at the window, and then blew with a great gust. He paused, holding up his hand and listening, and within him, swift as inspiration, the fire kindled.

"Just so it used to blow in the stone-pine in the garden at Capri," he said. "It was there I heard it first. That's no common wind, Violet! It's a message: it's a herald. The power is abroad and I hail it. Listen, isn't that, even to your ears, something more than the common wind! You know it is. Fear it and loathe it, or worship it and adore it. But don't deny it. Ah, the thrill of it! The splendid Pentecost."

Never had she seen him like this, and whether it was that his exaltation communicated itself to her, or whether there was something present there inherent in that sonorous sudden gale, she felt her very spirit shudder and flicker like the blown flame of a candle.

He sprang to his feet, and took hold of her arm.

"Come with me now to the chapel," he said. "We'll get Father Douglas. Yes, of course you know he's Father

Douglas. Join with me, Violet, throw scruple and struggle away. Who has the best time after all, you with your agonizings and fears, or I, who don't know what pain of soul or body means, whose every whim is gratified? Come and see: see if I haven't chosen well, see if you don't exult and glory in that power that I serve and that serves me! A midnight mass: you'll see me as an acolyte—I make a damned handsome one—and the book Father Douglas will use is the very book, the missal of wondrous blasphemies, that old Colin speaks of in his memoirs. I've got tepid about worship, but with you there it will be new again to me. It's in your blood, you're a Stanier just as I am. It will boil up in your blood."

She stood quite still, letting his hand still rest on her arm but sundering from herself the distraction of all the flood of desires and yearnings, of fears and of terrors, that had been streaming from her. She did not articulately pray, she did not implore and agonize for protection, she simply spread out her soul with an act of unreserved surrender to the spirit of God, and, in this turmoil within and without, let the peace that passed understanding seek her of its own accord and encompassingly hold her. Her only effort was to make no effort, to make herself utterly helpless. . . .

The timeless moment passed, and she knew that the stress of some spiritual crisis was over. The wind outside, which seemed to have been raging round the very fortress of her soul, died down and ceased.

Colin spoke again. But the ecstasy of direct inspiration had died out of his voice. For a little while he had been like one possessed; now he was himself again, terrible indeed but not terror itself, Satanic but not Satan.

"Violet, if you don't come," he said, "I shall go and get Dennis. I said I would go up and say good night to him, and he shall dress and come with me to the chapel. Rather like Abraham taking Isaac to sacrifice him: rather Biblical. It's you or he. I mean precisely what I say. He will obey me."

Violet's choice made itself without any question. But it was made under the compulsion of Love, and under Love's protection.

"Then of course I will come," she said. "You've given me my choice and there it is. But you won't like it if I come, Colin. I should only despise and scoff at what you believe in. And the power on which you lean is failing, and you know it. Where's the ecstasy that filled you just now? It has all evaporated: it has leaked away."

Rage and rebel as he might, he knew the truth of what she said, reading it in her quiet eyes, and her pitiful mouth. Definitely, and for the first time to his full consciousness, he had failed. Something stronger than the wind of the powers of the air had interposed between him and its inspiration.

He looked at her with quiet hellish eyes.

"I think you will be sorry for this, Vi," he said.

Some inner plane on which this scene had been transacted seemed to her to slide away again. She had been on it: it had sustained her. Now she was back again on normal levels, conscious only of a supreme fatigue. But the memory of that uplifting still held her. One power had englobed her, another him, and somehow, inscrutably, the two had come into direct contact, and at the touch his had been shattered like a film of glass.

"I do not think so," she said. "I think I shall be glad of it, thankful for it, as long as I live."

He turned on her, but his eyes were no longer bright with that quality with which he had heard the wind rise and roar.

"Do you suppose you've beaten me?" he said. "Are you really such a fool as that?"

She moved a step nearer to him, and pointed to the curtained door out on to the terrace.

"Colin," she said, "do you remember coming in at that door this evening and finding Dennis and me talking by the fire? You were jealous of him then and jealous of me, because you knew why we were so happy together. You wanted, in spite of yourself, to have a share in it."

CHAPTER II

DENNIS's holidays sped in an orgie of delightful amusements. There was the splendour of having a gun of his own, and being allowed to go out with the keepers and his father to blaze at rabbits and the pigeons among the trees in the Old Park. There was the splendour of a motor-bicycle given him by his father, and that of dining downstairs every night. But among all these experiences, there was none so enchanting as his father's companionship. . . .

Colin had suffered a defeat. He knew it, and he understood why, and learned a larger wisdom from it. He had been altogether too abrupt: excited and possessed himself, he had expected Violet to leap at once, in surrender and panic, over that huge gulf that separated them, when he asked her to come to the chapel with him. He should have known better, he told himself: it was demanding the impossible. The effect had been that, in her vital recoil, she had accomplished a supreme feat in the completion of her self-abandonment to the power of Love. She had made no reservation; she had cast herself on the spread arms of its sustaining force. It was quite consistent, too, that, the moment afterwards, when he had told her that, if she refused to come, he would take Dennis with him, she had said she would come. Love still upheld her and chose for her, and its force, he knew, had drained him of his, so that he no longer cared at that moment whether she came or not, or whether it was worth while even to fetch Dennis. . . . He could have done that, but it would have been a mere repetition of his original mistake. Dennis would no more leap to the sacrament of evil than Violet. The worship of evil demanded a dedication of the soul. . . .

Dennis must be wooed like some shy maiden. . . . His boyish heart was affianced to his mother, and its clinging tentacles, vigorous as young shoots of ivy, must be ever so gently detached, so that the boy would scarcely know that any detachment was going on, and laid, full of the sap of spring, round his father's encircling arm. Until that was done, Dennis would turn but a puzzled and incurious ear to anything of ultimate significance. Colin must abound in wholesome school-boy topics and interests, until the ivy clung close to him, and leaned on him for the support of its growth. Then, but not till then, could the education and enlistment of his instincts begin. It would be rather a bore, Colin thought: he would have to play golf with him, and go out to shoot the silly pigeons, and take him up to London perhaps to see the public-schools competition in racquets. Dennis evidently adored one of the boys who was playing for Eton, his senior by some four years. Colin wondered what sort of a fellow he was. . . .

A dozen guests or so came down next afternoon to spend a week, and before that week was over their numbers were redoubled; they settled on Stanier like a flock of gay and chattering birds. They were at liberty all day to amuse themselves as they liked, tennis and fishing and golf were diversions enough for them all: Violet, admirable hostess as she was, saw that they were occupied, and devoted herself to the dowagery element among them, which liked motoring to points of interest or going to see friends in country-houses in the neighbourhood. There was breakfast and lunch at elastic hours and no full or formal assembly met until dinner-time. Then there was the immemorial ritual of the house reassembling itself: old Lady Yardley in alabaster silence and immobility was the first to arrive in the long gallery, and the guests collected, and when all were there the major-domo opened the door into Colin's room, and he joined them. Just that one old-fashioned pompous moment was preserved: it was the Stanier use, like grace before meat. As he entered everyone stood up: it was only Colin of course, who next moment would be chattering like the rest of them or shouting with laughter, but just then he was Lord Yardley.

But most of the day, Colin would have had Dennis with him and often the boy dressed early and spent this last half-hour before dinner with his father. Very likely the two would be playing some game together when the summons of the opening door came, but on the moment Colin would jump up, leaving whatever fascinating pursuit was in progress, and become somebody quite different.

"Now, behave yourself, Dennis, just for a minute," he would say. . . . "We'll go back to our game afterwards, if we can. My move . . ." That was part of Dennis's education; just for that minute it was a solemn business to be Lord Yardley, the master of this magnificent inheritance, with its regal splendours. There was no other house in England like it, nor had there been for three centuries past, and it was his father's now, and would one day be his, and plenteousness would be in its palaces so long as he into whose hands it was given remembered to whom he owed it, and rendered affiance and allegiance.

So grace was said, and the diversions of the evening began. Dennis must not be pompous, but at the back of his mind the knowledge of his potential magnificence must consolidate itself. At dinner there was a place for him by his father, for that was Colin's order, and Dennis could see the charm that had been poured out on him in their employments together during the day now weave itself for these dazzling ladies. His mother, he knew, had not wanted him to come down to dinner when the house was full, but Colin had begged her, so it conveyed itself to his mind, to allow him, and Dennis secretly felt it to have been rather unkind of her to have tried to make him miss these wonderful hours. Of course there was a threat, veiled and not understood by him, behind this 'begging,' something about Dennis having nothing to do, while they were in at dinner, except say his prayers with Mr. Douglas and go to bed. Dennis had not understood that, for he never said his prayers with Mr. Douglas, but his mother consented to his coming down after that.

It was immensely amusing at dinner; there was his father, to begin with, whose gaiety was irresistible; Dennis had not known how fascinating he could be over nothing at all. Whether he asked a silly riddle, or told an absurd story, or just joined in the general chatter, he cast the magic of mirth over everyone. And all the time old Lady Yardley, silent and aware, would be watching him. Perhaps her neighbours would attempt conversation with her, but they were swiftly defeated. Her business was to look at Colin. Now and then he caught her eye and shouted something encouraging to her, and he would say to her neighbour, "Darling old Granny: I hope she isn't a nuisance. But she would break her heart if she didn't come down to dinner. Look, we're four generations. She and Aunt Hester and Violet and I and Dennis."

After dinner there were all sorts of amusements: one night there was nothing but cards, with bridge-tables for those who cared about those sedate joys, and old Lady Yardley's whist-table in the corner by the fire, which was its immemorial situation. Violet, Mr. Douglas and Aunt Hester were immolated there, and for the rest there was a delightful round game called poker. Once again his mother had suggested bed-time for Dennis, but again had Colin 'begged' for him.

"Give him half an hour, darling," he had said. "He'll get bored with it and won't touch a card for the rest of his life. Nothing like early associations. . . . Dennis, your mother says you may sit up for half an hour, so you and I will be partners, and you shall have a small salary, as long as I win."

"But if you lose, Father?" suggested the cautious Dennis.

"Then I shall sell your new dress-clothes, which I haven't pinched you for yet, and buy a hurdy-gurdy, and collect coppers in St. James's Square, till a copper collects me for obstructing your mother's motor-car on the way to church. You shall be the monkey on the top of it, and go to prison with me."

"Rather. I say, will you tell me how it goes?"

"You'll soon see. Where are the counters? Who wants money and how much? Oh, I think unlimited, don't you, Blanche? We're all so prudent, and we're all so poor that we shan't lose our heads. Let's all have a hundred pounds. That gives a false air of opulence."

Lady Blanche Frampton counted her portion with avaricious fingers.

"I haven't seen so much money for years," she said. "Colin, you've given me ten shillings short."

"No, I haven't, dear. Add it up again. Let's have six at this table and six at the other. Dennis doesn't count. He's going to bed in half an hour, if he doesn't sit up longer."

"But I want Dennis," said Lady Blanche. "I'll give you a pound for Dennis. He'd be a mascot, because you haven't played before, have you, Dennis? Or is poker part of a modern boy's education?"

"Yes, of course it is," said Colin. "The Head holds poker-classes for the sixth form twice a week, and the House Master for those under fourteen. Dennis, attend to me, 'Ich Deal' as the Prince of Wales said. Now, there are pairs and two pairs, Dennis, and a flush, and a straight. . . . Who's in? Everybody? Then who's shy, and has not put his mite into the pool? Oh, I believe it's the dealer."

An hour later, Dennis, instead of being in bed, had been started by Colin on his own, with a capital of ten pounds. Luck favoured him, and presently it had doubled itself. Then luck went against him, and he lost every farthing of his capital. Twenty pounds . . . he was Crœsus, and next moment penniless. The tragedy was quite appalling.

"Hullo, Dennis, cleaned out?" said Colin, observing this. "Poker's not so entertaining after all."

Dennis stiffened his rather drooping neck.

"I've enjoyed it tremendously," he said. "Rare good run for my money."

He gave that boyish cackle.

"And it was yours all the time," he said. "Sorry, Father, for losing it."

Colin had watched the tragedy and inwardly applauded. The boy was really plucky about it, and Colin respected pluck. It might be a virtue, but it was not connected with love. . . . How handsome he looked, with his flushed face and eager eyes, and chin slightly in the air, to show he cared nothing about the loss of that millionaire capital.

"Never mind," he said. "Now, Dennis, would you rather go to bed with a sovereign in your pocket, or shall I start you again? But if you lose it this time, you won't get a penny."

"Oh Lord! I'll go on," said Dennis. "Ripping of you, Father."

Another night there was a theatrical performance given by three actors of a play that would certainly never see the London footlights, and once again Dennis sat between his father and Blanche Frampton. The surface of the first act scintillated with cynical witty nonsense, light as foam, and the boy bubbled with laughter. But presently his laughter was not so frequent. Something began to shew through the surface, and a soft perpendicular wrinkle engraved itself between Dennis's eyebrows, and he puzzled out what seemed so clear and vastly entertaining to the rest of the audience. . . . Yes, soon he thought he had got it, and his brow cleared, but he didn't laugh: it just did not happen to amuse him.

Colin's attention had been about equally divided between the stage and the boy. The play was to his mind: it drew with deft distinctness the passion that exists only as a pastime and is a foe rather than a friend of love. The author had expended inimitable wit in its delineation, but before the act was over Colin was recognizing rather than appreciating the corrupt and subtle handling, and his conscious attention was more engaged with the effect it had on Dennis than with the entertainment he himself derived from it. During these last few days he had grown very proud of Dennis. There were his extraordinarily good looks to begin with; and he enjoyed himself enormously, but never boisterously. Everyone tried to spoil him, but no one succeeded: he was ever so friendly and well at ease, and without a trace of self-consciousness. His manners were excellent: there was no impression that he was behaving himself, he was perfectly natural with a winning boyish simplicity. Withal he was not grown-up and green-housed for his years, he was on the contrary extremely young.

Colin put his arm round him as the act closed with a frank emergence of polished indecency.

"Well, old boy, enjoying it?" he asked.

Dennis made one of those confiding boyish movements, fitting his shoulder close under his father's arm.

"I liked the beginning," he said. "But—but they're rather playing the ass, aren't they?"

Clearly he wasn't enjoying it. Colin had distinctly hoped he would: that was why he had let him come. It was disappointing, but it was no use boring the boy with these intriguing animals: the last thing he wanted to do was to bore him.

"Go away then," he said, "if you don't care about it. I thought it would amuse you."

"I expect I'm awfully thick," said Dennis.

"You are, my dear: you're thick and fat with that enormous dinner you ate. Did you like your champagne?"

"Rather. I should think I did. May I have some to-morrow?"

"You must ask your mother."

Dennis laughed.

"I'd much sooner ask you," he said.

"You're a wine-bibber. You'll get gout and delirium tremens, and your mother will say it's my fault. . . . Well, what about this next act? Are you going to stop or not?"

"I think I won't," said Dennis. "And will you come and say good night?"

"No: you'll be asleep."

"I shall keep awake, if you're coming."

"All right. Say good night to your mother, and tell her I've sent you to bed."

"But you haven't," said Dennis.

"No, but that'll make her pleased with me."

Dennis stole out, and Blanche gave a sigh of relief.

"That's a good thing," she said. "Dennis was as much out of place here, as I should be playing football with him at Eton."

"But you'd ènjoy that," said Colin. "You'd love being the one female in a crowd of handsome boys."

She laughed.

"Yes, my dear, we all detest competition as we get older. But why did you let Dennis come at all? Either he'd wallow in it, which would be extremely bad for him, or he'd be bored with it."

"I wanted to see which he would do. It would have been very interesting if he'd wallowed in it."

"You're no judge of character. You might have known he wouldn't," she said.

"Oh, do you think that children of that age have character? Aren't they more like white sheets of paper, ready to be written on?"

"Colin, you're an awful father! Fancy wanting this delicious, witty piece of muck to be written in poor Dennis's first chapter! I'm glad he's gone. I shall be able to enjoy it with a freer conscience. Oh, observe your Aunt Hester! She looks as if she was receiving early impressions, and finding them wonderfully agreeable. And, oh, look at your much revered grandmother! Did you ever see anyone so monumental?"

There she sat in the centre of the room, in a great chair of rose-coloured Genoese velvet. In this interval between the acts, the cut-glass chandelier over her head had been lit, and the blaze strongly illuminated that alabaster face, motionless, expressionless, inscrutable. And yet what sculptor's skill could have wrought a countenance from which every sign of feeling or even of consciousness was so expunged? In a face of stone some expression lurks in the sightless eyes and the shadows at the corners of the mouth, and an attentive observer will seem to see the expression change, and discover some fresh hint of what the sculptor divined in his living model and chiselled into the lifeless stone. But here there was no such elasticity of interpretation possible. The closer you looked, the more you were baffled. And yet there was no tranquillity there as on the face of the dead. Lady Yardley's face was immensely alive, but with *what* was it alive?

"Talk of white paper . . ." said Blanche.

Colin laughed.

"Not a bit of it. Covered with strange writing," he said. "Look!"

He leaned forward.

"Granny dear," he called.

She turned her head in the direction of his voice. Then came recognition, for the blank eyes brightened and the folded lips uncurled. There was Something there: it was as if Colin had caused characters written in invisible ink to spring up over the blank surface. But they faded again before they could be read, and presently she turned back and looked up the curtain in front of the stage, where the footlights were just rekindled.

"Gracious me: it's covered with writing!" said Blanche. "But quite unintelligible. What was it about?"

"It was about Stanier," said Colin. "Stanier is the only thing she is conscious of. You see I'm the incarnation of it to her. And I think she's beginning to see that Dennis will have something to do with it. But I really don't believe she knows Violet by sight."

Supper succeeded the play, and it was not till after one o'clock that Colin went upstairs. Dennis slept in a room close to his father's: the door was ajar and there was a light within. Colin went in, and there was Dennis propped on pillows and sitting up in bed, but fast asleep. His yellow hair was tumbled over his forehead, his mouth was a little open, shewing the white rim of his lower teeth. Clearly he had sat up in bed in order to keep awake for his father's coming, but his precautions had failed: sleep heavy and soft had come upon him.

Colin stood looking at him. There, indeed, in the unguardedness of slumber was the white paper. He looked extraordinarily young as he slept; his was the face of a child, still sexless, just a radiant piece of youth, holy in its innocence. Would it not be possible, without really waking him, to put into his soul now unprotected by the guard of its conscious self some suggestion which would, like a fruitful seed, lie buried there and take root and presently push some folded horn of growth above the soil?

Colin turned out the light by the switch near the door, and began to gather force into himself. It was not an effort of concentration at all, rather it was a complete relaxation. He had only to lie open and tranquil, like a dew-pond, and let it flow in from the air, from the night. Drop by drop at first, and then in ampler streams it came flooding in, making a tingling in his blood. More and more he must collect, attracting it with images of evil—how well he knew the process of it—till he was charged and brimming with it, and then he would direct it and turn it on that boyish figure that sat up in bed, not with an effort of will, but making himself, so to speak, just the channel through which it flowed. Throughout he must not think of himself at all, nor even of Dennis; he was no more than the reservoir which was storing what Dennis should receive. He must direct and convey that without quite waking the boy.

There was a hitch somewhere, an obstruction. At first he could not conjecture the nature of it. Then he perceived what it was. He was not surrendering himself thoroughly, some rebellious part of his soul, ever so faintly, was protecting Dennis's beautiful face and slack limbs, and standing between the boy and the force that was seething about him. It would not allow Colin to be the channel, it blocked the way. Was it pride in the boy as he was? Was it pity? Was it something more powerful yet? Whatever it was, it was there.

Colin clutched at it, to wrench it away. He felt it give, and he felt the force foam by it towards Dennis's bed.

There came from the bed some stir of movement, and a gasping breath. Then Dennis's voice, muffled and strangling, as if there was a hand on his throat.

"No, no!" it cried. "No—— Ah. . . ."

The boy's breath came thick and fast.

"What is it? Who's there?" he screamed. "Father . . . Father. . . ."

Colin reached up his hand for the switch and turned on the light. He did not intend to do it; his hand moved as if by some reflex action outside the power of his will, for there was something in that instinctive cry to him which set at work some uncontrollable mechanism, within him.

Dennis was half out of bed, his face bathed in perspiration, his eyes wide and terrified. With a leap he sprang to Colin, never pausing to think how it was that he came to be standing there in the dark, and clung close to him.

"Oh, it's you," he said, with his head buried on Colin's shoulder. "Thank the Lord! Oh, I say, I've been so frightened. Something came into the room: I don't know what it was, but something hellish. I say, it's not here now, is it?"

Colin patted his shoulder.

"Why, Dennis, what's the matter?" he said. "You've had a nightmare, that's all. I came in here a minute ago, and found you asleep with your light burning. I turned it out."

Dennis wiped his forehead with the back of his hand, raising a troubled face, out of which that sheer terror was beginning to fade.

"Was that all?" he said. "Are you sure there was nothing that came in? O-o-oh, I thought I was going to die of fright."

Strange was it that so few minutes ago it was through his father's presence and complicity that the terror had gripped Dennis by the throat, and that now it was that same presence which so quickly restored the boy's confidence. With his father there he knew that nothing could hurt him, not nightmare, nor phantom, nor the terrors that walk in darkness.

"Get back into bed, old boy," said Colin. "It's late, you know. You must go to sleep."

Dennis unwound his clinging arms and hopped back into bed.

"Oh, do wait two minutes," he said. "It's . . . it's awfully rotten of me, but I couldn't stand to be alone in the dark again this moment. I never had such a horrible nightmare."

"Well, just two minutes," said Colin. "And what was the nightmare?"

Dennis pulled his father down till he sat on the edge of the bed, and held his hand.

"I don't know what it was," he said, with a shudder. "It felt like the devil. But it won't come back, will it, when I go to sleep again?"

"Of course it won't. You're not frightened now, are you?"

"No. At least I don't think so. If you promise me it won't come back, I'm not frightened."

"Yes, I promise you that," said Colin.

Colin left a tranquil Dennis curled round in bed like a drowsy puppy when he went to his room a few minutes later. But he was not so tranquil himself. He had not imagined that any panic terror would seize the boy: he had only meant to plant a seed, a suggestion, ever so quietly, leaving it to mature. . . . Dennis would not come to love evil, so that, when the time for his choice arrived, he would choose 'wisely and well,' if it approached him with these strangling assaults of nightmare. Why had it happened like that, he wondered? No boy's soul, at that age, was of such virgin and stainless purity that the breath of evil suffocated him. . . . More likely that it was his own divided purpose, his own struggle against that obstacle which somehow he had himself set up against the free flowing of the stream he had directed against Dennis. Some force, he felt sure, had reached the sleeping boy from him; that he had intended, and he had felt it flowing through him. But had it reached him in some fierce torrent, raging at having been checked in its passage, and settling on him with claws and teeth? Had it been like some wild beast, which, having been shewn its lawful and desired prey, was held back from it?

He must not approach Dennis again like that, nor seek to hold back the power that he directed. It was no conscious scruple on his part which had blocked the channel: the obstacle seemed to have made itself, and planted itself there. It was of the same nature as the instinct that made his hand search for the switch and turn up the light at Dennis's appealing cry. He hated the boy to be frightened, quite apart from the fact that Dennis must of his own inclination welcome and cherish the power that was ready to protect him and be his friend even as it had been his father's friend, and the friend of old Colin. It had come to Dennis to-night as a foe of malignancy and terror: that would never do. . . .

Colin had slipped quickly out of his clothes, and now, before he got into bed, he drew up the blind, and throwing the window wide leaned out into the pregnant spring night. Thick and warm was the darkness, a floor of cloud covered the sky, and there would be rain before morning, the soft, fruitful, windless April rain which sent the sap flooding upwards through stem and branch till it burst into leaf and bud. The young growth needed not pelting showers and fierce suns; it prospered most in these still warm nights. . . . And Dennis was like these tender, sappy shoots: he must be left to grow quietly yet awhile, not drenched by deluge and speared by violent suns: these would only blast and wither him. . . . How panic-stricken the boy had been! That psychical onslaught had from its very vehemence been to him a hostile intrusion, not the advent of a protecting power. How instinctively in the shock and terror of it he had called to his father!

There was an irony about that: instinct was a blind ignorant force, else Dennis would have shuddered and fled from his father, not clung to him with arms close pressed, and terrified face hidden on his shoulder. And yet (here was the puzzling, the baffling thing), Dennis had been perfectly right. At that cry of his in the dark, Colin had had no thought but the answering instinct to comfort and reassure him. His hand had shot out, independently of his purpose, to flash on the light, and he had given the boy the protection he sought. He couldn't stand that wail of desolation.

What made him do that? Him, who had jeered and flouted Pamela to her self-destruction without a pang of pity, but only with devilish glee, who had let Nino die of fever with a shrug of his shoulders, who had worshipped evil and drunk of the derided sacrament of love, dedicating himself by rite and symbol, as by the daily conduct of his life, to his soul's master, how came there that disloyalty to his affiance? How was it that there flourished in the garden of his soul that despicable weed? He had not done it in mere careless pity, as he might have raised a corner of netting to set free a bird that was caught there, nor had he done it with the deliberate reasoning that justified it to his mind afterwards, when he perceived that it would never do to have Dennis regard this directed force as hostile and malignant. He had done it because there was no question of choice: an inward compulsion, not to be resisted, had made him. And thus Dennis's instinct was right. He called on him and he clung to him, exactly as he would have clung to his mother, because he loved her, and was certain of her love. Colin had given him, too, exactly what his mother would have given him.

There was no other conclusion, and instantly all Colin's nature was in revolt. It had been an impulse of love that had taken hold of him; he had leaped to the protection of Dennis's terror and of his innocence. He had denied his allegiance, he had rooted evil out of his heart for that moment, and . . . and how curiously sweet it had been to have the boy in his arms like that, and see the terror and trouble vanish from his eyes! There was no woman in the world whom he would have suffered to take Dennis's place at that clinging moment, no promise of physical rapture and consummation to follow that would have been so desirable as that comforting of Dennis, that sitting by him on his bed for five minutes while he tranquillized and composed himself.

He revolted and rebelled. It was not for this that he had grown proud of Dennis, delighting in his physical beauty, and in the sunshine of his boyish vigour, and in the grace and charm of him. He had enjoyed them with ever increasing zest because of the thought that someday Dennis would be one with him in his allegiance to the Lord of hate. He had seen himself bringing him to the tribunal of his choice, and beholding him choose as he himself, with never a moment of regret, had chosen. Who, in all the world of men with their callow consciences, their bloodless ideals, their cold duties, had prospered as he had done, or whose days succeeded each other in such procession of satisfaction? All that must be Dennis's: it was his unique birthright to be allowed to choose all that the lust of the eye and the pride of the flesh and the glory of the world could bestow with never an ache of compunction, or a sigh of pity, or a pulse of love.

Colin got up; the rain had begun to hiss on the shrubs below his window. He must have been sitting here for more than an hour, for the chimes in the church a couple of hundred yards away struck three. He had not been thinking consciously or with purpose: it was as if pictures had been spread out in front of him on which he let his eyes rest. Now, as he went across to his bed, there came an intenser focussing. It was well enough that Dennis should come to him as he would have gone to his mother, drawn there by the bonds of his love. Colin had meant to oust Violet from the boy's heart, and take her place, and, if nothing more at present, Dennis had given him a niche of his own there. He wanted Dennis's affection and confidence, for it was through them that he would most surely lead him. . . . It was natural, too, that he himself should delight in the boy's magnificent youth and abounding charm. But it was not well that his own heart should have gone out to Dennis like that. Whence had come that spark of soft authentic fire? Was it from some remote and infinite conflagration, the warmth and the light of which can penetrate the uttermost darkness?

Colin turned out his light, and curled himself up in bed as he had seen Dennis do.

"That would be a nightmare indeed," he thought. . . .

All that week and the two that followed Stanier outvied itself—for indeed there was no other competitor—in the splendour of its hospitalities. The great houses of England were now, for the most part, shut up, and the owners, crippled by the ruinous taxation, only lived in small corners of them, like picnicking tourists. Those who were fortunate let them to Americans or Argentines, preferring, like sensible folk, to live in comfort in smaller houses, rather than shiver in palaces they could not afford to warm, and which, after all, were very desolate abodes unless they were full of the life and merriment of guests. They sold their pictures, for who could afford to look at a Reynolds which hung unharvested on the walls, and not reap it into five hundred a year? They sold tapestries and ivories and plate; whatever could be alienated and turned into cash went to Christie's, and, like some monstrous insatiable reptile, America, gorged already with the gold of Europe, spat a little of it out, and took some Majolica or some Beauvais tapestry instead. Lucky indeed were the impoverished land-owners of England to find in their kinsmen across the Atlantic this delightful illusion that living in a castle conveyed culture, and to have somebody else's family pictures on the walls quickened the ancestral sense, and that to eat off Caroline plate was like a course of history lectures. . . .

Of hospitality as a kindly and sociable virtue, Colin had no opinion at all, that side of it did not concern him. Nor again did he in the least care, in itself, for mere lavish ostentation: he would just as soon, as far as personal inclination went, have had Stanier empty and serene in its established security as swarming with guests, some of whom he scarcely knew by sight, and for none of whom he had any real affection. Nor did the presence of two Royal personages, who had come down for three days directly after Easter, and found that they were able to honour him and Violet by staying for a week, give him any thrill of satisfaction. It was a matter of complete indifference to him whether they came or not, or whether they were so much amused that they stopped longer than they had intended. But what was to the point was that Stanier should carry on its tradition for magnificent entertainment, for that belonged to it, just as its legend did. It might be a deplorable waste of money, yielding an infinitesimal dividend of pleasure on the capital expended, but that could not be helped. Everything that could be procured to give gorgeousness must be there; one night, the Russian ballet danced on the enclosed terrace, and another there was a concert; whatever the diversion was, it was a matter of course that his guests should be thus amused for an hour or two, and it was Stanier that gave the *cachet* to the entertainment more than the artists.

When Stanier was *en fête* it was not to be supposed that the guests should be asked to spend the evening in polite or even impolite conversation, or in making words out of words.

They might do so if they liked, if they wearied of that there was the concert or the ballet. But every evening (for this was just as much a part of Stanier as the rest) there was old Lady Yardley's whist-table by the fire in the long gallery, and whoever was there, she had her two rubbers of whist. This was the Stanier use, and the presence of all the crowned heads in the world would not be suffered to interfere with it. One night Violet and a couple of guests played with her, another night Colin took his place there. That happened to be on the night of the Russian ballet, and, as the rubbers were unusually long, the other entertainment had to wait. When they were over, Colin, without explanation, escorted one of his Royal guests to the front row, and Violet the other. He rather enjoyed that: it was an object-lesson for Dennis to shew him that at Stanier the sovereignty of the house took precedence of anything and anyone else. He did not call Dennis's attention to it, but he let Dennis see. And on Sunday, of course, Colin read the lessons at morning service.

All this week, too, and with what infinite address, the education of Dennis went on. Even the mistake that Colin had fallen into, in thinking that the direct force could be brought to bear upon him as he slept, in such a way that he would not be startled at it, had turned out not so badly, for that night Dennis had leaped to him to seek protection in love, and certainly the boy was fonder of him than ever. He did not want Dennis's love in itself, any more than he had wanted Pamela's or Violet's, but he saw now into what an admirable weapon for his own use that love could be forged. Love should be the goad, fashioned by Dennis himself, with which, when the time was ripe, Colin would drive him where he would. Already Dennis would sooner please his father than please himself: if his father gave him, by way of test, some rather irksome duty of hospitality to perform towards his guests the boy would obey him, not grudgingly at all but with that alacrity and joy which is Love's obedience. . . . But it was no use forcing him to that of which his natural instincts warned him: "Let the young fruit ripen," thought Colin. In similar preparation, it was good that Dennis should see what the prosperity of Stanier connoted, and what its lordship implied. Dennis was by no means the sort of boy whom mere splendour dazzled, but he must be impressed by the greatness of that to which this magnificence was just a whim, a flick of the fingers to summon diversion for a fortnight of Easter recess. Dennis was enjoying it vastly, and without doubt it was dawning on him that some day he would be in his father's place, and if this sort of thing amused him, it was his to evoke, or if he had a mind for anything else, that would be his also. On the last night of the party, when all would disperse next morning, Colin meant to call his attention to that, and, very carefully, to the contract on which it depended. He knew now that Dennis would not leap to it, as he himself, at that age, would have done, but, so he reflected, the existence of Raymond, his elder twin, had even then schooled him in hate. Dennis had had no such schooling and incentive. . . .

But this was not all that that night had revealed. It had revealed in himself a tenderness altogether alien to him. Even though he had been in the act of loosing on the boy the force which was to befriend him, his mere physical distress had sufficed to make him abandon that, and give him the protection he sought. All this week that memory had lain in his mind, and, below the occupations of the busy days, he had impatiently considered it, cavilling at his own faint-heartedness. Probably, certainly indeed, he had done wisely: the power with which he had sought to surround Dennis must come to him, not in this nightmare guise, but as a friendly and protecting influence; and to have continued then directing it on him would have been a great mistake. It might even have done some mental or spiritual hurt to the boy, for his whole nature had been up in arms to resist it, and who knew what deadly struggle might not have resulted? For the force which he had turned on him was no pretty toy-like drawing-room mesmerism, you could not play with it and try psychical experiments. It was a thing deadly and potent. Even when it was not resisted, but welcomed and embraced, its passion could manifest itself in disturbing and terrible ways, and Colin shuddered to think of Dennis in the grip of it in such manner as he had before now seen Vincenzo possessed when he served at the rites in the chapel. And Dennis had not yielded to it, he had struggled and fought. . . . But that, and Colin knew it, had not been the primary reason for his abandoning that midnight assault. The primary and instinctive reason had been that Dennis called to him with the insistent and compelling voice of love. . . . Strange, indeed, that he should have hearkened to it, for the voice of love was most unmusical in his ears, and made not melody but exasperating discord. Just so had it been with him when he came unperceived, on the day of his return home, into the gallery, and found Dennis and his mother there, happy and content for no reason except that they were together. At that moment (how quick Violet had been to notice it!) he had envied them, though he knew precisely what the ground of their happiness was.

Love and he had nothing to do with each other. He did not desire to have any commerce with love, either in giving or receiving. He had chosen, and the reward of his choice was that he had everything else, as long as his life lasted, but that. He had always hated love, and never would he consciously or deliberately make terms with it. But it was as if some shadowy semblance of it in the shape of Dennis had come silently and burglariously up to his well-guarded house of hate, and opened the sash of some unbolted window. He wanted Dennis's love, because, as he had seen, that would be a useful weapon, but Dennis must not gain entrance to him. . . .

He must make his house more secure. He had been careless, not seeing to its safety. Not once since he had returned home had he been to the chapel or strengthened himself in his allegiance by sign or symbol. He remembered the glee with which he had built it, the glee with which he had found the book of wondrous blasphemies, and knew that the edge and keenness of his devotion was blunted. Was it this remissness which had allowed the wraith of Dennis to slip open the window-sash, or was it that this soft assault on his heart had caused the remissness? Of course during these last two weeks it had been almost impossible to attend these rites, but, as soon as the house was empty, he would make amends, with the intention of the abhorrence of love in his heart. At midnight now, the hour at which chiefly he used to love to attend the impious celebration, some entertainment was in progress, and he could not leave his guests, and, unlocking the door in his private study which communicated with the corridor, move along it past those infamous pictures with which it was decorated to the chapel. The altar with its black cloth would be blazing with lights, and presently Father Douglas robed only in that magnificent Italian cope would enter from his lodging followed by his server, tossing fresh clouds of incense into the air.

He must resist this stealthy menace of winged love. He must spread nets and lay traps for it, and, when it lay unresisting in his hand, squeeze it with strangling fingers till it ceased to flutter.

CHAPTER III

A FANCY-DRESS ball had been arranged for the last night. There were already some forty guests in the house, who, as Colin said, would form "a sort of nucleus," and a special train was coming down from town, arriving at ten and going back at three in the morning, and invitations had been sent to the neighbourhood for twenty miles round, with the hope that ladies and gentlemen would be Elizabethan, but begging the ladies not to be Elizabeth. Dozens of Elizabeths, he thought, of all shapes and sizes with crumpled ruffs and jewels off crackers were bewildering, and you collided with the Queen with improbable frequency. Instead Violet was to be the sole Elizabeth present, and Dennis was to appear as her young Colin in attendance.

Colin came into the wife's room in a wonderfully good humour that morning to talk over the manner of their appearance. For several days he had scarcely had a word with her.

"I think we won't stand by the door as host and hostess," he said, "and shake hands. One has to say to everyone how wonderful and charming they look, and guess who they are. And then they have to say how wonderful and charming we look and guess who we are and the entrance gets blocked."

"Oh, isn't it rather rude not to receive guests?" she said.

"Not a bit. It's perfectly proper swank. In fact, I don't want you and Dennis to appear till the special has arrived and everyone is in the ballroom. The Royals will be on their dais at the end of the room, and the rest shall be marshalled round the walls, and you and Dennis and I will march up the whole length of the room. And then we go straight into the Royal Quadrille. I've told them."

"Very well," said she. "But what about you? I don't even know who you're to be yet. You've always represented old Colin, at fancy-dress here, but you can't if Dennis does."

He laughed.

"Admirably reasoned," he said. "Too many Colins would spoil the broth, like too many Queens. But I'm going to complete the group just a little way behind Dennis. Merely

Mephistopheles: but he had something to do with it. Strictly Elizabethan too, though belonging to other ages as well."

"Oh, Colin, that's rather grim," she said. "Why produce the family skeleton?"

"Well, it's the skeleton on which the family has grown fat. Of course everybody thinks the legend is mediæval bunkum, but they'll play up. Dennis will be an adorable Colin: I made him try his things on just now, and if the real one looked as enchanting as he I don't wonder the Queen lost her aged heart. And as you've lost yours to Dennis, we shall have a real parallel. As for you, darling, you'll be an anachronism but that can't be helped. Elizabeth was an ugly old woman at the Colin epoch, and we can't call you that exactly."

She was silent a moment.

"I wonder if you'll be vexed at what I want to say," she said.

"How can I tell?" he said. "I don't suppose I shall care much."

"It's this then. Please don't get yourself up like Mephistopheles. It's for Dennis's sake I ask it. I want him to be among those who think the legend—what did you call it?—mediæval bunkum. Colin, do leave him to think that."

He sat there looking at her with that brilliant sunny smile, that alertness of perpetual youth.

"Well, a fancy-dress ball is mediæval bunkum, isn't it?" he said.

"But you aren't," said she. "All you do, all you are, has a tremendous reality for Dennis. Everything you do is perfect in his eyes."

"That's good. That's the right filial attitude. Are you as right conjugally, darling? Besides, what do you believe about the legend? Shouldn't a child learn its faith at its mother's knee? The legend is fairly real to you, isn't it?"

There was the spirit that mocked. But when Dennis was concerned she was not afraid of him.

"There are many things I believe which I don't want Dennis to believe," she said.

He laughed.

"What an easy riddle!" he said. "You don't want Dennis to believe that his father is an unmitigated devil. That's the answer, so don't trouble to say it isn't. And as I believe in the legend too, it would be nice to have our only boy one with us. That's the root of domestic bliss."

"I can't argue with you," she said. "You mock at whatever I say."

"But who asked you to argue?" said Colin. "I'm sure I didn't. But as we're on the subject I may as well say that my whole object in making a black guy of myself is to help Dennis to realize the legend. He has heard it, as everybody else has, but it's nothing to him. Though a fancy-dress ball is only a sort of play, a play makes a thing more real to you. Dennis will be Colin in the play, and he'll look round and see his dear Mephistopheles at his elbow."

Colin paused to light a cigarette, and spoke with gathering impatience.

"He's got to believe it sometime," he said. "We all begin, you and I did, by thinking it just a picturesque old story, but somehow it grows into us, or we into it."

"It's the curse of the house," said Violet suddenly. "And it's believing in it that makes it real. Oh, Colin, let Dennis grow up without it becoming real to him! Then it will stop, it and all the horror and the misery it brings. You're quite right: it grows into us. Don't let it grow into him."

He got up.

"Do you know, I really haven't got time for an ethical discussion just now," he said. "And why should I disinherit Dennis? That's what it comes to. You may call the legend the curse of the house if you like, but it's been big with blessings. You've got no sense of gratitude, darling. No family pride."

"Pride!" said she.

"Yes, I said 'pride,' didn't I? I wish you wouldn't make yourself into a damned echo, and force me to be cross. We won't discuss Dennis's future any more: we'll confine ourselves to the present. You and Dennis and I will come in as I have indicated. I want you to wear every jewel that you can cram on. Chiefly pearls, I think, but also that sort of large red plaster of rubies. Stomacher, isn't it? But you mustn't wear the Stanier sapphire. I want that for Dennis. You might give it me now, if you'll open your safe."

"But that's all wrong," she said. "The Queen never gave that to Colin till just before her death."

"My dear, you needn't tell me that. I suppose I know the history of Colin as well as you. But I want Dennis to wear it. I want it; that's all."

Colin had recovered his temper: he was all serenity and sun again.

"There's something queer about the stone," he said. "It never looks well on you: it loses half its light, whereas on me it blazes like a blue arc lamp. Everyone round looks blue, as in the Grotto at Capri. And I want to see what effect he has on it. . . ."

Who could be as devilish as Colin, she found herself thinking, but who had such charm? One moment he would sneer and mock, the next he had dropped all that and without intention and certainly without effort he was like a boy again, making plans and having secrets with her. Often during this last week or two that enchanting side of him had popped out unawares. One moment his mouth would be full of veiled insults and scarcely veiled hostilities, the next, as now, he would be eager and pleasant. . . . More particularly had she observed this when he was with Dennis; though she knew that in his heart he had contemplated the boy's initiation into all that was evil, she could not believe that it was not from his heart that, every now and then, there came up the impulse that made that soft light in his eye, that tenderness on his mouth. Could it be possible that he was getting to love Dennis? After all there had been that moment's jealousy (of that she made no doubt) when he had seen Dennis and her together. Was that the grain of mustard-seed? Poor little seed, if it was: it would find poisoned soil and corrosive moisture for its growth.

"I'll get you the stone," she said. "It's in the safe in my bedroom wall."

Colin perched himself on the arm of the sofa where she sat.

"Oh, there's no hurry," he said. "Let's have five minutes' chat. I haven't seen you all this week, and I haven't told you what an incomparable hostess you've been. I always recognize merit, Vi, and you've been most meritorious. The sapphire now: there is something queer about that stone. Pearls always shine with you like moons, but the sapphire gets as stale as a piece of mildew. It's because it was old Colin's, I believe. His getting it seems to me his most remarkable achievement. He can never have been more hugely inspired than when he made that stingy old woman give it him. All else that she had given him, his Garter, his estates, cost her nothing. But fancy getting her to part with something that was hers, and that was worth a ransom. And you can't look at it without seeing there's something in it you don't understand."

She laughed.

"You speak as if there was something magical about it," she said.

"Well, why shouldn't there be? I'm not such a shallow ass as not to believe in the supernatural. And the whole point of the supernatural is that you can't understand it. If you could understand it, it wouldn't be supernatural."

Suddenly he appeared to forget about the stone altogether.

"I want to ask you something," he said. "Did Dennis by any chance tell you that about a week ago he had the most awful nightmare?"

"Yes."

"Then tell me exactly what he said."

Violet thought a moment.

"He had gone up to bed, he told me, and, as he expected you to come and say good night to him, he didn't put his light out, but propped himself up with pillows to keep awake. He thinks that he must have gone to sleep, though he didn't know that he had. Then a great blackness, he said, came into the room and tried to force its way into him. He struggled and struggled, and called out to you. And then he found he was awake and you were there, and comforted him. He said you were angelic to him."

Colin turned quickly to her.

"What do you make of it?" he said.

"I make of it what Dennis made of it. That's simple enough, isn't it?"

She looked at him, and saw there was something more. The notion somehow branded itself into her mind like the touch of a hot iron. There was the conviction, incredible and terrifying, that Colin had something more to do with that visitation than to bring comfort. But what?

"Tell me your side of it," she said.

Colin's face changed: the impatience and mockery came back.

"Good Lord, how can I have a side?" he said. "Wasn't I right to comfort him? Or should I have scolded him for being frightened by a dream? Has he forgotten about it, do you think? I mean, does he accept it just as a nightmare and me as an angel?"

"I'm not certain. He was most frightfully scared. But it will wear off if he doesn't have another nightmare. You remain an angel anyhow: that doesn't wear off."

Still that irrational conviction of some complicity of his —how insane it appeared when she faced it—beset her.

"Colin, he mustn't have another nightmare," she said. "Terror is so frightfully bad for a child."

She saw Colin's fingers beginning to twitch. When he was getting angry or impatient they made the strangest little movements as if some electric current was jerking them.

"I'm responsible for Dennis's dreams then, am I?" he said. "Why else did you tell me he mustn't have any more nightmares? What's the meaning of that? Come, out with it; you did mean something."

She could not state what after all was the most fantastical notion. It would not bear examination: it was just as much a nightmare as Dennis's.

"I mean that you have the most extraordinary control over Dennis," she said, "his whole soul is devoted to you. Waking or sleeping he would obey you. You know that as well as I do."

Surely Colin had never been in so strange a weather-cock of a humour as he was this morning. At one moment he was ready to fly out at her with unbridled irritation, the next he was all sweetness and amiability. He put his arm round her.

"Vi, you and I are like Norns," he said. "Aren't they Norns who, in some dreary Wagner opera, sit in the dusk, and toss the shuttles of destiny to and fro? Dennis is flying from hand to hand between you and me. You catch him and weave, and then you toss him back to me, and I weave. There ought to be three Norns, though, oughtn't there? Who is the third? I don't believe we shall agree on the third."

All her unfathomable distrust of him came flooding back on her. His purring content seemed to her like that of some lithe savage beast, basking in the sun, who next minute might deal some shattering lightning-blow with unsheathed claws. Who could trust him? Who had ever trusted him that did not repent (unless already it was too late to repent) of such a madness? And yet she believed that he was getting fond of Dennis, with a quality of affection not proud only and paternal, but personal. She made up her mind to stake on it.

"I don't think we should disagree," she said. "We both love him——"

He pulled his arm away from her, and, looking at him, she fancied she saw for a moment behind the brightness of his eye that dull red glow, not human, which you can see in the eye of a dog. One glimpse she got and no more, for he rose.

"I think we've bleated long enough on the *vox humana* stop," he said. "Or shall we sing a short hymn before you give me the sapphire?"

She went into the bedroom next door and opened the safe that was built into the wall, and returned to him with the shagreen case. He took it from her without a word and left her.

The special train of saloon carriages, that brought the guests from London and ran without a stop into Rye, was on time, and by half-past ten the last of them had passed into the ballroom. The request that they should be as Elizabethan as possible was faithfully carried out; never was there such a one-period galaxy. No house but Stanier could have induced people to pour out into the country for a few hours, but how they flocked to Stanier! For the last fortnight this Easter fête had been the talk of the town; and no-one of the amused and amusing world, who was so fortunate as to be bidden to the final and crowning splendour, could afford to miss it, and no-one who was bidden could afford to fall below the standard of its magnificence. Glittering and bravely attired was the throng, a joy to behold in these dingy days when never were women so garish and slovenly, and when men all wear the same ill-inspired livery. Every great jewel-chest in London that night must have been void of its finest treasures, for here was their gorgeous rendezvous.

No host or hostess was there to receive the guests; they flowed in, jewelled and kaleidoscopic, and wondered where Lady Yardley was and where Colin was, and collected and dispersed again in shimmering groups over the floor. Some of those staying in the house appeared to know something about their absence, but could give no further information beyond that the hosts would be sure to be here presently and, acting as marshals and masters of ceremony, gradually began clearing the centre of the room. Back and back towards the walls they enticed the crowd, and soon it was seen that this was some intentional manœuvre to secure an empty floor. In a gallery above the door into the hall the band was stationed still silent; on a dais at the other end were seated the two Royal guests who had been here all the week, with others who had come down to-night. Then, at some signal given from the far end of the room, a dozen chandeliers, hitherto unlit, blazed out, and the hosts arrived.

Violet advanced some few yards into the room, with her retinue close behind her. She was dressed in a gown of dark blue velvet, thickly embroidered in gold with the Tudor rose. The tall white collar of her ruff was edged with diamonds, and round her neck were the eight full rows of great pearls, the first three close round her throat, and five others, each longer than the last, falling in loops over her bosom, the fifth being clipped to the stomacher of large rubies, and round her waist was a girdle of the same stones. On her head she wore a net of diamonds that pressed closely down on her golden hair, so that it rose in soft resilent cushions through the meshes of it. Just behind her came Dennis, in trunk of white velvet and white silk hose. Over his shoulders, leaving his arms free, was a short cloak of dark red velvet; this was buckled at the neck with the great sapphire, and on his head was a white cap with an aigrette of diamonds. In his low-heeled rosetted shoes he was a shade shorter than his mother, and his face, flushed with excitement, was grave with the desire to acquit himself worthily. A pace behind him came Colin, a foil to the sparkle and splendour of the others, for from head to foot, trunk and hose and cloak, he was in black. Black too was his cap, with one red feather in it. He was a little the taller of the three, and, standing just behind Dennis's white gleam, he seemed to encompass the boy with the protection of his blackness, and round the room as they stood there ran whispers of "The Legend: The Legend." But people looked not so much at the jewels and the clothes and the gorgeous colouring, but at those three faces, all cast in one peerless mould, gold haired and blue eyed, the difference of age and sex quite overcome by the amazing likeness between the three of them. Here indeed was Stanier itself: the splendour of its jewels, its wealth, its palaces, its story shrunk into insignificance in the marvel of its incarnations.

They paused there a moment, and then Violet gave three deep curtsies, the first towards the dais in front, and then to right and left, to the rows of guests marshalled by the walls.

There was Stanier in the person of its hostess saluting its visitors; Dennis and Colin stood quite still meantime, for they were but in attendance. As she moved forward again the full blare of the band shattered the silence, and the welcome was over.

With the departure of the special train back to town the ball came to an end, and no attempt was made to carry it on to a dwindling and fatigued conclusion. It ended, as it had begun and continued, in a blaze, and after it there was no flickering of expiring flames and fading of its glow. Last of all Colin and Dennis came upstairs together.

Colin had been watching the boy all night. Dennis had suffered a short experience of high self-consciousness when he entered the crowded expectant room, but after that it had vanished altogether, and he had merely enjoyed himself immensely, without being in the least aware who he was. The radiance of his youth shone round him like a fire, no one could look at him without a smile of pleasure that the world held such perfection of boyhood. All that Colin saw, and again and again his heart leaped to think that this was the son of his loins: no sculptor could have made so fair an image, no painter have found on his palette such colouring. Four generations of them were there that night, old Lady Yardley sat like some white alabaster statue of deathless age on the dais, then came Aunt Hester with a wreath round her head (Perdita or Ophelia, he supposed), outrageously flirting with every man she could get hold of, and succeeding, to do her justice, in getting hold of an incredible number, then came himself and Violet, and last the flower of them all. . . . The guests had had no greeting on their arrival, but the three stood at the ballroom door as they passed out, and it was with Dennis that they lingered. Frank and friendly but a little shy again at this multiplicity of smiles and greetings for himself, he stood there, erect and boyish, the bonniest figure in all that assemblage of beauty.

He tucked his hand into his father's arm as they went up the broad stairs from the empty hall.

"Oh, Father, wasn't it fun?" he said. "I wish we could have a fancy-dress ball every night. When shall we have another?"

"To-morrow, if we have one every night," said Colin.

Dennis cackled with laughter.

"It'll only be you and Mother and great-granny and me, won't it, to-morrow? I say, are you coming to talk to me while I undress?"

"And after that may I go to bed?" said Colin.

"Oh, if you like I'll come and talk to you, while you go to bed," said he. "I'm not an atom tired."

Colin looked at that radiant face, still fresh as morning, and for the first time he consciously noticed the sapphire that buckled his cloak. That gave the measure of his absorption in Dennis himself, for he had given him the stone to wear with a definite object. And now he saw how stale and unluminous it was. No blaze of light burned within it, its brilliance was dim compared to what it could be: it was splendid still, but no more than a shadow of its real self. He knew his own idea about the stone to be quite fantastic, but he felt a sudden spasm of anger with the boy that that great blue cornflower was so faded. Yet he felt he might have known it. . . .

"No, I'll see you to bed," he said. "Here we are; turn up the light."

The room flashed into brightness and Colin closed the door.

"Undo your cloak, Dennis," he said, "and give me the sapphire."

The boy stood in the full light of the lamp above the dressing-table, fumbling with it.

"Rather," he said. "It's like a bit of ice on my throat. I almost took it off during the ball, but I supposed it wasn't a thing to leave about. . . . Oh, I can't unfasten it: do it for me, Father."

He held his head up, smiling into his father's eyes; and moved by some uncontrollable impulse Colin kissed that smooth cheek. The boy was so splendidly handsome, of so winning a charm. "And after all," as Colin thought to himself, as if in excuse of the affection of that caress, "he's my own son. . . ." Then he raised his hands to undo the fastening at which Dennis fumbled, and even as he touched it, light seemed to dawn somewhere deep in the heart of the sapphire.

"There you are," he said, "there's the ice-bag removed. It doesn't look much like ice, does it?"

Dennis shook off his cloak.

"O-oh! It doesn't look very icy," he said. "Have I really been wearing that all evening? Why, it's alive, it's burning! Or is it only that it looks so bright against your black clothes? You ought to have worn it. Tell me about it: you said you would!"

Colin looked at the rays that danced in that blue furnace

that he held. It was scarcely possible to believe that this awakened lustre was purely an imagined effect, and not imagined surely was the counsel that its splendour gave him to tell Dennis a little more about his birthright.

"Well, it was the last thing and the most splendid that the Queen ever gave old Colin," he said. "He speaks of it in his Memoirs, which I'll shew you——"

"Oh do; shew me them to-morrow. I should love to see them. The old rip! Sorry, Father: about the sapphire."

Colin let his eyes rest again on the great stone, and then looked straight at Dennis.

"He says that his Lord and Benefactor caused him so mightily to please the Queen that she gave it him," he said. "You must learn to love it, Dennis, for he calls it the finest fruit of his bargain."

Dennis looked puzzled.

"His bargain?" he asked. "Oh, the legend. Then do you think he really believed in the legend?"

"Certainly he did, and wise he was too. You shall read how Satan came to him one night as he slept."

Dennis had taken off his tunic, and stood there stock-still, his face now more definitely troubled.

"Like some horrible nightmare?" he asked.

Colin came a step nearer, black as the pit and fair of face, with the stone gleaming in his hand.

"A nightmare? Good heavens, no!" he said. "Like some wonderful dream, if you like, but it was no dream. It was gloriously real. You can't understand yet what the bargain meant, for you're only a boy, and there's nothing that you really want which you don't get. But imagine what it would be, when you grew up, to have every wish gratified. . . . The bargain holds not for old Colin alone but for all those who come after, you and me for instance, who by their own choice claim their right to share in it. The legend is no fairy-tale, Dennis; it is sober, serious truth. It was a miracle, if you like, but the evidence for it is conclusive."

The trouble deepened in Dennis's eyes. When Colin first spoke of that visitor coming to his ancestor as he slept, there had started unbidden into his mind the remembrance of that nightmare from which his father had rescued him. And now again he felt that invasion pressing on him, and though it was surely his father who stood there, yet somehow his black robes and his red-feathered cap and that blue-blazing gift of Satan in his hand seemed to obscure him. It was as if some shadow had passed over him, and behind that shadow he was changing.

"Oh, don't, Father!" he cried. "I hate it! It's awfully stupid of me, but I do hate it. Please!"

There was no doubt that the boy was vaguely and yet deeply frightened: his voice rose shrilly, his hands were trembling. And once again Colin recoiled from the idea of Dennis's terror. When he had directed the force towards him before, in the defencelessness of his sleep, it was easily intelligible that the invasion of it should alarm him, but now, speaking to him in his own person, with the authority that Dennis's love for him gave, he had hoped that the boy would at any rate sip at the cup which he held out to him. But still he was troubled and alarmed, he was not mature enough yet to guess the lure of dreams and of desires. And yet that was not all that made Colin pause: if that had been all, he would have persisted, he would have induced Dennis somehow to taste the sweetness of evil, he would have pricked his arm to let just one drop of blood flow in which, so to speak, he could begin to write his name to the everlasting bond and bargain, to initial it at least. Dennis might be a little frightened, but the beginning would have been made.

What withheld him was not the wickedness of his intention, nor yet the unwisdom of frightening Dennis with it, but his own damnable squirming weakness in minding the boy's terror. It was cowardly, it was even apostate of him to recoil from that, but he wavered before it, he lacked firmness and indifference. He must get rid of that scruple and the hateful tenderness that prompted it.

There Dennis stood, his bare arms stretched out to him, half-imploring, it seemed, and yet, by that same action, keeping him off. The throat-apple in the soft neck moved up and down in his agitation, as if struggling to keep his panting breath steady, and the red flower of his mouth quivered.

The great sapphire slipped from Colin's hand and rolled on the floor. He let it lie there, unheeding or unknowing, and came close to Dennis, putting his arm round his neck. "Dennis, my dear," he said, "what's the matter? What ails you? Why, you're having the nightmare again while you're awake! This will never do."

The boy's attitude of defence, of keeping his father away from him, collapsed suddenly. He threw out his arms and caught his father round the shoulders.

"I'm an awful fool," he said. "I was frightened, and I can't think why. Just as if you weren't protection enough against anything. Oh, Father, you're a brick: I do love you."

Colin drew the boy down on the edge of the bed, and sat close to him.

"But what was the matter, my darling?" he said. "Tell me about it."

"It wasn't anything," said Dennis. "I'm a bloody fool —sorry. But, just for a second, it was nightmare again, and I thought somehow it wasn't you standing there. It was like some awful conjuring-trick. . . . And I wanted you. And I've got you. I won't be such an ass again."

"Sure you're all right?" said Colin. "We can't have you getting panics, Dennis, and being an ass."

Dennis laughed.

"You shan't," he said. "It's all gone. I say, I'm keeping you up. I must undress and go to bed, or you'll never get there."

Dennis got up, and stood there between his father's knees, erect and tranquil again. He peeled off his hose and vest, and put on his pyjamas. Just then his eye fell on the great sapphire that lay on the floor.

"Why, you've dropped the sapphire, Father," he said.

"So I see. Never mind that. I'll pick it up. Now into bed with you."

"How can I when you're sitting there? No, don't get up. I'll crawl in."

Dennis inserted one leg between his pillow and where Colin sat and drew himself into bed, curling himself against his father.

"There, that's all snug," he said.

"Good night, then," said Colin.

Dennis raised himself in bed, and kissed him.

"It's been a lovely evening," he said. "And it'll be just as lovely to-morrow with you and mother and me. I wish I wasn't going back to Eton on Thursday."

Colin, with the stone in his hand, went out and down the few steps of the corridor to the door of his room. Once again, and this time with a more direct and personal defeat, Dennis had routed him. Before, he had directed the force that governed and protected him on the boy as he slept, and who could tel in what fury of lambent evil it had begun to encompass him? But now, he himself, whom above all Dennis loved and trusted, had approached him with the same initiation, and yet all his love and trust had not given Dennis confidence: the spiritual semaphore of his instinct had hung out the red light of danger. The boy had recoiled from what he brought with a shrinking that was not reassured by the fact that it was his father who brought it. He had detected the nature of it, and all his affection would not suffer him to take it, even from the hands he loved, and this time Dennis had been broad awake, knowing well what he was doing. Here then was a more personal rebuff: it appeared that all Colin's trouble to endear himself to the boy (and with what success he had accomplished that!) was useless for the purpose for which he had intended it. Indeed it was far worse than useless, for in the process Dennis had somehow entered his heart, and for the second time he had been unable to persist.

The fault then, in great part, lay with himself. He made no doubt that if, with Dennis's love for him to assist him, he had reasoned and persuaded, telling him that in sober truth this ancient bargain was valid still, and that, when the day of his choice came, he could have all that had been so richly showered on his father, something of what he said would have remained in the boy's mind, quietly fermenting there. But he had failed to do anything of the kind: some incalculable impulse had seized him, and he had thought of nothing except to reassure him.

He stood in his room, the door of which he had not even closed, looking at the sapphire that blazed in his hand. That azure fire bade him go back to Dennis now, and, conquering this despicable softness in himself, tell him, with all the gusto of a splendid surprise (and he knew that a tongue of skill and persuasion would be given him), that the legend was alive to-day, that a power, mightier than the kings of the earth, was alert and eager to befriend him, at so cheap a cost, for the price was no more than that he should root out of his heart the sickly and sentimental stuff, the injurious weakness called love which saps the strength of a man and enslaves him to others. That was all that was meant by the bargain and the signing of the soul away. That was the true and the sensible way to look at it; and those who talked of it as being a consignment to the outer darkness and eternal damnation, were merely trying to frighten people by hoisting bogies. . . . Dennis would not understand, but that wonderful and impressionable thing, a boy's memory, would retain letter and form of it, till bit by bit he began to understand it, and then, from its having dwelt long in his mind, it would appear familiar and friendly. Dennis would already be half asleep, and his father would just sit and talk to him a minute or two, quietly and affectionately, sowing seed, and smoothing the rich fruitful earth of the boy's mind over it. . . .

He moved towards the door, opened it and went into the passage. And then, as his hand was on the latch of Dennis's door, he knew that even if he went in, with his intention hot within him, his expedition would be in vain. Dennis would sit up in bed, sleepily smiling, and welcoming the intrusion, on any or no excuse, so long as the intruder was he. Once more he would be disarmed by the defenceless.

The change that had to be wrought must begin with himself. There was no doubt that he had allowed himself to get fond of the boy, and for that reason he winced at the thought of the first incision. He must anneal himself to the gay ruthlessness with which he dealt with others, with which he had mocked Pamela to her doom, and jeered at his brother Raymond struggling with the broken lids of ice, before he attempted to deal with Dennis again. If only the boy was not so affectionate, how easy it would be! He had thought of Dennis's affection for him as a weapon in his own hand, but at present it was a weapon in Dennis's. Perhaps he would have to snap that, or, wresting it from him, turn it against him. At any rate he must anneal himself: he must weld the armour of hate against love. . . .

The general dispersal took place next morning; for an hour an almost incessant stream of motors left the door, and Dennis and his father were like ferry-boats conveying their visitors from the gallery where they said good-bye to Violet to the hall. Vastly as the boy had enjoyed this fortnight of crowd and turmoil, he got even gayer as it streamed away, and when the last had left he executed a wild rampageous dance in the hall.

"Hurrah, they've all gone!" he cried, "and now it's just us, Father. What shall we do all day? It's my last day, you know; you must let me have you all the time. What shall we do first?"

What was the use of spoiling Dennis's last day, Colin asked himself. The boy would be gone to-morrow for the next twelve weeks, and then would be the time to rout out the intruder. Indeed, that uprooting should begin to-night, that change in himself, that recantation of his recent apostasy. At midnight, when Dennis had gone to bed, he would renew his vows, and partake in the mockery of Love itself.

"Dennis, don't whirl round me like that," he said. "You make me giddy. And it's very grumpy of you, do you know, to be glad that your friends have gone? How many tipped you?"

"Oh, a frightful lot," said Dennis. "I'm rolling in riches. Will you come and play golf? Or tennis, do you think? Or what about potting rabbits? Or don't you want to be bothered with me?"

"We'll do just what you like," said Colin. "Sit down and make up your mind."

"Oh, but it's made up," said the boy. "Golf first: we'll drive over to Rye in the two-seater. I'll drive."

Colin paused a moment.

"You don't want to look at the Memoirs then?" he asked. "I'll read interesting bits to you, if you like."

Dennis's eyebrows drew themselves together. Some remembrance, was it, of his vanished fears?

"Oh, I'd sooner play golf," he said.

All day the two were together, and at dinner, for Aunt Hester had gone back with the rest to London, there were just the four of them, at a small round table in the dining-room, which last night had resounded to the gaiety of fifty, and blazed with the costumes of Elizabeth. And yet all that was essentially Stanier was gathered undiluted there; the splendour and the sparkle of these last days had been no more than a casual decoration it had plucked for itself and worn a little while and thrown away again. Last night old Lady Yardley had sat up till the very end of the ball, and all the week she had attended whatever entertainment was provided, but these unusual hours seemed to have made no call on her strength, and now bright-eyed and somehow terribly alive, beneath that immobile alabastrine sheath of her body, she looked from Dennis to his father and back again, as if searching for some assurance, some confirmation of what she desired. Of Violet, as usual, she seemed unconscious.

The ball of laughter and talk had been thrown hither and thither merrily enough all dinner time; Dennis and Colin were the chief performers, and Violet had taken but little part in it. All day she had wrestled with a secret jealousy; not once had Dennis, to whose last day at home she usually devoted herself, appeared to want her, and since their guests had left in the morning he had been exclusively with his father. It was all very natural: his exuberance wanted his golf and his rabbit-shooting and the activities of his budding manhood. And yet it was not the boy's fault that he had not spared her a half-hour out of his day, for at the conclusion of each diversion, Colin had been at hand with another. Was it simply for her discomfiture, and the exhibition of his own triumphant rivalry that he had done that? Certainly that would have been a sufficient motive for him, but she felt there was something else as well, a larger issue, an ampler cause. If it had been that alone, he would have had little oblique mockeries for her, would have called her attention to his success, would even have told Dennis to go and talk to her, and that when he had had a "nice talk" he was ready to fish or play tennis.

And then, like a blown flame, those little surface-jealousies went out. Was Colin planning some final employment for Dennis to-night? She knew he had sent for Mr. Douglas this evening, and had had some private interview with him, for she had unwittingly interrupted it, and seen the breaking off of their topic when she entered the room. . . . At the thought, that small green flame was quenched, and cold apprehension gripped her. As dinner went on she ceased to take any part in those gay crossing volleys, and became, like old Lady Yardley, silent and watchful and aware. She seemed to enter into the spirit of all those generations of silent and frozen women who were the wives and mothers of the race. They had always been like that who were knit into the line through which the legend was transmitted, and now she seemed to comprehend the nature of that vesture of ice that clothed them, for they knew that it was through their blood and the love of their conceiving bodies that the Satanic bargain was kept alive, and that their sons were the inheritors of the bond. Was that not enough to freeze the mother the fruit of whose womb would be dedicated to hell, who watched the growing strength and beauty of her son, and knew the consecration of evil to which, at his choice, he gave his soul? She would see him prosperous beyond all other heritors, beauty and health, honour and wealth, would be his, and her spirit would freeze and burn in the ice of knowing that all this was but the payment in dross for that which in the eyes of God was worth the ransom of the precious blood. . . . Would she get used to that, she wondered, so that the knowledge became part of her nature, and, as the flocks of grey-winged years passed over her head, she would become so one with Stanier, that the prosperity and continuance of the house would grow into the very fibre of her nature. It was so, she guessed, with old Lady Yardley: Colin and Dennis were the connotation of the world to her. Over all else the penumbra and eclipse of age had passed, and just that rim and nothing else was illuminated. Neither evil nor good, nor love nor hate perhaps, existed for her any more, the sense of Stanier was her only reaction to the exterior world.

Dinner was over and the coffee handed, and still Lady Yardley had not broken that frost of her silence. But now there came a sudden uncongealment.

"Stanier is itself again to-night," she said. "They have gone, all the fine folk who come like dogs when my Colin whistles to them. They lick his hand and he feeds them."

Colin turned to her.

"Granny dear, what nonsense!" he said. "And you shouldn't call our distinguished guests dogs. Didn't you like having them here? I thought you were enjoying it all."

That wraith of a smile dimpled her mouth.

"Yes, I enjoyed it," she said. "I enjoyed seeing them all doing homage to Stanier, to my Colin."

She looked from him to Dennis.

"And here is my Colin as he was when he was a boy," she said. "When he grows up they will do homage to him too. But before then he must know the legend instead of only hearing it. Read, mark, learn and inwardly digest. The prayer-book says that about the legend."

Colin pushed back his chair.

"Granny, you are charming," he said, "but we settled the first night that I was here that we were to have no prophesying at dinner."

"But I am not prophesying," said she. "I am only saying what you and I know and what presently he will know. It will be pleasant when we all know, for then we can talk freely. Shall I tell him now, Colin? Shall I break the sheet of ice?

I would be out in the sun then, instead of being cold. I will melt my frost——"

He took her stick and put it into her hand.

"Get up," he said. "Go and melt the frost by the fire in the gallery, where your card-table is ready for you. Now not a word more."

She rose, still smiling, as if content with what she had said. She had borne witness to what she knew, and what Colin knew, and whether he was sharp with her or not was insignificant compared to that. Leaning on her stick, she went out, followed by Violet.

Colin watched Dennis's troubled face as he came back to the table after closing the door behind the others. When first three weeks ago old Lady Yardley had 'prophesied,' he had been puzzled, but excited and fascinated. But since then he had learned something; waking or asleep he had seen the outline of a terrible shadow, and it seemed to be the same as that, whatever it was, of which she had just spoken.

"What does she mean?" he said. "What was all that about her telling me and melting the frost?"

"Dottiness," said Colin at once. "You discovered she was dotty weeks ago. And just now, you remember, she thought that you were me as a boy again. That wasn't very clear-headed, was it? And all the rest was just as muddled. Don't think anything more about it, Dennis."

That cloud did not clear away at once from Dennis's forehead. His father had clearly wanted to tell him something last night, and, by an unerring instinct, he divined that this same something lurked behind what he had just stopped old Lady Yardley from saying. It concerned the legend, clearly; some practical personal application of the legend. . . .

"Dennis, you're not doing what I told you," said Colin sharply. "You're thinking of Grannie's dottiness."

Dennis pulled in that sail of his mind which was still catching that mysterious breeze.

"Righto," he said.

"Come and sit next me then, you exclusive brute," said Colin, "instead of sitting at the other side of the table. . . . And you've liked your last day, have you, Dennis?"

"Oh, Father, it has been lovely," said Dennis, drawing a chair quite close to him. "Why, they all went away at eleven, and I've been with you ever since except when I had my bath, and even then you came in in the middle. Ten solid hours with you. Not bad."

"No, not very bad. You've made an elderly gent like me play golf and tennis and shoot pigeons. I shall have a rest-cure after you've gone."

"Do. Come and have it at Eton. There's a nursing home somewhere in the town. Elderly gent!"

"Well, don't rub it in," said Colin. "Come on, Dennis. We must go and play whist. You and I will rook your mother and Granny. And then, after being up till nearly four last night, you shall go softly and silently to bed like the Snark."

"Not silent. You'll come and talk, won't you?"

"Perhaps I'll look in, but I don't promise. I must sit up and do some jobs."

"Why?" said Dennis.

"Because you've prevented my doing them all day."

Colin smiled to himself as he said that. It was most emphatically true: he would concentrate on his jobs to-night.

Violet went upstairs with Dennis at bed-time, relieved of her immediate fear, for Colin made no move to detain the boy, and whatever he had planned for himself, he did not look for Dennis's partnership. Colin sat in his room when the others had gone up, and for half an hour, while he was waiting for midnight, he read and mused over the Memoirs of his ancestor. How symmetrical and consistent he had been till that senile ague of terror palsied him in the last year of his life! Never once in those fascinating pages was there a hint of any struggle in his soul, any stirrings of compassion or love which disturbed the poise of his undivided allegiance. Nor even at the end, did he waver in spirit, for it was easy to see that his belated pieties, his formal acts of pity and charity, sprang not from any turning of him in spirit towards God, but from the mere physical terror of his approaching doom. He only added cowardice, in fact, to his other sins, and went forth with a blacker load than ever. . . . So early, too, must he have initiated his two sons into the doctrines of the gospel, for long before the time came for their choice they were ripe and ready.

Colin dropped his reading. There was yet time to go upstairs and bid Dennis dress and come with him. But still the excuse held that the boy's soul was not ready for the sacrament of evil: he had to learn the sweetness of evil for evil's sake before he could take part in its worship. He would understand nothing:

the rite would be meaningless, or, worse than that, would perhaps disgust and horrify him, and it was not in disgust and horror that he must be drawn, but must spring with a leap of the spirit towards a congenial mystery. And still Colin knew that all this was an excuse only: and his reason for not fetching the boy was that obstinate intruder in his own heart, which made him recoil from the notion of Dennis being frightened or revolted. It was, in fact, himself with whom he had to deal: he must cleanse his own heart of the tenderness which was in bud there, and by the inspiration of evil root out that alien weed. He must concentrate his mind on defiance and hate. . . .

There came a tap at the door which led into the corridor up to the chapel. This was always kept locked, and the key to it, like a latch-key, he wore on his watch-chain. Otherwise the chapel could only be approached through Mr. Douglas's lodging. He opened the door and found Vincenzo standing there.

"Pronto, signor," said Vincenzo, and fell behind him as he walked up the corridor, leaving him at the door into the chapel, while he went through to the priest's dwelling to vest himself as server. Colin entered: the chapel was redolent of stale incense, soon to be refreshed and renewed, and blazed with lights.

Presently the priest entered, served by Vincenzo. He was robed in that wonderful cope which, once stolen from some Italian sacristy, had been bought by Colin in Naples. For a minute or so, he knelt with his back to the altar and then, making the sign of the cross reversed, rose and began.

Though he knew the ritual well, Colin closely followed the service in the vellum-leaved book on his faldstool. Douglas had copied this in his exquisite formal handwriting from the missal of wondrous blasphemies, illuminating the initial letters with appropriate decoration and sacrilegious parodies of holy scenes. Two years had it taken him, a labour of love, and Colin, by keeping his attention on the book, strove to devote his mind to the spirit of the blasphemy. He confessed his fallings and his lapses from his vowed life, he tried to root Dennis out of his heart. He let his mind dwell on evil and cruelty and hate. And now the new clouds of incense rose from the censer that Vincenzo swung, the altar gleamed through the fragrant sanctification, and the supreme moment approached.

Colin felt the stir of the power seething round him, but he knew he no longer went out to meet it with welcome and heart's surrender. All the pressure of his will was bent on doing so, but it was as if some grain of grit had got into the psychic mechanism of his soul: it checked and laboured, it did not respond with full smooth strokes. Why could he not be like Vincenzo who knelt there, his face working with some diabolical rapture? Vincenzo's hands were clasped in front of him, his mouth grinned and slavered, he shook and swayed in that fierce gale of possession. The priest's arms were raised now for consecration, and Vincenzo's eyes were fixed on them; in a moment more, on the completion of the act, he would pull the rope of the bell that hung by him, and the three muffled strokes. . . .

Even as Colin looked, half-envying him, half-horrified at the tension of the man's face, Vincenzo suddenly rose to his feet, with hands stretched out in front of him. He swayed as he stood, as if blown by a great wind, and then crashed forward and fell full length on the altar-step.

The priest, with the wafer still unconsecrated in his hand, turned at the thud of his fall. He placed the wafer back on the paten, and, beckoning to Colin, stooped down by the man's side. Vincenzo had rolled on to his face and lay there trembling and twitching. They turned him over; his eyes wide open seemed to be focussed in blank terror at something close in front of them, and at the corners of his mouth foam had gathered.

The priest felt for his pulse.

"What happened?" he said to Colin.

"He fell forward. . . . Well? Is he alive? Is he dead?"

"I can't find any flicker of pulse," said Douglas. "Can you get some brandy? I've got none."

"Yes, there's sure to be a tray in the gallery. I'll go and get it."

Colin nodded towards the altar.

"Take the vessels back to your room," he said, "and disrobe. I'll be back in a moment."

Father Douglas knew something of first aid, but it was in vain that they tried to restore the stricken man. The brandy, unswallowed, trickled out of his mouth again, the raising and lowering of his arms started no flicker of vitality.

"We must send for the doctor," said Douglas. "But——"

Colin nodded, understanding him.

"Yes, not here of course," he said. "We must move him. Now, for hell's sake, don't let us make any mistake which we can't correct afterwards. First of all, we must take his cotta and cassock off. . . . Get a pair of scissors, quick: we must cut the sleeves."

Colin was perfectly alert and collected; coolly and swiftly he thought over what was to be done. Just one glance of angry disgust he gave to that distorted whitening face, which was the cause of all this trouble, but for the present he needed all his wits to grapple with the dispositions which must be made instantly and without the possibility of correction afterwards. His brain was busy as they slipped the severed vestments off Vincenzo, and he began to see the road.

"Lay him down again," he said, when this was done. "We mustn't move him at all till we've settled everything. Cover his face, though; I hate those dimmed glass eyes. God, what terror is there!"

He sat down on the step with his back to the body. "I want to smoke," he said. "Nothing like a cigarette for filtering your thoughts. Now look here, Douglas, of course he mustn't be found here at all: no doctor or anybody else must come in here. Therefore it's clear we've got to move him. Luckily it's late: the servants will have gone to bed: we shall have the house to ourselves."

The priest's hands were trembling, he was utterly unnerved by the catastrophe. Memories of years long past when he was a priest of God, and when to the dying he gave the Bread of Angels for their soul's refreshment and support, stood before him like white statues, silent and aware. Now, he was priest of a creed that mocked and defied, and at the moment of supreme blasphemy this stroke had fallen. Was the visitation from God or from Satan? Under which king? He buried his face in his hands.

"The horror of it," he whispered. "The terror——"

Colin turned sharply to him.

"Here, take some brandy," he said, "as—as nobody else will. And you can enjoy your terrors afterwards. At present you've got to help. We've got to carry him away first. Good Lord, man, you're not frightened of the dead, are you? The world must be a jumpy place for you with its millions of dead generations. And Vincenzo worshipped Satan: what better death do you want for him? . . . Well, we'll talk theology by and by. Think, man, help me to make up a story that's question-proof. And we must be quick, too, these doctors have a trick of knowing how long a man's been dead. Perhaps he's not even dead: we're not doctors and we can't tell."

Colin smoked in silence a moment, frowning but bright-eyed. "Damned lot of use you are," he said. "But hold your tongue now. I'm getting at it."

He got up briskly and began walking up and down the black marble floor of the chapel.

"Come along," he said. "You've got to help me to carry him out down the corridor, and through my room and into the hall, and then, you'll be pleased to hear, all you've got to do is not to know that anything at all has happened. You'll come back here afterwards and put things away, and then get to your bed and sleep or lie awake just as you feel inclined. Look, there's the censer overturned, and burning a hole in that carpet, Spit on it or something. . . . My word, you're lucky that this didn't happen when you were alone with him but had someone with you who doesn't suffer from terror of the spirit. Now catch hold of him under his knees and lift him when I've got hold of his shoulders. Why, the man's as light as a child. That's the devout life."

Under Colin's directions they carried their burden with the slit cassock still over his face, and the arm hanging limply down, out into the hall, and laid him sprawling there, much as he had fallen. Then Colin twitched the cassock from the face, and gave it to the priest.

"Lock up that and the cotta," he said, "and bury them to-morrow in your bit of garden. Or weight them, that will be better, and make a parcel of them and chuck them into the lake above the sluice. And now go back to the chapel, make everything ship-shape, just as you would have done if this had not occurred, and get to bed. You know nothing, nothing."

Colin looked at his ashen face, in contemptuous pity. "You're all to bits," he said. "I suppose I shall have to come back and help you or you'll forget to lock the chapel or something. Wait a minute!"

He went to the telephone and got connected with the house of the doctor at Rye.

"I'm Lord Yardley," he said, as soon as he got a reply "and I'm so sorry to trouble you, but would you make all haste to come up to Stanier? My servant has had some sort of fit; he's still unconscious. Thank you very much."

Colin saw Father Douglas through with his part of the business and then waited in the hall, where he would hear the doctor's wheels. There on the floor lay the body curiously insignificant, and now he noticed that the famous picture of old Colin, with the supposed deed of bargain let into the frame, was on the wall just above where it lay. There was something rather suitable about that. . . . But he gave no further thought to it: over and over in his mind he conned what he was going to say: framing answers to any questions that might be put, and above all rehearsing his own initial statement. That was the important thing, it was that which he must make so familiar to himself that he really believed it to be true, for no doubt he would have to repeat it again at the inquest. Over all else, though it teemed with surmise and wonder, he drew an impenetrable curtain. Nothing else mattered just now but what he must say to the doctor.

Before he had begun to expect his arrival, he heard the crunch of motor-wheels, and undid the bolts of the door.

"Come in, Doctor," he said. "It is good of you to have been so quick. It's my servant, Vincenzo, who has been with me a long time. There he lies, exactly as he fell. I thought it wise not to move him in any way. I tried to get him to swallow a mouthful of brandy, but I couldn't."

"Very wise of you, Lord Yardley," said the doctor. "A man taken by a seizure should always be left till it is ascertained of what nature his seizure is. Now let me examine him."

Dr. Martin knelt down by his patient. He felt for his pulse, he listened at his chest, and with a light brought close he looked with narrow scruting into the eyes. Then he rose to his feet.

"I'm sorry to say I can do nothing," he said. "The man is dead."

"Ah, poor fellow—poor Vincenzo," said Colin. "It is terrible, terrible."

"Perhaps you would tell me exactly what happened," said Dr. Martin.

"Yes, yes. Let us come into my room. . . . Sit down, Doctor. Now let me think for a moment, my wits seem all abroad."

Colin covered his eyes with his hand a moment: the clock on the mantelpiece chimed the three quarters after twelve. He pointed to it, and spoke.

"Vincenzo always sat up till I went to bed," he said, "but often, if I was sitting up late, I would ring for him, and tell him he needn't wait. This evening when my wife and my boy went upstairs, I came in here: it must have been not long after eleven. I began reading the type-written copy of an old family memoir, got interested in it, and did not notice how the time went. When I looked up I saw that it was late: twenty minutes past twelve or thereabouts. I had not finished my reading, and so I rang the bell here, in order to tell Vincenzo that he need not sit up. Almost immediately I heard the noise of some heavy fall. The house had been silent for some time, and it startled me considerably. I went out into the hall which we have just quitted and found the poor fellow lying there. From the fact that I heard this noise immediately after ringing my bell, I suppose that he had been waiting in the hall, where he would hear my bell. I instantly rang you up, and remained there with him till you came. I thought perhaps he might come to himself, and I could be of use. It occurred to me to call some of the other servants, but since I felt sure that it would be safer not to move him, there seemed to be no object in that. Ah, yes, I tried to make him swallow some brandy."

"Quite so. You acted very wisely."

Colin looked imploringly at the doctor.

"It would be a great relief to my mind," he said, "if you could definitely tell me that there was nothing I could have done to help him."

"I am positive there was nothing. Probably he was dead when he fell. There is a question or two I should like to ask. When you rang me up, you said he had had some sort of a fit. Had he suffered from fits before?"

Colin almost smiled with pleasure at that question.

"He told me once that when he was a boy he was subject to them," he said. "He supposed he had outgrown them."

"I see. Of course this was not a fit, medically speaking. No sign of an epileptic seizure or anything of the kind. Sudden death: that's all we can say at present."

"And from what, do you conjecture?" asked Colin.

"It is quite impossible to say. That of course will have to be ascertained."

"You can form no idea?"

"One would imagine he had some terrible shock. There was an expression in his eyes of the most abject terror."

Dr. Martin got up.

"Now would you like to summon one of your men to help

us?" he said. "We must move the body, of course. Is there some room near at hand where we can place him till morning, when I will be back early to make all arrangements—some room which you can lock up and give me the key or keep it yourself?"

"Yes, there's the smoking-room close at hand," said Colin. "But there is no need to call anybody. I will help you."

They laid him on a sofa there, covering the face with a rug, and presently, after the key was turned, and Colin had taken it from the lock, he saw the doctor to the door. In his admirable way he had conveyed the impression of being terribly shocked and keeping a firm hand on himself.

"You can rest assured, Lord Yardley," said the doctor, "that you did all that could be done. You acted with great wisdom in not moving him, and in sending at once for me. I wish I could have been of any use. Put your mind quite at rest about that. You'll sleep I hope?"

Colin raised soft swimming eyes.

"I feel as if I should," he said. "Now it is all over I feel most awfully tired. Good night, Dr. Martin. Ever so many thanks."

Colin bolted and barred the door, switched off the lights in the hall and went upstairs. Passing Dennis's door, he saw that it still stood ajar, and a line of brightness was rectangled round it. He pushed it quietly open, expecting to see that Dennis had again fallen asleep while waiting for him to come and say good night. This time, however, the boy was wide-awake.

"Oh, Father, what an age you've been," he said. "What have you been doing?"

It was as if some shutter had been snapped down in Colin's mind. Behind it lay all that had happened in this last hour, bright and vivid as in some decked shop window but now cut off from view.

"Dennis, you little wretch," he said. "You ought to have been asleep long ago."

Dennis laughed.

"Oh don't be silly," he said. "You didn't think I was going to sleep without saying good night to you on my last night, did you? Come and sit down for two minutes."

Dennis wriggled away to the middle of the bed, leaving room for his father to sit on the edge of it, and put up his knees to form a back for him.

"I expected you to be snoring," said Colin.

"I never snore!" said the indignant Dennis. "As for being asleep, I didn't want to go to sleep. . . . Finished your jobs?"

"Pretty well. I can leave the rest till morning."

Dennis sniffed, wrinkling up his nose like a young terrier.

"Where have you been?" he said. "Your coat smells of Roman Catholic churches."

"Rot, my dear. Cigarettes."

"But it isn't rot. Well, never mind. I say, Father, we have had a ripping holiday. And to-day's been the best of all. And it's ever so much nicer here than in London. I love Stanier."

"That's a family affliction," said Colin. "I wonder what you'll do with it, when I'm dead and you get it."

"Oh, shut up. As if I should care about it without you."

"Dennis, what compliments!" said Colin.

Colin went to his room, and let that shutter in his mind rattle up and looked into that lighted window. Between the catastrophe and the coming of the doctor his acuteness had been entirely busy over the account he would be called upon to give, and there his cool ingenuity had served him well: his story had been coherent and consistent, and he had eliminated from it everyone but himself and the dead man, who could bring forward no conflicting testimony. But for the moment he looked only absently at that sensationally decked window, for he congratulated himself on his wisdom in rejecting that wayward thought of taking Dennis with him at midnight, only a little more than an hour ago, into the chapel. If he had done that, what face would Dennis be wearing now? Would he have curled down in bed so quietly and followed his father as he went to the door with the shining of his tranquil, affectionate eyes? Already he knew (and had shuddered to know) that there was in the legend something more than a fairy story, something alive and Satanic from the touch of which he shrank when it came near him. Colin would have told him that what he was to see in the chapel was the worship of that power which through the centuries had so wonderfully befriended the house, and while he quivered in the face of that initiation, there would have come this appalling, this unexpected stroke. The boy would have been distraught with terror; evil which, for its own sake, he must sometime choose as guardian of his soul and body, would have been to him for ever a force that smote its suppliant with death, sudden and terrific. It would have been disastrous if Dennis had seen that.

Colin looked into the lighted window. There, vivid as when the scene itself was before his amazed eyes, he scrutinized the image of Vincenzo, already writhing in the ecstasy of possession, and then falling forward like that. Why had that happened? What was its psychical significance? He had died, it appeared, of some shock or terror: panic yelled in his wide silent eyes. Had there came to him some appalling revelation of ultimate absolute evil, even as it had come to old Colin himself when, at his birthday feast, he had shrieked out, "No! No!" and with repelling hands had fallen dead across the table? Or had he looked in the eyes of God, and seen there the infinite love of Him at Whom he mocked?

Colin felt himself shudder at that thought. That indeed would be enough to shrivel the spirit of a man, like a burnt feather in a furnace. Hell could not contain such torment as to realize that, through the night and blackness of absolute evil, the love of God, still shone without change or dimness, even as the light of a steadfast star burns unblown by the puny violence of terrestrial tempests. . . . If there had come to Vincenzo at the moment of death only some vision or internal realization of the wrath of God, that surely, to one whose joy it was to mock and defy Him, would have been like a waved banner of victory, a sign that his mockery had reached its mark: God's anger would be a testimonial to his success. But it would have been hell indeed to know that all his defiance and rebellion had never caused the infinite Love and pity to waver, that for him still 'Christ's blood streamed in the firmament.' That would have been sufficient to glaze with the terror of utter and ultimate defeat, those dying eyes. . . .

"See where Christ's blood stream is the firmament" . . . Colin muttered the words to himself. They came, he remembered now, from the last scene in Marlowe's Faustus, just before the stroke of midnight, on which Mephistopheles came to exact the payment of Faustus's soul. That to Faustus had been the ultimate anguish, and what if it had been so too to him who now lay in the locked room downstairs?

Colin shrank from that thought, even as Dennis had shrunk from the terror of his nightmare. It was better to suppose that there had come to the man some fresh intuition into the power of evil, and that in the panic of his eyes was the knowledge that his time was come, and that he was eternally consigned to the protection of what he had worshipped. At that so easily the flesh might quaver, in the dissolution of the body from the spirit. That in comparison was a comforting thought: he felt himself at home there and not afraid. He himself had chosen evil for his good, and hell surely could be no other than the eternal severance of the soul from God. It was physical terror merely that had distorted Vincenzo's face: and with that thought there sprang up in him the desire to look on the dead once more, and convince himself that there was imprinted on it just the tokens of this natural cowering before the face of death. He had with him the key of the locked smoking-room, where the body lay, and now, taking off his shoes so that his step should be noiseless, he let himself out into the passage again. The switch was to his hand just outside his door, and at his touch the passage and the hall below flashed into light.

He paused after fitting the key into the door of the smoking-room. The great portrait of old Colin seemed to smile on him; on the floor in front of it was the rug on which Vincenzo's body had sprawled, it was crumpled into ridges where they had taken it up again. He entered the death-chamber. There on the sofa with its face covered lay the body, and standing there beside it he told himself again what he had come to see, namely the tokens of physical terror, the shrinking of the flesh at the touch of death. Then he drew the covering away.

Vincenzo's eyes were closed—perhaps the doctor had done that. The face was perfectly composed and tranquil, and looked younger than his years. He did not seem to be dead: it was more reasonable to think that he was asleep, and the mouth, slightly smiling, suggested that he dreamed of happy affairs, of friends, of home. In life there had been something a little sinister about his expression: now he looked contented and kind.

Colin covered his face again with a sullen spasm of misgiving. He feared that tranquillity, he hated the conjectured cause of it; death had stamped that face with terror, and something stronger than death had smoothed that terror out again.

He went upstairs. Had the events of the evening begun to get on his nerves, spurring them to unreal imaginings? Perhaps it was normal that, after death, the face should grow tranquil again. But its tranquillity was more disturbing by far than its distortion of terror had been.

CHAPTER IV

COLIN went into his wife's room early next morning and gave her his official version of Vincenzo's death. They were both agreed that Dennis should be told nothing of it, and before the hour for the removal of the body came, to await the inquest in Rye, he took the boy out for a final morning of rabbit shooting. He had slept well and woke with nerves quieted and refreshed: Dennis's ignorance, too, both of what had actually occurred and what was supposed to have occurred was in itself a healing to those troubled fancies of the midnight, just as this warm April morning was healing in its physical tonic to his nerves.

Indeed Stanier had never seemed so tranquil and serene an abode of prosperous peace, as now when he walked with this tall fair son of his along the terrace, and up the wooded slope beyond the chapel, where the ruby glass of the windows was penetrated by the gleaming sunshine, and shone like a fire. To be out of doors this morning was better than being within, and better it was to walk in the warm wind than to breathe stale incense smoke. Below them the broad lake glittered, and for a moment, in a gap between the rhododendron bushes along the sluice-wall, the figure of the priest, black against the vivid green of the young-leafed trees beyond, came into sight and vanished again. He had gone down there, no doubt, to do his part concerning the secret version of the events of the night: Colin was pleased to have caught that glimpse of him. Later, when Dennis had gone, he would have to see him.

But just for the present he let all that concerned the drowning of slit cassock and cotta slip down into the depths of his mind, even as those relics with the weight to sink them had dwindled into the darkness of the deep water, where once Raymond lay. Soon he would have to fish these problems and perplexities up again, and discuss them with the priest; but for an hour or two, till Dennis departed, he would keep on the sunny surface of this windy morning. There lay the house that he loved more than anything or anyone in the world; he could almost fancy himself, if this April day were only eternal, being happy here, as the deer were happy, browsing on the fresh growth of spring time, and letting that love of hate and of evil in his heart sink into quiescence, even evaporate away.

Would life lose all its effervescence without it? Supposing now that the whole history of the legend from its inception to his own passionate participation in it was a dream; supposing it rolled away like those moving mists which an hour ago lay fleecy and thick over the plain, and that with an opening of his eyes and a tranquil awakening he found himself just here, mounting the steep slope with Dennis, chattering by him, and the house gleaming rosy-red below, and that all which had given to him the thrill and the motive of life passed into unsubstantial nothingness, so that even the memory of it was elusive and hard to capture—would he look forward over the coming years as over a desert featurelessness of barren sand? . . . The notion occurred to him for just long enough to frame itself into a definite mental question, but the moment it presented itself like that, he saw that any answer to it must be inconceivable, simply because the question itself was so. He could not with deliberation even frame the question for, in itself, it presupposed an obliteration of all that which consciousness implied. He might as well ask himself what he would think about if his brain was incapable of thought.

He took Dennis down to the station after lunch, and on his return, meaning to ask Douglas to come to see him, was told that he had already asked if he could do so, and was waiting in his room. He went there, but had he met in a crowd away from Stanier the figure that rose on his entrance, he would scarcely have recognized it. The man's upright athletic carriage was bowed and bent, he stumbled as he walked, and the fresh-coloured face was a drawn white mask. So this was the diver with whose help he had to try to bring up to the surface the submerged burden of the night. . . .

Colin did not mind other people looking ill. Their weakness only emphasized to him his own superb health.

"Hullo," he said. "You look rather poorly, Douglas. I might almost say you look ghastly. Oh, by the way, I caught a glimpse of you this morning, telling your beads no doubt down by the lake. I take it then that you've done that little job. Is that so?"

"Yes, I did exactly what you asked me."

"Capital. Then all that remains for you is to realize that up till this moment you are not aware that anything unusual occurred. So much so, in fact, that you must listen to a sad piece of news I've got for you. Listen. My Italian servant,

Vincenzo, had a sudden seizure shortly after midnight in the hall. I had just rung my bell to tell him not to sit up, and it appears that he was waiting for that. He was in the hall in fact already. He got up, it would seem, to come to this room here, when a seizure took him and he fell. I heard the noise of his fall, and found him there, and, as one should never touch a man in a fit, I telephoned for the doctor, who said he was dead. There will be an inquest which I shall have to attend. Sad news, isn't it? I shall miss him. I thought I had better tell you. Any questions to ask? We'll take your sympathy for granted."

Colin moved quietly about the room as he spoke. He lit a cigarette and pointed to a chair.

"And now that I've taken that off your mind," he said, "let us discuss something quite different. Look at me, Douglas, and tell me, in your capacity as spiritual expert, black and white, what happened last night? Or, rather, what caused that which we both saw?"

The priest raised his eyes to Colin. Terror, deep and still as a summer sea, gleamed and darkled in them. The words came slowly at first, for his twitching mouth stammered as he spoke.

"I can tell you what happened," he said. "Just at the moment when evil and defiance were mounting in a blaze of triumph in his soul, he saw God. There is nothing else that can account for it. If he had seen Satan himself, would the terror that smote soul and body asunder have come to him? He might have fallen in a trance of adoration, but what cause would there have been for terror? There was cause only for ecstasy. But was that ecstasy which you and I saw on his face? I tell you it was the despair of final defeat. He was at the mercy of Him whom he had made his enemy. As I raised my hands in consecration, God came."

Was it the infection only of that mute panic in the priest's eyes that caused Colin's heart to beat suddenly small and quick, and his hands to grow cold?

"That occurred to me," he said.

There was a moment's silence. The clock ticked, and just outside the window a thrush sang.

Colin made a violent effort with himself. He attacked his fear, driving it before him.

"We're rotten Satanists, you and I," he said. "We ought to be ashamed of ourselves. As I tell you, that idea did occur to me, but I was, without knowing it, overwrought last night and excited. I, too, when I saw that terror in his face, thought that the sight of God alone, merciful and pitiful, could have caused it and I thought so even more strongly when half an hour later, I looked at his face again, and saw it was quiet and serene. But I needn't go into that. What I intend to do now and for ever from this moment, is to put that notion away."

"It doesn't matter if you put it away or not," said the priest. "It is true."

Colin made that silent, effortless relaxation, that opening of his heart to the power that he loved and served, which is the essence of prayer. He had just to remain like that, till it began to tingle and throb within him, till he was charged and brimming with it. Soon he spoke.

"Of course, the ways of God are inscrutable," he observed, "but I don't take the slightest interest in them. Of course, He'll win in the end somehow—it's such a score to be Omnipotent. But it isn't the end yet. I'm going to have a good long run for my money first. Besides, the notion is quite illogical: it doesn't hold water. You were the principal culprit last night, weren't you? Why, in the name of justice, weren't you bagged instead of Vincenzo?"

"I wish to God I had been," said the priest.

"Now will you explain why?"

"Because I am in hell."

"This pleasant room?" asked Colin.

The priest got up.

"Can't you understand?" he said. "Vincenzo has been conquered: he has made his submission. He saw the truth of what he denied and mocked: it was made real to him, in some manner inscrutable to us. And if that was the end of life, it was the end of hell also."

"Oh, I thought hell was eternal," said Colin.

"Every moment holds eternity," said the other. "Millions of years multiplied by millions of years are no nearer eternity than the millionth part of a second. Eternity isn't quantity, it is quality."

Something shone on Colin at that, as from an immense distance over stormy water there shines some steadfast beam from a harbour light. Instantly his whole will, strong in the power that possessed it, mocked and derided.

"Ah, fine durable quality," he said.

That abyss of terror in the priest's eyes was veiled for a moment.

"Yes, the quality of God," he said. "Nothing else but it exists at all."

Colin stretched himself in his chair.

"Oh damn," he said quietly. "I'm sure I beg your pardon Douglas, but when I try to impart a little lightness to your solemn gibberish, you flop back again. Let us quit theology or demonology, or whatever we're talking about—I'm sure I haven't the slightest idea what it is—and be a little more practical. Now I hear you asked to see me. What did you want to say?"

"I wanted to tell you that I am leaving Stanier to-day," said Douglas.

Colin raised his eyebrows.

"That's rather sudden, isn't it?" he said.

"Yes. It's very sudden. What happened last night was sudden and what it wrought in me."

"And so I'm to be left without my—my librarian at a moment's notice?" said Colin.

"It would make no difference if I stopped," said Douglas. "I could never do my office again."

Colin laid his hand on the priest's shoulder, and put into his manner all the winning charm which was his.

"My dear fellow," he said, "you mustn't think that I'm unsympathetic. You've had a frightful shock, and it has absolutely upset your nerves. It has had no effect on mine, as you see, but I quite understand that you're all abroad to-day. Now take a complete holiday for a month, and don't go near the—the library. We're having a divine spring, May is delicious down here. And then after a month you'll find you're yourself again."

Douglas shook his head.

"I couldn't possibly stop here," he said.

"Well, then, go out to Capri for a month or so. The villa is at your disposal, and, of course, you'll be my guest, though I shan't be there."

"That is kind of you," said Douglas, "but I couldn't do that either. I must go."

"But I can't permit it," said Colin. "You're part of Stanier now, a very important part too. Why, it's through you that old Colin's original designs are complete. I built the chapel he planned before he turned traitor, but what's the use of a chapel, without a priest? It's no more than an empty picture frame. Last night was very upsetting, I quite grant you that, but for a fit of the nerves you mustn't break up the very shrine of Stanier's hidden life. Do you suppose it was chance that caused us to meet? Why, we've often agreed it was the most miraculous design. You can't smash it up like that. Take a holiday by all means, but you must come back."

"I cannot stop here, and I can never come back here," said Douglas. "The place—how shall I say it—is saturated."

Colin moved a step away from him.

"I think your attitude requires explanation," he said. "Is Capri saturated too?"

Douglas faced him.

"My attitude is perfectly simple," he said. "For twelve years the worship of evil has been my spiritual life, and last night my eyes were opened to what I have been. Whether I can find salvation I don't know, but what I can do is to hate and loathe myself, and break of all connection with those who are as I have been."

"Ah now we're getting at it," said Colin. "The saturation you speak of—I am the saturator, I perceive. Is that it?"

"Yes: you and the evil which your worship."

Colin's blue eyes were still smiling and kind.

"I think you're inconsistent," he said. "Shouldn't the zeal of the convert inspire you to missionary work? A brand plucked from the burning ought surely to want to spoil the fire by pulling out another brand."

Douglas hesitated.

"I am afraid," he said.

"Not of me?" asked Colin.

"Yes. You have a power for evil that is terrible. The legend is true: I can't stand up against you. And yet . . ."

"Go on," said Colin.

"It's this, and these are my last words to you. I have watched you this last month, and you have changed. At least there is the shadow of change over you. Till last night you have never come to the chapel, and last night I could feel that you felt no true devotion. If I could hope to assist that change, I might stop, but it has nothing to do with me. You have let love approach you . . . Dennis . . . He loves you as you know very well, and there is something in you, crush and throttle it as you will, which goes out to him."

Colin suddenly shot out his hand at him. Never, not even in the days of Raymond, had he known so blistering and undiluted a stream of hate flood his soul. This man, with whom he had been knit in the worship of evil not only had thrown it and him aside, but he had seen and spoken of that which, like a disgrace, he had tried to cover up and excuse from himself.

"That's enough!" he said. "And let me tell you that you never spoke words more ill-advised for your purpose than these. It's the truth in them that damns them. Do you think I don't know that as well as you? And don't you see that if anything was wanted to encourage me to root that change out of my heart, it would be that you, you trembling renegade, should tell me of its shadow lying on me?"

He came close up to him again; there was not much of a smile in his eyes now, and he spoke with a cold and deadly concentration.

"I know that I've been weak," he said, "and it's a tonic you've given me for my weakness. There'll be no more complaint of my lack of fervour: what has frightened you has put resolve and courage into me. You, and your truckling submission! Why, I shall hear of you teaching in a Sunday school next. Perhaps you'd like Dennis to come and sit under you. I'll wring the weakness out of my heart as you wring the last drop of moisture from a wet cloth, and out of Dennis's heart I'll pluck the weeds of love and plant the flowers of hate there, thick as the spring daffodils on the hillside."

Colin broke off suddenly.

"Go away," he said, "while you have time. If you stop here you'll see something that will curl you up like Vincenzo. It won't be the face of God, but it will be something you can't bear. You're trembling in every limb now. By God, there'll be two inquests instead of one if you stop here! You're afraid of me, as you said, and that's very prudent of you."

How the power surged and foamed through him: it was like fire and wine in his veins, buoyant and intoxicating.

"I would kill you now," he said, "except for the fuss and bother that would involve me in. There's one mysterious death to be investigated already, and you may thank your luck that it is so.

It was true enough that Douglas had shrunk before him, holding up his arm as if to ward off some impending blow. But now he suddenly straightened himself up, as if new force had nerved him, and in the strength of that he stood steadfast and unafraid before the power that flickered in Colin's eyes.

"I was afraid of you," he said, "but it was my blindness that made me afraid. Now, *de profundis*, I call on God, Whom I have mocked at and defied, but in Whom you believe just as I do. I daresay you could kill my body, for that is mortal, it is weak with sin and defilement, but against me you are powerless as hate in the presence of love. You know that yourself. And one day you will be conquered and make your submission, too. You will go down into hell, as I have done, and find that God is there also."

He waited a moment watching, now without dismay, the furious impotence of the other's face. But no word came from Colin, and presently he moved to the door.

"Good-bye, Lord Yardley," he said. "And God will have mercy on your soul in spite of you."

Colin stood where he was, hearing Douglas's steps pass across the gallery and into the hall. His fingers still twitched with rage, he felt himself charged and crackling with the friendly power, and he had no doubt in his own soul that by the mere exercise of his will he could have brought to bear some disastrous force on the man who had just quitted him, that should exhibit itself in illness or misfortune, or in ways more swift and terrible. And yet though the mere opening of the sluice of pent-up evil would have done it, and though with every conscious fibre of him he hated and wished evil, he did not do it. For what might happen to Douglas was a side issue, not worth pursuing, and as regards the main issue, namely his soul's abhorrence of the power in Whose name Douglas had withstood him, he knew that he was defeated already. He had come up against something that did not fight him nor strive against him; it merely stood there, patient and pitiful, serenely existing.

He confessed defeat, but he did not acquiesce in it. Rather it stirred in him, as he had said to Douglas, a more determined antagonism, and took him farther than ever from any notion of submission. But Douglas was right in saying that there was a breach in his defences, and that in the breach stood Dennis, boyish and smiling and clad in that armour of love and innocence. Somehow he must be stripped of that, and wounded, and driven away from the crumbling wall of Colin's defences, else he would never be able to repair it. Of course the boy was not convent-bred, he was no pious barley-sugar little saint, but a high-spirited, vigorous fellow with a good leaven of mischief and boyish naughtiness, but that was nothing. His armoured innocence lay in his utter lack of the love of evil; when it came near him in the abstract, he choked and shuddered at it, instinctively recoiling. Dennis had no notion of hate, of the desire to hurt; the rudiments of cruelty, that bramble full of thorns and red fruit, which when it has taken root in the soul spreads over it quicker than any other lust, and chokes and stabs to death any growth that impedes it, had no existence in him. He liked enjoying himself, and there perhaps lay the seeds of selfishness, but selfishness was a negative quality, compared with the other.

And there, more impregnable yet, the very breastplate of Dennis's armour which covered his heart, was his propensity for love. Colin knew that, in these three weeks of his Easter holidays, he had made a sad mess in attempting to use that as a weapon in his own hand. He had thought that by making Dennis attached to himself he would be able to influence the boy to his own ends, and lay his soul open for the introduction of that which he intended to implant there. But a strangely miscalculated result had ensued. Easily, indeed, by the exercise of that charm which was his to command had he won the boy's heart, but, by some mischance of carelessness, he had let Dennis's love ooze into himself. That leak must be stopped up. As it was, his house of hate was not impervious to those soft April rains. Why was it, he wondered, that Dennis penetrated like this, whereas Violet, whose love for him still lived, could make no entrance? He could sit, so to speak, in the window and watch her streaming on the pane, and never a drop come in, but Dennis dripped from the roof, and entered through chink and cranny. Was it that with Violet's love there was mingled fear of him and horror, which cloyed its power of penetration, whereas Dennis was pure limpid water? Dennis had neither fear nor horror of him; he had clung to him in the midnight hour of his fear, as to a rock and a sure defence, unknowing that it was from there that he was assailed, and that he fled to him from whom he was fleeing. There was love in all its innocence, and its awful power.

Above all, then, he must kill Dennis's love for him. The weapon he had thought to forge out of that had only been turned against himself, and at the same time it was, in itself, Dennis's chief protection. Dennis loved no one, Colin was sure, as he loved him, and there was his cuirass of security, which must be hammered into fragments which should pierce and wound him, until he drew them out of his own breast, and cast them from him as poisoned things, which were the origin of all his woe.

"Yes, that damned Douglas was right," thought Colin, "and I'm grateful to him for warning me. I'll see to it."

He sat there a few moments longer, then ejected the topic from his mind altogether, and for distraction moved across to the window. The superb and luminous afternoon was already near its close, and the tide of clear shadow was creeping up the terrace. Below, the lake reflecting the sky was a mirror of steely blue: beyond, the plain was dim with the mists rising from its intersecting dykes. Its further edge and the line of the sea which bounded it had vanished altogether, for a sea fog hung over the Channel and was slowly drifting inland. Towards sunset in the chill of evening following on warm days like this, it often spread right across the plain, opaque and impenetrable, covering it completely, and, like a sea, lapped round the lower edges of the higher ground, turning its contours into bays and headlands. The hill of Rye rose above it like an island, and the tops of any tall trees in the plain would float like derelicts on its surface, but it submerged the featureless flat beyond, and till it dispersed again, with a rising wind or the warmth of dawn, it was bewildering and blinding, and a man caught by it unawares, where there was no path to guide him, might lose his bearings altogether, and wander half the night in aimless circles over pastures perfectly familiar to him. To-night, reinforced by the moisture rising from the dykes, the dense mist spread very rapidly and, even as Colin watched, the whole plain vanished before his eyes. From the sea, the foghorns were already hooting with hollow, long-drawn wails.

Colin turned from the window: the luminous west had grown pale, and this march of the shadows and the mists was rather a dreary spectacle. But within it was scarcely better. Two days ago at this time the house had been seething with life and the fancy-dress ball was yet to come. Then yesterday morning the guests had all gone, but there was still Dennis here, and what a festival they had made of his last day! Then had come that midnight catastrophe, of which the sequel had been the scene which he had just gone through, and the departure of Douglas: that was over, and there was no object to be served by brooding upon it. But above all it was the absence of Dennis that contributed to this mood of slack purposelessness, which was so unusual with him. Only this morning, as he trudged up the slope with the boy for the silly rabbit-shooting, he had, taking himself unawares, fancied that he could be content to expunge all that had given the zest and alacrity to life, and browse here animal-like, so long as he was at Stanier and Stanier was his. Here he was at Stanier, but for some reason mists, chilly and obliterating, had crept up round it, penetrating everywhere. Surely they had come before they were due?—it was not evening with him yet, but broad noon, and many years must pass before for him the sun set, and the frost of death came to him, and Dennis plucked the reins from his nerveless hands.

For a moment he let himself visualise what manner of impotence would be his at that hour. Just the power of hate would be left him, he thought, and even the red of that would be fading, like the sunset outside, into the grey encompassing mists, but surely as long as one touch of colour remained there he would be hating the very existence of Stanier because it was his no longer but Dennis's, and hating Dennis for the dawning pride of his ownership. How would he long then to summon some cataclysmic force which would annihilate heritage and heritor alike! What worse torment could there be for those uncharted æons that should follow, than to be condemned to exist, unseen and unheard here where he stood now, and be actively aware of Dennis in possession with sons growing up who would inherit after him, while he himself drifted impalpably about, surrounded by the warmth of life which yet could not thaw that ice-cold bubble that contained his consciousness? He must school himself to think of Dennis enjoying all that had been torn from him. Already Dennis was his potential foe, his supplanter. . . .

It was time to eject these comfortless imaginings: all that

he need retain of them was this new conception of Dennis, for that surely might prove an antidote to affection—and he went out of his room into the long gallery, where Violet, all alone, was seated at her tea-table. She put down the book she was reading as he sauntered up.

"Anyone dining to-night?" he said. "Or are you and Granny and I going to spend a quiet evening of domestic bliss?"

She poured him out his cup of tea.

"We shall be alone as far as I know," she said. "Would you like to ask Mr. Douglas?"

Colin paused: that subject was one of those he had meant to put away from him. But she should have it if she liked.

"Douglas has gone," he observed.

"Gone?" asked she.

"Yes, I said 'gone,' didn't I?" said Colin. "To spare you any more questions I don't know where he's gone, because he didn't tell me. Sometimes I thought he would be rather a good tutor for Dennis in his holidays a little later on."

He just glanced at Violet and saw she had understood.

"But that's all over now," he continued. "I shall have to conduct Dennis's holiday education myself. . . . Yes, the atmosphere of Stanier didn't suit Douglas. He was impolite enough to say that it was saturated with me and that he couldn't bear it for a moment longer. You're delighted I suppose, aren't you?"

"I saw very little of him," said Violet. "As you know, I didn't like him."

"How very unchristian of you. What was the fault you found with him?"

"I don't think we need go into that," said she.

"How reticent you are, darling," he said. "Sad, isn't it, that there's so little mutual confidence and trust between us. I wonder if you're glad that Vincenzo has gone, too. Would you feel inclined to come to the inquest with me, and say that Vincenzo was a lovable, God-fearing fellow who had nothing on his mind, no fears, no worries?"

She looked at him with a sudden spasm of alarm.

"Colin, what do you mean?" she said. "He didn't kill himself?"

He liked producing that look of terror in her eyes: he liked playing with her fears.

"Of course I haven't told you what really happened," he said, "for as you know, I am always considerate and should hate to shock you. Perhaps I will tell you some time. But suicide, no, it wasn't suicide. There's a little puzzle for you, Violet, to occupy your leisure, now that the duties of a hostess no longer take all your time. Vincenzo dies very suddenly one night, and Douglas finds he can't breathe the same atmosphere as me next day. . . . Ah, I guess what you're conjecturing, but it's wrong. I wasn't the cause, directly or indirectly, of Vincenzo's death. What a mind you've got, darling, to let that suspicion ever peep into it!"

Colin spoke with a soft deliberation: he was like a great purring cat with a mouse between his paws.

"You did think that, you know," he said, "just as you still think that I had, well, let's say the tip of a finger in poor Pamela's death. Altogether, I feel rather lonely and deserted this afternoon. Here are you, with dark suspicions about me, and then my old friend Douglas has gone, and my old servant (he was a friend, too) Vincenzo has gone, and then Dennis has gone, and all within twenty-four hours."

He put down his cup and sat down on the rug by her feet, clasping his knees.

"And I find so little sympathy," he said. "I believe you're not sorry that Douglas and Vincenzo have gone, and I wonder, I really do wonder, whether you're sorry that Dennis has gone."

There was a fiendish ingenuity, Violet suspected, at the bottom of this question. How well he divined her mind! How like him, as if he was some deft conjurer, to guess what was in it!

"Why, I miss Dennis most awfully," she said. "The house seems dead without him."

Colin smiled.

"Yes, very pretty and Madonna-like," he said. "But that wasn't what I asked you. I asked you if you were sorry Dennis had gone. That's a direct question enough: can't you answer it directly?"

She rose with all her nerves on edge. But that would never do. If she was to reach Colin at all, with the love that was the only efficient power she had, she must eradicate her fear of him, brushing aside all that she shuddered at, for that, cramped and clogged her movement towards him.

"The question is direct enough," she said, "but I can't give you a direct answer. You've made the boy devoted to you, that's beyond question, and sometimes I've been afraid, and wished he was not here. But then I've wondered whether I haven't misjudged you altogether. Dennis is just as sweet and innocent as he has always been. And then I've asked myself whether you haven't begun to love him. . . . Oh, Colin, if that's only so! You know I would give my life for that."

Colin jumped to his feet.

"If you think I'm going to listen to your damned sentimental maunderings," he said, "you're awfully mistaken. Dennis is devoted to me, that is perfectly true. I effected that for two reasons. One, which concerns you, was in order to cut you out, dear Violet. I've done that, and I've seen how you've writhed with jealousy once or twice under the knowledge. The second reason was more important. I made Dennis love me, in order that I might have unbounded influence over him, for, as you've often told me, love is infinite in power. No wonder you were afraid; but, as a matter of fact, I haven't used that influence over him, in the way that you expected. And now (perhaps this will be a relief to you) I'm going to change my tactics. I don't like love you know; I'm going to make Dennis sorry he loved me. He hasn't yet seen me with any—shall we call it with any clarity of vision? So important for a boy to form habits of accurate observation! He must get to dislike love, too, because it wounds him and makes him bleed."

There spoke the very spirit and essence of wickedness, and yet Violet felt that it struggled for utterance, fighting its way to his lips. His purpose was plain, but there was something which contested it, an impediment that threatened its free exercise. He, so she guessed, was aware of it too, for though he had never been in more deadly and bitter a mood, never swifter with those characteristic gibes that pierced and stung, she felt that there was an effort about them, as if the bow that shot them had to be strung again and again instead of being always ready. In superficial and trivial ways also, in the days that followed, that struggle, whatever it was, seemed to manifest itself in strange little indecisions which irritated him and made him unlike himself. One day, for instance, he would tell her that connubial solitude, with an immortal grandmother thrown in, was too delicate a form of happiness and that he would go up to London that afternoon, and an hour later he would have changed his mind, and told her to ask down a party for the week-end. Then, before she had done that, he would change his mind again, and say that he wanted nobody, and spent the day rambling about the park, or, in this hot spell of May weather, bathing and basking by the lake. Another day he started off to drive to Eton and see Dennis, to whom he had promised an early visit, but when that evening she asked him how Dennis was, he told her he had not been there.

They were at dinner, just the three of them, when he rapped this out at her, and it roused in old Lady Yardley some dim, disordered train of thought, for she began to speak in that level monotone which came out of her twilight mists.

"Yes, much wiser, much wiser," she said. "Let there be no force, not even persuasion. Let him come to it naturally: it is bred in the bone. Do not make him drink of the spring: he will be thirsty some day, and then he will go to it."

Colin turned sharply round.

"Go to what, Granny?" he said. "What do you mean? What are you talking about?"

"Aha, I am talking of what I know and what you know. We talk in parables that are plain to us. He knew, too—that man who never comes here now. Yes, and yet another. They have both gone. Only Colin and I are left now, and the chapel is empty."

She stopped as suddenly as she had begun, and rose, leaning on her sticks.

But all through these days, while spring every hour was weaving fresh embroideries, some black pattern was being worked, stitch by stitch, so Violet felt, into Colin's heart. Sometimes the needle was nimbly plied, and then, despite herself, she shuddered at the depths that lay beneath the bright surface of his gaiety, for it was when some black business within went well that his mood was sunniest. Such was the case when he came back from the inquest held on the body of Vincenzo. "There was an autopsy," he told her, "and though they rummaged about, so Dr. Martin told me, with great thoroughness, they could find no cause of death whatever. Visitation of God, that was all they could make of it, and I daresay they were quite right. He was like Enoch, apparently: he was translated. I wonder how Vincenzo would bear translation. I wonder what he was translated into."

It was difficult not to shudder at that.

"Colin, don't talk like that," she said. "You're terrible."

"Terrible? Why? I didn't translate him. And then I gave my evidence, and we were all very polite and complimentary, and bowed at each other with respectful and mournful little smiles. I told them just what I told you, and they all agreed I had acted with great wisdom and prudence. That was quite true: they had no idea how true that was; and then we all bowed again like—like a minuet. By the way, have you made anything of that little puzzle I set you about the departure of Douglas following so closely on the death of Vincenzo, and the reason he gave for it?"

Violet made no reply.

"Your manners are getting very bad, darling," said Colin. "I asked you a civil enough question. Now, here's another queer thing. Both the doctor and his assistant noticed a very curious smell about the frail earthly tabernacle of poor Vincenzo. What do you think that was? You'll never guess, so I'll tell you. There was a strong odour of incense. Now where can that have come from? I could throw no light on it. Can you?"

She got up.

"Colin, supposing I told them there was more about Vincenzo's death than they know?" she said.

"Ah! That's a great idea. What fun! Write an anonymous etter to the coroner. And what will you say it was that they don't know? . . . I thought that information about the incense might interest you. Consider it in connection with the puzzle."

Another day, it seemed as if things did not go well with the black embroidery, for he was savage and silent. Then it was she guessed that something was struggling with him for its existence, and that he stabbed at it, and tried to strangle it. Yet such days, lashed by blasts of his bitter tongue, were more welcome to her than those on which he was smiling and content and in harmony with himself.

As these weeks of May went by, Violet saw more and more clearly that she had no significance for him at all, and it was just that which gave the days their unspeakable tension. Sometimes she was the butt of his irony, sometimes he completely disregarded her, but, whichever it was, he was not concerned with her. She was just the traditional Stanier wife, whose duty it was to provide an heir; after that she might freeze. He knew she loved him, he knew she feared him, and he was quite indifferent to both. It was Dennis round whom all his thoughts and all this strange hidden contest centred, and unerringly she knew who were the combatants now beginning to come into touch with each other. On the one side was all that the legend stood for, the love of hate, and the hate of love. Colin, all his life, had been an apt pupil in that deadly school: perhaps no such scholar as he had ever graduated there. Already he had tried to use love as an instrument of corruption, and he had failed and changed his plan. Now, he was out to kill love, and in command of the black panoply he was arraying himself to fight against a young boy who stood there unaware that there was anyone but the father he adored coming to meet him. He had no defence except love . . . and yet was there a traitor in the very heart of his foes?

And she had to stand aside and watch. Of what use was it to warn Dennis? What form could that warning take? All he knew was that it was his father coming to him. If she could somehow throw herself between them, Colin would pass on over her, indifferent, scarcely even aware of her. One thing only perhaps she could do, and that was to stamp out her fear of him, for the only effect of fear was to paralyse. . . .

Thus, then, dimly and mistily, was the new situation forming. But it would not present itself like that: it would take shape, when Dennis was home again, in daily domestic ways, in ways cunning and cruel, in ways perhaps affectionate and winning. But they would all contribute to the end in view.

CHAPTER V

The Eton term came to an end in the last week of July, and Dennis found that, by leaving at some timeless hour, he could get down to Stanier by the middle of the morning. The idea was irresistible, for there would be time to have an hour or so bathing with his father before lunch, and keep the afternoon intact, and so, though the original plan had been to lunch with Aunt Hester, and, tipped and gorged, go on to Stanier afterwards, he telegraphed to her that he 'had to' go straight home, and sent a second telegram to his father to say that he would arrive at Rye at half-past eleven. He knew that Colin was there, for his mother had written to him a day or two before to say they had left London and were at Stanier.

The heat of the day promised well for the pleasure of diversions such as bathing, and the addition of excited anticipation made Dennis strip off his coat, when he had got into his train from London, and turn up his shirt sleeves to the elbow. These long summer holidays, with an extra week at the end in honour of a certain Royal visit to the school, contained an eternity of joys: not only was there Stanier to look forward to, but that visit to Capri with his father, which had been promised him. As the train neared Rye he hung out of the window to catch the first sight of the house glowing among its woods. There was just a glimpse of it, with its flag flying on the tower, and then the trees hid it again, and he must bounce across to the other side of the carriage to see his father standing on the platform, and wave to him. He would be there to meet him as certainly as Stanier was waiting for him on the hill.

The platform was rather full, and Dennis was still searching for Colin when the train drew up. He descended with arms full of agreeable impedimenta and then the very natural explanation of Colin's absence occurred to him: without doubt he had driven down in the little two-seater, and was waiting for him outside. He went through the gate of egress, but in the station yard there was no two-seater, nor any other conveyance from Stanier. Again an explanation was easy: his telegram had not yet been delivered. This was not quite the ecstasy of arrival that he had anticipated, but it was entirely his own fault.

The cab laboured up the long hill and jogged very sedately along the level up to the lodge-gate. At this rate he could traverse the short cut on foot more quickly than this deliberate quadruped would make the detour. Getting out at the lodge he struck across its park, arriving at the house before the cab came within sight. He ran through the hall and burst into his father's room. But the room was empty.

There was his mother, anyhow, in a shady corner of the garden below the terrace, and he hailed her, and next moment was running down the steps and leaping the flower-beds. She rose to meet him, and caught him to her, close and clinging.

"Dennis, darling," she said. "This is lovely. And, oh, my dear, what a heat you're in!"

"I know: I ran across the park and got here before the old cab. And where's Father?"

"He started an hour ago to drive up to London."

"Oh, how rotten! I think that's beastly of him. And didn't he get my telegram to say I was coming this morning?"

Violet hesitated.

"Yes, dear, he did get it," she said. "He thought that, having said you would come in the afternoon, you ought to have kept to your first plan."

Dennis looked impartially at this verdict.

"I suppose I ought," he said. "But as I found I could get here earlier, of course I did. And so he scored off me by making me come up in a cab, and going away himself. When will he be back?"

"Some time to-day. Late perhaps, he thought."

Dennis's sun was very certainly clouded, but sufficient brightness remained to illuminate a pleasant day. There was a bathe before lunch, and Violet took him to play golf, after a slight demur over the chance of his father arriving during their absence, and there was tea on the terrace, and a stroll through the woods with his gun. All these things had been rapturous in anticipation, and though nothing could quite rob them of their honey, it was not of that transcendent order. . . . Well did Violet understand that, and well she understood why Colin had suddenly settled to go up to town that day. Then came dinner, where his place but laid was unoccupied, and old Lady Yardley groping in the twilight which was darkening round her, now thinking that this was Colin back from school, now asking where Colin was.

But still he did not come, and about eleven Dennis, visibly perturbed and depressed, and his mother went up to bed.

"And you're sure he hasn't had an accident?" he asked.

"Yes, darling, quite sure. You mustn't think of that."

A bright idea struck Dennis.

"Oh, Mother, somebody must sit up for him to let him in," he said. "Mayn't I?"

"No, dear. I know he wouldn't wish you to. Go to bed, darling, and get a long night. You were up early enough to-day."

Dennis sighed.

"Well, I've had a ripping day with you, anyhow," he said.

Dennis's room looked out on to the front of the house, and before he got into bed he set his door ajar, and the window wide, so that by no chance could he miss the sound of his father's arrival, and, without turning off his light, sat propped up in bed, prepared for any length of vigil, for, in spite of the day-long disappointments, he was sure that Colin would look in on him when he came, and it would never do to miss that conference. There were millions of things to tell and be told, but better than any would be the fact of his father's presence sitting here on his bed, and after ever so long a talk wishing him good night and leaving him to fall asleep with the sense of him still lingering in the room.

It was not long before he heard the crunch of the gravel beneath the wheels of the motor, and he jumped out of bed to look out of the window and call to him. But they had been equally quick in letting him in, and Dennis had no more than a glimpse of him standing in the oblong of light from the open door, before it closed again behind him. But that was of no consequence: he would be here immediately, and Dennis leaped back into bed.

The minutes passed, but very likely Colin would want something to eat after his drive from London, before he came upstairs. Soon there came along the passage a step that Dennis knew, and his eyes, sparkling with the imminent joy, were fixed on his door, to see it swing open. But the steps stopped short before they reached it, and another door a little way down the passage was opened and closed.

"I suppose he thought it was very late, and that I should be asleep," said Dennis to himself as he put out his light.

He slept late next morning and hurried downstairs to breakfast. His father, dressed in flannels with his hair still wet from his bathe, was standing by the window, opening his letters.

"Oh, there you are at last," said Dennis, springing to him. Colin gave him a rather absent hand.

"Hullo, Dennis," he said.

"Hullo, Father. I say, how late you were last night, and you never came to see me."

"No. I managed to curb my impatience till this morning," said Colin.

"O-oh! Sarcasm! And have you been bathing? Why didn't you fetch me?"

"I didn't imagine you had forgotten your way down to the lake, if you wanted to bathe."

Dennis gave him one quick anxious glance. There was something wrong: perhaps the business in London yesterday had worried him, or perhaps his father was vexed with him, though it seemed very inexplicable, about that matter of the train yesterday.

"I'm sorry about my coming in the morning yesterday," he said, "after I had told you the afternoon. But I thought it would be so ripping to get here before lunch."

"Oh yes: that's all right," said Colin absently.

At this moment Violet came in, and Colin's manner instantly changed.

"Ah, Vi, darling," he said. "There you are! I got back very late last night, for I thought I would dine with Aunt Hester. She was quite delightful: also quite astounding. About eleven she went off to a dance in a short pink dress and a wreath of flowers. She promised to come down here to-day, and stop till I go to Capri."

Dennis pricked an ear at this.

"Oh, when will that be, Father?" he said.

"One of these days. . . . And then, if she likes, and you don't mind, darling, she can stop on here, though I really believe she would like best to come to Capri, and disport herself like a small, imperishable, highly-coloured sea-nymph. How she would astonish the islanders!"

Dennis gave a cackle of laughter at this picture. Best of all was the gay good humour in his father's voice. Colin turned to him.

"Dennis, she told me that you had promised to lunch with her yesterday," he said, "and that you sent a telegram saying you had to get down here. There was no compulsion on you to get down here that I'm aware of."

"Oh, but I wanted to get down here so frightfully," said Dennis.

"I see: anything you want frightfully has to happen," said Colin, "and I suppose anything you want not to happen, isn't allowed to. But in spite of that, next time you say you'll go to see Aunt Hester and then throw her over at the last minute, it's just conceivable that something may happen which you don't like. Go and put your mother's plate down for her."

This was all bewildering, but Dennis did as he was told, and having finished his breakfast came and stood by his father's chair.

"Well, what do you want?" asked Colin sharply.

Dennis flushed.

"Oh, nothing," he said.

"Don't hang about then. You can go if you've finished your breakfast."

Dennis had a spirit of his own, and one thing was perfectly clear to him as he left the room, namely, that if his father did not want to be bothered with him, he was not going to make any importunate requests for his companionship. It was a horrid state of things, but no doubt temporary: he could parallel it by the bleakness which sometimes fell upon his house-master at school, for no apparent reason. This paternal bleakness, unknown in those last glorious Easter holidays, was of course far more depressing, for it took all the colour out of life. He was absolutely ignorant what cause of offence he had given; throwing over Aunt Hester and coming by another train were clearly inadequate as the reason for it, and all he could do, while it lasted. was to be prompt and obedient, and above everything to spring to him, whenever his sun should shine out again, without any shadow of resentment or reserve. This treatment was wounding and inexplicable, but he must keep his hurt to himself, and most certainly he must not go to his mother with querulous wonder as to what it was about. It concerned his father and himself, and nobody else: it would be disloyal to his unshaken allegiance to make moan.

Dennis had ample opportunity for loyalty in the next few days, for he could do nothing right in his father's eyes. He scarcely saw him or had speech with him except at meals, and then, if he talked he was told not to jabber, if he was silent he was asked why he was so sulky. It was a heart-rending and inexplicable affair, and all the more puzzling because except with him Colin was in his gayest and most entrancing mood. Aunt Hester, who apparently had not in the least minded Dennis's conduct, received the most delightful welcome for an indefinite period, and Colin chaffed her and made much of her, till she beamed again. With Violet he was the same; only Dennis had the power to check his geniality and cause him to rap out a reprimand of some kind. In the evening the four of them, with old Lady Yardley, played their whist, and he was left to amuse himself as he best could. Even then he could not escape censure. If he watched them, a dreary enough occupation, he was asked why he didn't get a book and read a bit after his day of enjoyment: if he read it was supposed that whist was too old-fashioned for the young generation to interest themselves in. Once Aunt Hester intervened.

"Let him read or look on as he likes, dear," she said to Colin. "He can please himself, surely."

On that occasion only Colin was sharp with her.

"Dear Aunt Hester," he said, "perhaps you'd mind your own business. We're waiting for you to play."

And then, after the dismal whist, there was the dismal going up to his room, with the knowledge that the door would not open, nor his father look in and sit on his bed, and make delightful plans for the next day.

A darker phase succeeded.

In the following week an Eton friend came to stay, and now at least there was someone to play with. Jim Airedale was an engaging and good-looking boy, devoted to Dennis, and even in this eclipse, the two of them, with all the resources of Stanier to choose from, might entertain themselves with considerable enjoyment. But all went more grievously for Dennis than ever. Colin appeared to take a great fancy to his friend, and at dinner, on the day of his arrival, talked to him delightfully, with occasional interspersions of snubs for Dennis. No one—as Dennis was bitterly aware—knew so well the road to a boy's heart; he made Jim at ease in a couple of minutes, set him chattering in a couple more, and it was a hilarious meal that followed. After dinner he set Dennis down to play that weary whist, and took the other boy off to play billiards. When the whist was over, Dennis joined them and marked for them. Then at bedtime Colin took Jim up to his room, to see that everything was comfortable, and lingered there talking, while next door Dennis, half-undressed, sat on his bed, waiting for those merry sounds to cease. When all was quiet, he slipped out of his room to have a few words with Jim, and perhaps Colin was waiting for that, for as he passed his door, it opened quietly and there his father stood.

"Hullo, where are you going?" he asked.

Something in Dennis seemed to strain almost to breaking-point at the cold hostility of his tone.

"I'm just going to see Jim," he said.

"Well, then, you had better just go back to your room again," said Colin.

Next morning he took Jim off in the two-seater to play golf—Dennis would lend him his clubs—and they came back late for lunch, better friends than ever. Afterwards there was some rabbit-potting, at which Jim excelled, and Colin found occasion to say to Dennis, "I wonder if you'll ever learn to shoot like that." And there were dreadful games of lawn tennis, in which Colin, saying that he was the worst player of the four, must play with Jim, against Violet and Dennis. He really was the best, so of course they won. All this was sufficient to turn the boy's head, and Jim became slightly condescending to his friend. But when he said to Dennis:

"I say, you're father's pretty rough on you sometimes," with the intention of being consolatory and friendly, he found he had strangely miscalculated. Up went Dennis's chin.

"Rough on me?" he said. "What on earth do you mean? He's perfectly ripping to me."

Finally, on the last evening of that nightmare week, Colin made it impossible for Jim, after a decent allowance of champagne at dinner, to refuse a couple of glasses of port. He became rather tipsy, and when, with a rolling eye and a menacing sense of rising nausea, he hurried away to his room, Colin watched him go with a shrug of the shoulders. "Nice sort of friends you bring to the house, Dennis," he said. That seemed to round off the visit very pleasantly.

Colin was sitting up alone that night after the others had gone upstairs. He had been more brutal than usual with Dennis at dinner, and for the first time he had seen Dennis bite his lip, obviously to keep tears back. . . . But, in spite of all his pitiless persecution, he knew that he was no nearer to the attainment of his purpose. As far as Dennis himself was concerned, he had systematically and continuously hurt and wounded him in that attempt to which he was committed, to kill his love, but no failure could at present have been more complete. Often when the whip of his tongue had been cruellest, and his cunning to hurt most diabolical, he had looked at Dennis saying, "Well, answer me, can't you?" and Dennis had raised to him troubled and bewildered eyes in which no spark of hate smouldered. There was no meekness about Dennis; he could answer back with his head up, quite unsubdued and unafraid, but in vain Colin looked for any sign that his love was ailing or like to die. And occasionally when he relaxed, and gave him a kind word, love leaped sparkling to his eyes and his beautiful mouth. What confirmed this impression was the pride of the boy, for he never, as Colin knew, uttered to his mother a single word of complaint, or went to her for comfort. Little as Colin knew of love, he knew that here was the noble pride of love, which would never admit failing or blemish in the object of its high affection.

Colin opened the door on to the terrace and strolled out into the warm pregnant night There was something more indicative of failure than this impregnable loyalty of Dennis's, and that was his own unchanged affection for the boy. In every possible way that could be devised by his alert perceptive brain, he had wounded and injured Dennis's heart, and though there is no such royal road towards hate as to injure, he had made no headway at all. His devotion to hatred, his vow to himself, so faithfully kept, to all that was evil, had often made him bubble with secret glee to see Dennis wince under those barbed attacks, but all the time there existed that soft aching tenderness for him, so easy to stifle but so impossible to smother. Like eternity, as he had sneered to Douglas, it seemed of very durable stuff. All this fortnight's persecution had done nothing to break it up. Uninvited, it had entered his heart, and nothing could stir it. He could act as if he had no other feeling for the boy than this contemptuous aversion, but something ached. . . .

The night-breeze drew landward from the sea and sometimes it fell altogether, and there was dead calm, and again he heard its whispered approach in the trees by the lake, and presently it flowed over the garden and streamed on to the terrace. He tried, as he so often had done, to lay himself open to the spell that had woven the prosperity of Stanier; he thought of Dennis heir to all its glories and possessor of them when he had gone from this world, and at that the flicker of jealousy, a strange offspring of love and hate, shot up in his heart. But supposing Dennis died before he did. . . . Would he sooner see him lying dead, and know that he, at any rate, would never succeed to Stanier and its magnificence, or when death drew near to himself, see Dennis by his bedside, and picture him assuming what was his to enjoy no longer? On his deathbed surely he would entirely hate Dennis, and wish that he lay there in his stead.

At the end of the long façade there stood the chapel unused since Douglas's departure, and Colin going back into his room let himself into the corridor which led to it, turning up the lights as he went. He had not been there since the night of Vincenzo's death, and now it seemed to him that if he sat and meditated there, where so often he had made the consecration of himself to evil, he could arrive at some clearer and conscious realization of it. He told himself that he hated love, and delighted in hate, but no fervour warmed his creed. In that sanctuary of Satan the truth of that might shine more vividly on him, and he might get rid of that fancy that Dennis's eyes, eager and ready to kindle; or sad but without reproach, were watching him. Surely they would not follow him where Dennis had never been.

Colin sat quiet in his place looking at the altar. The faint odour of incense still hung about, but emotionally the place was dead. He thought of Vincenzo twitching and grinning as he knelt: he thought of Douglas, lifting high the consecrated elements, so soon to be a mockery and a derision, but his mind gave no welcome or greeting to the remembrance. . . .

Well, his deeds must atone for his lack of fervour, and presently he rose and went back through the silent house, and upstairs along the dim-lit passage.

Suddenly the desire came to him just to look at Dennis. The boy would certainly be asleep by now, for he must have learned that it was not much good to keep awake, on the chance of his father coming in to say good night. He would just open the door, turn on the light for a second and look at him and leave him. He told himself he wanted to remind himself that the boy would inherit all that he now loved and enjoyed; what he concealed from himself, stuffing it away out of sight, was that some human craving hungered for the sight of him. Dennis would be asleep; he would get no pleasure from what he did not know.

Colin opened the door quietly, and saw the room was light, and there was Dennis sitting up in bed. His face was bright with the unexpected surprise: and he stretched out his arms. There was something appealing and timid in the gesture.

"Oh, Father, how ripping!" he said.

Colin was helpless in the grip of that welcome. He tried to frame his tongue to some chilling reprimand, but none came.

"Dennis! Not asleep yet? And your light on? What does it mean?" he asked.

The boy broke out into a little bubble of a laugh.

"Why, I always keep it on till I hear you go to your room," he said.

"Why?" asked Colin.

"Of course on the chance that you'd come in, as you always used to do. I knew you would some time. Jolly glad I kept it on. Oh, come and sit down."

Against his will and his purpose Colin came up to the bed. Dennis wriggled aside to make room for him, and put up his knees for him to lean against.

"I can't stop," said Colin, sitting down. "It's fearfully late and you're a villain for being awake."

"All right: I'm a villain," said Dennis.

"And you wait for me every night?" asked Colin.

Dennis nodded. Just then he could not trust himself to speak, but his shining eyes spoke for him.

"What shall we talk about," asked Colin, "just for a minute?"

"Oh anything: it doesn't matter a bit, as long as it's you."

At that moment Colin was happy. But he had hardly realized that, before, just as he had heard the night-wind coming up and whispering in the trees by the lake, he knew that there was approaching the blast of hate and evil which he had tried to conjure up in the chapel. He leant towards Dennis, put his arm round his neck and kissed him.

"Good night, old boy," he said. "I won't stop now. Sleep well."

"Ever so well," said Dennis.

Colin clicked out the light, and went to his room. Already his brain seethed with images of evil, vivid and alluring, and fierce at this treason of his. They swarmed like a loyal garrison to that breach in his defences where Dennis had stood, and drove him off. They urged Colin to pursue, to go back to the boy's room, to let loose on him their assault, to defile and desecrate his innocence, to show him the ecstasy of evil, the charm of cruelty. What matter if panic or horror made nightmare round him? He would wake from them with new currents coursing in his veins, new desires stinging him to their fulfilment. Where was the good of his being heir to the legend if he did not enter into his birthright?

Fierce was the stress of that possession. Colin withstood it, feeling that if he yielded the very bonds of sanity would be loosed. If he went back to Dennis's room now, he would go as a devil unchained, ready and eager to perpetrate any spiritual outrage and desecration, and who knew whether the very balance and poise of Dennis's being, whom he had just left with all his serenity restored and the lamp of love bravely burning, might not be upset altogether? Already he was scarcely in his own control, and, maddened to an invincible lust of evil by the sight of that tender victim, he might let himself cross the boundary which separates the territories of human life from the untamed welter and chaos of prodigious forces which both threaten and maintain it. He had served Satan all his life alike in spirit and in works, and would serve him still, but while this stress, which seemed like some dervish possession, was on him, he could not trust himself with Dennis. Something of irremediable violence might happen, some fatal laceration of the fibres of the boy's soul.

The crisis passed, leaving him conscious only of immense fatigue. There had been a struggle, not between himself alone and this Satanic power, but between it and something in himself, but not of himself, which opposed it. He was too tired to think any more, and, throwing off his clothes, sank into the dark of dreamless sleep.

He slept late, and waking brought with it a certain incredulousness at his memory of the night before; what had happened seemed buried, at any rate, under deep layers of consciousness, so that he could not handle and examine it. Much more accessible was the memory of his weakness in going in to Dennis at all. Whatever fruits might have ripened from this fortnight's harshness to the boy, were certainly frost-bitten now, for Dennis knew, and hugged himself to know, that below these bleak cruelties the father he loved existed still. It was a foolish thing to have done, not only for that reason, but because he had weakened himself in allowing that spasm of affection to assert itself. But it is never too late, he thought, to mend foolishness by wise courses.

Dennis had finished breakfast when he got down, and he heard from Violet that he had gone for a morning in the water, leaving an urgent message for his father to follow.

"And the boy's radiant this morning," she said. "He told me you came into his room last night and were 'ripping,' so he said."

Colin was busy at the side table.

"Oh! What else did he say?" he asked.

"Just that. I am glad you did it. That couple of minutes made him forget all the woes of these holidays."

"Ah! He's forgotten about them, has he?" said Colin.

"Absolutely; they've vanished. Oh yes, he wondered if I knew when you and he were going to Capri. I said you hadn't told me."

"I shall go to-morrow. But how it concerns Dennis, I don't know, unless, as is highly probable, he's glad to get rid of me."

"But aren't you taking him?" asked Violet. "You promised to take him."

"Did I? Well, now I promise you not to. Entirely for your sake, of course, darling. You'll love having him here to yourself. You'll be able to make up lost ground. Now I don't want to hear anything more about Capri. I'll tell Dennis myself. Why should I drag a brat like that about with me?"

Before long Colin strolled down to the lake. There was Dennis's yellow head far out on the water, and his browned arms, glistening with wet, lifting themselves alternately as he surged back to the shed. By the time Colin had come to the smooth turf that margined the lake, he had got to land, and stood knee-deep in the shallow water, slim and shining with an April-face of happiness. He gave a great whoop of welcome when he saw his father.

"Hurrah, Father!" he said. "You have been quick. The water's lovely; let's bathe and lie about all morning. Oh, I say, I was diving just now, and found an awfully funny thing in the mud at the bottom. Looks as if it was lace of sorts. Catch!"

Dennis picked up a sodden grey ball which he had put on the bank and threw it at his father. At the moment Colin's attention was attracted by some water-fowl swimming at the far end of the lake, and Dennis's missile, wet and muddy, hit him full in the face.

"Oh, I'm sorry," said Dennis. "I thought you were looking."

The missile had fallen at Colin's feet, and he saw at once that it must be the lace cotta which had been torn off Vincenzo's body.

At the sight a horde of recollections drove in upon him; once more Vincenzo twitched and grinned, and the incense smoked. Those instincts of hate and cruelty which had dozed last night in the chapel, leaped up, bright-eyed and snarling. Then, too, this recovered relic had splashed him, the mud slimy and evil-smelling had dropped on to his white coat.

"Dennis, you're a damned nuisance," he said. "I'll teach you to behave. What the devil do you mean by doing that?"

He plucked two lithe shoots of willow from a tree that grew by the water's edge and stripped off the leaves.

"Come out," he said, "and stand here with your back to me."

Dennis looked at his father, and saw blind rage and fury in his face, as he peeled the willow wands.

"I'm awfully sorry, Father," he said.

"You'll be sorrier in a minute. Come here. I'm going to give you six of the smartest cuts you've ever had. It hurts more when you're wet."

Dennis stepped out of the water, and stood where his father pointed, and four strokes, savagely delivered, fell across his shoulders. He stood perfectly steady, gasping a little at the burning sting of them. As Colin slashed at him, he felt an exultant glee that at last he was hurting him to some purpose. He had spoiled the effect of his fortnight's cruelty by that concession last night: this should start him afresh, with no apostasy to follow. He saw the red criss-cross of the strokes and the weals rising on the boy's skin with some such ecstasy of satisfaction as he had seen Pamela standing in his room one night at Capri. And then in the middle of this chastisement he knew he could not strike Dennis again.

"That will do," he said. "Turn round."

Dennis turned and looked him straight in the eyes. In spite of the sharpness of the pain his face was in perfect control, his mouth was just a little compressed. And once more Colin knew that he had failed, for he saw there pain and bewilderment, mute reproach, but of fear not a trace nor yet of hate. With regard to himself he had failed also, for he had been literally unable to finish the punishment he had promised, and now he wanted to put his arm round Dennis's neck, and kiss him, and tell him that he knew what a devil he was, and beg the boy's forgiveness. . . .

The very consciousness of that failure made him rage again.

"Well, did you like that?" he said. "It hurt, I expect."

"Yes," said Dennis.

"Why don't you cry then?" asked Colin.

"I don't choose to."

Colin sat down on the grass and lit a cigarette.

"Well, there's another pleasure in store for you," he said. "I'm going to Capri to-morrow, and your mother says you think you're coming with me. That's an error on your part—that's all."

"Yes," said Dennis again. He walked to where his clothes lay on a bench and began dressing.

"Aren't you going on with your bathe?" asked Colin. "It will take the sting out."

"No, Father, I've finished," said Dennis.

Colin began taking his clothes off.

"Going to sulk, I suppose," he said. "But please yourself."

Smarting of skin, but far sorer at heart, Dennis walked quietly off when he had dressed, and skirting the lake went up along the bracken-covered slopes of the park that looked out over the marsh. He longed to confide in his mother, and ask if she could account in any way for this Pentecost of trouble which the holidays had brought, and which had culminated in this thrashing, but in spite of the comfort she might have brought from the mere knowledge of her sympathy, he could not tell her of that, not because it was a humiliation to him, but because it was a disgrace to his father, and that must never be known to her. The offence which provoked it was no cause at all; in the Easter holidays he might have done that until seventy times seven, and his father would only have laughed, and called him a little devil, and thrown the missile back at him. And the same policy of repression must be preserved about his other woes. In whatever manner his father treated him, that was an affair that concerned themselves alone: mere manliness forbade him to go whimpering to anybody, and more stringent yet was the prohibition that his own love for his father enjoined on him. It was impossible to complain: he had got to shoulder his own burden whatever injustice and harshness had laid it on him.

He waded through the waist-high bracken with the scuttle of rabbits about him. There were patches of bare turf between the clumps of fern; it was great sport to walk through the bracken with a gun, and get a pot-shot at a rabbit that bolted across these clearings. Often had he done that with his father, but to-day he had not the least inclination to fetch his gun. He wanted only, since speaking to his mother was out of the question, to be alone, and stare this intolerable state of affairs in the face, and he sat down in one of these open spaces, with the aromatic smell of the woodland round him, and tried to focus it. He smarted with the blows he had received and with the utter injustice of them, but most of all his heart cried out against the virulent glee in his father's face, when he told him to turn round again and asked him how he enjoyed it. If only he was like some other fellows at school who either disliked or just put up with their fathers, he would merely have been angry at this abominable treatment, and delighted that the beastly man was taking himself off to-morrow. But Dennis felt none of these natural sentiments; in spite of these harshnesses he would rapturously have gone with his father to Capri, if that had been allowed, unshaken in the faith (which for a minute or two last night had been so joyfully justified) that to-day or to-morrow his father would turn to him again, and be 'ripping' as no one else in the world could be. But his father—and what had he himself done to evoke this desolating displeasure?—had altogether changed to him, he disliked him, and he wanted to hurt him, and finely he succeeded. As the sense of this bitter tragedy grew on him, Dennis could bear it no longer, but rolled over on his face, and, for the first time in this awful fortnight, sobbed with the pain of his wounded affection.

After a while he sat up again: there was no earthly use in indulging in such sloppy tricks, and, pulling himself together, he walked back to the house. It was close on lunch-time, and he made himself neat, for fear of provoking sarcastic comments, and sat in the gallery over a picture paper. Presently his mother and Colin came in together.

"Well, dear, nice bathe?" she said to him.

"Yes, mother, jolly and warm," he said.

She came over to his chair, and leaned over him, putting her hands on his shoulders. Dennis could not help wincing at that.

"What's the matter, darling?" she said.

"Nothing. I scratched my back against a snag as I was bathing," he said. "Rather sore."

Colin heard that, and instantly he thought to himself, "Now I'll tell her: that will humiliate him." But on the heels of that came some sudden glow of pride at the staunchness of the boy. He guessed that he said that, not to spare himself, but to spare him, and, as last night, the yearning for him, the affection he had not yet succeeded in killing, pulled at his heart.

It was an unutterable relief to Violet when, next morning, with charming farewells to her and Aunt Hester, and with a nod to Dennis, Colin drove off to catch his boat at Folkestone. She had ached and mourned over her boy's misery, but at the same time she had rejoiced in that reticence he had observed to her, for there indeed was the banner of love flying bravely. If he had struck that, and come to her for comfort and with complaint, indeed there would have been no matter for wonder, but she delighted in the fact that he flew it still. But it was good that Colin was gone: poor Dennis had had a rotten time, and she longed to give him pleasanter days. Naturally, he had no inkling of the meaning of his tribulations, of the significance that underlay them, and she had no notion of telling him that, in her belief, a battle was going on that somehow centred round him, in which he, boyishly unheeding, was standing his ground in the face of black and bitter assaults. She knew well that it was not yet over, nor yet nearly over; he had but held his own, and fresh assaults, fiercer yet perhaps, would come. But just for the next few weeks there was truce, and she was thankful for that.

The summer days passed on: another school-friend came to stay with Dennis, and after him another, and Dennis seemed happy, though no one could kindle in him that abandoned radiance which Colin so easily lit. Colin had been away a month now, and, according to his plans, would be back for Dennis's last week at home. But one evening there came a letter to Violet saying that he was intending to stop on in the island for another fortnight.

She read this to Dennis as they sat together that night for a bed-time talk after old Lady Yardley's whist was finished, and Aunt Hester had hurried away in horror of the lateness of the hour and the fear of missing her beauty sleep. One piece of the letter was not for his ears: Colin asked if she was making up lost ground with Dennis, and supposed they had hatched plenty of conspiracies against him: he also sent a message to Dennis to say that he need not trouble to ink his fingers over writing to him, as his letters were quite illegible. Violet thought it unnecessary to deliver that message, but, reading out the postponement of his father's return, she saw Dennis's face fall.

"Then I shan't see Father before I go back to Eton," he observed.

Violet considered the dates.

"No, dear, you'll have gone back several days before he comes," she said.

The cloud deepened on Dennis's face.

"Did Father say anything about the letters I've written him?" he asked.

She laughed.

"Yes, dear, he did say something," she said, "about their not being particularly easy to read."

"No other message for me?" asked the boy.

Violet's heart began to ache for him.

"Let's see: where have I got to?" she said. "Wonderful vintage, he says, in the lovely hot weather they're having. . . . He's been bathing all the morning, and has had lunch, and is going to sleep. . . ."

"But no message for me?" persisted Dennis.

Violet finished the letter and tore it up. There was a good deal about Dennis, though nothing for him. But it struck her that these uncomplimentary comments were forced. In one Colin had first written 'the boy,' but had crossed that out and substituted 'the brat.' He had not thought of him as 'the brat' originally: 'the brat' was the image under which he schooled himself to think of him. The sentences had no spontaneous ring about them; they expressed what he tried to feel. She felt sure that her interpretation was no fanciful one.

Dennis had accepted her silence to his repeated question.

"And what else has he been doing?" he said.

"Dining out in the garden every night," said Violet, "and looking at them making the wine. The garden is a good deal burned up with the heat. Nothing else. The bathing takes half the day."

Dennis crossed from the far side of the hearth-rug and made a back for himself against her knees.

"It sounds awfully ripping and lazy," he said. "Father loves it, doesn't he? I should have liked to have gone with him for a bit."

"Perhaps another year he'll take you," said Violet. She felt no sense of injury in the fact that Dennis wanted to be out there with him, rather than at home with her. She thanked God that it was so, that all these wretched days, when his father had persecuted him, had left no stain on the luminous brightness of his affection. At all costs she wanted that to retain its shining quality. Even if Dennis suffered, he suffered in the cause of love: if he had not loved his father, he would have thought of him now as merely a very disagreeable person whose absence was a matter for congratulation. But even now Dennis wanted to be with him; he was disappointed that his postponed return would rob him of a glimpse before he went back to Eton.

"I wonder if he will," said Dennis. "I wonder——"

Violet felt that the boy was on the verge of speech. She drew him back against her knees, encompassing his shoulders.

"Yes, darling, what do you wonder?" she said.

Dennis drew a long breath.

"I wonder what made Father so beastly to me when I came home this time," he said. "I can't think of anything that I had done. I didn't mean to speak of it, but . . . but had I done anything, Mother?"

"No, darling," she said gently.

"Then it's not my fault, anyhow," he said. "That's something. Oh Lord, I have thought about it so much. So if it's not me, it's something that has just got hold of Father. . . . I wish it would let go. He came up to my room one night, you know, and was just as he used to be. I believe . . . I believe he's fond of me all the time, really. What am I to do?"

She wondered how near the truth he had come. The words, "something has got hold of Father . . . I wish it would let go," were extraordinarily apt. But she could not tell him that his father loved hate, and hated love, and that in her belief love was beginning to assert itself against that black dominion. To tell him that, to speak of the legend and of the choice which Colin had renewed for himself, might spoil the instinctive simplicity with which Dennis faced it all. She could not tell him that his father had tried to corrupt him, and, failing there, was trying to kill his love. The truth, baldly stated, might easily produce in him, if he understood it, just that atmosphere of horror in which love gasped for breath.

"Dennis darling," she said. "You can help your father in a way that nobody else can."

"How?" said Dennis quickly. "And what's it all about?"

"It doesn't matter what it's all about," she said. "But you can help him by doing just what you are doing. Go on loving him, dear. Never let yourself cease loving him."

"As if I could help doing that!" said Dennis.

He was busy next morning. He scribbled a long letter to his father, and copied it out with extreme care. No one could possibly say it was illegible. . . .

CHAPTER VI

IT was not until the first of the autumn shooting parties at Stanier was nearly due that Colin came back from his island, and from then till early in December a succession of guests passed through. Sometimes he went up to town with the party that was leaving, returning a few days afterwards with the new relay, and then again he was busy with his duties as host. Sometimes he stopped here in the emptied house, but even then Violet was never once alone with him for any private talk. He pointedly avoided all chance of this, and on the only occasion when she had attempted to break this ring of his seclusion from her, he had flamed into devilish anger.

"Oh, for God's sake clear out!" he said, "if you've come for a heart-to-heart talk. You'll know fast enough if I've got anything to say to you."

"But I want to talk to you," she said. "I haven't seen you since you left here in August."

He gave her one furious glance.

"You'd better go," he said.

Dennis, she knew, wrote to him, for sometimes she would see that laborious and legible script on one of his letters, so different from the cursive scrawl which he gave her. Colin certainly read these, but he never wrote to the boy, and one day there came to Violet, at the end of one of Dennis's letters, a postscript without comment. "Father has told me not to write to him any more." There was no reply to be made to that: Dennis had stated it without comment, and without comment it had better remain, for they understood each other on the subject which it concerned. And yet, for some reason which she could not justify and could scarcely even define, Violet felt that, underneath the harshness of that injunction, there lay not so much the desire to wound as the deliberate intention of so doing. Colin had sat down and thought of that: it had not sprung from the open garden of his mind, but had been reared with deliberate care. It had not been derived from instinct, but from craft; that waspish little prohibition was no spontaneous product. She might even regard it as a missile discharged not in offence but in defence. . . . And then he never spoke of Dennis: not once did the boy's name pass his lips. To her who knew him so well, and had so often shuddered at what he was, this carried the same interpretation. He wanted no suggestion or reminder of Dennis to come near him, not even to her did he mention him, though it was just here that she was most vulnerable to the taunts and gibes that wounded. It was not like him to spare the most sensitive spot for fear of hurting her; it was much more probable that, somehow or other, he was sensitive there himself, and forbore from a contact at which he would have himself winced.

They were alone for a few minutes together, one evening early in December. Old Lady Yardley's whist, at which her nurse had made the fourth, was just over. These sepulchral games were now, in the dimness that was falling ever duskier over her mind, no more than the mere approximate symbol of a game; she held her cards and played them quite ortuitously, and smiled as she gathered the random tricks. But after a few hands of this phantom game had been dealt and disposed of, she was quite content when told that her two rubbers were over, and that she had won them both, though she would whimper in some vague distress if she thought she was not going to get her whist. Even Colin had become now to her a shadow among shadows; just occasionally some faint ray from her mind illuminated him, but for the most part he was but a piece of that grey background, ever receding, of the visible world. To-night, however, some thought of him quickened her, just as she was being wheeled out of the room, though all evening she had seemed unconscious of his presence, for she turned in her chair and said, "My Colin is coming back from Eton before long, and it will be well with Stanier again."

Colin had got up and was half way along the gallery on his passage to his own room, leaving Violet there. But at this he came back, and stood in front of the fire.

"When does 'her Colin'—I suppose she means that brat of yours and mine—come home?" he asked.

Violet gave him the date, some five days before Christmas.

"I suppose you've made a calendar, as one used to do at school," he sneered, "and tear the days off as they pass."

"Oh, no: I can remember without that," said she. "There are eight days more."

"And what happens at Christmas?" he asked. "The usual ntoxicating family fathering?"

"Aunt Hester's coming," said Violet, "and my mother."

"Very exhilarating," observed Colin.

"Then why don't you go to some friend for Christmas, if you feel like that?" said she. "There's no reason why you should be here, with a handful of women."

"There is, if you'll excuse my contradicting you," he said. "I must make Dennis's Christmas happy and joyful. And after all I have a certain right to be at Stanier if I like. Or have you planned to give Dennis a taste of what it will be like to be master here, when I'm out of the way, just as my father gave you and me a taste of it one year, after your discarded Raymond was out of the way? How well I remember that somehow! Raymond was still at Cambridge, and my father made you and me hostess and host at a big party, before Raymond came down. Perhaps you've counted on my absence at Christmas, knowing how exhilarating I find the company of my aunts, and are asking a large party with Dennis to play host. Sure you haven't?"

The question was too preposterous to need an answer, and he continued:

"I shall be here for Christmas with your permission," he said, "just to give Dennis a treat. You may have him alone a bit first and—and tonic him up for so much pleasure. He kept writing to me when I was in Capri, saying he wished I was here, and that he was sorry I should not be back before he went to Eton. There was a sarcastic touch about that which made me laugh."

Violet shook her head.

"No, you're wrong there," she said. "There was nothing sarcastic about it."

He looked at her with a sort of malignant pity.

"You make me feel sick sometimes," he said, "with that sort of remark. I suppose Dennis thought it a positive joy to be thrashed by me.

"You thrashed him?" said she.

"Do you really expect me to believe he hasn't told you that?" sneered Colin, "and that you haven't wept over me for it?"

"It doesn't matter to me whether you believe it or not," said she. "Dennis never said a word about it. What had he done?"

Colin smiled. "Nothing very particular——"

"And so you thrashed him! That was brutal of you."

"Thank you for that kind word," said he. "But I wish you wouldn't interrupt in the middle of a sentence. I didn't thrash him for what he did, but for what he was."

It was just on occasions like these, when Colin, as now, was in his most fiendish mood, that she felt this sudden pang of compassion for him.

"Oh, my poor Colin!" she said. "That's what is the matter with you. It isn't what you do; it's what you are."

"The noble art of tu quoque," remarked Colin. "But it's a rather meaningless art. Don't my actions express me pretty well? I fancied I shewed myself fairly frankly to Dennis in the summer."

"No, you only shewed him what you're trying to be," said Violet.

"You shall explain that in a minute," he said. "I was saying that I gave a sincere exposition of myself. I hate Dennis, you see: I hate the fact of his existence. Stanier will be his when I've gone to hell; probably the knowledge of that will be what constitutes hell for me, and I allow it will be damnable. But until then I can make it pretty damnable for him."

Colin took a cigarette.

"But there's more than that," he said. "I hate love, and, if you're right—thanks for the hint—Dennis loves me. I'm going to kill that, not only because I abominate it, but because it will help to wither Dennis's soul. I want to make him like me: I should delight in him then. I might even be pleased to know that Stanier would be his. Is that all clear? If so, you might explain what you meant when you said I only shewed him what I'm trying to be."

She looked at him as she might have looked at some sick child.

"It's very simple," she said. "You're trying to hate Dennis, and you're trying to make him hate you. You're acting as if you hated him. But you're not succeeding."

She felt that she had never known him till then, so nakedly his soul leaped into his eyes. She had no physical fear of him, it did not seem to matter if he struck her or if he killed her, but at that moment she looked into the nethermost pit, and her spirit cried out for the horror of it. That reacted on her physically, she knew she turned as white as paper, and that her heart fluttered in her throat like a bird ready to take wing, but all that was a secondary effect. She knew that she had spoken truly and she knew also that he recognized that, for otherwise he would not have flamed into that icy fire of anger.

He took a step towards her, and she saw him clench his fists, so that the knuckles shewed white on his brown hands.

"Stand up," he said. "Are you mad that you speak to me like that?"

With a violent effort she controlled the shaking of her knees, and stood in front of him with her hands hanging defencelessly by her side.

"No, Colin, I'm not mad at all," she said.

He drew back his arm as if to strike her.

"I'll give you one chance," he said. "Are you sorry?"

"No. If you're going to knock me down, do so. I shan't tell Dennis."

She looked him perfectly straight in the face, waiting for the blow. And then suddenly she perceived that her defencelessness had beaten him.

"You'd better go," he said. "You haven't made things easier for Dennis, I may tell you."

Instantly all her courage which had sufficed for herself surrendered.

"Colin, it's nothing to do with him," she said. "Do what you like to me, but don't strike me through him."

"I think that will hurt you most," he said.

There was no use in saying anything further, and she moved towards the door.

"I am going back to London to-morrow," he said.

Violet heard nothing more from him during the days which intervened before Dennis's arrival. As he knew the date of that, she expected him to come back that day, but there was still no sign from him, and she and the boy had to themselves these few days, before her mother and Aunt Hester came. Out of doors there was windless and sunny wintry weather: every night there was a frost, and the bare trees were decked with the whiteness of it, which lay thick over the lawns and grassy slopes till the sun resolved it. Below on the marsh there was spread a mantle of dense mist through which the rays could not penetrate, and when, on the third day, a breeze from the east folded it up, the whole plain from edge to edge was dazzling with the glistening fall of the hoar frost. On the lake, the lids of ice shooting out from the shallow water had already roofed the whole surface, with a promise of skating imminent, but this wind, with a veiled sun, though chillier by sensation than the briskness of the still, clear frost, melted the frozen floor, and brought up flocks of grey clouds, and that evening the snowfall began. For two days and nights, beneath a bitter wind, it fell without intermission, lying in thick drifts in hollow places, and giving the yew-hedge an unbroken coat of white: then, as the wind dropped, and the snow ceased, the sky cleared again, and a great frost, black and of exceeding sharpness, set in. Once more, and this time very swiftly, the chilled waters of the lake were congealed and the surface was dark like steel, and transparent as the water over which it lay. Two days before Christmas it already bore at the shallow end, and Dennis frenziedly began hunting for skates.

"There must be some, Mother," he said, "if one only looks in the right place. You find them with broken golf-clubs and old croquet-mallets . . ." and he ran off to explore suitable regions.

There had been no further talk between them about his relations with his father. Every morning he asked if there was any news of his coming, but there had been none. Violet had suggested his getting some Eton friend to stay with him, and then only distantly, Dennis had answered with, it seemed to her, a recollection of last holidays. "Oh, I think I won't, thanks,' he had said. "Father may come any day, mayn't he?" . . . Apart from that he had said nothing whatever, and to Violet every day of Colin's absence was so much remission. Old Lady Yardley seemed to accept the boy as being Colin back from school again. . . . And all these days seemed to Violet like hours of calm, lit with a pale cold sunshine, which preceded some inconjecturable tempest.

Aunt Hester and her mother arrived that afternoon, and Aunt Hester instantly had her snow-boots unpacked, and went for a walk, while the light still lingered.

"I hate seeing the windows shuttered and the lamps lit, my dear," she said. "It makes me feel that I am being put in a box, and I'm too near my latter end to waste my time now over boxes. But if you get a bit of a walk while they're shutting up, the box seems pleasant enough when you get back to it. And I'll be ready for my tea, too."

Such Esquimaux practices, of course, made no appeal to Violet's mother. She brought down from her room her Patience cards, and an altar-frontal which she was embroidering for Winchester Cathedral, and hoped to have ready by Easter. Of the two, for immediate employment, she settled on the altar-frontal, as she had a vague idea that she and Violet must have a great deal to say to each other, and it was impossible to talk while you were playing Patience, or, rather, it was impossible to play Patience if you talked. She had grown a shade greyer, a shade more ladylike, a shade more inaccessible. But she always did everything slowly.

"Dennis will be quite a big boy," she observed. "I have not seen him since last year at this time."

"Yes, he's grown a great deal," said Violet. . . . Could it be possible that Colin was not coming for Christmas?

"And Colin is well?" asked Mrs. Stanier.

"I hope so. He has been away for the last fortnight, and the wretch has never even said when he will be coming back."

"It is a pity that he should miss Dennis's holidays," said Mrs. Stanier.

Violet had no sympathetic contribution to give to this sentiment, and her mother moistened her lips with the tip of her tongue. They got dry and a little cracked in this very cold weather.

"I have brought a wreath for your father's grave," she said. "I made it entirely from flowers in my greenhouse. My gardener is very clever at getting me plenty of flowers throughout the winter."

Violet rummaged her mind for some ardent rejoinder.

"That is always nice," she said. "Flowers are a guarantee that spring will come. But the poor things will wither very quickly when you put them out in this icy air."

"Yes, dear. But I should feel very remiss and hard if I did not always put a wreath on your father's grave whenever I come to Stanier. I daresay it will not be for many more years that I shall do so."

Violet laughed.

"Dear Mother, what nonsense," she said. "Why, there's my grandmother who was married before you were born: she plays her whist still, and walks in to dinner."

"Her mind I suppose is now completely gone?" said Mrs. Stanier. "She did not recognize me at all last time I was here.

And occasionally she mentioned your father as if he was with me still."

The arrival of tea interrupted this lugubrious interchange of thought, followed by Dennis, triumphantly clashing a pair of skates, which were screwed on to boots, the leather of which was perished and wrinkled like withered funguses.

"They're old enough," he said, "but they're all right. I'm going to put them on to my boots, so that they'll be ready in the morning. I found them in a cupboard upstairs."

Instantly it occurred to Violet whose those skates had been. For more than a dozen years now there had been no skating at Stanier, probably the last person who had skated on the lake was Raymond. . . . Almost certainly the skates were his, for they were workmanlike blades, screwed on to the boots, whereas the rest of them used to shoe themselves with strange antiquated wooden concerns, or skates with keys and catches which invariably came undone. But Raymond had spent a winter's vacation once at Davos, and Violet remembered his laughing at her, when one of her skates unclasped itself and slithered across the ice. . . . Somehow, with fantastic disquiet, she hated the idea of Dennis using Raymond's skates.

"Aren't they too big for you?" she asked.

"Lord, yes," said Dennis, "but they're better than nothing. Hefty skates, too. I wonder whose they were?"

Mrs. Stanier put a small saccharine lozenge into her tea.

"The lake has not borne for many years," she said. "I think we used to have harder winters once than we have now. The last year it bore . . . ah, dear me, yes."

The return of Aunt Hester from her tramp in the snow was a welcome advent. She professed herself vastly refreshed, and had a very pretty colour in her cheeks.

"Nothing like a frosty air for giving you an appetite," she said, "and they say that the microbes all get killed in it, though for my part I never believed much in microbes. Everything's microbes nowadays: if you've got a pain in your stomach from eating what you shouldn't it's a microbe, if you covet your neighbour's wife they'll make it out to be a microbe soon. Give me a good strong cup of tea, Violet dear; I hope it's been standing. What's that you're working at, Margaret? A shawl for cold evenings?"

Mrs. Stanier drew in her breath with a sound of shocked sipping.

"No, Hester, it's an altar-cloth for Winchester Cathedral," she said.

"Well, I couldn't see the pattern, and it looked to me like a shawl. And when's that wretch Colin coming back? I thought I should find him here."

"I've not heard a word from him," said Violet. "I've been expecting him for some days."

"Well, I shall have to flirt with Dennis till he comes," said Aunt Hester.

"Rather," said Dennis. "There's the telephone ringing, Mother. Shall I go and see what it is?"

Dennis ran into the hall, leaving the skates which he was transferring to his own boots on the floor.

"Yes, who is it?" he asked.

There was a moment's silence.

"Hullo, is that Dennis?" asked his father's voice.

"Yes, Father."

"Well, tell them to send down to the station to meet the 7.30 train. I'm coming by it."

"Oh, ripping," said Dennis. "I'll tell them."

Colin rang off again without another word.

Colin's train was very late: he did not get up to the house till they were half way through dinner, and came in as he was. He was clearly in the best of spirits.

"Don't get up, anybody," he said. "Violet darling, how goes it? And Aunt Hester and Aunt Margaret. And Granny. An awful journey; they always cut off the heating apparatus when it's more than usually cold."

Dennis waited for a greeting, but there was none for him: Colin ignored him altogether, as if he had not been present; to all the others, no doubt in intentional contrast, he was extraordinarily cordial. But as he spoke now to one and now to another, with affection for Violet, with extravagant compliments for Aunt Hester, and sympathetic enquiries about the Girls' Friendly Society for Aunt Margaret, who was a pillar of that admirable institution, Violet saw his eyes, as they flitted by Dennis, pause on the boy's face from time to time with a look that peeped out like a lizard from a crevice and whisked in again. And then for the first time he spoke to him.

"Any tipsy school-friends coming this Christmas, Dennis?"

he said. "My word, that was a beauty you treated us to in the summer."

Dennis raised his eyes to his father's, and even as they met, Violet saw that look pop out again, instantly sheathing itself in the iron of Colin's voice.

"No, Father, I haven't asked anybody these holidays," he said quietly.

Colin paid no more attention to him, till the women got up to leave the table. Then he watched him to see what Dennis would do.

Dennis stood by the door he had opened, not knowing whether his father expected him to go with the others or stay. But his hesitation was enough.

"Perhaps you'd kindly shut that door," he said. "You can leave yourself on whichever side of it you like."

Dennis shut it, and came back to the table.

"Looking out for a drink, I suppose?" said Colin, rising. "Ring the bell when you've finished, I'm going into the other room."

Dennis went to the door again to open it for his father and followed him.

Colin sat up late that night, thinking of Dennis and of little else. He thought of him, as he always did now, as his survivor and supplanter, who, in all probability, would rule at Stanier for twenty years after he was dead, unless he himself lingered on like his own grandmother till all the fires of life had grown cold. Then possibly he might out-live his son, and possibly there might be enough heat in his grey embers to chuckle at that, for he would sooner be the last of his race than be succeeded by Dennis. Who would come after him, he wondered, in that case. He knew there was a small homestead in the marsh, just outside his property, where there lived a farmer called Stanier, with a brood of scarecrow children. Perhaps they would establish their claim, and there would be a romantic sequel to these centuries of direct line and ever-increasing prosperity. But he would sooner have them reigning here than Dennis.

Of course there was another chance: the leaven of evil might yet work in the boy—for he was young still—and turn sour that sweet milk of love with which he dripped. But he meant to make no more experiments with regard to that. Dennis must come to it because he loved evil: he would only struggle against it and abhor it if he was forced to it. Besides, Colin knew he could not do it: he could bully and ill-treat him, striving to kill love in him, but the ultimate direct initiative was beyond him. He could wish him dead, he could wish him corrupted, but he could not take on himself the actual sacrifice. It was his own fault, he had allowed Dennis to enter his heart, where no one else had ever been, and now, with all the vigour of his evil soul, it was as much as he could do to stop his advance. But never would he allow that love was stronger than he: he would fight it till it lay bleeding and helpless at his feet.

It had grown cold in his room: he fancied there was a draught from the door which led into the corridor to the now disused chapel. But, as he tried the door and found it shut, the notion came to him to visit the chapel where he had not been since last Easter, and he fetched the key and turned up the lights. It would be Christmas Eve to-morrow, he remembered; last year they had held a midnight mass there, and the sacring bell had rung simultaneously with the peal from the church near by. It was bitter to-night in the chapel, and he shivered as he stood there. In the air there still hung the faint stale odour of incense, and faint, too, and hardly to be recalled, was the thrill of satisfied evil with which once he had knelt there. There was the step off which Vincenzo had rolled when the slavering ecstasy in his face was struck from it by that mortal terror. How horrible to think that perhaps he had seen God at that moment! Poor Vincenzo!

Colin had a sneering smile at the thought of that. God did not come to you unless you permitted it, for otherwise there was no such thing as free-will. Vincenzo must have had a weak spot somewhere: he must have loved somebody for his own sake, and that perhaps gave God a permit. He must be careful then. . . .

He went back into the silent house, and upstairs. He saw that Dennis's door was ajar, and that there was a light within.

Morning brought no such deplorable disaster as a thaw, and soon after breakfast Dennis came into the gallery with his skates in his hand. Colin was by the fire, looking at the paper, and glanced up at him.

"Skating?" he said.

"Yes, the lake bears," said Dennis.

Colin looked at the rusty skates on the boots he was carrying. "Where did you get those?" he asked.

"I found them in a cupboard," said Dennis. "They were on a pair of very old boots, so I took them off and put them on mine."

It flashed through Colin's mind that they were Raymond's. He had meant to stop Dennis skating just for the mere sake of spoiling his enjoyment: now he rather liked the idea of his doing so."

"Well, don't go out through here," he said, "and let in the cold air. Go round by the hall. Perhaps I'll come presently."

Colin put the paper down. On just such a morning as this, clear and sunny after a night's hard frost, had Raymond gone down alone to the lake, and he himself had strolled after him, in time to see the white face already blue-lipped rise out of a hole in the broken ice, where the lake lay deepest, and sink again before his eyes, as he leaned on the parapet by the sluice and asked him if it was not rather cold. The ice was always treacherous near where the stream came out of the lake. . . . Some inward certainty took possession of him. Preposterous though such a coincidence would be, he found himself believing that Dennis was now gaily tramping over the hard frozen snow to his death, and that he would be there to see it. Out of the window he saw the boy running down the white slopes beyond the yew-hedge, with his great coat on that reached nearly to his heels, and his breath smoking in the bitter air. . . . Three minutes later he was walking down over those same slopes.

Dennis had gone into the bathing-shed to put on his skates; presently when he got warm he would divest himself of his great-coat, but it was too cold for that yet: besides it would make a fall the softer. He tried the edge of the lake, and found it firm as a floor beneath him, and soon he extended the field of his manœuvres.

Colin heard the ring of his skates as he came down to the lake; he did not go to the bathing-shed, but kept straight on along the retaining bank, hidden from Dennis's view by the rhododendrons. He felt it was all going to happen as he expected: the chain of coincidence was already strong, for was not Dennis alone on the virgin ice, just as Raymond had been, and was he not (marvellous that!) wearing the skates which Raymond had worn? There would be no more struggle to hate the boy, no more looking on him as his survivor and supplanter. Things did not go well with those who crossed Colin, and who shuddered with nightmare at the approach of his protector.

There came a sudden crack, sharp as a rifle-shot, from the lake, and he heard a splash. The open gap in the rhododendron bushes, where the sluice-gate stood, was now only a few yards in front of him, and he ran there. Ten or twelve yards from the bank, where the water was deepest, there was a jagged hole in the ice, and Dennis's cap floated on the bubbling water. Next moment he rose: only just his face thrown back appeared above the water, for his coat heavily weighted him. His eyes were staring with fright, his mouth already blue with cold. He saw Colin.

"Father!" he called.

And now in a moment Colin would be rid of his supplanter. It had happened without plan or effort of his, and he had only got to stop still for a few seconds and fill his mind with images of hate. He hated Dennis, and smiled to himself as he repeated that, while he met the boy's eyes.

Dennis still looked at him: he had clutched a rim of the broken ice in one hand, but it broke as he tried to raise himself, and, still struggling, his head sank a little lower in the water that now covered his chin and mouth. And then with a flood that bore all opposition way, the knowledge burst on Colin that he loved him, and already perhaps it was too late. . . . He knew well, too, that it was risking his own life to jump into that deep water, paralyzingly cold, and swim out to him, and he knew that life was sweet, and he believed that death would be to him the open door through which he must go into the outer darkness of damnation. But swiftly he tore off his coat, for his arms would have to be strong for the two of them.

"Hold on, old boy," he shouted. "We'll have you out in a jiffy. Don't be frightened."

And those were sweet words to Dennis, and sweeter yet to him who spoke them.

Colin vaulted over the parapet of the sluice breaking another hole in the ice, and before he had come to the surface was striking out for the boy. He did not know whether the water was hot or cold; all that he was conscious of was the stark necessity of reaching Dennis. Before he got to him the boy's head had disappeared, and plunging downwards he dived after him. There he was, still struggling but slowly sinking, and Colin caught hold first of his hair, then got an arm round him, and looking upwards saw the glint of the sun on the open water. Furiously kicking downwards he rose to the surface, pulling Dennis with him. But the boy's thick coat was a terrible drag and got heavier every moment as the water soaked into it, and, few yards as they had to go, he thought for a moment that they would never reach the shore.

"Kick out for all you're worth," he panted. "We've got to get there. It's just a few yards, Dennis."

At last a rhododendron branch growing out over the water came within reach, and he caught hold of it. This brought him to the edge of the unbroken ice again, and, letting go of Dennis for a moment, he brought his elbow down full on to it, and broke another yard of passage. Then Dennis came within reach of further branches and felt the steep sides of the retaining bank beneath his feet. Next minute they had dragged themselves out of the water.

Colin turned to the boy, his teeth chattering with cold, and, now that Dennis was safe, his heart was hot with the tide of hate, momentarily driven back, but now flowing swiftly.

"You damned little idiot," he said. "I suppose your plan was to drown me."

A revulsion of feeling not less than that which seized Colin drove over the boy. All the time that they had been struggling in the water, with that strong arm upholding him, his heart had sung with the thought that his father had risked his life to save him, and now bitter as the icy water itself were his first words to him.

"Take off that coat of yours and run," said Colin. "After all my trouble you needn't stand here and freeze."

Colin was now the more exhausted of the two, and after they had trotted some fifty yards together, Dennis staggering and hobbling in his skated boots, he had to stop.

"I can't run any more," he said. "Go on."

He was terribly white of face, and his breath came in short panting sobs.

"That's likely," said Dennis. "Here, catch hold of me, Father. Give me your hand."

Colin's spirit rebelled, but the flesh was weak, and he let Dennis tuck his arm in his, and pound away up the hill. The boy's vigour and young blood had reasserted themselves, the colour came back to his cheeks, while the elder man, after his frantic struggle for them both, was growing every moment more exhausted. But presently they came to the level paving of the terrace, and Violet from within saw them pass a window, and rushed to the door to open it. Colin was now near collapse, but between them they lifted him into the warmth.

"Ring the bell, Dennis," she said. "What has happened?"

"I was drowning," said Dennis, "and he saved me."

A few hours in bed encircled with hot water-bottles and blankets soon restored Dennis, but the cold had taken a much firmer grip over his father. For several days, without ever being dangerously ill, he was in danger of so being, for his vitality, which had always been so serene and vigorous, failed to recuperate him, and repel the effects of that icy struggle and its sequel of exhaustion. Never before in his life had he known a day's sickness: now it seemed as if the spring of his vital force was drained. He made but little resistance; he let himself lie passively there while nurses and doctors fought for him. But all the time, as he lay there, and so slowly recovered his strength, a struggle more grim than that to which others could minister had laid hold on him. The exuberant vitality of his love of hate had suffered a shock to which that of his chilled and exhausted physical frame was not comparable. That vitality, never before seriously threatened, but always bubbling with energy, had collapsed at the moment when he vaulted over the sluice and crashed into the ice on his way to save Dennis. He, who loved life with every fibre of his being, and with every fibre of his being hated love, knew well enough that he risked his life and betrayed his vow of hate, when he did that. A moment before he had been smiling at this wonderful coincidence which would rid him of a survivor and supplanter, even as in identical manner, and at this same spot, he had been rid of that elder twin of his who stood between him and the lordship he coveted. And then came the humiliating collapse of his hate, before this assault of love.

And now as he lay here hour after hour of sunny wintry days and fitful sleep, it was not so much that he thought all this over, as that it was presented to him from outside, like a picture on the wall, which too was painted within his eyelids, so that when he closed them the images were still there. He saw himself, risking everything for Dennis's sake, not because

Dennis was his son, for that for many weeks now had been a solid ground of hatred, but because he loved the boy. With whatever incredulity he tried to counter that, it always slipped under his guard and stabbed him. He was forced to admit it to himself for the wound it made bled, but instinctively he covered it from others even as from Dennis himself, to whom, the moment after the danger was over, he had addressed those bitter and railing words, which came hot and fluent from the instinct of his soul. But still the flickering fire of hate, doused for that moment with deep and icy water, was alive, and day after day he refused to see the boy and Violet. And though, as his bodily strength returned, that fire burned more bravely, there was always present the knowledge that he had betrayed the Lord and Benefactor who all his life had done such great things for him. Was it in revenge for that betrayal that he had physically collapsed like this? Was it a warning that those whose souls were dedicated to evil had better not have commerce with love?

There was but a day left out of Dennis's holidays when Colin came downstairs for the first time. He had debated with himself whether to keep himself withdrawn till the boy had gone, but this would deprive him of the opportunity of testifying that he still hated him. He must put himself right. . . . And all the time, for other reasons than these, he knew he wanted to see Dennis. Not even to himself would he admit that, but in some closed cell the knowledge lurked.

Aunt Hester and Mrs. Stanier had gone: there were only Dennis and Violet at lunch when he came in. Neither had seen him for these two weeks, nor had they any clue as to his attitude towards them, except such as was implied by his refusal to see them. They were not left long in doubt.

They had both risen on his entry.

"Ah, Colin," said she, "this is splendid."

He turned upon her the full bleakness of his face.

"We'll take the splendour for granted," said he. "Ah, there's Dennis. It's splendid, isn't it, Dennis, to have got rid of me for all your holidays? That's what your mother means."

Dennis looked at him unwaveringly. The moment when Colin had leaped in after him was so far more real than anything else that could be said or done in the whole world.

"But she doesn't mean that, Father," he said, "nor do I."

"Oh, you've learned to contradict in my absence, have you?" asked Colin.

Dennis was still radiant.

"Sorry, Father," he said.

The meal went on in silence, till Dennis, over-anxious to give no cause of offence, made a terrific crash with his pudding spoon.

"If you can't eat your lunch decently, you had better leave the room," said Colin.

Dennis took this to be a general objurgation, not a command.

"Sorry, Father," he said again, and went on with his pudding.

"Did you hear what I said, Dennis?" asked Colin.

Dennis got up at once, but stood by his father's chair a moment, scarlet in the face at this public ignominy, and very nervous, but determined to speak.

"I've never thanked you yet, Father," he said, "for what you did for me. I can't do more than thank you, for there's nothing else I can do for you. But if there was——"

Colin wheeled round in his chair.

"Damn you, go away," he said.

CHAPTER VII

The rigour of the winter abated, and a rainy January was succeeded by a long spell of warm caressing weather, borrowed from May-time, so mild and sunny was it. The trees were bursting into early bud, the sallows were hung with catkins, primroses were a-bloom, and all over the marsh the ewes were with young. No shepherd there remembered so early a lambing season, nor one more fruitful.

Colin had spent a month on his beloved island, recuperating, and that very successfully, after his illness. Then one day, after a week of London, that longing for Stanier overcame him, and he drove down alone, with no plan but to stay there as long as he was content. He would find there only his grandmother, and she now kept to her room entirely, and no more preposterous rubbers of whist would be demanded in the evening. "After all, she has played two rubbers every night for seventy years," thought Colin, and tried to work out the portentous sum of the total. But on his arrival, her nurse came down to tell him that she was mysteriously aware, it seemed, that he was coming, for she kept restlessly muttering to herself, "Colin will be here soon": perhaps she would be quieted by the sight of him. So, rather grudgingly, for it must surely be a sheer waste of time, he went up to see her. There she lay in bed, pallid and immobile, with her pearls round her neck, and looked at him with that disconcerting, unwinking gaze, behind which there seemed to lie some frozen consciousness and knowledge. She was still repeating, even while she gazed at him, "Colin will be here soon," but suddenly she stopped and gave that smile which looked as if it was the blurred reflection of something very far away, and she muttered no more.

Surely the spell of Stanier, thought Colin as he left her, that nameless magic of the legend and its gift, had so penetrated her, that now, when the ultimate mists thickened about her, that was the last illumination, dimly piercing the cold shadows, that shone on her. She still had some consciousness of him as the inheritor of it all, and he remained the last link, now wearing so thin, of her connection with the visible world. He could imagine that; the spell of Stanier was strong, and it would not be so still, he thought, as he closed his dying eyes on its splendour and his doom. A long way off that seemed, on this young morning of spring.

He had started early from town, and the day was yet at noon when he arrived, and, reserving himself for a long outing after lunch, he wandered about the house, soaking himself in it, and inhaling its associations. He went into Violet's rooms, he went into the room where Raymond's dead body had lain, and thought of that fortunate morning which brought him his inheritance. Dennis's room he passed without entering, and some twitch of exasperation took him at the thought of Dennis.

He was for ever checking that truancy of his mind, overhauling it and bringing it back when it went on these illicit excursions. It would be long anyhow before he saw the boy, for in the Easter hoildays he would be in Italy again, and assuredly Dennis should not accompany him.

He went down the broad staircase into the hall, with the portrait of old Colin facing him, with the parchment of the legendary contract he had made let into the frame. '*O bonum commercium!*' he thought, and the picture smiled back at him across the prosperous centuries. Near by was the smoking-room: that too was a place where the dead had lain, and he recalled how he and good unsuspecting Doctor Martin had moved the remains of Vincenzo there. Then came the long gallery with the sunshine pouring in, and outside the terrace and the yew-hedge, where, beneath the summer night, Violet had said she loved him. There he had walked with Pamela too. . . . That silly Pamela: she might have been alive to-day and young still, if she had only not been so reckless as to love. You never know into what dangerous places love might lead you, into depths of unsubstantial air, or depths of icy water. And there, none too soon for his appetite, the door of the dining-room was opened, and his new valet whom he had brought from Italy told him that he was served. The boy was rather like Nino. . . .

He drove out after lunch in the little two-seater that went lightly over the roads in the marsh rough with the scourings of the winter storms, out past the golf-links and along the sandy road towards Lydd. He intended to walk home across the marsh, and presently he got out for his tramp. The dykes were full of water, but it was always possible to find a way over footbridges and culverts. It might be devious and zigzag, but you could progress in the required direction, and how more pleasantly, after the grime of London, could he pass a couple of hours than by strolling through the pastures bright with the young growth of spring, and populous with anxious ewes, and new-born lambs? There was Rye on the edge of the plain, and above it the woods of Stanier, with a glimpse of the house among them. That would be his general line, and with half the afternoon before him he would strike the Romney road before dusk and follow it along to the outskirts of the town, where his car would be waiting for him.

He had been walking for an hour with the sunlight warm on him, and the larks carolling in the lucent air, when the brightness began to grow dim, and looking up he saw that the sky was veiled with mist, through which the sun peered whitely. A little breeze had sprung up, and from seaward there was drifting in a fog off the Channel, where already the sirens were hooting. The warmth of the day had drawn up much moisture from the marsh into the air, and now, in the chill of the veiled sun, it was rapidly condensing into one of those thick white mists which, while Stanier on its hill still basked in sunshine, enveloped the lower ground. It was annoying, for he had still a mile to go before he struck the road, and he hurried on, to cover the ground as quickly as he could. But before he had gone half that distance the mist thickened to so dense an opacity that it was impossible to see more than a yard or two ahead. But, before it closed down on him, he had seen a gate some hundred yards in front, which was clearly the outlet from this pasture in the direction of Rye, and he walked, as he thought, straight towards it.

Presently he came to a stop. Instead of there being a gate in front of him there was a broad dyke. He followed along this to the left, but it seemed to run on indefinitely, and retracing his steps he tried the other direction. This brought him to the gate, through which he passed, and, orientating himself from it, he started off afresh. But now he had no visible mark to guide him, for the encompassing mists had closed their white walls impenetrably round him. Before long in this baffling dimness he knew he had lost his bearings altogether: whether Rye was to the left or right of him or straight ahead he had no idea: he must just hope to find gates or foot-bridges across the dykes till he came to the road, searching blindfold for them. And it was growing dark: the daylight of the clear air above the fog was fading.

He had passed, ten minutes before, a shepherd's hut put up for lambing, and now he determined to retrace his steps to this, and see if there was anyone there from whom he could get guidance, for at this season of the year the farmer or his shepherd often sat up all night, as once old Colin had done as a boy, for the needs of midwifery. But now he could not find the hut, and, giving up the search as vain, he thought that he would again retrace the steps of his fruitless exploration, and push on as best he might. Then with a sudden springing up of hope he saw a gate close ahead of him, but when he came to it he found it familiar in some bewildering manner. The staple was stiff just as was that of the last gate he had passed through, and on the lowest bar of it was caught a piece of white sheep's wool, which he had noticed before. He must have come round in a circle to the point from which he had started when the mist grew thick.

This was all very uncomfortable, and he paused, wondering what to do next. If he could not find his way across a mile of pasture, it would be mere folly to attempt to go back on the course he had come. It would have been infinitely better to have gone into that shepherd's hut when he had the chance, and waited for the mist to lift; now the wisest thing would be to try again to find his way back there, for it was somewhere close to this gate to which he had inadvertently returned.

He set off, and now with a clearer recollection of his bearings he met with better success, and presently he found the hut again. There was no one there, and there was no door to it, but at rate there was a roof to cover him, and wooden walls for shelter, and inside there was a pile of straw, dry and plentiful, into which he could burrow for warmth while he waited.

The moisture of the mist was thick on his clothes, like dew on fleece, and his face and hands were chilled and wet with it. His long walk had tired him, and the relief of finding shelter and rest was great and he sat down on the straw and made himself as comfortable as he could. What time it was he had no idea, for he was without matches, and it was now so dark that he could not see his watch. The doorless entrance was but a glimmering greyness against the blackness of the interior and he wondered whether, even if the mist cleared, he could find his way home before morning. Perhaps there was a moon, but time alone would show that, and his thoughts began to stray in other directions.

It was an odd adventure: just so had old Colin, when a shepherd boy, passed the night in some such hut as this, probably within a few hundred yards of where he himself now sat, and that certainly had been no unfortunate experience for him, for on that night the splendid fortunes and prosperity of the house of which now he himself was head had been founded. Health and wealth and honour and all that his heart desired had been granted to his ancestor on that night of the legend, into the inheritance of which he had entered by his love of evil, and his hate of love. . . . And then the thought of Dennis came up like a bubble to the surface of his mind, Dennis whom he hated and had tried to corrupt, and who was the heir to all his splendours.

Colin was getting drowsy in the warmth of his straw-bed; for a moment, as token of that, he thought he heard Dennis's voice, and that roused him again. But sleep was the most reasonable manner of passing these hours of waiting, which might be long; and it was certainly better than thinking about Dennis. Thicker and thicker, like the mists outside, the dusk of sleep darkened round him.

He slept soundly and dreamlessly, and woke, after some interval of the length of which he had no idea, into the full possession of his faculties, so that he had no puzzled bewilderment as to where he was or how he had come here: this waking consciousness dovetailed precisely into that which had preceded his sleep. Probably he had slept long, for he woke alert and refreshed, warm and comfortable under the straw that he had pulled over him. But close on the heels of his waking there came the conviction that he was not alone here. He had gone to sleep alone, far away from the haunts of men in the isolation of the mist, but while he slept someone had come.

He sat up, and turning looked towards the blank doorway. It was still faintly visible, a dusky oblong in the blackness, but now it framed the figure as of a man, which stood there in the entry. Some shepherd was it, who, like himself, sought shelter?

"Hullo, who is that?" said Colin. "I have lost my way, and am sheltering here till the mist clears. Lord Yardley from Stanier."

There was silence, then very quietly a voice spoke:

"I know who you are," it said.

Colin felt his breath catch in his throat, and a pulse beat there. This was not the voice of a shepherd come here for the lambing or for shelter, and a fantastic notion flashed into his head. Here was he, sleeping in a remote hut in the marsh at lambing-time, even as old Colin had done, and he asked himself whether some renewal or re-enactment of the legend was at hand. The idea scarcely seemed strange, so intimately did the belief in the legend beat in his blood. It was no shepherd who spoke. . . .

That shape in the doorway seemed to him rather larger than it had been at first: perhaps it had moved a silent step nearer him. It had outlined itself a little more clearly now: the shape of the shoulders and the head was more sharply defined; round the head there was a faint luminousness like the halo the moonlight casts round a man's shadow on the grass.

In the silence that followed Colin asked himself whether he was still asleep, whether the whole adventure was a dream, whether he would presently wake up and find himself in his bed at Stanier. And then the voice spoke again, and he knew that, whether he dreamed, or whether indeed he was awake, the substance of things unseen was in manifestation.

"Why did you save Dennis?" asked the quiet voice.

The question was utterly unexpected. But whoever this was, he had no claim to be answered. His Lord and Benefactor, if it was he, knew that his soul was set on evil and hate. And what right had any other power in heaven or earth or in the dark places to question him? Why he answered at all, he did not know; his voice seemed to take it upon itself to do so.

"I saved Dennis," he said, "just simply because I chose to. It was my own business, and my will is free."

"You might easily have been drowned," said the voice. "Did you consider that?"

"I knew I was taking that risk," said Colin.

"And did you consider what doom awaited you?"

"Yes."

"Then why did you save Dennis?"

Colin began to catch a glimpse of the purport of the question. But nothing, he determined, should make him give the answer that he felt was required of him. Besides, such an answer, he told himself, was not true. He had been guilty, at the most, of a momentary weakness.

"I saved him, I tell you," he said, "because I chose to. He was my only son. Was it not reasonable that I should wish him to live and continue my line?"

He was definitely uneasy now. His uneasiness irritated him into flippancy.

"Perhaps you are a bachelor," he said, "and so you can't be expected to understand that. In any case I don't know what right you have to ask me, and I have no other answer for you."

Once more there was silence. Then the quiet voice spoke again.

"Why did you save Dennis?" it asked.

The question was beginning to frighten him. He felt as if he was on the rack, and that each time the question came some lever was pulled, some cog clicked, and the ropes round his wrists and ankles were getting more taut. He could just feel the strain of them which would presently increase.

"Why did you save Dennis?" asked the voice again.

This time Colin clenched his teeth. Whatever torture might be in store, he would never answer that. There was no actual pain yet, only the anticipation of it. But surely years had passed since he found his way through the mist into this shed. It could not only have been last evening, as the dusk of this present night began to fall, that he had come here and covered himself up in the straw.

"It was on that very spot that you let your brother Raymond drown," said the voice. "Why did you let Raymond drown without an effort to save him?"

For a moment that relieved the tension.

"Because I hated Raymond," said Colin. "Because he stood between me and my inheritance."

"But you hate Dennis too. Will he not inherit all that is yours?"

"Yes, I hate Dennis," said Colin.

"Of course. You tried to corrupt him. You tried to make him miserable. You tried to kill his love for you. We are agreed on that then. You hate Dennis."

The voice was silent again. The figure surely had moved closer, for now it towered above him. The faint luminousness round its head was brighter: he could see the boarding of the hut and the grey glimmer of the straw where he sat. And then again the voice spoke: Colin knew what it was about to say.

"Why did you save Dennis?" it asked.

At that the pain began, some hot shooting stab of agony. But he could bear that and worse than that. Every moment now seemed to have a quality it had never possessed before: the seconds which he could hear his watch ticking out were not long exactly: they were eternal.

The tension relaxed again.

"You hated Nino," said the voice, "when he turned his back on you and your wickedness, and let him die. Did you not hate Nino?"

"Yes, I hated Nino then," said Colin.

"And you hated Pamela. You mocked her, and drove her to her death. You were never sorry. It amused you. Did you not hate Pamela?"

"Yes, I hated Pamela," said he.

"And you hate Violet. You hate the whole world. You hate the love which has been squandered on you. Do you not hate love?"

"Yes, I hate love."

Again came the terrible pause, and he bit his lip, and tried to brace his muscles against the wrench that was coming.

"Why did you save Dennis?" came the question.

The ropes were tight now, and the pull made him gasp and cry out.

"In God's name, who are you that torture me?" he screamed.

"You will know presently, when I have broken you."

Colin clenched his hands tight, still utterly steadfast and untamed.

"Don't imagine you'll do that," he said. "If that's what you expect, you're wasting your time."

Again the silence of eternity fell.

"Do you believe in God, Colin Stanier?" said the voice.

"Yes," said he. "You know that."

"And do you hate God with all your heart?"

"Yes," said Colin.

The figure receded a little. Perhaps, he thought, now that he had made his final and complete repudiation, which surely included all else, the torture was over, for the cruel wrench of that repeated question came no more, and he sank back utterly exhausted on his straw-bed, and sleep, or some such anodyne to sensation, came over him. Then once more he came to himself, alert and wholly awake.

Outside the mist had cleared, and he could see through the empty door-space the pasture covered with thick dew, and a few scattered sheep with their lambs beside them. It must be close on dawn, for in the east there was a long line of cloud, flushed red with the sun that had not yet risen on the earth. For the moment, with a pang of exquisite relief, he thought he was alone, and that the inquisition of the night was over. But how terribly real a dream could be! Dennis had known that when he woke from his nightmare, and threw himself into his father's arms for protection. And this dream, even though he was awake, had still that quality of eternity about it.

He sat up. And then he saw that the figure was by him once more, close to him now. It was still a shadow, dark and undecipherable, in spite of the flushed twilight of the coming day.

"Why did you save Dennis?" it asked.

The torture shot through him again, more poignant than ever to his racked spirit. He bowed his head, and felt the drops of agony grow thick on his forehead. But still he made no answer.

He raised his eyes, as if in obedience to a command, and saw the lines of cloud red in the dawn. And the voice spoke:

"See where Christ's blood streams in the firmament. One drop would save your soul." But you would never call on Him, Colin, because you hate Him."

He could not answer, so rending was the torture. He waited, writhing and stiffened against what was coming.

"Why did you save Dennis?" asked the voice.

At that the full fierceness of mortal agony was let loose on him, and that agony was eternal: it had existed before ever time began. The evil of all that he had done, the utter depravity of his soul, with its lust for hate and its hate of love, was torn and wrenched by the inflexible power of that which had made him so lightly vault over the parapet of the sluice, and strike out across the icy water towards Dennis. With all his force, with all his will he resisted, but his force faded, his will faltered and collapsed, and with a wail of pain he surrendered.

"I saved him because I loved him," he cried. "I give in, you devil from the pit. For Christ's sake don't torture me any more!"

The rending agony in which he writhed ceased, the strain relaxed. Blinded with sweat and tears he looked at the figure that stood close to him now, but still it was no more than a shadow to him.

"Who are you?" he sobbed. "Why have you tortured me like this? Are you my Lord whom I have served so well? Who are you?"

At that the shadow brightened into a beam that dimmed the lines of morning, and filled the hut with a radiance on which he could not look. And once more, for the last time, the quiet voice spoke.

"I am Love," it said.

THE END